Acknowledgements

It's important for me to acknowledge the fact that without my husband, Willie's encouragement, advice, editorial skills and technical genius, working long hours formatting the book, with all its illustrations, there would be no book.

I have always loved gardens, but then how could I not? Both my grandfathers created gardens, very different gardens, which I grew up exploring. My father followed in their footsteps and could usually be found with seed catalogues close by. My mother balanced the influence of the cultivated plants with her knowledge of wild flowers and trees and nature in general. I was lucky to have two friends who were professional gardeners and through them discovered more of the lives, enthusiasm and dedication of the professional gardener. They are all now gone but their influence has remained.

My sisters Judy and Jean hunted out old family photographs and information and are themselves lovers of gardening and gardens.

So this book has, rather like some seeds, taken four to five years to germinate, encountering periods of growth and dormancy, researching the period of the book, checking details and researching.

My MSc in Peace and Conflict dissertation provided me with the opportunity to further my research into the importance of gardens and gardening and the more I read the more I realised how powerful the urge to create a garden can be no matter what the situation and however dire.

A special thanks to author, Rosie O'Hara, who read the final draft and gave me valuable feedback.

Sheila O'Hare and Hugh Mills for their generosity in reading my book before publication and offering such helpful support.

All the gardens I've fallen in love with and dreamt of creating and all the people I've met visiting gardens or working in them. And also last, but not least, George the cat who assisted by lying across the table close to the computer and occasionally removing sentences he did not approve of and Rosie the collie who quietly watched the progress of the book being written, hoping that at the end of each session there would be the call to play football.

Ultimately this book is about love and connection to the natural world. I hope in reading it you enjoy it as much as I enjoyed writing it.

Garraiblagh House 1945

Contents

PART FOUR
Post-war

PART FIVE
WWII and after

PART SIX
Decline

PART SEVEN
Rebirth

'The oak stretched out its roots. It felt the slight vibrations of the foxes as they moved to and fro. It felt their uncertainty. The oak knew all about change.'

All images and text are copyright © 2020 Jenny A. Methven
All rights reserved.
This is a work of fiction.
ISBN: 978-0-9933950-8-6

The Lost Garden of Garraiblagh

The lost garden of Garraiblagh

PART ONE

Loss

'There are always flowers for those who want to see them.'
Henri Matisse

Chapter One

1980 — 1983

IN THE ROSE GARDEN the thorns grew. Roses, normally able to blossom, were trapped beneath thick stems and spreading suckers that smothered the pinks and magentas of the old scented roses. The garden was becoming wayward, unsure of its direction, sometimes fighting against the man-made structures of trellis and pergola, as though trying to draw attention to itself and appeal to the humans, who no longer cared whether it existed. The house stood forlorn, boarded up and empty of life. For the first time in its history it felt lost and forgotten.

And its isolation attracted a new use. Under cover of darkness shadowy figures whispered. Canisters and cans were heaved along the old pathway: loud discordant sounds in the otherwise tranquil setting. The scent of mint and sage betrayed the route with only the silent, watchful eyes of the badger crossing his habitual path and the wild rabbit in its burrow as witnesses. The smell of man on the air and other subtler scents caused the animals to retreat further. A wary darkness pervaded the garden, at odds with the aged tranquility.

Then one night, a starless, moonless night, the sounds changed. Harsh, angry voices, muffled discussions: swearing, guttural and vicious. Then came an explosion.

The world of the garden shook and then the most awful silence descended. It was as though all sound had been blown out of the world. A fox and vixen lay, awkward and silent, with bloodied fur. Their whimpering cub trying to move closer on the two remaining legs; nuzzling its parents as it died. The rabbit shook its head, one ear detached, but still alive. The old ash tree, scorched on one side, no longer gave shelter to the nesting rooks. Instead, a black confetti of feathers lay on the ground, broken branches like whitened bones.

A hole in the ground gaped open, deep and earth wounding. Plants, soil, stones, had all been re-arranged in a hellish parody of garden design.

Glass and nails studded the trees and guillotined the heads of flowers. Of the humans who had plotted and planned in the evil darkness there was little. A finger here, a foot there: pools of viscous liquid and particles of flesh creating a new covering for the garden instead of plants. The smell of burnt flesh, smoke and cordite hung in the air and suffocated life.

The army and police were soon on the scene. Not new to them, the sight of carnage, but a way of life. The forensic piecing together of human parts and death creating chemicals took place slowly over the next few days. Silence and the abandoned police tape fluttered in the breeze. The garden's natural inhabitants left to mourn: watchful eyes in burrows, untrusting.

The oak tree continued its watch over the gardens and the badgers pushed suspicious noses out of their sett to test for safety. Plants gained blood and bone meal in a new, more ghoulish way.

For the plants in the garden the old ways were gone. It was

the survival of the fittest. Garden plants vied with weeds and wild flowers. One invading the space of the other, territory was taken and then given up depending on the season with occasional cross–border, cross–plant bondings. The garden receded into itself.

Fuchsia and crocosmia continued to flower in the hedges. Garraiblagh house built by Amelia and George Henderson over a century before had not only lost its walls, but its soul. Jagged shards of glass from the conservatory mixed with carpet and curtains left flapping in the wind.

Rose and Peter were on a cruise when the notification of the bomb came through.

'Darling, we can't deal with it. It's up to you, Fleur.'

Fleur listened, tight-lipped, as her mother made it clear she wouldn't and didn't want anything to do with Garraiblagh. At the same time no one else wanted to make a decision about selling the devastated property.

After one particularly long distance phone call with Rose, Fleur, in frustration, asked, 'Why Mum? Why don't you care? I want to know.'

'I care, Fleur but not in the way I think you do. I moved away. I cut my ties with Garraiblagh and Northern Ireland and its awful difficulties. It sometimes felt that it was the garden that my mother and my father loved. I was there but, a poor second. It's a place on the other side of the world now, a little back water, surrounded by violence and death.'

At that point Fleur felt like hitting her mother. She wondered how a place could affect people so differently, how she could yearn for the garden and the people she had known in Garraiblagh while her mother ...well, her mother was her mother and Fleur realised that there was little reason in trying to make sense of her. Her coldness had not been focused purely on Garraiblagh and Northern Ireland. She as her only daughter had not fared much better. She thought about her mother's words and realised something else. Garraiblagh and her grandparents had given her the feeling of contentment that she had not, she realised, really experienced from her mother or her father. So she owed it to them to go back and see what could be done for the old place.

'Well,' she thought to herself, 'I have never done anything conventionally. Why be different now. Bryony and I will go to Garraiblagh.'

The lure of the old garden was pulling her and in the back of her mind was the thought that she might see Kevin and Bryony might finally meet her father.

Garraiblagh garden 1983

The garden was on its own, abandoned by humans, but the animals still harvested, dug, created, nested and burrowed. New trails were created and old ones reclaimed by badgers and foxes as they explored further into the old formal gardens now there were no humans to expel them. Winter rain and snow bit into the metal frames and wheel barrows that had been left, rusting them into the colours of the dying crocosmia and bracken. Cabbages flowered and died, hedges grew, wayward, enjoying their height, inviting new visitors in to share their cover. Daffodils and snowdrops clustered and spread, finding their way into the herbaceous borders where only the strongest and hardiest plants survived.

Seed pods full to bursting spread their seed across the garden, creating intriguing combinations.

Raspberry canes broke in the wind, their fruit eaten by foxes and birds who in their turn deposited the undigested seeds in areas of the garden set aside for flowering plants. Creeping buttercup and nettle took their chance and began their slow but effective march across the open flower beds. It was a sad rebellion.

It had been a long flight to London and Fleur and Bryony, now an energetic three year old, had stopped over with friends before getting the flight to Belfast.

It had not been an easy journey. The heavy security at Belfast airport and at regular intervals along the journey had disconcerted Fleur. Bryony had pointed to the soldiers carrying guns and asked about the men in their lorries wear funny clothes.

Fleur was glad when she eventually drove the hired car up the drive. The trees and rhododendron shrubs had closed over, and at times she felt the branches rubbing against the car. Weeds covered the gravel.

But then she saw the house.

'Oh God, no!'

She drove the car the last few yards and stopped. The front of the great house was gone. The remnants of police signs were visible from the explosion. She realised she was gripping the steering wheel so hard her fingers were becoming numb. The lime avenue was still there, but no longer cut and pleached, the trees had created their own protective glade and were shielding some small flowering plants beneath them like young children. She struggled to hide her tears from Bryony.

'Time to get out and look around,' she said out loud more to herself than Bryony.

She whispered to herself, 'You know this place and it still knows you. You will come to no harm here.' But still she shivered even though the sun was shining as she put on the jacket she had brought with her.

With tears in her eyes, she lifted Bryony down onto the ground and took her hand as they slowly moved around the corner of the house to the side facing the gardens. She thought back to where each of the rooms had been sited. Walking over the remains of the drawing room wall she crunched over broken glass until she came to the staircase. The back of the house had, bizarrely, missed some of the force of the blast.

Fleur looked down at her hand. She noticed blue and red light flickering across it. At first she couldn't understand, but then she looked up. The stained glass staircase window was still mostly intact. Two pieces of red and green glass lay on the ground and Fleur picked them up. Holding the red one up to her eyes she said, 'Am I looking through rose tinted glasses still?'

It was clear, as Fleur walked around, that others had come searching in the debris and had left after enjoying themselves. The sound of a car brought Fleur back from her reverie and she lifted Bryony into her arms again, gingerly making her way to the driveway.

John Adamson the solicitor got out of his car and introduced himself. Coldly and without emotion, he explained the situation.

'As you can see there was a great deal of damage to the building's structure. It is not a case of rebuilding, it requires demolition. That just leaves the considerable acreage and a very overgrown garden which could be easily ploughed up and made ready for development. It's a prime site for more housing.'

Fleur held back the tears.

'I'll leave you to consider what to do. You can contact me at the office, Miss Johnson.'

The grey suited solicitor turned with a brief goodbye and got back into his car and left.

'We're going for a little walk around, Bryony.' Fleur added angrily to herself, 'That man would have got on well with my mother.'

Fleur found that she and Bryony had walked to the old family graveyard, surrounded by trees. She opened the old wooden gate and walked along the now overgrown path. Beneath a magnificent magnolia was Timothy's grave with its small headstone. She knew he had been Amelia and George's second son, born dead, shortly after the family had moved into Garraiblagh. Fleur knelt down to read the inscription and looked at the other gravestones. Amelia and George Henderson, Ted and Florence Henderson and her grand-parents, Daisy and Tom Guthrie.

'Well, what do you think I should I do?' she said aloud to them. She had expected some form of response; an idea would pop into her head to solve the problem of Garraiblagh. The ancestors would have a way forward. But there was only a deathly silence, she knew it was hopeless.

The walls forming the field borders were now moss covered with age and no longer protected or divided areas. The natural order was changing. New paths and routes were being trodden down by the unseen animals no longer fearful of crossing into the garden. In the soft earth banks there were badgers' claw marks where worms and other insects had been excavated.

The dead inhabited the garden in many forms. Selling it would be difficult. All she could do for the moment was leave it. In the future when Bryony was older she would look again, perhaps persuade her to come to Garraiblagh and make decisions.

Fleur had brought her camera with her to take reminders of the world that she had loved so dearly. The house was not safe enough to investigate further but the gardens were what she was most interested in anyway.

The garden which had been hopeful when Fleur had arrived, sank back. Its hopes dashed. The wind sighed in the trees and Fleur realised that she could hear no birdsong.

'But I can't help you, garden! I wish I could, but I can't! I live in New Zealand and I don't know what I can do for you!' she cried.

A breeze caught the plants, rustling leaves and seed pods as though commenting on what she had said.

'I don't know what I expected. Perhaps in my dreams to see Kevin waiting for me, to have changed his mind. Things don't happen like that. And he doesn't even know he has a daughter.'

Fleur wandered around the grounds, stopping frequently to take photographs. Getting on the plane back to New Zealand was one of the hardest things Fleur had ever had to do. On the long journey home Fleur began to draw, memories of Garraiblagh, imaginary characters who inhabited the place. She would put together a story of the garden of Garraiblagh for Bryony. In her pocket Fleur held memories of the garden: seeds of agapanthus, petals pressed between pages of a novel.

Fleur carefully drew the garden from memory, as she drew she walked the paths in her memory. She had decided that the children book would have a child, named Bryony as its main character. As she drew, the illustrations brought to life the garden. Small details found their way into her pictures that she had forgotten. Somewhere in her mind was the thought that if she drew her daughter into the garden then, perhaps one day it would happen in reality.

Chapter Two

1985

DAVY KENNEDY FOUND the old estate and garden when he had been out on one of his regular cycle rides. In spite of the fact that it had been neglected for a good many years, his trained eye saw some interesting and rare plants. It became clear to him very quickly that it had been a plantsman's garden.

He enjoyed his job in the Botanic Gardens in Belfast. It was a haven of peace compared with what went on outside the gates. He liked to get out of the war-torn city whenever he could. He was tired of the helicopters constantly circling above the city day and night. He tried not to venture into the main shopping area, which meant making his way through the barriers and searches. The sound of police sirens and explosions unnerved him as he thought about his parents back in Coleraine. A realisation began to dawn on Davy that leaving Coleraine wasn't going to be enough. He had to get out of Northern Ireland. He wanted to travel: more precisely to seek out rare plants, to become a plant hunter. To do that he needed some working capital and his job as a council gardener did not pay enough to generate such money.

His discovery of the old garden offered not just a sanctuary from the madness, but to Davy it also offered a way of supporting his plans. He had carefully watched the area for several weeks before making his decision.

He'd been in Belfast for two years. He'd thought that moving down from Coleraine to take up a post in the Botanic Gardens would give him some freedom from small town life, but now he had ambitions to leave Ireland altogether.

Working with plants had saved Davy from an aimless life experienced by many of his friends of drinking, chasing women and humdrum jobs. He had not been sporty or particularly social as a teenager. He was happier growing fruit and vegetables for his mother and aunts. His mother understood Davy's interest and encouraged him. His father, on the other hand, was wrapped up in his work as a police officer: a demanding and highly dangerous occupation that robbed Davy of any relationship with his father. His father had coping mechanisms. He liked things black and white: well-polished shoes, routines, rules. The house was a fortress. The reinforced door could never be answered without determining who was there from an upstairs window. The car could not be driven without first checking the chassis for explosive devices.

Unsurprisingly, in recent times the tension between father and son had grown. The parting of the ways came when Davy's father found some cannabis hidden in the garden shed. No one else had access to the shed. He knew it was his son's.

Davy's interest in plants had led him naturally on to discover cannabis. He much preferred its effects to the alcohol his friends consumed. His father as a police officer only saw the law. Davy knew it was time to spread his wings and grabbed the opportunity of the gardening job in Belfast.

But now two years on, it was the old deserted garden on the

northern outskirts of the city that was the focus of Davy's attention. Not only was it perfect for growing cannabis, the rare plants left behind by the plantsmen of Victorian times could be re-cultivated and sold to nurseries and collectors. It was to be Davy's way out to a life as an international plant hunter.

'Who's going to be bothered these days if I cultivate a bit of cannabis anyway?' he thought.

The walled garden was perfect with its own tiny micro-climate: a good stone wall for heat and protection and still some sections of one of the old glasshouses still standing. The area, he thought, looked too derelict and dangerous for prying eyes.

The smoke from his joint circled around as he considered the crop growing to its full height to be dried and harvested, ready for sale. As he smoked, he thought, with a satisfied grin, some things were just meant to be! In a haze he saw images of himself in Africa and along the Amazon collecting rare species and even writing books of his adventures.

Davy's confidence in being hidden from prying eyes was mistaken. Unknown to him his business venture was being watched. Hidden from view cameras, installed on an army watch tower some distance away, were occasionally focused, not on the nearby houses, but on the disused garden.

On one occasion a lone bramble caught Davy around the ankle knocking him off balance as he moved carefully through a bank of nettles. Reaching out an uncovered arm to steady himself he found nothing to hold on to and landed heavily amidst the stinging plants. There was laughter from one of the watchers.

"E looks as though 'e's doing some sort of rain-dance down there.'

'No one wades through nettles like that unless there's a reason.'

The camera followed Davy up to his growing crop in the old greenhouse.

'Looks like 'e's been raidin' the budgie seed!' said another.

'That's marijuana!' said a soldier looking through binoculars. 'You can't grow weed usin' budgie seed.'

'I know that! Thicko!'

'But he is growin' marijuana. Let's just see what happens.'

The watchers, there to monitor more deadly intentions, watched Davy's movements in amused detachment. It was a form of light relief to the soldiers when there was a break in more deadly activities.

Davy, happily unaware that he was being watched, found the derelict greenhouse a perfect place not only to grow his crop, but to sit and dream his dreams with a spliff.

The garden too, watched Davy, with a growing concern about his illicit activities.

His crop was growing well. Just a few more weeks and he would harvest. He smoked the last of his joint and went on checking the plants. He thought he saw a movement and turned. There was nothing to see. But there was a scent mixing with the aroma of his joint. Vaguely seductive. Unsettling.

He returned to the plants. A slight breeze was catching their leaves. Davy hesitated. He had never encountered any breeze disturbing his crop. He checked but could find no source. There was the scent again. Roses? But where? There were no rose bushes nearby. Davy suddenly felt unaccountably unnerved and moved out of the greenhouse to look around.

'Hey, look at this! Matey, the gardener, is behaving very strangely.'

'Too much weed.'

'Could be, but 'e looks spooked.'

The third watcher leant forward and stared at the screen intently.

'I'm not sure that 'e hasn't got a reason. Look at this.'

A tall figure appeared to be standing close to Davy, but slightly out of focus. Each time Davy moved the figure moved with him. It had an air of authority. The watchers could see Davy put up his arms and begin to wave them around in protest. Then he began to run.

The cameras followed as Davy grabbed his bike and cycled frantically down the old estate drive and out of the gates. When the cameras panned back to the greenhouses, the menacing figure was nowhere to be seen.

'Where'd 'e go? 'E can't have moved that quickly. There's nowhere for 'im to hide.'

The soldiers never saw the strange figure or Davy Kennedy again. Soon the cannabis grew wild and without close attention withered and died. The garden returned to its dying slumber.

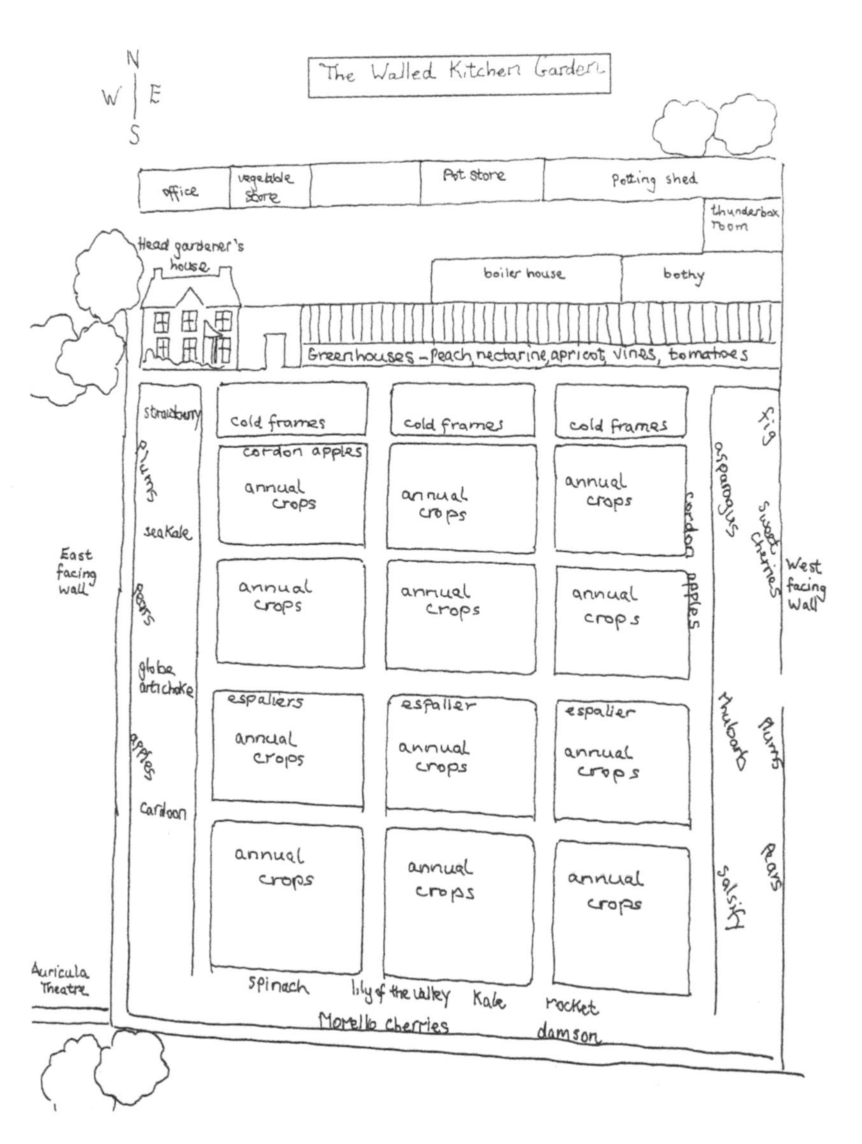

James Black's design layout of Garraiblagh's kitchen garden 1870

PART TWO

Beginnings

'Life begins the day you start a garden'
Chinese proverb

Farmland before Garraiblagh was created : 1869

Chapter Three

Spring 1869, Belfast

THE HARE STOPPED in her tracks, smelled the air and then with a long loping movement disappeared into the field of tall grasses and cowslip. The scent of bluebells from the nearby wood hung in the air, mixing with the blackthorn blossom and a slow murmur of a breeze passed through the trees circling the old fields. In the distance the water of Belfast Lough shimmered beneath a blue sky as hare made her way, past the old standing stone that marked the ancient people's sacred place and into the next field, relishing the freedom of this place that she and other creatures had always enjoyed. She sniffed again, her eyes wide. Change was in the wind. She smelled something she couldn't quite identify. She could not determine whether it was good or bad.

Amelia could not help herself. She knew it had become an obsession for her but then, so were the linen mills for her husband,

George. She had dreamed of a garden for so long she could close her eyes and be there in her imagination. The scents and the colours, the textures of leaves and petals, all tantalisingly just out of reach in reality. This had to be the place.

She sat forward staring through the carriage window, as though in doing so she could make the horses move faster as they drove out of Belfast. The clatter of the hooves on the cobbled roads reverberated around the carriage. Cranes lowered their huge bundles onto the quayside of the busy docks and the sound of men's voices and engines hung in the air while the smoke from the red brick chimney stacks mixed with the bright sunlight to create a rosy glow. Belfast Lough and its busy port were full of sailing ships arriving and leaving.

Amelia searched for trees, plants, any life beyond industry and commerce which she found so suffocating.

George, sitting opposite her with his cigar alight, glanced across at one of the ships, then checked his watch and nodded to himself.

'That will be the Ariana leaving for Hamburg. If we can interest them in more linen it will increase our reach further into Europe.'

Amelia nodded, but without interest. She looked down at the information sheet on the land they were going to view, her fingers carefully opening the page to see the description. The paper was now well thumbed and she had to smooth it down with her hands, hands that she wanted to use to grow plants, to create a garden.

George Henderson lifted up the Northern Whig[01] and opened it. She looked at her husband's hands. They were good hands she thought. Strong and capable. Those of a man who did not need to make his living through practical work.

'I see that the top stone on the Albert Memorial[02] has been put in place, but it will still be some time before the structure is complete.'

---

01 Belfast-based unionist daily morning newspaper (1832-1963).

02 Albert Clock in Belfast. Completed in 1869 in memory of the consort to Queen Victoria.

George noticed the silence from his normally enthusiastic wife and dropped the newspaper to his lap. He looked at Amelia, his brows furrowed, trying to understand her mood.

'I hope our house will not be dogged with similar delays when we come to build it.'

'George, do not even suggest it!' Amelia said in exasperation, her feet stamping on the floor.

'I'm sure it will all work out well, my dear, I'm only teasing!'

Amelia was not in the mood.

He sat back against the well–padded seat, taking in the expression on his wife's face, a combination of worried excitement and hope. She was wearing her best hat, the one with the velvet ribbons; her lucky hat but worn with her sensible green wool dress and cape. Her paisley shawl was one that George had bought her on their honeymoon after spending a glorious day looking around gardens in Rome. The gardens had been breathtaking, even George could acknowledge that and he understood the power and prestige that the owners of such gardens wielded, as much as the complex engineering of fountains and terraces. They had both fallen in love with the gardens, but it was Amelia who had been enthralled with the plants, their colours, shapes and scents. He remembered her, walking along the paths, reaching out to touch a petal or leaf, recognising a name or greeting a plant almost like an old friend.

Amelia became aware of George's stare and looked across at him. She assumed he was probably thinking of some business deal. It was rare that he was not preoccupied these days, but today was important. She noticed the creases around his eyes, the lines made from laughter and now, more and more, and the lines between his eyes from business worries. She had been captivated by his rugged good looks the first time she had seen him, his deep brown eyes full of passion and excitement and his chestnut brown, curly hair escaping from under his hat. Amelia felt herself relax. This project was something they both wanted, even if in different ways.

'I think it was your smile that first attracted me,' she said. 'You had just rushed into the bookshop looking for some obscure engineering text.'

'I was already late for a lecture! Then I was very late,' George said. 'It had never occurred to me that a girl could be working in a bookshop even if, as I discovered later, her uncle owned the shop and the accompanying printing press. Your bookshop became my second home in Glasgow,' George said wistfully. 'I would have made it so, even if it had not been so close to the university! The books were not the only items of interest there,'

He arched his eyebrow and focused his brown eyes on his wife, in a way that she had not felt for some time. George's work and a prolonged stay in her in–laws' home had brought tensions.

Amelia felt herself blushing.

'What has made you think about our meeting, Amelia?'

'I suppose you were the first person that I really talked to about gardens. Or, perhaps I should say the only person who listened. My father certainly didn't. He felt it was quite unsuitable. I suppose it is because you didn't patronise me and we could discuss books and ideas and dreams. You didn't laugh and particularly, you did not laugh when I told you about my dream to have a garden.'

'And now here we are, looking for your garden,' said George.

George sat further back into the seat, allowing himself to enjoy the memories. He knew that he had become very wrapped up in business. He saw now in this moment that he could lose more than a business deal if he did not concentrate more on his wife.

He leant forward and took her hand, kissing it.

Amelia laughed. 'It is a long time since you have done that.'

'I know, my love. I will try to be less absorbed in business, but it is the business that will allow us to build our home and garden — when we find it.'

'Given the discussions we have had it could be a very strange mixture of styles and ideas,' said Amelia.

The carriage followed the road, moving from cobbled street to hardened earth. The lough was almost the same colour as the sky, magical. The start of hedgerows and green fields relaxed Amelia, her head no longer echoing with the noises of industry.

She thought back to the first time she had travelled to Belfast after their honeymoon six years ago. From their cabin on board the ship Amelia had stood with George's arms around her shoulders; the early morning light illuminating the surrounding shoreline and countryside as the ship negotiated the channel into Belfast's harbour.

She had been used to bustling cities and Belfast had been so much smaller than she had expected, but with an obvious energy. It seemed to beat with excitement. In the years since then, Belfast had proved itself. It was now a match for Glasgow, Dublin and the English cities and George was a part of that tremendous change. As a woman she was not.

Today was hopefully going to be the start of changing all that, the promise of something she had longed for. Her garden. George looked at his wife. He had known soon after he had met her in the bookshop close to the university in Glasgow that he would marry her. He had not wanted someone who would be a quiet, well behaved and submissive wife and George was glad that Amelia was not. She was his equal in so many ways and he relied on her. However he knew that it rankled with Amelia that she could never, as a woman, be accepted in business circles especially in engineering and shipping. He knew she needed an outlet for her talent and energy and horticulture was her passion. George noticed the determined set of his wife's jaw. He knew that there would probably be arguments about the garden and the house and how they should proceed on aspects of the building, but that was for the future and in any case, they understood their combined strength.

'I do hope this is the right place,' Amelia said.

'From what Grant has told me it sounds the most probable site that we have looked at.'

'I think Mr Grant must be becoming a little frustrated with our search by now,' said Amelia.

'Mr Grant is being well paid to act as our agent and to find these locations for us and Mr Grant knows that!' said George. In that comment Amelia could see the steeliness of the successful business-man that her husband was.

George gazed into the distance and then laughed and commented, 'Do you remember the place that we viewed last year? You almost lost your shoe trying to walk across the first muddy field!'

'And you fell into that pile of thistles, helping me to retrieve it,' giggled Amelia.

George laughed at himself and then said more quietly, 'We will find the right place. You will have your garden and I will have my estate. I know it sounds pretentious, but I want to show the world what we can do.'

'Mr Darcy's house,' smiled Amelia.

'Perhaps not quite that large, my love.'

Amelia laughed. 'I know I am still entranced by Jane Austen's stories, but if it hadn't been for her description of Darcy I might not have noticed you when you came looking for your engineering books!'

'So I should also thank Jane Austen for your obsession with gardens!'

'Jane Austen and others. I had a lot of time to read! Travelling around as the daughter of a colonel in the Engineers, I have lived in so many places, but never had one that I could really call home'.

'But, my love,' George interrupted, 'would your interest and knowledge of plants and gardens have been as great if you had not?'

'True and I hope that I will be able to obtain some of the plants

I have seen and bring them to our garden.'

'Well, the house is certainly full of gardening journals! I'm not sure if they aren't quite subversive. My mother commented on the number of journals the other day. She said that perhaps they were inappropriate reading for a young married woman.'

George then realised what he had said. He saw his wife begin to bristle and the blue eyes flash. George knew that he had stirred a hornet's nest.

'And your mother is concerned at my reading gardening journals? Why should I not! Am I supposed to sit quietly at home with my embroidery or worse still, make visits to people I find boring!'

Amelia's stare bored into George. She was not someone to take for granted he knew and he also knew that his mother found her too outspoken.

'Amelia, I shouldn't have said that. You know I want our own house as much as you do.'

'And garden' added Amelia, still angry.

Amelia thought back to her early years, moving from posting to posting as her father, a military engineer, worked on projects. She had been overwhelmed by the colours and the shapes of the plants and their settings in India. At home she had spent hours planning gardens, writing stories about them in the same way that other children might have drawn treasure maps and plotted pirates' adventures across the sea. When her father, for many years a widower, was away she was looked after by her Indian aya. She had become independent in ways that her Scottish cousins had not. Later, she had spent hours drawing and painting the plants she saw and had kept a journal of those she had seen. While in India her father had hosted Mr Hooker, the plant hunter. Amelia had listened with rapt attention to his tales of the plants the party had found. She had been delighted when Mr Hooker had complemented her on a drawing she had made of a particular rhododendron. In her often solitary existence she had dreamed of the gardens and parklands in the novels of Jane Austen novels and developed a deep and romantic attachment to gardens in her adolescent years. Her father's decision to send her back to Glasgow to stay with her uncle and aunt had not been one that initially she had wanted, especially as she was sure that it was in the hope that she would find an appropriate husband. In that respect she felt very like a Jane Austen character.

But it had many compensations. It had enabled Amelia to listen to lectures given by Mr Hooker[03] and Mr Fortune[04] in Glasgow. A number of the plants they described she had seen for herself and she was curious as to how they had transported them back to Scotland on such long sea journeys. She was grateful that living with her aunt and uncle had given her the opportunity of spending time in the nearby Botanic Gardens, close to the university and she regularly read and drew amidst the colour and scent of the carefully planted flowerbeds. Her time in Glasgow had even allowed for a short plant gathering trip into the Highlands with her aunt.

Amelia smiled as she came out of her reverie and commented to George, who was again deeply engrossed in the Northern Whig.

'Do you know that I had planned to be an earnest young female plant hunter until I met you!'

'I do hope marrying me has not been a disappointment!'

'No, never that, George dear,' said Amelia.

They both laughed. Their current house just off the Malone Road in Belfast was in reality a shared property, albeit a shared mansion. George's parents had welcomed the newly-weds to their home and while both George and Amelia were grateful for their support, they wanted their own home. The Henderson house was first and foremost a building. The garden was relatively small and only there to provide a decoration for the main interest of the house.

03 William Hooker, English botanist and illustrator 1785-1865.

04 Robert Fortune, Scottish botanist and plant hunter 1812-1880.

Amelia wanted her own garden. And house. She wanted the freedom to create. She intended to be practically involved in the garden, something else of which her mother-in-law did not approve. Amelia smiled to herself. She would enjoy shocking her.

She saw the city of Belfast disappear into the distance behind them. Unable to keep still she focused on the scenery. It was early May and the white thorn hedges were full of blossom and the trees were wearing their new bright green canopies. It was unusual for her to be out in the carriage during the week with her husband. Normally George would be at his office in the main mill and she would not see him until he returned in time for dinner.

Initially, after she had first arrived in Belfast, time had hung heavily. Her mother-in-law was mistress of the house and she was expected to accompany her on social visits. This did nothing to improve the relationship between the two women. George, becoming increasingly aware of the difficulties, had come across information on the new Belfast Botanic Gardens and had suggested that they become shareholders, something that Amelia seized on with joy. Since that time Amelia had visited the gardens frequently, taking Ted, their young son, with her whenever she could. She hoped that he, too, would love the plants and the closeness to nature that their future home and garden would provide.

Ted was only four but George had decided that when they had found their own home a nanny would be necessary, given the social engagements that he and Amelia needed to attend befitting an owner of two productive linen mills.

'Perhaps we should have brought Ted with us? He enjoys carriage rides, particularly with both of us,' said Amelia.

'He will be happy to stay with my parents. You know how much they love him,' responded George.

'Yes,' said Amelia drily, 'I often wonder if he knows we are his parents!'

George sighed. This was not the conversation he had hoped for on the way to view the property.

'When we find our land and he can see the building work, then he will have something to interest him,' George asserted.

Amelia made no reply but was determined that when the house and garden were complete Ted would have as much freedom as possible. Amelia knew she should feel more agreeably towards her in–laws. They had been welcoming and pleasant and they had been only too delighted to have the opportunity to spend time with their only grandchild. And, she remembered it was because of them that she and George had been able to see Mr Charles Dickens perform in the Ulster Hall in January. She had even been able to get the great writer to sign one of his books.

A change in the sound of the carriage wheels confirmed that the road surface had become less well used. Overhanging branches scratched against the sides of the carriage on the increasingly uneven and narrow roads, the only vehicle they met was a donkey and cart that respectfully pulled in to allow their grand carriage to pass. Small green fields and the occasional roadside cottage flitted past on their journey.

It seemed to Amelia that they had travelled for hours, but when George took out his gold pocket watch and flicked the top open he looked at it with satisfaction. 'We're on time to meet with Grant.'

Amelia was finding it increasingly difficult to sit still. The information that they had received from Mr Grant had sounded promising. A property of twenty acres laid out in fields which had been left to return to wildness since the previous owner had decided to move to England, upset at the incidents in the south of the country and the proposed changes in Irish land registration. There was also a small farm that could be included in the sale.

The carriage drew to a halt just over the rise of a hill. Beech and poplar trees quivered in the slight wind. A tall, well–built man came over to the door and raised his hat to Amelia.

'Good morning Sir, Madam. The next part of the journey is along a narrow track. I have brought the pony and trap. It will make it easier to view the property if you would care to follow me?'

Amelia and George climbed into the open cart where they were given rugs to cover their legs.

The sunken lane they drove along was indeed narrow with a mixture of ash, hazel, poplar and holly trees and on either side the trees curved over to create a green guard of honour with sunlight dappling the trap and its occupants. Amelia noticed the primroses, their pale yellow flowers in the hedgerow.

After a short and bumpy ride they arrived at a flat field, full of swaying grasses and wild flowers. George helped Amelia down and arm in arm they followed their agent. The field carried on in front of them for what seemed be an age and in the distance there was Belfast lough, glittering blue in the sunlight. The sun had now risen high above them and they could feel its warmth reviving them.

The couple saw the open fields surrounded by woodland and felt a pulse, a heartbeat through their carefully shod feet. An old oak tree gave shade as they scanned the countryside. This was what they had been looking for. They both began to feel that the house and estate that they had dreamt of could be realised at last.

George Henderson squeezed his wife's hand. Amelia looked up at him and in that glance was the combined hope and excitement they felt. George drew Amelia aside.

'Let me discuss the details of the property with Grant. He would not understand if you were to start quizzing him on business issues!'

Amelia was prepared to concede and began to make her way across to the edge of the field and trees. Bluebells and wood anemone carpeted the woods and around the field edges dog violets were still in bloom, half hidden by the grasses and mosses. It occurred to Amelia that the natural beauty of the wild flowers should be preserved, at least in some areas. She could see George looking at a large map that the agent had brought the two men's heads together as they discussed an issue. It was some time before George moved away from Mr Grant and walked towards her.

'Look at the view, George! The lough sparkled in the distance and small plumes of smoke could be seen rising from closer to the lough shore.

'See there, Amelia. It's the Belfast to Bangor train. Can you see it down there on the south side of the lough? It looks like Ted's toy train from here!'

'We are quite some distance from Belfast here, aren't we?' asked Amelia. 'Would that make it too difficult for you to get to the mills?' Amelia said this hoping that her husband would brush the suggestion aside, otherwise why had they come to view the property in the first place, but she wanted to show him that she understood the importance of his business.

'From where we are I can be in Belfast quickly enough. The roads are to be improved soon. It must be the right place for our home. I know others who have built properties only to find themselves being crowded by even newer properties and even commercial premises. I do not want that to happen to us.'

'We are on a nice height here aren't we, not too high for it to be windy and there is shelter from the trees. Look at the view all the way down towards the water,' said Amelia.

'I agree,' commented George as he looked around him, 'and the land looks good, but I will want further verification of that.'

'I think we could be happy here, George.'

'I agree, my love.'

Leaning against his shooting stick George called to Mr Grant.

Amelia walked as though in a dream, bending down to collect flowers as she sought to examine the land from every viewpoint. She could hear the agent informing George of the acreage, but it became a mere babble. She arrived back with George carrying a bouquet of wild cherry blossom, alkanet, primrose, herb-robert, bugle and cuckoo flower.

'It is such a perfect place! 'said Amelia, sighing.

'I have asked Grant to check everything thoroughly. We have been here before, Amelia. We can't let our hearts rule our heads. I want this to move as quickly as possible but, everything must be right. I don't want to find that we have bought a place that does not suit our needs or is in some way lacking. I did not see any source of water, did you? We cannot buy this property, no matter how attractive it may be if we do not have water and enough of it to serve our needs.'

Amelia nodded slowly. She did not want to countenance any difficulties, there was something about this place but she knew she couldn't explain it. She held on tightly to her embroidered shawl and flowers, muttering a silent prayer that all would be well.

A dog fox and his vixen watched from their den among the hazel bushes beneath the old oaks. They knew about humans. Going back into the den they nuzzled their cubs and sniffed the air. They would wait and see. They did not want to have to run again, but they would if they had to. Their ancestors, the ones who'd survived, had done. The oak stretched out its roots. It felt the slight vibrations of the foxes as they moved to and fro. It felt their uncertainty. The oak knew all about change. It had felt the tremors of other animals that had grazed the field, the humans who had lived in the cottage many years ago and had had to leave when a distant landowner had forced them out. The tree had grown from an acorn left behind by a squirrel long ago. It remembered seeing old wooden ships sailing up the lough with their sails full in the wind. Many of its kind had been cut down to make these ships, but the oak had remained, witnessing it all and now, what else? It would wait, it had no other option. From its height it watched the cart and then the carriage move off into the distance towards the noise and bustle of Belfast. The vibration with these humans seemed positive. They'll be back, it thought. A place certain of its power to weave its spell over all who came there, it beckoned, ready to work with humans and it hoped, to keep the balance.

The old standing stone close to the tree had long ago become a boundary marker for those who had divided the land into fields. It leant a little to one side, not clearly visible any more among the brambles and grasses. But, quietly, it was still a place for old beliefs and a small posy of buttercup, dandelion, primrose and thorn flowers lay decorating its base, placed by an unknown visitor.

Back in their carriage Amelia could contain herself no longer. 'Well, what do you think?'

George began. 'Well....'

'Well what? Don't keep me in suspense.'

He fixed his eyes on hers. 'Did you like it?'

She threw herself back against the cushions. 'Yes! I knew as soon as the pony and trap stopped and we stood in the field.'

George took out his leather-bound notebook and began to list the items that would require attention. He wanted so much to be able to give Amelia her garden and to provide for his family. He also knew that he would have to be careful not to be too enthusiastic in case the sale could not be progressed. He knew Amelia well enough to know that she was already planning her garden. And, he knew, that he had found it hard to think of anything negative about the land and imagined the house he wanted and the imposing driveway and gates. As they drove back to Belfast the land that they had seen imprinted itself in their minds and their hearts: Amelia imagining the garden and the plants.

The couple had travelled through Europe on their honeymoon and now, courtesy of the expanding linen business and his new interests in ship building, they could afford to create a house and garden that would reflect Amelia's interest in gardens and, also for George, emphasise their new found standing in society.

George, linen mill owner and engineer, had the unshakeable belief that all aspects of nature could be moulded by human power. The evidence was all around. He did not doubt the possibility that a house and garden could be created from their ideas. He had become a successful businessman through his determination and ability to find solutions. This was just another element to be dealt with. While George wanted Amelia to have her garden he wanted an estate to be there as much as any jewels worn by his wife and other family members to present the essential message that they were people of substance, people of consequence and taste.

The garden would be Amelia's project. He had the mills to run.

George knew she had her treasured book, Mrs Loudon's[05] book on gardening for women, as well as magazines. He was surprised at her knowledge and slightly disconcerted at the sense of independence it seemed to give her. She did not look to him for advice and ideas on plants or the ideas she had for a garden. There was a steely determination when ideas for the garden were mentioned.

In talking to Amelia George realised that he did not know much about plants at all, apart of course from crops like flax that he had grown up with. His own family had built up their business over the generations from small flax farming to owning first one mill and, now with George, in charge of two more large mills. At the same

05 Jane Loudon (1807-1858). Author of Science fiction novels and gardening manuals.

time he could appreciate the beauty of plants in a landscape.

He was proud of his wife and her ideas and he would not, as some of his friends did, condescendingly mention their respective wives 'little projects.' After all, George thought to himself, did not the Queen herself take a great interest in gardens and gardening? He knew that he also needed to smooth things between his wife and his mother. His mother did not have the understanding or the interest in plants that Amelia had and she could not understand her daughter–in–law being more ready to pore over a plant catalogue than discuss the latest fashions or gossip.

Chapter Four

Summer 1869

THE WATER DIVINER STOOD, clearing his mind of everything except the question. His role was to find water, underground springs that could be useful for a water supply to the house and the gardens.

Stepping out, holding the hazel rod in front of him slightly raised. He asked the question silently. 'Is there water here?' He walked slowly, in a straight line across the field. He had made a rough plan of the fields so that he could note where any point needed to be mentioned. The slight adjustment in energy and downward movement of the wand brought him to a stop. Marking the position with a small flag, he kept walking until again, a change in the hazel rod's sensitivity shifted and the rod confirmed a further spot.

For several hours the water diviner walked across the fields, criss-crossing and checking the points he and the hazel rod had decided on. The owners of this new place would have access to water, but not in enough quantities for a large house and garden. A large mansion and a garden would take much more than he had found. It was a shame he thought. The place was interesting.

He settled himself down among the grasses to eat his lunch. He brought bread and cheese out of his satchel, and, quickly devouring it, he laid his head on the empty bag to enjoy a short sleep. Waking suddenly as a bee landed on his hand he stood up and looked around, still half asleep. Something had disturbed him, more than the touch of the bee. He reached for his rod and walked across the field, among the poppies, buttercups and ragged robin. Something had affected the rod too. He looked down at the hazel and felt the vibration. It didn't feel like water, he knew how to identify water. Then he noticed the stone. It was half hidden, close to an old oak. Kneeling down he pulled the grass and weeds away to take a closer look. Granite, he thought, from the rough texture. He traced his hand over the surface facing him. A slight indentation, a spiral. He sat back on his haunches. An ancient place. He rubbed his chin. How would the place feel to have its solitude broken?

The report from the water diviner had come to the agent. This was not the news he had been expecting and now he had to inform George Henderson. Making his way across the courtyard of the mill he found the noise and bustle did nothing to make him feel less worried about the meeting. The office was furnished in dark wood, with a large, well-polished desk at its end near the window. A clock ticked quietly on the wall.

'Good morning, Grant. Take a seat. So what progress has been made?'

Grant did not feel it would help to draw out his answer in first discussing the positives. George Henderson had a reputation for being a difficult man if not given the facts as they were, accurately and clearly.

Grant took a deep breath and began.

'There is a problem Mr Henderson. The water diviner, a man of great skill in that area, has been over the acreage and while there is some water there is not enough on the property to supply a large house and gardens.'

George put down his pen and pushed back his chair. Grant opened his notebook to locate a page that did not exist. The focus of the dark eyes in the bearded face was intimidating.

'Do you have any suggestions as to how this could be remedied? I am paying you to find solutions. I suggest you go and look at the property again and come back to me by Friday. Otherwise we'll both have my wife to deal with!'

Grant knew he had been dismissed in no uncertain terms. He left the mill feeling as though he had been shredded. George Henderson was half his age, but there was such an air of authority from the young man that he was glad that he did not work full time for him. However, George Henderson was a coming man and he must be satisfied.

George was not looking forward to informing Amelia. In spite of what he had told her, he knew that she had been making drawings and thinking of ideas that would suit this property. He arrived home to find Amelia waiting for him.

'George, I have had a wonderful idea! Do you remember that statue...?'

'Amelia, wait, I have something to tell you.'

'Are we nearing the signing of the contract?' she asked.

'No, my love, we are very far from it.'

Amelia looked at him. 'Why so?'

'The water diviner has been out to see the property. He has found some small amounts of water, but not enough to service the house and gardens, I'm afraid.'

'Surely there must be a way around it. I can't bear it. Not another property that isn't suitable!'

'Well, it has been our decision to build a new house and create a garden from nothing. If we were prepared to buy an estate that has already been constructed there would not be problems such as this.' George said in his defence.

'And do you believe that's what we should do? Give up on building ourselves and buy someone else's place, someone else's ideas and preferences!'

'No, I do not, Amelia. I am as keen as you that we build and design what we want. I am telling you what the problem is and that currently I do not have an answer. I have told Grant to come back to me by Friday with a solution.'

'I do feel sorry for the man. He cannot magic water, can he? He cannot have had an easy interview with you!'

'He didn't, but I'm hoping that it may make him try harder to find a solution. If he can't we may have to let this property go. I'm sorry, Amelia.'

Grant lost no time and early the next morning he rode his horse out to the property, down the sunken lane and out onto the first field. Dismounting, he looked around and turning to his horse, commented, 'It is a beautiful place. It would be hard to find anywhere better.' Moving to the saddle bag he extracted a plan of the fields for sale and a wider map of the area, along with the points marked by the water diviner.

The farm that could be included in the sale had a water source, but taking water from there would be counter–productive. He realised that he was focusing on the southerly aspect of the land, towards the lough, obvious because of its beauty. He made himself turn round and face the north. He checked the map he had brought with him. Off to one side towards the north–west there was an old scutching mill. Mounting his horse he made his way back along the track and around the edge of a further field close to the road until he reached the edge of the stone building. There was no sign of activity.

At the back of the property was a substantial river with a section that had been diverted for the use of the mill and the retting ponds[06].

Grant walked his horse around. Long grass and thistles grew where once there had been clear pathways. The old homestead appeared derelict, but then suddenly there was a ferocious bark and a black and white collie raced towards him with its teeth bared. Grant held hard on the reins 'Whoa boy, whoa!' Grant was so engrossed in ensuring his animal did not bolt that he did not notice the old woman. She stood, wrapped in a woolen shawl, smoking a pipe. 'Come Bob!' The collie retreated obediently to her skirts.

'Who are ye and what do ye want?' she demanded.

'I'd like to speak to the owner.'

'My husband is passed this ten year an' me son is out workin' the fields.'

'Are you still growing flax then, I saw no sign?' said Grant.

'No, 'tis too much for him an' we have no others to help any more. He's just growin' tatties and cabbage.'

Grant introduced himself.

'I am here on behalf of a Mr Henderson who might be interested in purchasing your property. He is keen to acquire a significant amount of acreage.'

'An' why would he want to do that?'

'He and his young wife wish to build a home.'

'Grand people, eh! Too grand to come an' ask fir themsels!'

Grant looked at the old woman. There was a pride there that he could understand. It would be difficult to give up the property, even though they were not working it to much effect currently.

'I cannot give you a definite answer, but I will speak to Mr Henderson. If he is prepared to come and meet you and your son, would you be prepared to discuss matters?'

---

06 For submerging flax to separate the flax fibre from the stalk.

'Me name is Mrs Murray. Ye will need to let him know who he will be meetin' but I will want to meet the wife. There can be no possible agreement without that.'

John Grant remounted his horse in thoughtful mood. He was unsure whether he could convince Mr Henderson that a meeting would be necessary. It was not that George Henderson would feel above that sort of thing, but John Grant knew that George Henderson was a man on the way up and was making his way up through hard work. He surmised that he did not have much free time to negotiate with small farmers and difficult old women.

Friday arrived and Grant opened the door to George Henderson's office and stopped in surprise. He had never seen Mrs Henderson in her husband's office.

'I have asked my wife to be here because I want her to hear what you have to say first hand, good or bad so do not delay. What is the outcome of your further investigations, Grant?'

John Grant placed a map on the desk and unrolled it. It was the first time George and Amelia had seen the land and its connection to the wider area around it. The agent drew his finger over the map to the north of the proposed estate and tapped it on a small area including buildings and a river.

'This is an old scutching mill with associated building and homestead. It is not currently in use, but what it does have is a water supply,' and Grant moved his finger again to point out a river running around the property. 'It would be possible to use the river to expand the water supply to your land and, it could also offer a business opportunity if the scutching mill was put to use again.' Grant stood back, pleased with the information he had brought so far.

'You have been careful to tell us of the positives.' said George.

'What are the difficulties?'

'The owner, Mrs Murray, an elderly lady of fixed opinions, will only countenance a possible sale if you and Mrs Henderson meet with her and her son at the property.'

'A widow?'

'Yes,' responded Grant, 'but I believe she will be a shrewd negotiator. 'My assessment is that she knows her mind and it would not be wise to take her for a fool.'

'And I would not expect that to be the case,' snapped Amelia. 'She sounds interesting.'

George looked over at Amelia and saw her brief nod.

'Really Grant. I am very busy!' sighed George. 'Very well, make the arrangements please.'

George and Amelia exchanged their carriage for a small pony and cart as they had done when they first visited the site. John Grant accompanied them on horseback. George leant forward as they approached the old scutching mill and the house.

'It is sad to see this,' said George looking at the derelict nature of the property. 'I remember visiting my grandparents' mill as a young boy. There was so much life about the place.'

Mrs Murray stood in front of the house door, arms folded. John Grant noted that she had obviously made an effort, wearing what looked to be her best clothes. Her son, tall and gangly, looked to John to be in his early twenties. He shifted uneasily around in his Sunday best, clearly happier to be out in the fields than entertain well-to-do strangers.

Amelia moved forward to shake Mrs Murray's ungloved hand and felt the strength in it. Amelia looked down. Mrs Murray's hands were rough and red. The older woman noticed Amelia's glance.

'I could not houl' from pulling out a few weeds in the herb garden while I awaited ye.' Amelia noticed a small area carefully fenced, full of gaily coloured plants.

'I would have done the same if I had had the good fortune to have a herb garden, Mrs Murray.'

'May we go and look?'

Mrs Murray relaxed.

'Aye, but it's a wee bit muddy an' ye may find the plants will pull at your skirts, Ma'am?'

'I do not mind that.'

The two women followed an earthen path around the side of the house and to the left, leading to a hazel fence leaving George, Grant and the son to stand around awkwardly.

A smile brightened Mrs Murray's face as she held open the gate for Amelia.

'Yon's me herb plants. I've worked at them many a year, ma'am. I make tinctures and creams fae 'em. That's the way of it.'

The women, turned, realising the men were left behind. 'Why don't you and Mr Grant speak to Mr Murray while Mrs Murray shows me her herbs, George?'

'Take the gentlemen to the parlour, Tommy an' listen to what they have to say. Mrs Henderson an' I will be there in a piece.'

Mrs Murray started down the main dividing path, beds of herbs on either side.

'I'll speak plainly ma'am. I'll be heart-scairt to leave me herbs. I've spent many a year adding to them.'

Mrs Murray stroked the leaves of the plants as she led Amelia along the paths, pointing out the unusual herbs and offering Amelia leaves and flowers to smell.

'I do admire your garden! I have always loved plants and it is my dearest wish to have a garden, one of my own.'

Mrs Murray turned to look at Amelia, the wrinkles around her eyes showing the weather beaten face as she looked searchingly into the younger woman's face.

'A garden of yourn? But if ye are hopin' to buy the land yonder tis not just a garden. This is a wee garden an' I can manage it mesel, though I'm no longer a young 'unlike yersel. I'm surmisin'ye have in mind a much larger effort an' if the garden is so large ye'll not be fit to plant it yersel?'

'That is true and I know my limitations, Mrs Murray. I know we will need a professional gardener,' Amelia said and added, 'my mother–in–law believes my interest in plants and gardening is unnatural.'

'Unnatural? Tut, tut!' The old woman shook her head.

'I should be content to be the wife of a businessman.'

'Oh, aye? How'd a young lady like yersel become interested in plants?'

Amelia found it easy to talk to the older woman, to describe the plants she had seen on her travels, her love of gardens.

Amelia lifted an apple mint leaf between her fingers and felt its softness and then the scent.

'The plants all look so strong! How do you manage it?'

'The moon, ma'am, an' I believe the aul ways an' the fairies help.'

Amelia looked at the woman. She was not sure how to respond.

'I saw all sorts of different methods of cultivation when I lived with my father in different parts of the world. I suppose I just didn't expect it here. I would like to learn more.'

The two women moved to the old wooden bench near the top of the herb garden and were soon deeply engrossed in discussion.

Amelia plucked up her courage. 'Mrs Murray, if I spoke to my husband, would you consider selling your property and as part of the sale. We could offer you a cottage on the estate where you can re–create your herb garden. I admit I would be keen to learn from you as part of the agreement.'

'I would need to puzzle at that an' ask aroun', ma'am!'

'Around? Who would you ask?'

'The aul fairy folk a'course. From the thorn tree on the hill o'er there an' spend time in the herbs.'

Amelia looked at the older woman. The conversation she had had initially had been one that focused on the cultivation of the plants and the woman clearly knew what she was talking about, but this was different. Amelia paused.

Mrs Murray chuckled and winked at Amelia.

'Ye'll no doubt now be thinkin' that ye have spent the last wee while talkin' to a mad woman.'

Amelia shook her head slowly. 'No, I think I can understand what you're saying, Mrs Murray, I assure you. The evidence of your method is here to be seen! Touching your plants there is an energy that makes my fingers tingle but I can't explain it.'

'This is not for explainin,' ma'am. Women understand. It's them men that like the explainin'! I'm sure they're in there explainin' away.'

John Grant shook his head to himself as he drafted the agreement. It was not that the agreement was difficult in the sense that it would not work, but it showed him a side of George Henderson that he had not encountered. He would not ride roughshod over other people, he would listen and he would be fair in his dealings, not something he had seen much of in business of late. It also showed that there was an unusually close relationship between the husband and wife. John Grant had seen many where that was not the case.

The agreement drawn up handed ownership of the land to the Hendersons. Beyond this, it agreed that the scutching mill would be brought back into productivity. Mrs Murray and her son would be provided with a cottage rent free on the new estate close to the home farm. The established herb garden would be kept at the scutching mill, but cuttings and divisions would be taken and transferred to the new estate so that another herb garden could be introduced there with advice and support from Mrs Murray.

Tommy Murray would be offered a post, overseeing the newly productive scutching mill. He and his mother would also be relatively rich with the sale of the land.

The river would have a separate channel for the mill. A new wheel was to be built and the fields ploughed for flax once more. The main river would be left fresh so that it could be channeled towards the new estate and home.

Back home in Belfast George and Amelia were hardly able to contain themselves. George carried a rolled up map from the carriage.

Lighting a cigar, George felt a degree of relaxation for the first time in weeks. He looked over at his wife and realised that the negotiations for the scutching mill would not have been so immediately successful or as full of added elements as it was if she had not been there.

'Now we need a name for our home!' stated Amelia, clapping her hands and rolling out the map on the carpet between them.

'You really are a remarkable woman, Amelia Henderson!'

Amelia laughed. 'That is what you say now and I shall remind you of that in the coming days and weeks.'

She dropped a cushion from the chair onto the carpet beside the map. 'Will you join me Mr Henderson?'

'You really are a most forward young woman, my wife!'

George dropped to the floor beside her and took her in his arms.

'Promise me one thing?' George asked.

'What?'

'No pipe smoking like Mrs Murray.'

Amelia laughed. 'No, but I might have a word with her fairies! Now what about the name?'

'The townland[07] is *Garraiblagh*. I think that has a good sound to it,' said George.'But we have the opportunity to create a name that says something about the garden and the plants we will have,' said Amelia.' What do you suggest? It sounds very ordinary if we just call it '*the house of flowers*' or '*the place of flowers*,' said George.

'I know. What about the name in Irish?' suggested Amelia.

'*Teach na bláthanna* means house of flowers but it's a bit of a mouthful. There are already wild flowers here in the fields and the woodland isn't there? In Irish a flowery wood would be *Coill scothanachta*. We could call it *Kilscohanagh*?' said George.

'On thinking about it, it might be unlucky if we introduce a different name. There's something about *Garraiblagh*[08] that I like. Can we just keep it?'

George moved the map onto the sofa. 'I think perhaps you are right. Garraiblagh it is. It is time for us to celebrate I think. Let's mark the moment, Lady of Garraiblagh.' He took her in his arms again and began kissing her more urgently.

The land that had now been chosen remained unaware of the changes to come. The badgers followed their traditional moonlit path across the fields and through the hazel and hawthorn hedging to their sett. They had had a successful night's feeding and the cubs danced around before their parents. The stream which meandered down close to the eastern boundary found a fox lapping in its waters;

07 Pre-Christian term used in Ireland to identify a small area of land.
08 Pronounced Garryblah. Garraí Bláth. English translation - Flower garden

then pulling long grass from the banks. The hare sniffed the air again. Humans, it thought. It might be time to move on or could they be worked with?

The first stones were delivered, brought up from Belfast on a succession of open wagons pulled by teams of strong, large-hoofed horses.

The noise alerted the creatures of the surrounding woodland and meadow: humans and then the string and posts marking positions, the deep spade cuts and the wheel barrows. Their land, their homes were being invaded. Fox and hare moved further into the surrounding wilderness. The old gorse bushes which had spread across from one side to the other were gouged out, leaving a gap. There was no longer a way across hidden from sight for the small animals.

Chapter Five

Garraiblagh 1870

GARRAIBLAGH WAS NOW TAKING SHAPE. A small sandstone gate lodge guarded the entrance to the newly constructed front drive. From the gates there was a vista across lush, green fields to the lough. The large elegant wrought iron gates ensured that no one would be in any doubt that this was to be an important property. Amelia had suggested the leaf and flower design, based on the flax flower and this had been translated into bosses and curlicues that the local blacksmith had felt honoured to make. The narrow lane that Amelia and George had first driven down had become the farm entrance to the north of the property.

The grounds of the estate wrapped themselves around the solid red buildings spreading out to the front and south, making the most of the views across the lough and the sun, while the northern aspect, to the rear of the house was where the outbuildings were; including the well sized coach house and stable block. Small, terraced cottage accommodation close to the sunken lane, leading on to the home farm, was used as servant accommodation for those who worked in the garden and on the farm. A Head Gardener's house, a substantial three bedroomed property, denoting the status of that position, was situated in the corner of what would become the walled garden and awaited its occupants.

George and Amelia now occupied their new home.

The interior was a showcase for all that was best in modern Victorian style. Marble fireplaces, decorative plaster work, a formal staircase and another at the rear for the servants. Linens, from George's mills, were used to advantage in the upholstery and curtains, bedding and tableware. Wallpaper featured the newer floral designs of William Morris, designs that Amelia in particular liked.

Amelia sat in her study, composing a letter to a cousin in Glasgow.

Well, it is finished and I can't say I am unhappy to have left my in-laws' home. It is everything that George and I hoped it would be. The drive leads up to the front entrance with a porte cochere and from there into the house.

The rooms facing east include the breakfast room and morning room. The drawing room and the adjoining conservatory will face south and we have glass doors that will open out directly onto the veranda. George has his billiards room and a study. I have the conservatory and a delightfully sunny study of my own, where I am writing this letter to you. We both share the library and as you can imagine it is already full of books. The dining room is large enough for us to open it out into the drawing room to create a wonderful space if we wish to have a very formal gathering. George is sure that we will be entertaining a great deal and it is certain that he will see the estate as important to his ambitions.

Ted has a nursery and a bedroom which look out towards the farm. He is delighted with this view and when not actually outside, playing with the farm cats and visiting the cattle, he has a model farm to play with in his bedroom.

We will not have to go to the bother of an ice house in the grounds. There will, instead, be an ice cellar adjoining the rear of the house; so much more convenient to the kitchen and the pantry area. The servants have rooms in the basement and on the top floor.'It is the garden though on which I am yearning to see work commence. So many dreams and ideas are bound up in it.

We have engaged a head gardener of renown from Scotland — James Black — to take charge of the work, but I will be sure that he understands whose garden it is.

The family of foxes drew back from their vantage point overlooking the new buildings. The smell of humans now grew stronger and they had to remain alert. But, even the changes had brought some positives. Careless workmen left food, soon carefully hunted and retrieved gratefully by the growing fox family.

The ground changed; no longer the waving greens, yellows and ochres of grasses. Now the earth had been uncovered, laid bare to deep browns, puddled and muddy in the rain.

Amelia and George, aware that they needed advice on the practical aspects of creating their garden had wasted no time in appointing a Head Gardener. They had heard of James Black by reputation on their trips to London where they had visited the Royal Horticultural Society's Great Spring Show in Kensington with its nursery exhibits and model gardens. James Black was known to be a passionate, if rather autocratic designer and ruler of gardens, but he was the best and that was what they wanted. They, in particular Amelia, wanted someone who could translate her ideas and dreams. George had offered James more money than he was earning in his current work but it was, for James Black, more than the money. It was the opportunity to create something from the very start that appealed most. He accepted with little hesitation.

James Black had completed his apprenticeship in Edinburgh Botanic gardens, studiously working his way up through the ranks of gardeners and on occasion, managing to obtain a place in a plant hunter's team exploring the Himalayas and other exotic places. His love of plants, the unusual and the beautiful was combined with an intellect that easily understood both the practical and the theoretical.

James had worked in a number of large estate gardens in Scotland over the years but now aged thirty seven he was looking for something different; a garden that he could mould from the start, not just one that he adapted. There was a lot about this commission that intrigued him. He also had an idea that he might be able to convince the Hendersons that a gardener who was also a plant hunter could be very beneficial, both for the garden and their standing in society.

He walked the land of this new estate. Spring was a good time of year to visit. It had been a good spring and the weather was warm. Midsummer was on its way and then autumn would provide the quiet time for him to begin the physical changes to make this a garden. Through his feet he could feel the subtle changes in level and automatically calculated a rough estimate of the different areas. More precise and complex calculations would come later. Every so often a plant in flower or a grass caught his eye and he focused on the story that plant could tell him, dry or wet conditions, rich or disturbed earth, acid or alkaline. He searched for the nettles, the bare and stony ground, felt the soil between his fingers, adding spit to it, balling it between his fingers to sense its structure. In his head a picture was constructed. Stopping to study the old oak tree which he sensed marked a boundary, he sat down in the long grass and opened up a leather bound journal in which to make his notes. As he began to draw and make comments, he noticed out of the corner of his eye a movement and a feeling that he was being watched. He kept his head down and waited. Another rustle of leaves; then a flash of red fur. James tore off a piece of meat from the sandwiches and threw it into the undergrowth. A stronger rustle and this time, he could see two dark eyes and a black muzzle watching him.

'Don't worry, Reynard, this will be the boundary. I would nae hae ye an' your family put out o' your hoose. Your clan hae been aroon' fae a lang time. I ken what it's like tae have tae uproot an' I will nae bow tae any maister either.'

James' ideas transferred themselves to the large sheets of thick paper that he kept in his study. He knew the owners wanted formality, distinction with no expense spared, but he also understood that they had a deeper connection to the land they had bought and he respected them for that.

It was not often that he had the opportunity to create from scratch. The ideas flowed onto his pages. It was every gardener's dream.

James approved of the plan for the house. It was not too showy and was solid. There would be space for some attractive climbers on its walls and the kitchen garden, positioned and walled in the way that he had advised would work well and produce what was required.

James looked again at the letter he had been sent by the Hendersons, detailing the work. They had picked a good site for their home.

'I wonder if they realise what will be needed?' he said to himself as he filled his pipe.

Smoking his pipe he relaxed against the tree trunk. It would be his job to walk the precarious line between the reality of the climate, soil and aspect and the dreams of the owners.

All his initial measurements had been taken and noted: watching the arc of the sun as it moved across the land, and noting its path, the shade and the sun. Now he wanted the land to talk to him. He picked one of the grasses in his hand and played with it between his fingers as he gazed across the land to the lough.

Bringing his focus back to the present he noticed the stunted trees near the stone wall. He saw that the trees were bare of ivy — deer, sheep, rabbits were grazing. James noticed the nettles clustered close to the hedge where the ground was slightly raised. He wondered about the animal that had probably died there in years gone by, trying to shelter in the snow. He moved position to a small hill and considered the possible plants and features that he could place there.

The willow trees directed him to the wetter ground. They would be useful, but too wet for building any structure. The hard, compacted soil near the field entrance was covered in nettles and dandelions and James could see that the area around the old stone wall was full of yarrow and thistle.

A cluster of rooks perched like examining magistrates in the branches of the oak a little way off and cawed their query to this human intruder.

'Aye, it is to be a garden. There will be rich pickings, I imagine, and given that you are all here I imagine there are lots of worms in the soil.'

As if in response the birds, following each other took off out of the tree, muttering.

James lifted his satchel and moved to the corner of the top field close to the oak. The high pitched sound of the tree creepers and their echoing song, eerie even in the daylight followed him as he walked. There was a magic in this place he thought but then chided himself. A foolish idea, but then he had seen many strange things in his time.

The sandstone pillars and spherical tops of the main entrance stood at a bend in the road and reaching out along both sides a high brick wall, announced the boundary of the estate. The ornate iron gates opened to a sweeping graveled drive through woodland. Care had been taken to remove only the trees necessary to create the road. James acknowledged to himself that he had been correct to push for this. It gave the impression that the estate had been there for some time and traffic no longer needed to be directed down the old sunken back lane that had already wrecked a few wheels and axels on carts.

The gatehouse now had its new residents, an elderly couple, the Elliots. George had got to know Ben Elliot from the Henderson mill where until recently the man had been one of the night watchmen. Following a chance conversation with Ben Elliot George had offered the couple the gatehouse to see them through their later years. The couple had jumped at the opportunity to leave Belfast and already Mrs Elliot had placed a number of pots of geraniums near the entrance, giving it a warmth and colour. Ben Elliot wearing a rough woolen jacket and trousers touched his hat and waved at James as the carriage started up the drive. The old man closed the gates firmly and moved stiffly back to the cottage.

James saw ahead of him the sight of Garraiblagh House. The last time James had been to Garraiblagh the house had only been at the level of the third course of stone. This was his third visit and today would be the day he would put the final plan for the garden to the Hendersons.

It was good to see the reality. The soft red sandstone building stood as though ready to be dressed. A wisteria and a clematis would soon give a lived-in feeling to the house. James thought to himself that the house sat well in the landscape. The sound of the gravel under the wheels became more pronounced and then the carriage stopped under the portico at the front door on the west side.

James Black stood at the front door wearing his best Harris Tweed suit. He did not enjoy wearing formal clothes but he had long ago made a point of ensuring that the families he worked for understood that he was not a servant. He was a professional with standing in his field and would be treated as such.

James used the heavy brass knocker and awaited a response. A young maid opened the door, and he stepped into a spacious hall, where a young boy was busily chasing a black cocker spaniel. He removed his hat and a quick glance showed him the wealth on display in the silverware and the ornaments.

'Come this way please, sir. The master an' mistress will be with ye shortly.'

The maid swished past him to show him in to the library, taking a quick admiring glance at James' red hair and beard. A grandfather clock ticked in the background as he took the offered seat in an old wing-backed chair near the fire. He sensed that this was a favourite room. The warmth did not just come from the flames leaping in the grate, but from the colours of the carpet and curtains and even the spines of the books. He began to sweat in his heavy tweed. He noted that the sun was now feeling its way across the window sill and curtains. The large bay window had a built-in window seat below it. It looked surprisingly comfortable, as though it really was used for sitting on not just for show. Thinking through his designs he was glad that he would be able to point out how the garden would be seen from such rooms and how the vistas would change and develop depending on one's position and the time of year.

He could hear the muffled voice of the maid chastising the young 'master Edward' as he and the dog had nearly collided with one of the ornaments. This was a house which had a great deal of money spent on it, but he recognised it was also a home. In his experience that was unusual in houses of this type. He wondered about the person who had managed to combine the different aspects.

James stood up to get away from the heat of the fire and looked around the book cases and was surprised to find some less well known books on plants. Plants were already on display in wardian cases.

The door opened and George and Amelia Henderson entered with an air of excitement and anticipation. James had not expected this. He was used to dealing with people with money and only money, with no imagination.

'Good morning, Mr Black! It is good of you to meet with us. As you can imagine we are very keen to begin the work on the garden and landscaping, now that the house is complete,' said George Henderson.'

'Good morning Mr and Mrs Henderson. As ye know I have made some preliminary visits and have drawn up suggested designs, based on your ideas. May I show ye some of the information on this plan?'

Amelia smiled and spoke to the maid, 'Martha Jane, please bring in the tea now.'

Turning to James, she smiled, 'I'm sure that you could do with some refreshments. It's quite a journey out from Belfast and I gather you have been further afield in the last few months?'

Amelia noted the tanned face of the gardener.

'Thank ye, ma'am. Yes, I was on a trip to the Himalayas where we brought back some exquisite examples of rhododendron. I would like to think that some of them, when they are ready, could become part of the planting here.'

'Oh that would be wonderful! I remember seeing some when I lived in India.'

'So ye have both lived abroad?'

George shook his head.

'No, it is I who have lived abroad,' said Amelia. 'My father was a military engineer and I spent much of my childhood in different parts of the world. The plants I saw remain very strong memories for me.'

James realised that he had very quickly begun a conversation on plants. He had expected a slow introduction, a careful discovery of everyone's positions, explanations of terms and plants and then details of the project.

George laughed. 'You can see, Mr Black, that my wife is a keen and knowledgeable gardener. The garden is her province.'

James looked at George. There was no sense that he was patronising his wife. He was proud.

George pointed to the table in the centre of the room and quickly moved a couple of books and a newspaper that lay on it.

'Please lay the plan out on the table,' said George.

The plan stretched out across the table with Amelia securing the edges with small, ornate paperweights. James' eye was caught by one which he recognised was an image of the Great Exhibition at Crystal Palace.

James started. 'Now, the first thing I want to say is that the site is good, both in terms of the soil structure and the aspect. There will be a need for water pipes to feed fountains and other functions in the garden and the water diviner has marked locations of springs, but it is clear that the water from the river will be essential.'

James' experience as a gardener had shown him not just how to introduce plants into a garden, but how to introduce people to their positions in his plans.

James drew a pencil out of his leather satchel and adjusted his glasses.

'With ye agreement I will show ye.'

James had debated how he should present the information he had prepared. He had made some delicate watercolours of some special plants and detailed maps of designs and patterns for particular areas of the garden. James Black had learnt the advantage of a well presented plan in convincing owners of his ideas. He had taught himself to paint and to draw.

He understood that the making of the garden and the time for it to mature could be difficult for the couple so anxious to see their dreams quickly realised. James knew that they would accept the need to buy in larger, more mature trees and plants rather growing from very young saplings and seedlings.

Amelia moved the ruffles of material on her sleeves away from her wrists in order to lean forward and look more closely. James was suddenly aware of the light floral scent that she was wearing.

'So, Mr Black, if I walk out through the front door there will be a lawn directly opposite me with flowerbeds? What will be in them?'

'This area will get the morning sun so, depending on the season there will be dahlias and peonies, surrounded by hostas and irises.'

'And if I walk beyond the lawn and the more formal planting I will come to a bluebell glade?'

'Yes, the front door will show more formal planting around it, but it is not the main garden area — that will be the area seen from the drawing room windows and the morning room. The conservatory will also be accessed from this south facing area. The building is new. I am aware that ye would like it to seem less so...?'

'Yes, we would like the house and the grounds to look as though they have been here for some time and I admit that I am impatient to see plants in blossom,' said Amelia.

James Black nodded agreement. 'That is understandable. Climbers around the front door on the west, which will be east facing would soften the effect. Virginia creeper and honeysuckle would do well there. The wisteria will complement the stone on the south facing side of the house.'

James was surprised at Mrs Henderson's knowledge. He was forced to alter his focus to include her more in his explanations. James was beginning to see that although he had been appointed for his knowledge and skills, Mrs Henderson at least would want to have a greater say than he was used to. Mind you, he thought to himself, Janet, his wife would be pleased to hear that her husband had had to listen to a woman's view on the garden.

James described changes in level, down from the house to one level with the herbaceous border then to a further level and another beyond, before ending with the circular pond and fountain. There would then be a change of vista and a sunken area in which an oblong pond would be sited.

Pointing to the plan on the table Amelia queried the round shapes on both sides of the steps leading down from the house.

'Yes. Below the house there will be changes in level to give more interest and at each level there will be topiaries — box hedging with at their bases will be cyclamen and snowdrops followed by primula and lavender. The herbaceous borders will run the length of each level — roses and peonies and foxgloves in deep reds, magentas and pinks providing the central ground with deep blue delphiniums, agapanthus and larkspur towards the back. Lady's mantle, zinnia, day lilies, lavender and evening primroses will be arranged throughout the planting.'

'Oh! That will be fun!' said Amelia with delight.

James, encouraged by the response continued, 'the planted area on the lowest level close to the statue will be in a range of cooler colours involving white climbing roses, lamb's ears and white foxgloves, lavender and marjoram.'

Amelia and George nodded their approval.

'And we would like a summer house. We hoped that it could be constructed to face the lough. The position close to the old stone in the corner of what is currently the field seemed to us to be possible, something rustic?' said George.

Amelia brought out one of her gardening journals from the bookcase to illustrate the point.

'I see no problem with that Mr and Mrs Henderson. We can discuss the details of its structure.'

The door opened quietly and the maid entered with a tray.

'Ah, thank you, Martha Jane.'

James and the Hendersons sat down for tea. Amelia looked curiously over at James Black. She was intrigued. He was about ten years older than them but had a youthful and energetic air about him. His colouring made her think of a Scottish hero from the past, perhaps out of one of Sir Walter Scott's books.

She and George had spent time considering which gardener would be best and they had obtained much information about the different people whom they considered for the post, but Amelia wanted to find out more. If she was going to ensure that the garden really worked for her then she must know how this person worked.

'You're from Fife originally, Mr Black? I visited Falkland and the gardens there once but I know little of the area.'

'Yes, my family worked for generations down the coal mines of Fife, long dark hours tunneling into the depth of the earth. My father managed to move up into the daylight to farm work. So I grew up with two different views of the world — the industrial, dark and dangerous subterranean world and the agricultural with fields looking out across southern Fife to the Firth of Forth. I suppose my father taught me my love of nature. It had saved him from an early grave, Mrs Henderson. From an early age I loved every plant I could see and learned to identify even the complex ones. A seed merchant cousin in Leith found me work and I began as a garden boy in a local estate, Fallowfield.'

James thought back to his time as a young gardener, images coming to his mind as talked to the Hendersons. The head gardener at Fallowfield had seen that James was keen and found him a place on another estate on the other side of Fife to further his training. This garden was a teaching garden. The head gardener was well respected and did not use the young workers as slave labour, as was often the case.

Amelia saw that James Black was momentarily lost in thought and sought to bring him back with a further question.

'How did you enjoy your time at Edinburgh Botanic Gardens?'

'It was a fascinating time for me. I had met David Douglas[09], when I was a young gardener at Fallowfield where he was assisting the head gardener,' James smiled at the couple and continued. 'It was through my conversations with him that I became fascinated by plant hunting. So when I gained the opportunity to study at the Botanical Gardens in Edinburgh a few years later I found myself with Mr Douglas and joining his first expedition.'

Amelia, for her part, could see clearly that James Black was a man of sensitivity and had thought carefully about their garden ideas. She was keen to work with him. This gave her confidence to make her intention clear.

'Mr Black, the plans that you have created are wonderful, but it is important for to understand that I will wish to have practical involvement in the garden.'

"Practical? In what way?' James' heart sank. The dream project looked at risk. George heard the change of tone in James Black's voice, but decided that he would not intervene, at least not yet. Amelia had made clear that the garden was her domain.

'I don't want everything to be done by others. I don't want to feel that I cannot pick a plant or add a feature. I want it to be possible that I can ....' She didn't finish her sentence.

James looked across at the young woman, her hands describing her feelings, her eyes shining as she thought of the pleasure of working with plants. He understood that feeling of contentment, but also excitement. At the same time James thought back to other gardens where owners had involved themselves and chaos had ensued. Gardeners being ordered to do one thing by the head gardener and then being countermanded by the owner, often only to achieve a

09 Scottish botanist and plant hunter 1799-1834.

very momentary glory or to appear strong in front of visitors.

It would grieve him to have to end the work on this garden now, but he had reached a point in his life and career where he no longer felt he could or would twist himself and his ideas and those of the gardeners working for him to accommodate the whims of an owner, however seemingly pleasant.

George watched, ostensibly fascinated by the decorative paperweight in front of him. While he knew how much the garden meant to Amelia, he also understood the issues that James Black was facing. George knew he could not operate his business successfully when someone else could change or reorder what he had decided. Could a garden be any different?

'Mr Black?'

James realised that he had stopped listening as he had been thinking.

'May I make a suggestion, Mrs Henderson?'

Amelia nodded carefully, wondering what was about to be suggested.

'This is your garden and it is important we understand each other.. I have drawn up plans which are based on your ideas and informed by my knowledge. Could it be agreed that if you believe any changes should be made as we go along that you work thorough me so that the staff receive instructions from me, in order to avoid confusion for the staff you understand. I will only disagree on horticultural or cultivation grounds; if it would not grow or be amenable to the soil and the growing conditions.'

James glanced at George Henderson in the hope of enlisting his support. Amelia answered quickly to avoid any intervention from her husband.

'Mr Black, rest assured, I will do nothing to undermine your authority, but I would like to have practical opportunities to garden.'

'I see,' James considered for a moment and pointed to the plan.

'The conservatory is a large area. No plants have been suggested or bought for it. I would suggest that you are wholly responsible for the conservatory. My staff can assist whenever you need them.'

Amelia noted the use of the phrase 'my staff'. She noticed George slightly inclining his head at James' suggestion. As she had been listening to James Black, she realised that in appointing an eminent Head Gardener, she would have to give him his place. This man was nobody's lackey.

'Very well, Mr Black. That would seem to be a positive way forward.'

James breathed an inward sigh of relief. He would see that it worked.

Chapter Six

Garraiblagh garden 1870

JAMES BLACK WALKED down the line of gardeners. What he said to them now would set the tone of the garden, would make the difference between the garden flourishing and dying. He had seen it, experienced it, in his work in other estates. It was like an unseen fungus or injury to a plant which was at first unnoticeable, but continued to infect the plant unseen, eventually affecting the leaves which then didn't grow properly, flowers that were distorted and fell before their time.

James had learned that, as with plants, the growing conditions were important and he was going to make sure of that for his gardeners. He wouldn't mollycoddle them, and they'd be treated fairly and given opportunities. Not for nothing was he a member of the Ancient Order of Gardeners[10] and his gardeners would be too.

James was pleased to have Freddy here in Garraiblagh as his assistant head gardener. James could breathe more easily for that.

10 A society founded in Fife in the 17th century to share knowledge and provide mutual aid to gardeners fallen on hard times.

Freddy McPhee stood first in line looking around him. It had been a very rough crossing from Glasgow and Freddy was no sailor. Now he was in Ireland he did not plan to make frequent trips back to Scotland. He and James had a long history of friendship behind them and had supported each other through good times and bad times. He liked the look of this place. In some ways it was not so different from his home and besides, if James was here then Morag, James' sister, would not be content to stay in Scotland too long. She would want to visit her beloved brother and Freddy hoped, visit his assistant as well. There was a question he wanted to ask Morag now that he was to have a cottage of his own. He hadn't been sure what to expect of Ireland. He was a highlander and had met James there. Would these Irish people be like lowlanders? Freddy had been brought up in a strict family; tenant farmers in the wilds of Banffshire. He tended to see things in black and white and James Black and he had had their battles. James Black was a hard man to say no to. But his loyalty to the man was beyond question. With the other gardeners, he thought he would just have to sup with a long spoon, to begin with. James had brought Freddy over from Scotland, stealing him away from the large estate in which he had been assistant gardener. Freddy was someone he knew he could rely on, who had the same passion for plants and landscape that he had. A bachelor, for the moment though he'd seen the way Freddy looked at his sister Morag. Freddy and Morag would be good for each other, but his sister could be stubborn.

Next to Freddy stood Willie McAlpin, otherwise known as Peachy; another whom James had brought with him from Scotland. There was not much Willie didn't know about peaches and soft fruit. He cosseted them and spoke to them like his children and they blossomed and ripened under his care. James wanted to expand the growth of soft fruit in the garden and Willie was the man for that.

Freddy and Willie were James' strength and as the three of them looked across the fields James knew he had made the right decision. James was aware there might be differences in outlook. Religion and politics were never far away among the gardeners and this was Ireland. But he had no time for ideologies. Gardening was the only ideology he wanted from these men.

James had picked Ignatius O'Kane from a number of men who had applied locally for a job in the garden. He was sturdy and intelligent, the youngest of five sons to a local tenant farmer. When the advert for gardeners went into the local paper O'Kane had been the first to respond. James had been grateful for such an immediate response to his advertisement and was intrigued by the sturdy young man who had stood before him. His deep blue eyes were quick and intelligent and James watched as O'Kane looked around him. He could almost see the questions forming on the young man's lips.

For Ignatius it seemed like the answer to his prayers. He had read of the exploits of plant hunters and had visited the Botanical gardens in Belfast whenever he could get a lift on a cart going into town. Ignatius was clear that he did not have much experience of gardening, but he did know soil and the basic needs of cottage garden flowers and vegetables. Now he would be part of a great garden, being led by a renowned head gardener.

James looked over at Paddy Cleland. Just seeing him there with the wheelbarrow and hoe made James smile. There was something essentially happy and good natured about the man and James had learned that having someone like that helped in many ways, provided they could also do a day's work. Paddy Cleland had come from Belfast. The head gardener at the Botanical Gardens had recommended him; though James had been warned that he would have to maintain tight control as Cleland's jokes could rub people up the wrong way. Cleland's experience of glasshouse work would be invaluable.

James noticed that Vallelly stood a little apart from his fellow gardeners. Tommy Vallelly was older than the others. He had been a journeyman gardener for many years and now wanted to settle in one place. He brought with him much local experience of different weather and growing conditions which James valued. He had worked at the Mullyglass estate under Ferguson, but from the little Tommy had said the conditions there had been poor.

William Scott (Scottie) was good hearted, but needed a bit of prodding. His slow, methodical way of working was useful when it came to the annual plants and their propagation. James was accustomed to gardeners who were better in communicating with the plants and animals than humans and Scott's gentleness would be an asset. The only drawback was that he chewed tobacco and spat wherever he pleased. A habit James detested. He hoped the Henderson's were never witness to his spitting.

Billy McGonigle had been working as a jobbing gardener and about to give up and try his luck in America when he had met James Black by accident. Billy McGonigle had told himself he'd give this garden a year and if it wasn't right then he'd be on that boat to America. He had no ties to hold him.

James stopped and looked at the men. These were the first of the team. Others would be needed, but James was of the view that he should get to know his gardeners in small numbers first. That way he could ensure that any problems, whether in their work or their ability to work with others, could be easily dealt with.

Armstrong was standing at the end of the line with his head down, fingering his hat which he held in his hands. James thought back to his interview. Freddy had joined him to interview the young man and they would have waited a long time if Freddy had not noticed that Matthew Armstrong was quietly waiting outside the office, not wishing to knock on the door. He was a big country boy who would be learning the craft and that meant carrying out the spadework until he could be trusted to begin on more complex tasks.

James knew that would involve heavy, back breaking work, but James had a feeling that Matthew's natural intelligence would soon mean that his skills as the gardener would grow with the garden.

James took a step up onto the terrace to ensure he could be seen and heard by all the gardeners. This was the beginning. Over the next years they would be creating a garden of excellence. He turned to see Amelia Henderson walking down the steps to meet him.

James Black had informed Amelia that he would be speaking to the gardeners in the morning. He had asked whether she would be able to meet the gardeners to be formally introduced to them.

She had agreed with enthusiasm, keen to meet the gardeners whom she had seen working so hard. Amelia's suggestion that the gardeners be provided with tea and cake to celebrate the formal beginnings of the garden was agreed by James, though he didn't want the gardeners to think that this would be the way of things to come. James looked at the men gathered in front of him.

'You men are lucky enough to here at the start of something remarkable, a great garden. You may be thinking that there should be more of you. I know you have worked hard, each and every one of you. There has been a lot of pressure and I thank you for what you have already accomplished. You have been hand-picked to get this off to the right start, not just any start. More men will join you but I believe in getting it right from the start. I expect the best and I have the best in selecting you.

I would now like to formally introduce you to Mrs Henderson who is herself a knowledgeable gardener. None of us would be here if it was not for her vision.'

Amelia stepped forward.

'I would like to second what Mr Black has said about you and your work and I would now like to invite you all to tea and cake in the conservatory.'

The gardeners looked at each other, unsure whether to move or not. It took Freddy to encourage them to follow James Black as he accompanied Mrs Henderson back to the doors of the conservatory.

The work began with the garden area outside the front of the house in order to ensure the house would be appropriately decorated for visitors. The lawn opposite the entrance was carefully levelled and seeded, around the perimeter hostas and day lilies were planted beside peonies with larkspur and irises further back in the border to give height and depth. An archway, constructed to look as though it had come from an old Roman villa, was created and clematis trained around it. Beyond, the area that would become the bluebell wood waited anxiously for the gardeners to work with it.

Amelia watched from the drawing room window as the lines and shapes were made with string and sand.

An avenue of pleached limes now led away from the central path towards the edge of the lawn and the lower grouping of yew trees. Young lime trees had been obtained and carefully transported on carts to the lawn where, with their roots covered as though they were limbs in heavy bandaging, they were carried into position. It amazed Amelia to see how the trees began to define the vistas and fascinated to see the men shape the garden both horizontally and vertically.

In the evenings, after the gardeners had finished, she put on her galoshes and with George and Ted they walked the perimeter of the areas under construction, imagining the finished project. A circular pond had been dug at the end of the avenue and they awaited the statue of Venus which was to be placed at its head. The statue was one that George and Amelia had fallen in love with on their travels in Italy and had vowed it would find a place in their garden. A further pond was being constructed on the lower level and would feature fish and water lilies.

Young Ted was given a wheelbarrow and spent most mornings carting small amounts of soil from place to place, being spoken to patiently in most cases by the gardeners when he quizzed them.

James Black liked to see the boy in the garden. He could see the similarity between father and son in their stance. He would have liked a son to carry on his work but that had not been possible. He understood how precious life was. Working in nature had helped him to come to terms with the endless cycle of birth and death, but he still mourned the loss of his own children.

Herbaceous borders and a less formal area with azaleas and rhododendrons began to take shape. Colours and scents that James had experienced when on the plant hunting expedition to the Himalayas, began to populate the lower reaches of the gardens and the drive way. Now placed in an arbour at the end of the row of pleached lime trees and surrounded by roses and clematis stood an ornate sundial.

The plants seemed happy. James watched for their reactions to being planted. When he noticed a leaf become limp or a neighbouring plant becoming invasive a new position was found or an existing plant dealt with firmly so that it knew its place. Each section that was planted was put together with the consummate skill and artistry for which James Black was noted.

James was determined that nothing should hold up this first level of planting. It would be added to in the next few years, but the essential framework had to be in place. Time was not counted in hours, but in completion of each part of the plan.

Each evening James also made a final walk of the garden, checking on progress, making notes and drawings. Janet Black had become accustomed to not seeing her husband back in the house until the light had almost left the sky. She was becoming worried. He wasn't giving himself time to rest.

She and James had moved into the Head gardener's house with the minimum of difficulty even though the area around it was still part building site. Janet had coped with several house moves during their thirteen years of marriage and was now a very accomplished house mover. As she looked around the newly constructed house she felt at home. She had never moved into a new house before; one that she could put her own stamp on. It was a new life, with new opportunities and she was proud of her husband. Janet smoothed her auburn hair back from her face then lifted her arms to fix the strands more closely into the clip at the back and straightened her back from washing the pots. Janet looked out through the windows anxiously waiting for sign of James. She could see that there was still a lot to be done and she mused on the different gardens she and James had lived in and those she had known as a child. Her father had been head gardener of an estate in the North of Scotland and it was through the chance visit of Mr Douglas, the well-known plant hunter to the estate that she had met James, a young gardener who had been part of his recent plant hunting expedition. It had been love at first sight for her. She had noticed the tall young man with red hair and listened to his talk of places and people. Janet had then plotted ways in which she could meet up with the young gardener, eventually finding a way of bumping into him on the path towards the drive of the house. She had noticed his eyes first. Deep blue and full of fun; a mouth that promised much and a strength that she found captivating. The young gardener had found reasons to make his way to the northerly estate on a number of occasions after that. Her father was happy that his daughter would be marrying into the profession. Janet's musings were cut short by the sound of the front door closing. She wiped her hands on her apron and hurried to meet her husband.

'James, you're late back. Tak' a seat and I'll bring your supper.'

James murmured his thanks and slumped down in the chair. Janet's stew was soon devoured and she waited for her husband to finish before she enquired about his day.

'Ach Janet. I want it jest richt, ye ken?' With his kith and kin James spoke his native Scots, but with all others he had learnt to modify his accent to make himself understood.

Janet didn't say anything, putting her arm round her husband's shoulders.

'It'll a' be fine, Jamesy, ye ken that!'

'Ach, mebe, but I need to change a piece of the planting on the plan and let Freddy know the morrow.' James pored over his plans, penciling in additions and crossing out elements that had not been possible.

Janet watched quietly from her chair near the fire until she could no longer stay silent.

'Jamesy tha's enough! You ken you're falling asleep. You cannie keep gayin' at this rate.'

'You dinnae understand, Janet,' James growled. 'I cannie leave things half done. The weather has been kind to us so far, but any heavy rain could be catastrophic to they smaller plants an' some of the earth-work yet to be finished.'

James' concerns were real. She couldn't gainsay them. She had watched over the years the way in which James dealt with his work and knew that he was a perfectionist. But she also knew that he was particularly on edge this time.

She considered her next words carefully before voicing them

'Jamesy, there will be no garden if you fall ill.'

'I am expendable. All gardeners are! The plans are complete. Another head gardener could carry on.'

Jamesy, the Hendersons wanted ye! They ken your reputation.

I've nae heard any bad reports o' their treatment o'those wi' whom they work.'

'That may be my love, but Mrs Henderson wants this garden so much. I dinnae want to disappoint her.'

'Ye'll no' disappoint them, Jamesy. Ye've Freddy workin' wi' ye an' Willie. There is no better team. Ken wha' ye've accomplished in the past. I'm going to make you a cup o' tae an' when I return ye'll be sittin' beside the fire.'

By the time Janet had returned James was fast asleep and in a deeper sleep than he had managed for several days.

Amelia watched from the house with fascination as James ordered, explained, lifted an errant plant here and a sapling there, before standing back to review the whole. She now understood why James Black had been so uncertain on the question of her practical involvement in the garden. The planning and the planting, the knowledge and the skill that it took to create the garden was not something she had fully appreciated. She also understood that it made it no less her garden. She and George had found the land, loved the possibility of a garden and then provided James Black with their ideas.

'Good day, Mr Black. Mr and Mrs Henderson will be with ye soon.'

'Thank ye, Martha Jane' James was once more shown into the library to await the Hendersons. He felt more comfortable now he knew the names of the staff in the house and at the farm. He was no longer an outsider.

James turned from looking out of the window as he heard the door open.

Amelia and George entered.

'Mr Black, what wonderful progress you have made and please thank your gardeners for being so tolerant of Edward. I know he has been plaguing them with questions and trying to help them in his own way.'

'Thank ye, madam. Ye son is no' in our way. It's good to see a young one out and about enjoying himself. I have brought the garden plan in so that we may go over what has been done on paper before I suggest going out into the gardens themselves to see the planting.'

James unrolled the plan. The initial comments from Amelia had made him feel less anxious.

'The gardens at the front of the house are coming on well. Trees have been sourced that can be put in position to create the effect that they have been there for some many years. I will be employing the technique used by the head gardener, William Barron, on the Earl of Harrington's estate. It has proved reliable in other places.'

James put down his notebook and became serious.

'I am aware that the stonemasons will soon be commencing work on the walls for the kitchen garden. I spoke briefly to the foreman yesterday and he did not seem to understand the importance of the bricks.'

'In what way, Mr Black?' queried George Henderson.

'The bricks must be red and must be of the type that can be built strongly enough to accommodate the plants and the structures that will be attached to them.'

'Why particularly red?' queried Amelia, intrigued.

'The colour will help the heat from the sun to be retained during the day and to be released in the evening. Building the wall without consideration of the gardening needs could be a costly mistake. Mr Henderson, could I ask that the stone masons discuss what they are doing with me? It does not require your involvement.'

George agreed happily to James Black taking on responsibility for this aspect of the work.

James met with Mr Carraher the stonemason: both men examining each other for signs of weakness.

'We are on a strict deadline tae complete the gardens, Mr Carraher.'

'As are we, Mr Black. I have a large squad of men ready to begin the walls.'

'And I am grateful that ye are ready to start. There are however some elements that I need you and your men to understand. My gardeners will be preparing and planting the middle sections of what will be the walled garden. We cannot lose time by waiting for the walls to be complete. I will ensure that the men stay out of the areas ye are working on, but I need to come to agreement with ye as to which part of the wall you begin on.'

'And why might that be?' bridled Mr Carraher.

'If the first wall that you construct protects the garden from the west wind that would help with our planting.'

James and the stonemason looked at the plan in front of them.

Mr Carraher took his pipe from his mouth and shook James' hand. He could see that James Black knew his business as he did himself. Carraher respected a fellow professional. James breathed a sigh of relief.

Stonemasons still worked to complete the lower northern sections. The high brick wall was taking time to ensure the double skin to the wall and the correct amount of buttressing. Changes to the brick courses as the levels changed were carefully monitored and approved by James, just as his involvement was closely checked by the master stonemason.

The walled garden required the gardeners' full attention. The different sections of the garden were marked out and metal arches and hoops set into the ground where needed. Starting from scratch, the ground was dug and heavy carts of manure were brought round from the farm leaving their trails of straw and dung.

Workmen were busy digging trenches to take the heating pipes for the greenhouses in the walled garden. They would not be ready for another couple of months to allow time for the framework and glass, the complicated pulley system for ventilation and the glass pieces, carefully placed.

James was impatient to have all aspects of the kitchen garden ready as soon as possible to make the estate as self–sufficient as possible. Until then he would ensure that as much as possible of the ground could be prepared and developed. At the same time he and the gardeners had to ensure that the formal gardens were completed.

It was imperative that the kitchen garden begin producing the food for the estate as soon as possible. It was after all going to be the powerhouse of the garden. Box hedging was used to differentiate the sections of the kitchen garden and fencing was erected to carry the espalier trees. A small orchard of apples and pears, damsons, greengages and mulberries was also being created.

The rain started in the middle of the night; the wind forcing it hard against the window panes. James woke, disturbed by the noise. There was something unsettling about it, something that worried him.

'What's wrang, Jamesy?' mumbled Janet half asleep.

'Naithing, lass, it's naithing. Jest the rain,' James got back into bed and tried to sleep.

The next morning Janet had breakfast on the table and was just dishing up the porridge into the bowls when James opened the front door. What met him, horrified him. 'Och, no, it canna be!' Janet heard the anguish in his voice and came to the door.

''Where's the water fae?' A torrent of water was running down past the door and on down the paths though the walled garden.

'I dinnae ken lass but I'm about tae find oot!'

And James hurriedly put on his boots and his oilskin coat and went outside. It was still raining hard and the wind was pushing against him as he stood surveying the garden.

Following the flow of the water back up the slight incline he noticed that some bricks had been knocked out of the more recently built section of wall. He ran round and through the gate leading out onto the back lane and the bothy where he found Freddy, soaked to the skin and directing the gardeners. Each man was out with a shovel. They were digging into the back lane in an effort to redirect the water away from the garden and into a grassed area.

'Where's it coming fae, Freddy?'

Freddy shook his head and as he did so, rain was shaken from his head and his hat like a dog shaking itself after a swim. 'I dinnae ken. The first I knew o' it there was water tryin' tae flow under the door of the cottage and when I got down to the bothy, Matthew was standing there in his bare feet, swearin' that the water was trying tae drown him in his bed! I reckoned if we dug a ditch here we could stop it goin' into the main garden and that wid gie us some time tae find oot wha's amiss.'

James nodded. 'Right, on ye gae wi' this and I'll take a look further up.'

Gathering his coat and hat around him James faced into the wind and rain and made his way up the back lane, the rain and water flowing fast around his boots. By the time he reached the top of the lane where it met the road he was beginning to despair that he would find anything that could be the source of the problem. Then he saw it: a cart with only the back wheel visible. James hurried over. The rest of the cart had toppled over into the river and its heavy load of stone had spread out across the river. There was no sign of the owner but a horse lay dead, still in its harness.

'Och, ye poor animal,' whispered James to himself. He looked further at the beast. 'I think ye were dead afore ye went in tae the river. Blast the man who let ye become sae bad. You're just a bag o' bones!'

James surveyed the river bank and the area surrounding it. It was clear that the cart and its goods had blocked the river. Normally that wouldn't have caused the problem but the torrential rain had swollen the river and the water had taken a new route down into the estate.

James hurried back to tell Freddy of his find. 'Blaggard, the bratach salach! Fae daein' that tae a horse!'

'I'll leave word wi' Maguire, the farmer. He'll likely know whose cart it is. He can sort oot that end. If Cleland and Armstrong stay here wi' ye, I'll take O'Kane an' Valleley and McGonigle into the kitchen garden to see what the extent of the damage is there.'

James looked at what had been the carefully dug beds and where there had been seedlings beginning to push up their leaves. He could have cried.

James checked the worst damage. Some of the box hedging had survived and in its turn it had protected some of the plants being sheltered by it. In other places the small hedging plants had been hurled down among seedlings leaving holes to fill with water and seedlings crushed or damaged.

By late afternoon the rain had stopped. The men worked on until the light began to dim. Exhausted and soaked through they had managed to save a number of plants and to reinstate some sections and paths.

Janet had been watching from the gardener's cottage. Wisely she had decided that the best way she could help would be to make a big pot of soup and have it ready for the gardeners when they stopped.

Matthew Armstrong and Paddy Cleland were ordered to bring out benches to the front of the gardener's cottage and the pot of soup and the home baked bread was placed on the table brought from the kitchen. For the first time that day the gardeners relaxed.

Word had got through to the stonemason by the next morning that part of the newly built wall at the side had been demolished by the flood. The stonemasons work lay in ruins, bricks crushing plants as they had been bowled over in the storm.

Mr Carraher shook his head at the damage to the wall. 'I'll have to rebuild that section, I can't just fix those bricks at the base.'

'I did nae think ye would be able to, Mr Carraher. It is a shame wi' all your careful brickwork tae.'

'Aye, well. At least ye and your men managed to stem the flow as quickly as ye did. You've a brave group of workers here, that's for sure.'

'I have indeed and I'm glad o' them all.'

The day of the rain had affected everybody in the garden. It had seemed that everything they did in the garden had been charmed, that nothing could go wrong, but that event had shown them that that wasn't the case.

Early every morning the gardeners were found making their way from their stone bothy into the garden onto the gravel paths. Each with specific tasks for the day, they wheeled their tools in the barrows, the sounds of fork and spade banging against each other: each tool shining brightly after its careful cleaning and oiling the previous evening. No one wanted Mr Black or Freddy McPhee to find them with muddied spades or unsharpened clippers at the beginning of the day. The gardeners could see the different areas of the garden coming to life and felt pride in their involvement and there was a stronger bond between them all after having to deal with the crisis.

James watched them go as he made notes in his book. He would be walking the estate to check on the progress they had made in the different areas. It pleased him to see the anticipation and pride the gardeners had in the work ahead of them. The flood had destroyed some things, but it would not wreck the scheme of things.

Nevertheless, the flooding had made James even more nervous than he had been beforehand. He found he was slipping into his Scots tongue more frequently than usual and he only hoped it wouldn't happen when he was with the Hendersons in case they could not understand him. James knocked firmly on the front door of the house.

'Good morning Mr Black, come into the library,' smiled Martha Jane. 'Mr and Mrs Henderson will be with ye now.'

James made his way into the library and went to the window. 'Thank goodness the flooding didn't get as far as the formal garden,' he muttered to himself.

The door opened and Amelia Henderson followed by her husband entered the room.

'Mr Black, how are you and your gardeners? You have all done such sterling work in managing the flooding.'

'Aye, thank you, ma'am. We are all fit and able. I am very glad to say that we have managed to reduce the damage as far as possible and Mr Carraher has been able to continue with the brick work, as you will see.'

James led the couple through the formal flower gardens to the door of the walled garden and the newly painted door.

James stopped. 'The men have prepared the beds and are now beginning to plant out onions and other vegetables. There is much still to be done as you can see and we have been lucky with the weather since the flood.'

It was a hive of activity.

'There is as much going on here Mr Black as there would be down at the docks or in the mills,' said George Henderson in admiration. James Black warmed to his theme.

'We are using one of the greenhouses to propagate the vegetable seeds and the tomato plants and we have trained plum and fig on the west wall while here on the east wall there are pears. Seeds and seedlings are being planted out in their rows in the central beds while on the north facing wall have trained morello cherry trees with redcurrants planted below along with gooseberry bushes.'

Amelia looked around in wonder and felt as though she had walked into a description of a garden from one of her books.

'Are you all right, ma'am?' asked James, noticing her startled look.

'Yes. It's just that it has taken my breath away! I had hoped, always had a dream of having a garden like this and you have made it come true, Mr Black!'

'I'm glad you approve, ma'am, but it is not finished yet and the weather may cause us more problems yet. We have still to work on the south facing wall where the nectarines, sweet cherries, peaches and apricots will go. A grape vine will be established for the glass-house over there,' said James pointing to a metal structure not yet complete. 'There is one last section to show you.'

The group followed James like a horticultural pied piper back out of the walled garden and to the lawned area to the left of the house. 'This area here will be our cutting garden. It is not immediately in the public gaze. We will be growing for arrangements here so plants will be kept in rows for ease of management.'

'Which flowers will you produce here?' asked Amelia.

'We want to cultivate flowers with scent, form and colour for as much of the year as possible. Peonies, some roses, larkspur, zinnias, snapdragons, stock and sweet peas among others for the summer. For the winter there will be some Christmas roses and then in spring, Oriental hellebores with their range of pinks, magenta's and deep reds, tulips, narcissi, aquilegia. And of course, the immortelles — the helichrysum or strawflower and statice for use in the dried flower arrangements.'

Head Gardener's House, 1871

Chapter Seven

Garraiblagh 1871

JANET STOPPED POLISHING the table in the sitting room and opened the front door of the house to breathe in the fresh air. She was happy. She could feel the warmth and energy of this place. It was a place of contentment. She could not describe it further. She just knew. It felt for her as though she had come home and with James beside her she felt more at peace than she had done in a long time.

They had weathered their ups and downs during their years of marriage. Months of separation when James had been away on plant hunting expeditions or times when she and James had been left in an isolated house on some large estate — James could talk forever about plants, but human feelings had taken him much longer to be come comfortable with. Somehow Janet's memory was jogged. Her mind went back to the time of Isobel, their eldest daughter's death. They had so wanted children. Janet shivered and closed the door. She began smoothing the duster over the table top as though clearing a memory to see more closely. She and James had been the happiest people in the world when Isobel had been born. Then came the outbreak of diphtheria and Isobel had been taken from them at only a year old.

David had been born a year later and then Robert the next year. They had been two and three when scarlatina took them along with their cousins.

She and James had kept going as people did. Each had mourned their children in their own way and she felt that James' plant hunting trips had given him at least some respite from thoughts of their children.

A robin landed on the doorstep and gave Janet a quizzical look before proceeding to hop further in.

'Here, oot ye' gae! There'll be mair worms oot there. It's gai unlucky fae ye tae come by the hoose, ye should ken that!'

Janet knew she was superstitious, but that came from her parents and grandparents. She would always greet a magpie with 'Good day sir. How's your family.' Then carefully count. Janet cornered the robin, lifting it carefully in her hands, feeling the intense energy from its small body as it struggled to free itself.

'There ye gae! Gae an' annoy they gardeners. Find some worms, but leave some for the soil.'

Janet smiled to herself, putting aside the memories and went to put the kettle on the range.

James might be the well-respected gardener and plant hunter, however in the family Janet had her own ideas about the plants that were to be kept in the house. She had inherited an aspidistra from her mother. While it was not the most attractive of plants as James often reminded her, she liked it and it reminded her of her parents' home. This new home of theirs, airy and light was a far cry from the dark old house that had been her own childhood home in the north of Scotland, the house in which the aspidistra had thrived.

Once her pots and pans and kitchen equipment were clean and

in place and a pot of soup ready for when it was needed each day, she felt able to explore beyond the walled garden: each day finding a different route. It was on one of her walks that Janet found the standing stone and Mrs Murray.

Janet nodded a greeting to the elderly woman who was busily collecting herbs and digging up roots. She made a colourful picture with her red skirt, green shawl and wide brimmed hat with feathers stuck in its brim. Mrs Murray stood up slowly, adjusting the pipe she had in her mouth.

'You must be Mrs Murray,' said Janet.

'Aye, I am. Ye'll have heard o' me from ye husband, nae doubt,' and she searched Janet's face for confirmation.

'My husband has mentioned ye. I'd hoped to make your acquaintance myself, I am interested in herbs an' I came looking fae some tae make a salve fae broken skin. James' hands get many cuts.'

'Aye, ye'll find this is a good place an' the plants ye need grow well aroun' the ancient places.'

'Would you teach me the ways of the herbs?' asked Janet. 'My grandmother worked with them in Scotland though she used the heathers and the rowans too.'

'Come an' visit me, Mrs Black. 'My door is always open.'

By July Janet's plants were flowering and she and James had begun to feel relaxed in their new home. The pressure of the initial months of long, hard work had paid off and everything in the garden was working to a rhythm.

James was master of the gardens. His gardeners were picked and trained by him and he demanded perfection in all the work carried out. Those working for James understood this and while he could be a hard taskmaster they knew they were learning from the best.

James was never the sort of head gardener who resented a member of staff moving on to a new more challenging place. It was how all gardeners with ambition like himself got on. He realised that the Ancient Order of Gardeners did not yet operate in Ireland but he resolved to change that. He knew how important it was to have support of such a benevolent fund with practical financial support for ailing and elderly gardeners and how strong the networks had been in Scotland and then in England to improve understanding of gardening methods.

One of the first visits James made when he had first arrived at Garraiblagh was to the Belfast Botanical Gardens. Making contact with others in similar positions was key and, it was also a means of checking who, as a young gardener, might be available for work at Garraiblagh; working as part of their training. The skills and expertise gained in working in the Palm House would perfectly suit Garraiblagh.

James had also made sure that he knew about all the estates within riding distance. Usually an easy relationship was built up between the different head gardeners. They were an elite band who might be rivals in many ways and would express annoyance when one of their gardeners was poached to another garden however they were bound together by their vocation and professional standing.

Samuel Ferguson the head gardener of Mullyglass estate had kept an eye and ear open for information on the progress of Garraiblagh and had heard the rumours, rumours about this new garden that could grow to be the best in the north. He had to admit it rankled with him. The gardens at Mullyglass had been greatly admired for many years. He did not want to relinquish that notoriety. Who was this James Black?

Mathew Armstrong had lived in the local area all his young life. He knew the twists and turns of all the lanes, the places where the rabbits had their burrows and where the badgers had their crossings.

He knew about crops and in particular, flax. His family had worked the fields for generations, planting and harvesting the blue flowered crop. He knew about the back breaking hand pulling, the stacking of the beats into stooks, wary of the weather, the retting and the scutching in the small mill with its water driven wheel. But the gardening work at Garraiblagh was something different. The cycle of growth and harvest in the fields was something he understood; a garden was more complex. The move to work at Garraiblagh meant that he was able to move out of the family cottage, leaving a little more space for his four younger siblings. Two of his older brothers had already left and moved to Belfast and the shipyards. The family rarely saw them now. Long work hours and lack of money meant that they thought hard before making their way home for a visit.

Matthew had taken some time to get used to the garden and the other people working on the estate. As an unmarried young gardener he lived in the bothy with other under-gardeners and yet had more room than he would have had at home.

One of the things that had surprised him was the variety of vegetables in the kitchen garden. He'd been shown around by Tommy Valleley, an older gardener in his forties, who enjoyed making sure Matthew understood how much he had to learn.

At first Mathew had felt confident he would recognise vegetables. After all carrots were carrots and cabbage was cabbage and everyone knew potatoes. His eyes widened as he was shown rows of globe artichoke, cardoon, sea kale beet and beans. The feathery fronds of the asparagus and the scaled spears fascinated Mathew. The vegetables all went up to the big house, so he had no opportunity yet to taste any of these strange new vegetables and fruit. Yet Mr Black had told him that he would need to learn what the vegetable plants should taste like, otherwise he would not know when they were ready to crop. It was a puzzle to Matthew how he would ever find out.

Mathew buttoned up his jacket and knotted the scarf around his neck before adjusting his cap. The lower half of his trousers were now wrapped in heavy cotton tied with twine to protect them. Today was the day he had to weed around the central flowerbeds and the ornamental pond. It was not his favourite task. Statues were new to Mathew. There were two statues of lions near the house and there was what he had been told by the others, was a fancy sundial in the arbour among the roses. But the one statue that he did not like was one of a woman near the pond where he would be working. He had been taken aback by the lightly clothed female figure carved in stone and had tried to avoid her gaze. Try as he could to weed and work with his back to her it didn't work. He felt her eyes on him.

'Looksy, Miss, ye'll catch your death of the cowl' out here. It's not like them Italy places ye come from an' I can't work wi' ye looking like that. Here, put this on for pity's sake.'

Mathew solemnly took an old jacket he had found in the bothy and placed it around the statue's shoulders. 'That's better. I'll get on with my work now!'

Tommy and Paddy walking their wheelbarrows down the path noticed Mathew weeding by the statue and called over to him.

'How's your sweetheart today, young Armstrong?'

'Ach, away with ye boys, I'm busy!'

Seeing the statue with a coat draped over her Tommy couldn't resist. 'In the name of all that's holy! Does she need a hat an' scarf, boy? She looks like a barley buggle.[11]'

Mathew turned his back and pulled furiously at the weeds. He could hear the two of them laughing as they walked into the distance. He knew he'd be in for some leg pulling when he went back to the

---

11 Scots name for a scarecrow.

bothy for a cup of tea.

Beyond the fenced and walled areas, still in the wild areas of the fields the plants watched too. The tiny hearts-ease looked at the brightly coloured faces of their cultivated cousins given pride of place in the flowerbeds. Field poppies of yellow and red saw the larger furred and magnificent specimens of the oriental and opium poppies opening their full petalled flowers

The smaller field and hedge flowers knew the struggle they had to keep their place among the grasses and the animals that walked over them frequently. The gorse did not have any such concerns. It knew its power and its place. Sharp dagger spikes put off the human marauders and the yellow flowers with their seductive scent supported them. Their explosive seed heads ensured that they could not be easily contained. Small animals came to the gorse for protection which it gave freely.

The transformation from fields to cultivated garden was miraculous. James and the gardeners knew how much work had been needed over as the last two years and how much still needed to be done. At last James was content with what he could see. He had spent the morning traversing the garden, moving from one viewpoint to another, flowerbed to walkway, ensuring that all was as it should be. Amelia had followed the work being carried out and was under no illusion as to how much work had had to be undertaken. George Henderson was under no illusion as to the financial cost.

The herbaceous borders imitated those seen in the great estates with deep blue delphiniums standing tall at the back of the border with allium and peonies in front, all carefully arranged as though for a community photograph while shrubs and trees gave it a sense of permanence and history.

From the house and in particular, the bedrooms, the garden's design was shown in a different aspect. The pattern of the parterres were a source of continued delight to Amelia who, while brushing her hair or reading on the window seat, couldn't help but find her eyes caught by their beauty.

Decorative parterres, careful steps and stages at which to stop and admire the man–made elements painstakingly followed the different levels of the terrain, some carefully engineered to present the most interesting aspect. The plants knew their place. They decorated, divided and screened and the gardeners adjusted and cosseted them through their different stages of growth. They blossomed. Garraiblagh was growing into a mature garden. Armfuls of cut flowers of every hue were provided for the table, larkspur, gladioli, chrysanthemums and dahlias. Lily of the valley were cultivated for corsages and sweet violets for the dressing tables of Mrs Henderson and any female guests.

A rhythm of work through the seasons and changes of weather settled over the garden and Garraiblagh.

The summer house was now complete. Its rustic exterior complemented the surrounding woods to the rear. From the front there was an uninterrupted view of the lough and at the sides there was a pergola of roses and clematis. Russian vine flowers flowed over the top making it a dense wall of foliage and sweet scent. The summer house windows and door were made up of small panes while the door itself for all its charm had a stout lock.

The interior was simply furnished with a wide chaise-longue, covered in a flowered fabric. While cushions were strewn over its comfortable seating, a small simple desk held a number of books and writing materials and beside it a straight backed chair.

For Amelia in particular this summer house was her retreat: as close to being in the garden as she could be without formal convention getting in the way. It emphasised to her that the garden was her domain. This was the place that Amelia came to paint and several of her watercolours were lying on a bench awaiting decisions as to framing. The summer house was also where Amelia kept her garden diary. She had decided soon after moving in that she would make an illustrated record of the garden. Her small sketches and watercolours of views and details of plants accompanied her writings, which set out her feelings and also practical aspects such as the weather and the seasons.

It was a hot Sunday afternoon. The sky had been cloudless for hours now and Amelia had completed all her daily tasks. The garden beckoned. On Sundays the garden was reserved for the Hendersons alone. The gardeners did not intrude. She walked down across the lawn and along the herbaceous border, stopping to collect some flowers as she went. Nearing the pergola decorating the entrance to the summer house she felt her heart racing. Opening the door of the summer house Amelia removed her hat and linen jacket. It was still too warm. As she was beginning to undo the buttons to the top of her dress she heard George's footsteps.

'You have had the same thought then, my darling,' he moved over to her and cupping her breast in his hand bent and kissed it. His hands then made their way down to the bottom button and released her from the stays of her dress. As his fingers began exploring her, Amelia touched George and felt his hardness. He drew the curtains across the window and door then moved the cushions from the chaise longue and soon they were wrapped in each other's bodies.

Later as George and Amelia walked, flushed and arm in arm back up to the house.

Amelia thought of the evening ahead, bringing her back to everyday responsibilities The Johnstones from Mullyglass are coming to dinner.

George grimaced. 'I had hoped we could have a quiet Sunday. It has been so busy recently.'

'They have been very kind to us, George, and it is time we returned that. Mrs Mullan has prepared a wonderful menu. In this heat we decided on a menu that would show as much of the produce from the garden as possible so there will be celery and globe artichokes as well as figs from the greenhouse and I must admit I am looking forward to showing off our garden, both in its plants and its produce.'

As the gardens at Garraiblagh settled into its seasonal rhythms so too did the lives of the Hendersons. Regular dinners and balls were attended and Garraiblagh's reputation as a setting for these events became well known. James and the gardeners were kept busy not only with the normal planting and maintenance but also the need to ensure a range of flowers, not only for the table but for corsages and as posies for dressing tables. The delicate task of ensuring that sweet violets were available was overseen by Freddy, who grew them in leaf litter dressed with soot in a cold frame.

Chapter Eight

Winter 1873

AMELIA LOOKED OUT from the bedroom window. The trees were still only a tracery of branches creating patterns against the sunless sky. This was not her favourite time of year and she hadn't been feeling well for a few weeks now. It could be the extra entertaining and rich food from the festivities but somehow she sensed it might be more than that.

Throwing on her heavy woollen coat and hat she left the house. She breathed in the cool air and smelled the scent of wood smoke and noticed Ignatius O'Kane wheeling old branches away towards the kitchen garden. She could walk down to where the new flower bed was being dug but decided on impulse she would visit Mrs Murray in her cottage. She felt in need of female companionship. Snowdrops had pierced the top soil and were now clearly visible beyond the green of the lawn. Amelia stopped. That scent. She sniffed again, definitely an exquisite scent, but where from? She continued along the path with the scent strengthening until in front of her she noticed a tree or what a large shrub was really, she supposed.

Yellow, gingery spidery flowers. 'Witch hazel, of course! I should have known!' Amelia said out loud to herself. Breaking off a stem she walked on to the Murray cottage and knocked. 'I have brought you some witch hazel!'

'Thank ye, ma'am. Mr Black has nae caught on. Least he hasn't so far. I collect bark from it to make one of my preparations for the bruises.'

Mrs Murray looked at Amelia searchingly.

'Come away in ma'am an' I'll mak ye some tae.'

Amelia sat down and felt the sudden urge to fall asleep. When Mrs Murray returned she found Amelia sleeping in the old armchair with a cat on her lap.

'She needs this,' Mrs Murray thought to herself. 'It's not goin' to be a great year for this'n.'

Amelia woke with a start.

'I do apologise. I don't know what came over me.'

'Dinnae fuss, ma'am, rest yoursel.'

'I haven't been feeling well and I thought a walk and a visit to you would do me good, but I have abused your hospitality and fallen asleep!'

Mrs Murray took the younger woman's hand.

'Do ye have ony notion wha has made ye feel ill, ma'am?'

'I'm not sure, but I think I might be expecting and I hardly dare hope it is so. We always wanted Ted to have a brother or sister.'

'Ye hae tae keep up your strength, ma'am. If ye are, ma'am, mak sure ye call on me services as a midwife. I'd be honoured to help.

Amelia left Mrs Murray's cottage comforted and eager to talk to George.

Mrs Murray closed the door with a knowing look. She returned to her herbs in thoughtful mood. She had learned many things over the years and her sensitivity to the herbs had brought her understanding of other elements.

Amelia was enjoying her pregnancy. She had had a couple of sudden pains recently but they had not lasted long and she felt well, so full of energy. George watched his wife happily going about her tasks in the conservatory.

'It will be time soon, my love. How do you feel?'

'I have spoken to Mrs Murray and she will assist at the birth.'

'Only Mrs Murray?' asked George.

'Yes, I feel fine.'

'Don't you think we should ensure that Dr Semple is there too?'

'Why, George? Mrs Murray is as experienced as anyone. She's held in high regard by the mothers of the area.'

George did not want to lessen his wife's confidence but he was not going to accept her views so easily.

'Nonetheless my love, I think that as soon as it starts Dr Semple must be contacted.'

Amelia looked at her husband's worried features and relented.

'Very well, George.'

Doctor Semple and Mrs Murray worked throughout the night.

Amelia looked down at the baby wrapped in the lace shawl beside her. He had tried so hard for life. It should have been so perfect. This son born in their new house surrounded by nature, and the colours and shapes of the garden but instead he had had no heartbeat, no life.

George bent down and touched his son. He was used to being able to control what happened in his life. He found the utter desolation of this hard to bare. Words were difficult to find.

For Amelia it seemed that this son had been of the garden, of the love of the garden and now he'd been taken. Nature was unpredictable.

Burying Timothy in the garden was the only thing to do. They wanted to keep him close, to let him be in the place he had tried to reach: to play and laugh and grow up in. His tiny body was placed in the dappled shade of a small glade in the lower part of the garden. His brother Ted watched from a distance. The hushed atmosphere of the house made Ted scared, afraid of something he didn't understand and there was something threatening about the wind in the high trees and its rustling whispers.

James Black stood in the potting shed with the materials around him. The death of the Henderson's baby had brought back memories of his three children. Death was never something that could be understood. At least in putting together the wreath for the wee mite, Timothy, he felt he was doing something. Weaving the straw into a circle then covering it methodically with moss and binding it he thought about the colours he would use. '*The immortals*' — helichrysum and statice — would form the main elements. It would last for some months and not die within the days after the burial. Hopefully, a small comfort.

He stood back to look at the finished circlet. Reds and yellows, oranges and pinks with the purple mauves and cream of the statice. All the colours of life and for him the circle of life was what kept him going. He believed in Nature, its wisdom and its rules, but no longer in a god.

Ted looked at the gravestone and traced his small hand over the lettering. He hadn't seen this mysterious brother and now he was under the ground. He could make out some of the words but not all. He knew that his mother always talked about this brother. The wreath rested beside him. Ted's hand reached out and pulled one of the flowers out, slowly removing the petals one by one, creating a pile on the ground.

James, walking back from checking on the lower field, saw the young boy sitting beside the grave stone.

Unsure, he watched. Ted pulled out another petal and then heard a movement. He turned his head.

'Hello Mr Black.'

Ted then looked down at his lap and the wreath with the missing flowers and looked up again at James Black, this time with fear in his eyes.

'I didn't...'

'Don't worry lad. I'll not tell anyone. We can fix the wreath. You can help me. Can I sit down?'

Ted nodded and waited for this adult whom he knew from the gardeners could be very stern, but who had only been kind to him.

James looked at the boy, who held in his hands tight to his side as though ready to fight. He was so small to have to cope with this and James remembered how it had felt when his younger brother had died many years ago in Fife. He had been about the same age, but he had other brothers and sisters to share the grief with. This lad was on his own and though he did not fully realise it consciously, heir to a large estate and business. Ted waited for James to say something and when he didn't he took a curious sideways look at the older man.

James had learned that sometimes talking wasn't the best thing and he got out his pipe and began to fill it.

'Father has a pipe, but he doesn't smoke it much. Sometimes he lets me put the tobacco in it for him'.

There was silence.

'I don't have my brother. He's gone, Mother still talks about him and Father is sad. Mother said that I would have someone to play with when the baby was born but now,' Ted shrugged his shoulders and James Black steadied the boy with a firm hand, 'now I won't have anyone.'

Chapter Nine

Garraiblagh 1874

JANET FOUND IT was not only the garden that was blooming. She was pregnant and, like Amelia Henderson, she found herself visiting Mrs Murray in the cottage. Mrs Murray was well known for her healing and comforting herbal teas and preparations and Janet had begun to feel concerned about the impending birth after Mrs Henderson's tragedy.

Janet's pregnancy was not easy. After the three older children had died she and George had not considered risking more. Nevertheless they were both delighted when Janet had announced she was pregnant, though both were also aware that at forty she would have to be careful.

It was early spring, and that helped James feel positive about the birth. New life around him was beginning to blossom and soon they would have the child they had never dared hope for.

Mrs Murray met James at his front door.

'I've sent for the doctor, Mr Black. I would like him to be present for the birth.'

His excitement at the birth of their baby was now replaced with fear for his wife.

James returned to the garden, but did not stray far. Sitting on a bench at the bottom of the garden beside the apple tree, he noticed the warm yellow of primroses clustered close to the gate. Anxious for something to do James collected the flowers along with some tiny dog violets to take back for Janet. He smiled as he thought of Janet and her preference for wild flowers. He was eager to present them to Janet after the birth of their new child.

As he entered the house James sensed there was something wrong. It was as though the warmth had left the place. On hearing the door close, the doctor came down the stairs. James knew from his ashen face that there wasn't good news. Another still birth he thought. Janet and he would have to be strong.

'Mr Black, I'm so very sorry,' the doctor said. James made to raise a hand as if to say Janet and he had known such grief before.

'We were unable to save your wife. It was a difficult birth and Mrs Black was too exhausted to fight any more.'

James dropped the posy as his body went limp.

'Och, no, no my Janet, no my Janet!' he pleaded. 'I-I must see her.'

The doctor held his terrified gaze.

'Mrs Murray is with her. Give her a few moments.' The doctor steadied James with both hands. James collapsed into the chair with his head in his hands and then as though just remembering what the doctor had said

'But the bairn? The bairn tae?'

'You have a healthy son, James!.' The doctor forced a weak smile.

This was the home that he had hoped to share with Janet for many years. He was angry.

They had wanted this child, so much. The delight he had seen in Janet's eyes had been reflected in his own. Janet had been happier than she had for a long time. Now, she was deprived of seeing her child, or ever looking out on the plants and flowers, on the world, again.

Mrs Murray called to James.

'Your wee son needs ye, Mr Black. He's a brave wean wi' a grand set of lungs.'

Brooking no argument she placed the bundle of baby in James Black's arms and he reached out a finger to his son's hand.

Mrs Murray watched James. She'd seen it before many times, but still her heart ached for him. They might have had their differences over plants and the way to grow them but she knew too that this was a good man, capable of great love. That had been clear from his wife and Mrs Murray could see it in the way the gardens at Garraiblagh flourished. He was a man close to nature. He would survive and he'd care for the wee one.

It was Freddy's suggestion that he ask his sister Morag in Fife for help. While Freddy may have had his own reasons for encouraging James to invite Morag over to Ireland, James could see the sense in Morag moving to live with himself and Rory. He knew Morag had wanted to spread her wings for some time. It seemed to suit all parties. So when he wrote to his young sister she did not hesitate to accept. Within two weeks she was being driven up the avenue in the dog cart. The sight of her brother holding his baby son in his arms reduced Morag and James to tears.

The house was full of reminders of Janet. Her china collection, her pots and pans even some clothes that James would not part with. Morag often wondered how second wives could ever cope in the home of a widower. She doubted that James would ever remarry.

Her young nephew was an easy baby to manage. Morag's delight in looking after Rory was always tinged with sadness that he would never know his mother. Soon the gardener's house was decorated with window boxes of geraniums, their reds and oranges highlighting the red stone of the house. Morag was determined to make this a happy house again.

Among the first visitors to the house after Morag's arrival was Freddy. Freddy was excited to show Morag around the garden and eager to explain the role he had played in its creation: always careful to give James his place. Freddy tried to take as much of the responsibility for the garden as he could from James though he also knew that to take too much away would be just as wrong. James needed to grieve in his own way and his own time.

James was glad of his sister's company and her practical assistance. She had been close to Janet and she was able to create a routine in the household that was not that different. Rory was full of smiles and seemed oblivious to the tragic loss of his mother.

Every Sunday afternoon Freddy and Morag would step out together. They usually walked up to the old standing stone and home by the woods. Soon they were holding hands and then one day Freddy sought a kiss which Morag returned.

'Fred, we need tae talk, y'ken?' said Morag.

'Aye, aye, we do. I ken rightly lass.' They sat down on a fallen log from which they had a clear view of Garraiblagh house and the lough beyond.

'I came here to help James and wee Rory. For nae other reason.'

'Aye, aye,'

Morag was unaware that it was at Freddy's suggestion.

'So I dinnae want tae mislead ye, ye ken? I could nae leave James an' Rory.'

'Aye, I ken that, Morag.'

'I like steppin' oot wi' ye, mak no mistake aboot that, Fred, an'

I love the place, tae.'

'I'm glad,' said Freddy taking Morag's hand.

'But I dinnae..'

Freddy held up his hand to stop Morag.

'Morag, I'm goin' to be bold an' ye can chase me.' Freddy took a deep breath. 'Would ye reconsider once Rory is up a bit?'

Morag bit her lip and looked at Freddy. 'Wha's a bit?'

'Och, seven or acht?'

'Nae, that's too young. Ten, shall we say ten? But I will nae move awa' fae here until Rory's full grown.'

They sealed their agreement with a second kiss. James was informed of their plans. He was delighted that Morag and Freddy would have a future together, but relieved that they had Rory's interests and his own close to their hearts.

Chapter Ten

Garraiblagh 1875

JAMES RECEIVED THE SUMMONS to come to the house with a degree of trepidation. It was not that he was concerned that anything was awry with the gardens, but he had come to realise that Amelia Henderson was enthusiastic about ideas and stepping up to the front door James wondered what this would be about.

The door was opened by Martha Jane the parlour maid.

'Good morning Mr Black', she said cheerfully.

'Good morning Martha Jane I believe Mr and Mrs Henderson are expecting me.'

'Just Mrs Henderson. She'll join you in the library.'

James' heart sank. Within a few minutes the door opened. Amelia Henderson swept in. Her usual enthusiasm apparent in her swift movements.

'Good morning, Mr Black. I have just read a most interesting article and I wondered if it would be possible to include a similar planting here at Garraiblagh.'

Amelia placed the gardening journal on the polished table top and spread it open. Excitedly she pointed to the illustration, a hand drawn image of flowers in a circle.

'May I?' James asked and brought the drawing closer.

'It's a botanical clock,' interjected Amelia.'

'Yes,' said James hesitantly.

'A watch of Flora,' commented Amelia confidently and with a touch of impatience.

James scanned the individual plants that were illustrated. The feeling of trepidation that he had had earlier in the morning on his way to the meeting deepened.

'They are all named and the timings are given for when the individual flowers open and close. Wouldn't it be perfect?' Amelia sighed.

James took a deep breath, trying hard not to be too obvious. He was going to have to tell her.

'Mrs Henderson.'

Amelia looked up, 'Yes?'

She saw the blue eyes and the frown and for a moment was lost.

'Yes, Mr Black?'

'It is indeed a perfect arrangement.'

'That is what I thought!'

'It is perfect and as you know Mr Linnaeus was a remarkable man and contributed much to our understanding of plants however...My understanding of the flower clock is that it was more a theoretical idea than a practical one.'

'Why so? It seems so clear. Here the African marigold opens at seven in the morning and here, the scarlet pimpernel flower closes at two o'clock.'

'Yes, may I explain further?'

'Please do Mr Black. Take a seat. I have been very remiss in my excitement. I will ring for tea.'

James was glad of the few minutes further to gather his thoughts.

He did not want to be hard or unfeeling in his responses. He liked Mrs Henderson greatly and had come to realise that she was the strongest ally he had when it came to matters in the garden. They had worked well together. It was just that sometimes her enthusiasm and her theoretical knowledge did not always match the reality of gardening.

James noticed that she was now watching him intently, something that discomforted him.

'I would have difficulty explaining the issues,' he started, 'to someone who did not have your understanding of horticulture.'

Amelia smiled but was not taken in by the flattery. A good start, thought James. He continued, 'Linnaeus created his clock for a more northerly setting and as well as that, I am aware that it has been tried in large botanical gardens elsewhere and it has not been successful. Linnaeus is correct in the fact that flowers open and close at particular times of day, but different factors can affect that.'

'I see, Mr Black,' Amelia looked downcast. 'You are, I believe, trying to let me down gently.'

'Mrs Henderson, there is another issue. The plants chosen you may have noticed, are a very strange mixture!'

'I did wonder, but I suppose my enthusiasm got the better of me.'

James pointed to the list. 'Scarlet pimpernel, a tiny flower between much larger dianthus and tall hawksbit and then water lilies! Colours, sizes, wild, cultivated and even in the case of the water lily, the need for water.'

'Oh, dear, I have made a fool of myself.' Amelia laughed self-consciously. 'How silly of me.'

James looked across at Amelia. She sat there framed by the sunlight coming through the window. Her auburn hair accentuated by the green wool dress she was wearing. He smiled and realised that he would never be able to imagine her unconnected to plants. Her passion for them was real. He felt a pang of guilt at having dashed her enthusiasm and sought to make amends.

'I have a possible alternative,' he said.

'Do you? I would so love to work at something different, something practical, in the garden, something worthwhile...' Amelia did not finish her sentence.

James noticed a brief clouding over of her normally open expression.

He wondered.

She was not a hot house flower to be kept in a wardian case. She was a beautiful herbaceous plant. He hoped that all was well between her and her husband. Very selfishly he did not want discord that could affect his position or the development of the garden but more than that he did not want her to lose her vitality and there was the loss of the baby not that long before the death of his own Janet.

'One element we do not yet have in Garraiblagh is a proper herb garden. I wonder, could that be something that you would design? There are the obvious designs for herb gardens, but I have been wondering about a herb maze. This meeting is very fortuitous as I was going to ask your advice on this.'

'A maze?' queried Amelia with interest. 'Doesn't that have to be high, like Hampton Court?'

'Not necessarily. It can be much closer to the ground as it would be in the case of the herbs. I could offer advice but I was hoping that you would consider designing the maze?'

'If I design this I would want to undertake the planting of it as much as is possible. I know the very person to assist me. Mrs Murray has an extensive range of herbs that she has grown at the scutching mill[12].'

James looked at her. 'I wasn't aware that Mrs Murray was a gardener as well as her other accomplishments.' At the word

12 A mill where the flax stalks are crushed to remove the fibre for use in linen-making.

'accomplishments' James raised an eyebrow.

Amelia realised her mistake. 'She is of course not a trained gardener but has learnt the ways of her ancestors in growing herbs that are useful.'

There was a distinct pause before James Black responded. He was well aware of Mrs Murray's ideas on planting and they had had several short and to the point discussions on the subject. James did not completely reject her views and he knew she had some followers, even within his own team of gardeners. He had seen what some of the newer, innovative practices could do to enhance the plants' ability to withstand insects. He was also very aware that Janet had thought highly of the woman and Janet had been no fool.

'Of course you are at liberty to consult whoever you wish, Mrs Henderson.' Still James Black worried at letting this eccentric old woman run amok in his garden.

Amelia realised she could not leave the conversation in this way.

'Your idea is such a good one, Mr Black. I'm afraid I got carried away. Of course you will be the final authority on any suggestions.'

James knew that he was being difficult. He had averted one difficulty, but was about to create a new one. He saw that through their conversation about the herb maze Amelia's brightness had returned and James felt a strange delight in being responsible for this. He did not want to take away from that.

'Of course Mrs Murray's knowledge of herbs would be useful, Mrs Henderson. I will leave you to consider the idea and consult with Mrs Murray.'

'Wonderful. I will draw up some ideas and arrange to meet with you.'

James left the meeting feeling somewhat uneasy. He realised he had no alternative and also that Mrs Henderson's happiness was important to him.

Amelia wasted little time and met with James two weeks later. As he waited in the library he thought of the first time he stood there and awaited the Hendersons with a degree of trepidation six years before. Things had changed a little since then. Amelia walked in, and greeted him then laughed as she held out a rolled paper in her hand.

'It is my turn to seek approval from you, Mr Black! I have been wondering about a centre piece for the herb maze and I have a proposal. What about a topiary animal? Ted could help too perhaps?'

'That's a good idea. Perhaps Master Ted could decide on the animal and we would then decide if it can be shaped from box or will require the blacksmith to make a metal frame around which we can twine ivy.'

In truth, Amelia was finding her son difficult. Ted had had several tutors and several tutors had left. He could be stubborn and while bright, was not interested in history or Latin. He hung on his father's every word when the subject of shipping was discussed. George had spoken to Ted about his studies and while he worked with his latest tutor it was not with any enthusiasm. Amelia hated to see Ted so lost.

'I've got something to show you, Ted, Some new plants that might interest you!'

Ted could think of nothing less interesting than his mother's plants. He was now ten and plants were only for gardeners and his mother. He had more important matters to consider.

'Do I have to, mother?'

'In this case, yes. You can go and do what you want afterwards, which I assume will be something close to the pond?'

Ted nodded and Amelia laughed. 'Just be careful. The pond is deeper than you think and you haven't learnt to swim yet.'

Amelia led Ted in through the white painted glass doors into the conservatory. The scent of pelargoniums and jasmine filled the air. Amelia breathed in the perfume. Ted wrinkled his nose.

'This place smells of flowers!' He tried his best to hold his breath.

'Don't be silly, Ted. Come with me.'

'I wish we had parrots in here. I could teach them talk. It would be a proper jungle then and I could have adventures.'

Amelia led Ted to a feathery leaved plant with small purple coloured pompom flowers, Ted waited. He could see nothing spectacular about this.

'Try touching a leaf, Ted.'

Ted gingerly put out a finger, unsure of what to expect.

'What is supposed to happen?' but as he said that he noticed the leaf begin to fold in on itself at the spine as though praying.

Ted reached out a finger again and again. The leaves closed over.

'Oh boy!'

'It's a sensitive plant. They're shy and don't like being touched.'

Ted, for once was slightly interested.

'And now, come and see this!' Amelia beckoned to her son to follow her further into the conservatory where she pointed to several strange looking sundew and pitcher plants.

'They are very strange looking, but what is special about them?'

'Look closely,' Amelia pointed to a fly hovering above the sundew plant and watched fascinated as one of its leaves clamped shut on the fly that had landed.

'Now there definitely should be parrots and it could be a jungle.'

Ted had decided that there were aspects of plants and gardens that could be interesting and he definitely hadn't realised that plants could kill things. He couldn't wait to tell his friends.

The idea of deciding on the centrepiece topiary was accepted by Ted with some lack of eagerness but in spite of himself he began to consider which animal he wanted to see.

The mist was clearing from the lough leaving a watery paleness in the sky. James, well wrapped up in his heavy coat and muffler waited for the Henderson line ship with anticipation. He clapped his gloved hands together in an attempt to warm himself. The damp was insidious and he could see his breath in the cold air.

He had written to his contacts in India before winter had set in last year requesting a number of exotic plants. Now they were about to be unloaded. He had faith that the plants would have been properly prepared and packed in wardian cases for their long sea voyage, but there was always the possibility some air had got in or an insect had been missed in inspection.

The noise of the chains being slipped down into the water and the shouts of the men directing and clearing was deafening.

'Mr Black?'

James turned to find a crew member addressing him.

'Where do you want us to put the cases sir?'

In the noise James motioned for the man to follow him. Once loaded on the cart, James and the driver made careful progress away from the docks and the lough. As the cart made its way slowly along the roads and away from Belfast, James considered what it must have been like when Mr and Mrs Henderson had first made their way to the land that would become Garraiblagh. Not for the first time he congratulated them. They had made a good choice. He had long come to understand that there was something special about Garraiblagh.

It was nearly an hour later that the slow moving cart approached the estate. The calm, sure footed carthorses had been directed to the main drive of Garraiblagh, rather than the farm lane which James felt would be too rutted and bumpy for the cart's precious cargo.

Amelia saw the horses rounding the last bend in the drive and rushed from the house to meet the cart.

'How exciting this is,' she exclaimed. 'I do hope the plants have survived the long journey well.'

'We will soon know. I believe it will be best to open the cases in the conservatory. We do not want to shock the plants too much when they are open to the cold air,' said James.

Opening the cases in the heat of the conservatory it was clear that most plants had survived well.

'The wardian cases have done their job,' said James satisfied. 'We will need to keep the plants here for a few days to allow them to acclimatise before moving them to the greenhouses. I trust that will not inconvenience you too much, Mrs Henderson?'

'I will enjoy seeing them here, could we perhaps move them to one side to allow for movement through the area?'

While some of the more established plants may have resented the newcomers such as the mimosa, they also understood that their power and fame was now well established and they enjoyed the positive remarks from the exquisitely dressed people who were shown around by Amelia and George.

As the garden developed it further seduced its owners and James Black got his wish to make expeditions to far off places, bringing back exquisite plants and the sort of notoriety that the Hendersons revelled in.

The walled garden rolled up its sleeves and within its walls it worked hard to provide the varied vegetables and fruit which the cook and her kitchen turned into the gastronomic delights the family expected for their regular dinner parties. The hobnail boots worn by the group of gardeners clattered on the brick and dust paths as they moved their wheelbarrows around could not intrude on the tranquility of the main pleasure grounds.

The high wall not only kept out possible thieves and strong winds, but kept this workaday level of functional gardening separate and out of sight.

Peaches, apricots and nectarines luxuriated in the warmth of the glasshouse wall with the metal trellis giving them the support they desired. From there they would watch the garden while feeling cosseted and special. They were the silent recipients of whispered conversations. Sometimes about the master and mistress: sometimes about trysts between others. Eating one of them was like gaining the innermost knowledge of the garden and always, there was Willie McAlpin, guarding them from harm.

Part of the garden relished its notoriety and its leaves and plants moved gently in the breeze, congratulating themselves on their pedigree. A formal part of the garden with trained roses looked across the lough to the wild hills of county Down in the distance with their infinite variety of blues and lilacs and sometimes wished that it had that same freedom as the heathers on the mountains.

Chapter Eleven

James Black 1878

THE AGREEMENT THAT HAD BEEN MADE at the beginning worked well. The more the garden grew and developed the more James Black and Amelia understood their roles and responsibilities. The conservatory had been agreed as Amelia's domain. She would decide on the plants and maintain them.

Gardeners would be called in by James when Amelia required heavy work to be undertaken. The conservatory was little used by other members of the family and for her; it was a private space of warmth and colour.

As she turned the brass handle and opened the glassed door, she breathed in the scent of jasmine that wafted through to her and she closed her eyes in delight. The bottle palm branches brushed her dress as she made her way into the conservatory. She liked the idea that the palm trees would stand sentinel, making the entrance intriguing. Jasmine had been allowed to run riot around the doorway. Amelia had arranged the area so that it would not be a simple space and to this end she had abutilons of reds, yellows, blues and whites spreading their branches towards the roof. Their different petals fascinated her, the almost papery rounded ones and then the delicate white and blue. It seemed as though the plants always welcomed her and it was mutual. Gardenias and pelargoniums crowded onto shelving along with large leafed plants of varying colours giving the conservatory an exotic feel.

Light flowed in from the roof and the windows. There was that feeling of warmth from the hot water pipes that kept the conservatory at a pleasant temperature. Well upholstered metal seats were placed in a small group around a table, often used by Amelia when she had female friends for tea. It was also where Amelia brought her gardening journals to read and make notes on. When she came across a new variety or plant for the conservatory it was her decision alone whether she would purchase it. When it came to the rest of the garden she consulted with James Black who only ever disagreed on sound horticultural grounds and on these grounds Amelia was always willing to give way.

Staging had been built into one section so that Amelia could pot new plants, trim and gather seeds. She realised that without the staging at waist height she would be hampered by the corsets she wore and might even have difficulty getting up. She had visions of herself as a sheep left helplessly rolling on her back.

How many more pea pods are there to be shelled, Mrs Mullan?' queried Annie, the kitchen maid.

'As many as are needed an' don't be cheeky!'

Annie did not look forward to the morning arrival of vegetables and fruit from the garden. It seemed to her that it would be much simpler just to have cabbage and turnip and potato.

'Hurry up wi' those peas, there are French beans to top an' tail after that.'

Annie moaned.

'Be grateful the blackcurrants are finished otherwise ye would be toppin' and tailin' them an' then helpin' to sieve them!'

Annie remembered the time-consuming task of removing the tiny tops and bottoms of each currant ready for Mrs Mullan to place in the heavy saucepan and add sugar. The bubbling mixture of currants smelled wonderful, but Annie had had to spend ages scrubbing her hands to remove the deep purple colour.

The years since Janet's death had not been easy for James Black. The first years after her death James watched his son grow fearful that he too could be taken as his older sister and brothers had been. As Rory grew beyond the very early years James began to relax. It became clear that even at a young age, Rory was as fascinated by plants as his father. Morag spent time walking Rory around the less public areas of the estate and the bordering countryside. She, like her brother, had grown up on the land and she knew the wild flowers, many of whom were the same as those that grew near the family home in Fife. One particular area attracted her, the old standing stone. It felt a good place to be and Rory could safely scramble around it and pick flowers. She could see that he was likely to follow in his father's footsteps. The area around the stone felt warm, alive with an energy that brooked no negativity.

While the garden had flourished there had been a part of James that had just wanted to stop when Janet had died, find solace somewhere, anywhere but Garraiblagh. The garden that he had wanted to create and had put so much into had, in some way, been complicit in her death. At first everywhere around him reminded him of Janet and her delight at the move to Garraiblagh with it new home and then the unexpected pregnancy. He felt the garden had tricked them both.

He knew that if it hadn't been for Morag he would have found it difficult to manage. He loved his son dearly, but he knew that Rory needed a mother figure. 'Rory,' said James, smiling to himself, and savouring the name of his young son. In Rory he saw so much of Janet and he was pleased to see that Rory had taken an interest in the garden and his father's plant hunting adventures. He was loath to go on plant hunting expeditions now, but both Morag and Freddy had persuaded him that the trip was important. Amelia Henderson had also done what she could; reassuring James that if Morag needed anything for Rory it would be obtained. She also had a shrewd idea that there was a part of James that needed this expedition. The trip had yielded many new varieties and species and helped him see things with a new perspective. James' journey to India had been exhausting. True, the plant hunting trip had been successful but packing the plants, labelling them and sealing them in their wardian cases had been a delicate and time-consuming task. A lot of money was tied up in the trip. He was just glad that the ship being used to transport the plants was one of the Henderson line.

James sat in his cabin, relishing a cup of fine Indian Assam tea, checking through his plant records. He could relax now until they arrived back in Ireland. The plants in the cases were sealed. Any tampering with them en route could cause the plants to die. He was looking forward to seeing Rory and had brought him several curiosities that he thought might intrigue him.

Freddy and Willie had come down with the cart to meet James and help collect the cases. Despite having to go slowly to ensure no damage to the wardian cases[13] they made good time.

At the entrance to the walled garden a small, curly headed boy

---

13 A sealed glass case allowing plants to be transported. Invented in 1829 by Dr. Nathaniel Ward

was waving wildly at him. James jumped down from the cart and ran. Scooping up his son in his arms he held him tight.

James Black was still enjoying the work at Garraiblagh but in the back of his mind was the warning from his old gardening mentor to be careful. James knew that as a gardener, even one with a reputation such as his, he was exposed to uncertainty and insecurity. His house was part of the property and if his style of gardening went out of favour, he could well find himself looking for another job. He did not think that the Hendersons were so fickle, but he had learned to be wary of the landowning class. He thought back to his early days when he'd been invited into the Ancient order of Gardeners. It had changed somewhat in its focus since then, though it had been very useful in providing him with introductions to important contacts in the world of gardening and through his weekly subscriptions, built up the security of a sum of money should he and his family be left without employment. He made sure his gardeners knew about the scheme but there were also those who could not be persuaded to contribute to the scheme. Living close to the soil had the drawback of detaching many from more material concerns. Sadly he had seen too many old gardeners ending up in the workhouse. They seemed to hold to the belief that they would continue to be fed and watered like their plants. James felt strongly that part of his work in Ireland was to ensure that as many gardeners as possible would know how the Ancient Order of gardeners could help them. To that end he had begun to hold meetings in different locations. In most areas his work was met with a positive response however, on estates such as Mullyglass the head gardener was less enthusiastic. His care for his gardeners left a lot to be desired.

James re-read what he had just written and looked at it critically. Other head gardeners had put together books of advice. He hoped that his would be a little different, combining practical tips that might be found in such volumes as Thompson's Gardener's Assistant, yet dealing with more complex issues and providing advice and information on the more exotic and rare plants that he had had much experience. He had also included some tales from plant hunting expeditions he had been on. Now that Garraiblagh was understood to be a teaching garden, it required a higher public profile for its head gardener. James had become used to sharing advice in such journals as Gardener's magazine and Gardener's Chronicle[14] and he was keen to find other ways in which his professional expertise could be highlighted.

Checking his pocket watch he put down his pen. The new prospective apprentice would be here shortly for interview. James always interviewed the new apprentices. At fourteen they entered a three year apprenticeship. In return for their work they received instruction from the head gardener as well as free board and lodging.

Sam Mc Bride sat up beside his father on the cart. His father was never one for too much conversation, but for whatever reason he was making an effort as he drove his son to Garraiblagh. The cart bumped along the old track that came into the north gate of the estate and then past the farm. It had been a long journey of an hour with old Buster the horse.

'We are to meet Mr Black at the entrance to the walled garden.'

Sam looked around him. He was used to farm buildings and fields but this was like a village. There were cottages and barns, sheds and paddocks. Sam twisted round in his seat to catch a glimpse of a carriage and a man polishing it. A woman was ushering some ducks along a laneway.

'There's the house, Sam.'

14 English horticultural periodical founded 1841. Now Horticulture Week.

Sam's eyes widened. The house could be seen beyond the farm and the buildings.

'It's like a palace.'

James Black stood at the corner of the garden office. He had seen the old cart making its way along the lane.

'Mr McBride, welcome. You've made good time.'

'As I mentioned in me letter Mr Black, me uncle was a gardener on the Cleeborn estate. He alus had a notion that a son o' his would be a gardener like himsel, but the damnable thing was he never had any sons. So he took a keen interest in young Sam here an' alus thought Sam would fit the bill.'

While the two men talked Sam looked around him, hoping he wouldn't be noticed and occasionally stole a glance at James Black, trying to get a sense of what he was going to be like as a boss.

James turned from talking to Mr McBride, catching Sam unawares in his evaluating glances.

'I have a cup of tea for you before you start on your homeward journey. I know you'll want to be on your way before the light lessens. A cup of tea for you too, young McBride?'

James nodded. 'So young fellow, you will be starting at the bottom, hard work I'll not pretend, but a worthwhile apprenticeship if you put mind and your back to it!'

'Sir,' mumbled Sam.

'He can do a brave day's work, Mr Black. I would not have brought him to ye, if he didn't.'

'Well, I'll let you say your goodbyes to your father. Come back into the office when you've done that.'

With a few last admonitions to his son, Mr McBride mounted the cart without further ado.

Sam left the office, just in time to see his father and the horse disappearing round the bend of the lane without a backward glance. He wouldn't see him again for many months.

James knew from experience that homesickness would settle in but that if Sam was kept busy it would wear off. He walked Sam down the path and through the open gateway where he saw a number of gardeners busy in the walled garden.

'I have clay pots for you to work on. They need to be scrubbed clean and then stacked according to the numbers on their bases.'

The young boy looked at the pots of all sizes, littering the floor of the shed, many covered in soil and moss.

'You can use that brush there and the old sink is in the corner and here's your apron.'

James handed the boy a heavy leather apron. Sam reached out for it and put it over his head, feeling its smooth heaviness. It almost reached his feet.

'I'll introduce you to the other gardeners later when we stop for a bite to eat. But I'll tell you now. Pay no heed to anything the others tell you, I and Mr McPhee give the orders. If you have any questions ask Mr McPhee. He'll sort your accommodation.'

Sam looked at the flower pots. He'd never seen so many. He sighed and picked up one which was near his foot. Lifting it up he moved it around in his hands till he found the number. Most of the pots were covered in mossy earth. Sam rolled up his sleeves and began to scrub. The apron protected him from the worst of the water and mud. The wire brush was less forgiving and scratched his hands mercilessly when it missed a pot. Sam believed in having a way out, an alternative, in case he needed it. He had learned that there often was no choice for him in what he was told to do by his father or others in authority but he liked to think out possible ways in which he could get himself out of unpleasant situations. While he scrubbed he thought how long it would take him to get home if he walked. He was strong and he could do it but what about when he got home? Would he be welcome? Would he have to leave home and go to Belfast? At the moment, Sam decided as he caught his hand on the wire brush again, the alternatives were probably worse than the apprenticeship.

Sam was just finishing his mug of tea when he saw Billy the Tree at the door.

'Sam McBride, Mr Black wants ye to get the long handled short spade.'

'Where is it?'

'In the tool shed, o' curse. Move yersel!'

Sam hurried to the tool shed. He looked along the rows of implements

'A long handled short spade' he said to himself. 'Damned if I can see it!'

It was then that he noticed there was a darkening of the light at the door. He looked round to see Billy and several of the other gardeners smirking.

'Found the spade yet, young'un?'

'Naw,' said Sam, looking worried.

'Ye'll not find wan in this garden,' laughed Billy.

'Thanks for that,' said Sam and watched the men laugh at him.

Willie McAlpin walked into the peach house and took a deep breath. The scent of the ripening peaches was one of his favourite smells and he loved the work that it brought. He turned, remembering he had young Sam with him.

'Come on in, young fella, but don't touch enythin', just watch unless I tell ye to do somethin.'

'Aye, Mr McAlpin,' said Sam

Placing the trug on the wooden staging Willie moved over to the plants, checking each leaf and fruit for possible insect damage and to see whether the peaches needed to be faced.

'Come here lad an' see this.' Sam moved carefully in case he bumped into anything.

'Got ye wee skitter!' Willie said aloud. Sam thought Willie was referring to him until Willie turned a peach to show him an earwig.

'Now watch this.'

Willie took one of the old, hardened broad bean stalks and cut it into lengths with his pruning knife. Slowly and methodically he hung the pieces on wire beside the vulnerable fruit.

'That should do it,' he said with satisfaction. 'Ony of ye eariwigs in there the morra an' ye'll be gone!' He shouted as he flicked the earwig away.

Sam chuckled, feeling a little less tense and smiled.

Rubbing his hands Willie launched into the next part of the work, placing white card behind the fruit to face them.

'Why ye doin' that, Mr McAlpin?'

'To mak sure the sun gets to 'em. We don't want any peaches stayin' hard because they haven't ripened in the sun!'

Tidying things into the trug Sam noticed the white fur of a rabbit foot

'Mr McAlpin, what's this for?' queried Sam.

'For the peaches, I'll show ye when the time is right. Well, that's done but there's still a piece of time for us to go an' check on the matoes an' figs afore the bell goes for our break. Remember boy, Mr Black will test ye on what ye've seen.'

Willie looked at the boy with a stern gaze and then relented.

'So, how're ye settlin' in?'

The young boy looked at the older gardener, not sure what to say.

'Are they takin' a rise outa ye?'

'A bit,' said Sam.

'Huh! They'll tire of it. We all had it. What sort of a hame d'ye come frae?'

'Me mother an' me father an' the five others an' Jed. I'm the eldest', he said standing a little straighter.

'Yer family must be proud of ye fir gettin' this job.'

'Aye, but there's a lotto larning, isn't there?'

'Ye'll get the hang of it. Who's Jed?'

'Me dog, but now he'll be Conor's dog as I'm not at hame. I s'pose he'll forget me.'

'Ach, don't fret. Once ye get settled, ye'll get down to visit 'em an' show off yer larning.'

The boy perked up. It was the first time he had heard time off being mentioned.

'Mrs Mullan's grand. She gave us a wee bun when I took the vegetables up to the kitchen'.

'Oh, she did, did she? You're lucky but min' ye manners an' don't get greedy. Let's go an' see the cucumbers.'

James took the nicotine from the cupboard in his office and with it the glass container, wick and methylated spirits and made his way to the tomato house. Checking the leaves on the tomato plant he saw the white fly clustering on the leaves and when disturbed, flying in a small cloud. He didn't like using nicotine, but it was the best way to deal with the pest. James poured the meths into the glass container and lit the wick. He placed the small metal cap on top and added the nicotine. The fumes from the nicotine were dangerous and highly poisonous so James quickly left the greenhouse, closing the door sharply. It was an effective method of dealing with the insects that he disliked because of the potential dangers.

'Mr Black!'

James looked round to see Ignatius hurrying up the path.

'Aye........ what is it?'

'Could ye come please? There's a problem with the new plantin' at the front of the border.'

'Och aye, very well, I'll come now.' James frowned, wondering what the problem could be. He thought they had got the combination of plants right, perhaps there had been some insect or rodent damage.

Willie finished his bread and cheese and got out his pipe.

'Right lad, we'll go down to the cucumbers in a wheen a' minutes. Ye can red up in here. We dinnae want ony rats nor mice living wi' us.'

Sam swept the floor and put away the bread board and knife.

'Did ye see the trug an' me secateurs?'

'No, Mr McAlpin. Haud on, I'm thinking they were left in the tomato house 'cos we were goin' tae be going back there! I'll go an' get 'em.'

'Thanks lad.'

Sam ran across the gardens towards the greenhouses. The black and white garden cat appeared in front of him, rubbing itself against the box hedging, determined to get attention.

James walked into the bothy muttering. 'What a to–do about nothing! Ignatius thought he saw some leaf damage in the herbaceous border. There wasn't anything. Anyway I've put nicotine in the tomato house. So remind everyone to stay away.'

Willie dropped his pipe. 'The 'mato house! Young Sam has jus' gone o'er there tae get the trug he thinks is there.'

Both men ran.

Sam stroked the soft fur of the cat that purred its approval and wound its way around Sam's legs in an effort to make him stay.

'I've got tae go, Lupin. I've got t'get Mr McAlpin's trug. See ye in a wee while.'

He raced on towards the greenhouses.

Sam suddenly stopped.

It wasn't the tomato house, he remembered. It was the peach house! That's where he'd seen the trug. He took a breath and then ran on, this time swerving round to the left toward the taller glass building of the peach house. He turned the brass handle and hurried in.

Yes, there it is he said to himself before grabbing the basket and making for the door.

'Outa the way, cat!' muttered Willie as he and James ran on, their hobnailed boots sending up dust and grit from the path.

The men looked across at each other with grim faces.

James was the first one at the door and was just about to turn the knob of the door when he heard whistling. Sam appeared around the corner swinging the basket.

'Sam McBride!' shouted James as Sam stopped in his tracks looking scared. 'Thank the lord!' breathed James.

'Wha' have I done, sir?'

'Nothing. Nothing at all. We thought you were going to the tomato house?'

'I was, but then I membered the trug was in the peach house. Do you want me to go into the tomato house now?'

'No!' both men shouted.

Sam realised as he pulled his muffler up around his neck and his cap as low down over his ears as he could that he had been in the garden for six months and he no longer thought of his 'way out'. Mr Black had told him of plant hunting expeditions and the people and animals he had encountered. Now Sam's plan wasn't so much an escape plan as a dream — to work hard enough and learn enough to go plant hunting like Mr Black. At night while he wrestled with sleep he imagined finding a plant. He hadn't decided what yet, but this plant would be named after him or maybe Garraiblagh. Mr Black had told him that he was breeding a plant that would be named after him and he was writing a book. Now Sam had plans and until then he'd have to put up with Tommy Vallelley's snoring and Billy the Tree's jokes.

Gradually Sam began to get used to the routine. Woken at daybreak, it was his job to collect the logs for the stove in the bothy. He managed to sleep but Tommy Vallelley's snoring meant he had covered his ears with his jumper. Listening to the others grumbling it sounded as though Tommy's snoring annoyed everyone.

Sam was glad that it was summer. Even though it was still cool in the bothy at night. He determined that he would keep as many clothes on as he could. He wasn't looking forward to winter even with a stove that the gardeners kept well banked up over-night.

At home he had shared the loft with his five brothers. 'At laist here,' he thought, 'I might get a night's sleep wi'out them'uns muckin' about as long as I cover me ears from the snoring!'

Mr McGonigle usually made the porridge. While he, Sam, as the apprentice ran up the lane with a jug for some milk from the farm. This was not something Sam minded. It gave him the chance to stroke the farm cats while he waited and chat to the dairy maid.

Putting on his leather apron, Sam went next to the boiler room to stoke the fire which kept the greenhouses warm.

Chapter Twelve

1885

Amelia found James Black in the kitchen garden.

'I've just received this booklet, a catalogue of daffodils from Mr Hartland's nursery in Cork. I wondered if you had seen it?'

'I have, Mrs Henderson. There certainly seems to be a wide range of daffodils. Although some of the names are somewhat confusing. The slope below the western side of the house would be a good place to plant some daffodils for the spring.'

'I agree. I do so like this one. "The Rip Van Winkle'. It is a most intriguing name! I would like to be involved in the planting of the different bulbs Mr Black.'

'Certainly Mrs Henderson. I'll let you know when the bulbs arrive.'

Amelia set off back to the house in good humour. She was looking forward to planting the bulbs and also seeing the very different shapes and colours. She had recently been reading about the narcissi family and had another idea which would require further research.

She was angry. It had been such a simple thing to ask. Her jaw tightened and her eyes flashed. Silence vibrated around the room.

'Why not?' Amelia asked George in such a way that it would make any, but the most courageous or stupid respond.

Amelia focused on the deep red of the schizostylis in their vase in the corner of the drawing room. She allowed her gaze to move to its six petalled flower and the buds still to come out. The red seemed to reflect her anger. In an effort to calm herself down she looked out across the garden and the fields towards the lough. She made use of the silence. She knew that she had shocked him with her vehemence.

'I know the Browns. Their parents were friends of my mother and father for many years. They are experienced travellers and will be well looked after given that they are attached to the British embassy in Paris.'

'But what about your duties here? And what about us, Ted and I? Do we mean so little?'

'You know that is not the case. But you have already made it clear that you do not have the time to spare to travel with me.'

George looked uneasily at his wife.

George was about to say something when Amelia spoke. 'Do you remember I once told you I had wanted to be a plant hunter before I met you?'

George remembered and nodded. He remembered too that he had never wanted a wife who would be docile and boring.

'And would you rather have been a plant hunter than marry me?' countered George with a frown on his face, trying to gain the upper hand.

Amelia sank back. 'Of course not, George. You know that. You have had your adventures, travelling to different countries, even during the difficult times before this new German Empire. Am I not to be allowed a small adventure?'

George sighed. 'It's different for a man, Amelia. Surely you must see that?'

'No I don't, George. Women are travelling. Look at Marianne North and I was reading about Mrs Nina Mazuchelli in India, the first European women to see Everest. I only wish to go to France, admittedly not the most accessible area, but just France. I have been reading a great deal about narcissi recently. We have ordered some very beautiful varieties from Cork for the garden. It set me thinking and I found this book on the different varieties that could be found in Europe. The particular one I want to find is the Narcissus triandrus, a dwarf variety of daffodil which is evidently also known as 'Angel's Tears'. It can be found in the wild on one of the islands off Finistère in Brittany. I want to find the daffodils and bring home some bulbs that we can plant here. To do that and see the flowers in bloom we need to travel in spring. Collecting off-sets would be possible in early summer but part of the attraction is to see them in flower.'

'Could we not have someone obtain the bulbs and bring them back or send them?' asked George with a forlorn look.

'We will stay in the embassy in Paris for the first few days and then take the Paris — Brest train. From there we will take a carriage to Quimper. The Browns are keen to see more of France than merely the capital city and its environs. I know what I need to do to successfully bring back any bulbs and if I have any queries before I go I will ask Mr Black.'

'I will want to communicate directly with Mr Brown and with the embassy. I know you have your heart set on this Amelia, but I cannot countenance you travelling across Europe in these times without assurances that you will not be put at risk. I love you. I hope you understand my concern.'

'I do, George but remember I have travelled before.'

'Yes, as a young person and as part of the Army! A very different situation. Let me think about it and write to Mr Brown.'

Amelia accepted that the conversation had gone as far as it could, for the moment and resolved to invite the Browns to stay while they were in Ireland visiting relatives.

George saw Amelia and her maid, Maud and Mr and Mrs Brown onto the boat at Belfast. It was going to be a long journey down to London and then the channel port for the crossing to France, but George, after a long and detailed conversation with Mr Brown, felt reassured.

Daisy found Paris lively and for the first couple of days she reveled in the change from Ireland and Garraiblagh. There was much to see and do and in spite of herself she found she looked forward to the visits to the Opera and elegant cafés. Amelia enjoyed the company of the Browns and listened with interest to their tales of life in the Diplomatic service. However, spending a prolonged period with the couple on the rail journey from Paris and the subsequent carriage ride from Quimper to the Brittany coast was beginning to test her patience. She had come to the conclusion that they were very worthy, but dull and she thought of the conversation she could have been enjoying with George. Amelia's mood improved as they came into Benodet with its ancient buildings and the harbour close to the old church. Seeing the size of the small boat that would carry she and the Browns over to the Iles de Glenans and St Nicolas Island almost made Amelia reconsider her plant hunting idea. However, the water was calm and the sun shone in a deep blue sky. Arriving on the island, Amelia was speechless. A lane ran from the small pier to a grass area and beyond that hundreds of tiny daffodils in different stages of flowering covered the ground. They were so pretty with their pale yellow, almost white petals pulled back like miniature wings. She thought she had never seen anything so beautiful. Mr and Mrs Brown found a place close to the top of the island to rest and admire the view, leaving Amelia to make her way through the daffodils. Kneeling down among the plants she opened the carrying box that James Black had constructed for her to store the bulbs. Soon she was using the small spade and trowel that he had thoughtfully included. Her collecting was soon completed and closing the box she looked up from under her straw hat to take in the view cross the fields to the white sand and turquoise sea beyond. Amelia carefully took one of the flowers and pressed it into her book. She had read somewhere that the ancient Phoenicians had brought the tiny narcissus to the island. There was little time to make extensive drawings as the boatman had warned they needed to be aware of the tides and she could see the Browns were laying out the picnic from the hamper they had brought with them. Seeing seashells on the beach Amelia picked up a handful to bring home, a further reminder of her adventure. The picnic of cold chicken and Brittany cherries and local cider was, as the Browns explained, to celebrate her plant hunting success. She was glad that she had made the trip and began to feel that perhaps the Mr and Mrs Brown were not as dull as she had begun to believe they were. Now that Amelia had obtained her bulbs though, she was keen to return home. She missed George and Ted but knew that she had much to thank the Browns for. Two days later Daisy and Maud set off on their return journey from Paris, boarding the ferry at Dieppe.

Amelia stepped off the boat train at Victoria station. Maud, her maid, had hurried to ensure a porter would collect their luggage. Amelia was glad to be on the return trip to Ireland. She had sent a letter to George telling him of her plans, but was unsure how reliable the postal service was: she and Maud would stay overnight in London and then travel north.

At first Amelia thought she was dreaming. George stood in front of her on the platform.

'I thought you were too busy to travel?'

'I decided that my wife, the plant hunter, should be welcomed back in style! And, Amelia, it was too long to wait for you to return to Belfast. I missed you my love.'

'Oh George, I am so glad to see you!' She collapsed into his arms.

'Come I have booked us into Claridges' for the night. I have sent Maud on ahead with Peter, my valet.'

On the return to Belfast Amelia and George did as they had done on their return from honeymoon. They watched as the boat brought them into Belfast Lough and then into the port itself. This time the noise and bustle had increased and there were many more dockside buildings and factories than there had been on that previous occasion.

'We're home', said Amelia as she and George kissed. 'It is a good place to be.'

Amelia carried the box of bulbs down across the lawn and through the walled garden to the garden office. She knocked politely at the door. James Black opened the door in surprise. 'Good morning Mrs Henderson. I didn't expect to see you here so soon. How was your trip?'

'Interesting and I have something to show you, Mr Black.'

Amelia placed the box on the table sited at the office entrance and opened the lid. The look of triumph on her face said it all. James lifted out the bulbs and examined them carefully. 'They are in very good condition, ma'am.'

Amelia described the island and the daffodils covering it and showed him the pressed specimens she had. James smiled. 'They are very attractive, are they not? They will be planted out to your instructions, Mrs Henderson.'

'Thank you Mr Black.' Amelia turned to go and then looked back at James. 'It was fun being among those beautiful plants. I can understand why you enjoy plant hunting.' They smiled at each other like co–conspirators.

Walled garden

Chapter Thirteen

Winter 1886

THE BLIZZARD BEGAN EARLY in the morning and the ice bit into the plants that were usually strong enough to withstand the cold.

The walled garden with its winter white blanket covering was still. A few robins hopped from cabbage stalk to stalk. Closer to the wall a slight shifting of snow on top of the wall caused miniature avalanches and occasionally a shout of annoyance from one of the gardeners as cold snow slid down their necks or over their heads.

Ignatius and Billy well wrapped with mufflers and additional sacking tied over their trousers and boots made their way down the path.

Occasionally there were the sounds of shrubs, their branches weighed down, and cracking as they could no longer tolerate the heavy load.

The imprints of rabbit, hare and fox paws showing their preferred secret routes made visible for once, the hidden occupants of Garraiblagh. The two men had become firm friends, their love of plants and nature was central to this, but also their love of music; Ignatius on the fiddle and Billy on the whistle. The two hummed a new tune they had heard as they walked, frequently having to stop to knock snow off their boots.

'Here, wha's thon o'er there, Billy?'

Billy wiped the snowflakes from his lashes and stared.

'Looks powerful like someone's left their jacket, just dropped it on the ground. Thon'll take some drying out! I'll get it.'

A young man's body lay huddled into the wall, his face pale and cold.

'Go an' get Mr Black, Ignatius, shift yersel! I'll houl on here. We'll be needin mer' help to move this boy.'

James arrived with Freddy following behind.

'We need to get the lad into the warmth. He's lucky to still be alive. Bring him up to the office. Freddy, go to Morag and ask her to bring some blankets down and some hot soup.'

The men carried the limp body along the path, slipping at times on the ice.

Morag held the door of the office open to let the men in. She had already cleared the bench and placed in near the stove.

'The poor soul. He's hardly grown. There's nothing of him.'

'Where are you from lad?'

'Belfast,' he whispered.

'That's a long way to be travelling in this weather,' commented James. There was no response and the boy kept his head down. Morag placed the bowl of soup in front of the boy and handed him the spoon.

Hungrily he took it and loaded it with soup. 'Ah, ouch,' and dropped the spoon.

'What is it?' queried Morag.

'Ach, it's hot, it's burning.'

'You're so cold it feels that hot, take it slowly,' suggested Freddy.

'What's yer name?'

The boy put the spoon to his mouth again and took a sip then another.

'What's your name, lad?' Freddy asked again.

The boy looked up at him as though debating whether to say anything.

'Me name is Johnny Coyle.'

'But where' yer family?' asked Morag. 'They must be mighty worried about ye.'

The boy hung his head and would say no more.

'Well,' said Morag, 'take some mair soup. Ye don't look as though ye've had a sup tae eat in days.'

Johnny lifted the spoon again and took the soup, trying hard not to look as hungry as he felt. He'd meant to get out of Belfast and just keep on going. He didn't know where he was. He'd been reluctant to give his name worried they'd know what he was and throw him out, but this woman's accent wasn't local. He couldn't place it. In the short time his family had been in Belfast after moving there to try for work, he'd found out what happened if you were the other sort[15].'

'So, Johnny, where were ye going when the snow fell an' ye found yersel in Garraiblagh?'

'Family, up the Glens.[16]'

'You've a brave way tae go then.' remarked Freddy.

James motioned to Freddy to come outside.

'I wonder if this is related to the riots in Belfast? said James.

'But they were months ago,' responded Freddy.

'And you ken as well as I do Freddy, that nothing ever stops at a precise moment. That trouble has been festering for a lang while. I

---

15 Phrase used to describe people in the north of Ireland of a different religion.

16 The Glens of Antrim on the north-east coast.

would be surprised if it hae stopped. We just have nae heard aboot the incidents. If Mr Gladstone[17] tries to introduce anither Home Rule Bill[18] there'll be riotin' an' worse. I'll hae to inform Mr and Mrs Henderson, but I'd like to ken a little more o' the lad's story first. I would be loathe to have him transferred tae the Workhouse.'

' The workhouse?' said Freddy.

'Well, that would be the obvious place, but I'd raither that was no' the case. I'll hae to hae a think aboot it.'

'He's said he wants to travel on to find his relatives,' said Freddy.

'I'm nae sure I believe that. He must hae been desperate to get oot o' Belfast in this weather. He won't be in any fit state to keep walkin' for a good while.'

In the office the warmth of the soup and the blankets was having a gradual effect. The boy's eyes were closing and he had lost the ghostly pallor he had had before.

'James,' said Morag, 'he cannot stay like this. Bring him to the cottage and I'll get a bed ready for him.'

'Morag we ken nothin' aboot the lad. Would ye hae him in the same house as Rory?'

'Would ye leave a young lad on his own who has nae family?' said Morag. 'I'll sit up wi' him if it makes ye feel easier.'

James relented. Morag left the office with instructions to bring the boy to the cottage. She would go ahead and prepare a bed for him.

Morag sat beside the boy as he slept. She was glad he had fallen into an exhausted sleep almost as soon as his head had touched the pillow, but now he seemed to be having a nightmare. He was making sounds, moving his arms over his face, she wasn't sure whether to wake him or not then he let out a cry and she leant over to place her hand on his shoulder.

---

17 William Gladstone (1809-1898), British Prime Minister

18 Proposal to give Ireland a degree of self-government under British rule.

'There, there, ye're alright.'

Johnny sat up in shock, still held by the nightmare and unsure of his surroundings.

James, alerted by the cry, came rushing into the room. His immediate concern had been that something had happened to his sister.

'Johnny has hae a bad dream. Try an' get some mair rest lad.'

Johnny woke as the light flooded in through the window. Hearing the sounds of people talking and smelling what he thought was bacon; he found his way down the stairs and into the kitchen.

Rory was busily eating his porridge and stopped to stare curiously at the stranger. Morag turned from the range where she was frying and wiped her hand on the apron.

'Take a seat. Ye need some breakfast.'

The front door opened and James came in, rubbing his hands together. He unwrapped his scarf from his neck. He'd been out checking on the greenhouses and the boilers. 'It's still snowing and it's banking up against the walls. Well, young Johnny, I don't think ye'll be travelling far today.'

The breakfast finished, Morag took Rory out of the room.

'Now, Johnny, tell me if I'm wrong. Did you leave Belfast because of the trouble there, the riots?'

Johnny nodded, miserably. 'Aye, sir. I couldn't take it no more. I jest wanted a job. Me uncle had told us all at hame that it was great in Belfast — jobs fae everywan. I had the notion I'd go to me uncle an' aunt and try me luck. When I got to Belfast there was rioting an' they didn't want us to work. I was afeard.'

'What about your aunt an' uncle?'

'I tellt them I was going hame. They weren't that bothered, but ma family willna be able tae feed another at hame either on the farm.'

'Are ye a hard worker?'

'Aye, I am, sir. I'm strong too; though I might not look it at the moment. I...' Johnny began and then thought better of it.

'What were ye about to say?'

Johnny took a deep breath and looked at James.

'I got a gardening apprenticeship on Clark's estate up on the north coast. I had near two year done when me uncle came up to visit and tauld us about the city,' Johnny sighed. 'I don't know what to do. I can't go back now, they wudnae have me. I've burnt me bridges there right enough. I was stupid. I thought I'd get mair money in the city, y'see.'

James looked at the boy thoughtfully.

'We all make mistakes, y'ken? I've made a fair few myself over the years. Well, we have a position vacant for an apprentice gardener. You might be the person I'm looking for. Mind it's hard work and long hours and if you leave there will be no coming back and there'll be no reference.'

'I don't mind that, sir. I won't let you down!'

The mahonia and witch hazel sent out wafts of deeply beautiful scent from their yellow and orange flowers.

It was difficult work in the garden as hot beds were put together. The worry of the constant supply for the big house both for food and suitable flowers continued throughout the colder months. The family entertained on a regular basis and Sam, when he got a chance, now that he had moved up a stage and was able to harvest some of the vegetables, listened to Mrs Mullan and the others in the kitchen as they described the food they prepared. Even Sam knew that if there were any problems in the garden and the fruit and vegetables did not appear at the kitchen door it would be a disaster. Mr Black always looked calm, but he had seen even he had a frown the other week when the potatoes weren't as unblemished as he wanted.

Christmas 1886

November had been chilly but sunny and Amelia and George had made several trips into Belfast, present hunting for Christmas, returning with large beautifully wrapped boxes from Robinson and Cleaver and Anderson and McAuley. The short dark days of winter were difficult for Amelia and she was glad to have her mind involved in preparations for Christmas.

The snow began almost unexpectedly: falling slowly at first, a few slight flakes, but then heavier flurries.

James Black and his team were well prepared in the garden. It was always a busy time.

'I don't think we should leave anything to chance, men. That snow looks as though it could last and I don't want us caught out with no vegetables lifted.'

'Valleley and Jones, collect the cauliflowers please and hang them up in the shed. They'll keep alright in there.'

'McGonigle, how is the pineapple doing?'

'I'm keeping my fingers crossed, sir. It looks good, but I don't want any last minute difficulties with the heating or the snow breaking a glass in the roof!'

'Cleland, check on the rhubarb and the seakale in the forcing shed and make sure the fire is still burning and none of the candles need to be replaced in there. They looked as though they were coming on well when I last checked, but we can't take anything for granted.'

'Mr McPhee, I'd like you to check on the celery. It's been well covered. If it seems good, pick two or three and cover the rest up again. Mrs Mullan will be pleased if we can offer that for her salads.'

Helichrysum and decorative leaves which had been drying in the potting shed came into their own and took the place of many of the cut flowers in the indoor flower displays.

It would have been Timothy's thirteenth Christmas and his

brother Ted was now twenty one. There were no young ones to share Christmas with. It saddened Amelia. She had imagined the house full of children, but Timothy's death had put an end to that.

Amelia realised that she needed to be out in the garden. She had something to do. Amelia put her coat and hat on and collected a trug and secateurs from the cloakroom where she always had some basic gardening tools.

There were some early witch hazel flowers and a little mahonia and then, sheltered from the worst of the snow by the branches of a fir tree, was a pink rose. Its colour brightened the whole area, and there was something so wonderful about its strength and vitality in managing to flower in the depth of winter. It seemed a pity to pick it, to sacrifice it, almost, she thought.

'Mrs Henderson.'

Amelia turned without having cut the stem.

James Black, his coat buttoned up to his chin, a thick scarf around his neck was holding his hat down over his face in the snow that was now thickly falling.

'Good morning, Mrs Henderson. I was on my way to find you.'

'Good morning, Mr Black. It certainly looks as though we may have a white Christmas.'

Snowflakes were falling and lodging in James' beard and on his muffler and coat. Amelia thought he looked a little like a dressed Christmas tree or maybe even a passable Father Christmas.

'You were looking for me?'

'I have been keeping straw flowers for you,' as he held out a covered basket and lifted a corner of the blanket material. The bright warmth of the colours seemed to flood the cool white all around them.

'Oh, they are beautiful!' said Amelia as she wrestled to take a glove off. 'I do love them. I have such memories of the wreath you made for Timothy with them.'

'Yes, and forgive me, but I thought it was likely that you would be visiting your son's grave and might like some of the Immortelles to brighten it up.'

'Oh thank you! Mr Black. Would it be possible for you to show me how to make a small wreath to put on Timothy's grave?'

'Would you like me to make one for you?'

'No, I'd like you to show me how to do it if you would. I want to make it myself but I don't want to be alone while I do so.'

James and Amelia walked past the glasshouses where Ignatius and Paddy, under Freddy's supervision were putting the finishing touches to the huge garlands of holly and ivy before they were to be taken into the house.

The potting shed had Christmas roses newly potted and ready. There was something about the earthy smell that reassured Amelia.

James brought over the materials to make the wreath and began to instruct Amelia.

'I'm so glad we've been able to do this. It really feels as though I am giving something to Timothy. Thank you for your help.'

Amelia looked up at James. She had not noticed the sadness in his face until now, so caught up in her own thoughts as she had been.

'Ah, I'm so selfish. Mr Black, this must be a difficult time for you.'

James dropped his head and busied himself sweeping up the remnants of the wreath making.

'Aye, aye, it is. I will be visiting Janet's grave on Christmas Day with Rory. Janet wasn't so fond of the snow. She liked the summer.'

James replaced the baskets and suddenly needed to be somewhere else to hide his discomfort.

'I'd better be checking on the preparations in the garden. We have our lists for the kitchen from Mrs Mullan and Mr Russell and Mrs Henry will be awaiting the garlands and the plants for the main rooms in the house.'

'Yes, of course. Thank you so much for your help and

consideration.'

And Amelia picked up her gloves and left the shed, regretting that she should hadn't been more sensitive about his wife and her death.

'Mr McPhee, would you take O'Kane, Armstrong and Cleland to oversee the hanging of the garlands?' said James and then added, 'and take McBride with you too.'

James saw Sam's face light up at the opportunity to see inside the big house and to help with the decorations.

'Right, lads,' said Freddy. 'Let's get these garlands up to the house and whatever you do don't let them fall in the snow!'

Patrick Russell the butler met the gardeners at the door. Despite his name Patrick Russell was English and Freddy found conversations with him, even though few and far between, uncomfortable. In the privacy of his cottage he often had Morag and James in stitches with his impersonation of the pompous butler. He had to be careful in such situations as these to keep his voice even and not to let himself be riled. It took a great deal of effort.

'Good morning Mr Mc Phee, I've had the staff put down sheets on the floor so please stay on them if you would! You have a garland for the staircase and the fireplace here in the hall? And one for the drawing room?'

'We do, Mr Russell. I think it would be best to dress the staircase first,' said Freddy, wishing to ensure that he had some authority on the subject.

Moving behind them, with a mop as ice dropped from their leggings and coats, blown by the wind into drifts of snow, came Martha Jane the house maid. As Freddy took charge, ordering the gardeners in the difficult task of attaching the heavy garland he stepped back. At the same time, his mind was diverted from the task in hand and the mop caught under Freddy's feet.

There was a crash as Freddy landed in the bucket, backside first and was unable to get out. Sam burst out laughing and as he couldn't be stopped was ordered out of the house.

The dressing of the rooms with the garlands continued in silence as Freddy moved carefully to avoid the wetness seeping further into his clothes.

The light was beginning to lessen as the gardeners completed their task. Standing back in the hall they took one last look at their handiwork.

'Happy Christmas,' announced Mrs Henry the housekeeper as she brought mince pies in on a tray.

Back in the garden, Freddy regaled the gardeners, including James Black with his impersonation of Mr Russell. 'That man! I prefer the company of carrots.'

He noticed Willie MacAlpin and Sam McBride sharing a private joke.

'What's up wi' youse?' Freddy demanded.

'Nathin, Mr McPhee, 'nathin at all.' Willie burst into shrieks of laughter joined by Sam.

'Only Martha Jane toul' us ye sat down wi'out bein' asked by Mr Russell. Ha ha!'

'Oh aye, oh aye. Very funny I'm sure!'

At that all the gardeners burst into laughter, including James Black.'

'That is good that you prefer the carrots, Freddy because I'd like you to take some carrots and potatoes out of the clamp. Young Mathew can take them up to Mrs Mullan.'

George watched the snow falling as the evening began to gather. It had been a long day, a difficult one. This Christmas was special as it was the year of Ted's twenty–first birthday. Collecting the tree for the house had become a tradition and George's job, assisted by Ted. Both were provided with axes by James Black and they set off to the forest behind Garraiblagh. After a lengthy discussion about which young tree to cut father and son dragged the tree back on a sled, tied with rope, laughing as they stumbled over snow hidden roots.

Tin stars, fir cones, and a strange collection of glass ornaments were brought out ready to decorate the tree and added to them were the fragrant slices of dried orange and apple and nuts were strung together. While Amelia made tiny parcels of shiny gold and silver paper, each with a sweet in them. Since coming back and initially living in Glasgow she had enjoyed the winter Christmas. The tree glowed with the intricate decorations, caught in the light from the wood fire.

In the moonlight with the snow still falling heavily, the badger lumbered slowly across the old farm track and into the woods where it began to use its claws to ease out insects and worms for its ` Christmas feast.

Chapter Fourteen

1887

AMELIA ENTERED the drawing room. It was clear to George that she was anxious to discuss something with him. He just wondered what she was about to suggest.

'George I have been wondering about Garraiblagh.'

'That sounds very all encompassing, Amelia, what in particular?'

'I was thinking of a celebration.'

'A celebration. That sounds intriguing, my dear?'

'Yes, Margaret Forbes was here with Kitty Johnston and Abigail Black this afternoon and the subject of garden fetes arose. Apparently the Smiths had one last summer, I don't know why I wasn't aware of it, but anyway they did and it was a great success.'

Amelia sat down on the deep ruby red velvet chair opposite her husband.

'So I thought we could have a garden fete, a show, a way of showing off Garraiblagh and I...'

'And you?' asked George, raising one eyebrow.

'Well, I told them that we were organising one here. I know I should have waited but really, Margaret was being so obnoxious and insinuating that it would be an impossibility for such a place as ours!'

'I'm surprised at you Amelia, I didn't think you rose to that sort of baiting. You normally don't care a fig for what people are saying.'

'I know but it is the garden! It was as though our garden was not worthy after all Mr Black's work. And Margaret Forbes! She is such a difficult woman. We'll show them... won't we? Please say that it is possible?' said Amelia as she leant forward and reached out for her husband's hand.

George laughed. 'It isn't often that you plead for anything, Amelia, and I'm inclined to think that I would have done the same thing if I'd been in your shoes. I assume that you want Margaret's face to be as green as it is possible?'

Amelia chuckled. 'Most certainly.'

'So when were you thinking of having this?'

'I'm not sure yet, but it would have to be during the summer.'

'Have you mentioned it to James Black yet?'

'No, of course not. I wouldn't do that without consulting you first.'

At which George raised one eyebrow and fixed her with a stare.

'Be diplomatic when you do, my love. He may not be so keen to have people trampling over his grass and flowerbeds.'

'I will be and I know I need to be very nice to Mrs Mullan and her staff as we'll be providing teas.'

'I don't envy you your discussions, Amelia. I'm just glad I'm managing linen factories.'

Amelia decided that it would be best to meet with James Black in the garden. She found him deep in conversation with Mr McPhee.

'Mr Black, I wonder if I could have a moment of your time?'

James nodded and removed his hat. 'Of course, how can I help you, Mrs Henderson?'

'I may have agreed to something that you will not approve of,' said Amelia deciding that the best way of approaching the subject would be to throw herself on Mr. Black's mercy and confess the error of her ways.

James' mind considered a variety of horrors as she began to speak.

'Forgive me, but in a moment of weakness I have agreed that we will have an open day, a fete at Garraiblagh.'

'A fete?' James now had images in his head that suggested frivolity, stalls and fun fairs. 'In the garden?' he said looking around.

'Not just that,' said Amelia hurriedly, as she saw James' face cloud over. 'It would be an opportunity for people to admire the gardens and the estate, with perhaps guided tours from you?'

James made a non–committal clearing of his throat and looked sideways at Freddy McPhee who stood, suitably stony faced.

'Mr Black, I will take you into my confidence. I was informed by a person who shall remain anonymous that they had been to a garden fete at another estate, well known to you. They had then remarked that it was a pity we did not have the gardens that could host such an event ourselves.' Amelia slumped down on the garden bench. 'I'm afraid you'll think I overreacted.'

'Mrs Henderson, I am aware of the estate that you allude to, I think. In fact I went to their open day. I can say with no false modesty that Garraiblagh can host a superior garden fete. Would you agree, Mr McPhee?'

'Oh, aye, Mr Black. Superior, very superior.'

'However,' began James. 'I wonder, have you thought about an open garden rather than a fete?' James still had visions of trampled grass, lawns that would take ages to mend, flowers and shrubs broken. 'An open garden would show off Garraiblagh and focus on it rather than having to resort to elements that might be found in a funfair.'

Amelia felt chastened. Had she allowed her anger to get the better of her? Was a fete really the best way forward?

'In fact,' James continued. 'I made some notes when I was at that estate's garden fete as to how such an event or similar one could be more effectively run.'

'Oh, I see,' said Amelia, now feeling as though her idea had been well and truly flattened.

James realised that he had to now convince Amelia that an open garden would be a much more elegant and appropriate way of showing off Garraiblagh.

Amelia found herself being bombarded in the nicest possible way with the reasons for an open garden and by the end, found herself agreeing.

'Then may I suggest that we hold a meeting to discuss the details? We will have to work out a timetable for the day and also ensure that you are happy with the guided talks and walks on the garden.'

Amelia rose from her bench a happy woman and began to walk back to the terrace. James and Freddy walked steadily around the corner of the rose arbour and then stopped. A large grin lit up James face.

'It all comes to he who waits, Freddy, eh?'

'Aye indeed, James. Indeed it does.'

'We'll show that Ferguson fella at Mullyglass what a real garden looks like. I hoped Mrs Henderson would get riled by the Smiths and she did, by Jove!'

'She's a great woman and no mistake, James.'

'She is that, Freddy. Now let's get our heads together.'

The open garden could not have come at a better time for James. They wasted no time. That night after James had met with Amelia, the preparations began in earnest.

'We will need a marquee for the quartet in case o' rain an' also somewhere for people tae take their teas. That will mean extra tables an' chairs.' said James. 'Freddy I want you to talk to Patrick Russell about that.'

'James, do I hae to be the one tae speak to that English windbag? Ye ken he and I aren't on the best of terms.'

'Freddy, it has to be ye.' Freddy knew there was no argument. The embarrassment of the Christmas decorations still inhabited his dreams.

'Mrs Henderson has asked if it would be possible to have a small plant stand where people can purchase some plants. I'm wondering who would be best to man that stall. Any thoughts, Freddy?'

'I think Ignatius O'Kane is our man. Sensible. Ye definitely don't want Paddy Cleland. Ye ken what he's like with the jokes. He'd probably tell some poor unsuspecting person that they've just bought a ten foot rose or a flyin' cabbage plant and they'd believe him!'

The flyers were printed and delivered to local shops and Church noticeboards. Individual invitations were sent to the friends and acquaintances of the Hendersons.

Morag Black lifted one of the flyers from the table and read it aloud.

"The grounds of Garraiblagh estate will be open to the public on the 10 July. There will be a display of the unusual and rare plants for which Garraiblagh is famed and there will be garden tours conducted by Mr James Black, Head Gardener and plant hunter."

'Well, I'm glad to see your name is mentioned James. It is as it should be. It certainly looks grand enough. "A quartet will play in the garden where teas will also be served."

'Mrs Mullan will be busy in the kitchens. I must get out my best hat and coat.' said Morag as she placed the flyer carefully on the mantelpiece.

Biddy O'Hara, the local postmistress and gossip noticed the paper sitting on the grocer's counter. 'Let me have a look at that,' she said as she was handed her carefully wrapped parcels of tea and flour. 'I hear the grounds will be open for all to see, and there will even be music an' opportunity to purchase some plants.' commented

Mr James the grocer.

'Oh,' said Biddy, as she quickly scanned the flyer. 'I'll take it with me and study it at home.' She tucked it into her willow basket and left the shop, trying not to allow Mr James to see her excitement about the Garraiblagh event.

At home setting her basket on the kitchen table she took the flyer into the light by the window of the cottage. She knew she wouldn't be the only one of the locals who would be curious about the famous garden, but Biddy also wanted to get a peek at the house if she could.

Sitting down with Freddy, James went over the plan for the open day once again.

'The palings need to be in place as soon as we are up. They must be done first. People need to be clear about where they can walk and where they cannot. I need you, Freddy to be in the kitchen garden. The fruit and vegetables in there are likely to be a temptation to some I would think. And Willie McAlpin will watch the glasshouses along with young Sam McBride.'

'I'll have Tommy Vallelly stationed near the rose arbour. He will need to ensure no one goes into the summer house or decides to take any roses home with them.'

'What will we do with Willie Scott, James? He's no very good with people. Great with plants but no good with people he doesn't ken.'

'Let's put him in the walled garden, down by the fruit bushes. All he has to do is nod and say hello.'

Amelia and George Henderson formally opened the gardens for viewing and then moved among the gathered throng of invited friends and acquaintances. It was clear after the first talk given by

James Black that he had built up a following. Word had got round that he could tell a good story about where some of the plants had come from and how he had been on hunting expeditions to distant lands to find them. Freddy found himself answering questions on a wide range of subjects, from growing lettuces to people marvelling at the exotic plants in the conservatory.

Biddy O'Hara walked along the main path and gazed at the deep borders of flowering plants. Yes, they were very pretty, but she preferred her marigolds and larkspur. She was curious about the fruit and vegetables being grown. Mrs Mullan the cook had been overheard describing a particular dessert involving blackcurrants and raspberries to a customer in the shop. Biddy had no fruit bushes, but she would dearly like to grow some fruit to make puddings like Mrs Mullan. She might not like the idea of the people in the big house, but she did like the idea of showing off to her neighbours.

For Biddy it had been a successful afternoon. Her hat back on her head, but slightly awry, she walked solemnly towards the drive, carrying a redcurrant cutting and two raspberry canes. She had had a glimpse inside the big house and she had gossip that would keep customers going for some time.

She still didn't hold with growing grapes in hot houses and as for that gardener telling her how the peaches had to be fertilised! Well, she'd never heard the like. What goings on in a garden!'

James noticed the stocky figure of Mr Samuel Ferguson, the head gardener at Mullyglass. A man who considered himself James Black's rival. He smiled to himself. It had been a good day and James had been especially pleased that the head of the Botanic gardens in Belfast had come all the way to Garraiblagh.

'Good day, Ferguson. I'm glad you were able to come.'

Mr Ferguson, his thumbs hooked into the top pockets of his tweed jacket, nodded in response and rolled back on his heels, his double chins tucked neatly into his uncomfortably tight looking collar.

'The garden's lookin' well, I'll say that for your gardeners, Black. I suppose they would have to be with ye off gallivanting round the globe looking for your fancy plants.'

James widened his mouth in what he hoped would approximate a pleasant smile and might also help him remove the image that he had in his head of a rotund Ferguson buried head first in a compost heap. It was, however, a pleasing image and difficult to shift.

'Aye, I'm glad ye approve of the garden. We work hard to ensure it always looks its best. I hope ye find some unusual plants on your tour. Please let me know if ye require any advice. Good day to you, Ferguson.'

James bowed his head, turned and walked back towards the crowds who were admiring the ponds on the lower lawn.

Chapter Fifteen

1890

JAMES TOLD RORY STORIES of the famous plant hunters, their daring adventures and the strange and wonderful plants they found. Rory sat round eyed, listening. And, when as occurred on several occasions, James Black joined a plant hunting expedition to China or the Himalayas, Rory waited excitedly for his father's return. There was always some exotic artefact that his father presented to him.

As the years progressed Rory, with his mother's colouring and gentleness became a well known figure around the estate and the surrounding area. He had a ready smile and his blue eyes usually managed to convince the cook that he was in dire need of food, something that rankled with Morag who had heard comments that she did not feed the growing boy enough.

Maps, books on gardening and history formed Rory's reading. There was never any question that he would not follow in his father's footsteps, but this did not mean that he did not have to serve his apprenticeship like anyone else.

Now sixteen Rory was ready to leave the estate and obtain experience elsewhere. James had carefully investigated the different estates and their specialisms and decided on the estate that he had trained in in Scotland, where as an under–gardener he had met David Douglas.

It was a difficult parting for father and son. Rory's work in Scotland and then anywhere else in Scotland or England would only allow very irregular journeys back home. The hope was that Rory would return and prepare to take up his father's role as head gardener at Garraiblagh, when the time came for James to retire, but that was some years off.

In the years that followed, James tried hard not to seem unduly concerned about his son as he watched for the postman and was usually the first to greet him.

'He's been offered a position at Kew,' James read out proudly to Morag and Freddy. 'He will be working in the tropical house, at least initially. I wonder what he'll make of that?'

'Is there any word of him coming home?' asked Morag.

'No, there isn't,' said James and he scanned the rest of Rory's letter as though he might find information there that he had missed in his first reading.

'Ha! He does mention a young lass he's met by the name of Alice.'

'Hmm!' said all three. A girl in England was a mixed blessing. It contained the threat that Rory might stay in England.

Chapter Sixteen

Eighteen – nineties

GEORGE AND AMELIA were disappointed when Ted did not share their interests. They had hoped that being brought up at Garraiblagh he would want to nurture the garden and estate. He knew how much his parents cared for Garraiblagh and understood that but he saw Garraiblagh as very secondary to the family's business, a place that reflected their standing in the world of business not horticulture. In his thoughts there was the frequent feeling that his parents felt more for the garden than for him, that it reflected their love for each other. At times he felt as though it was like a sibling that he felt jealous of. It unsettled him, but at the same time made him more determined to have his mother think well of him.

When Ted married in 1894 at the age of twenty-nine, it was understood that he would carry on the family business with Florence, his new wife, at his side.

Amelia greeted Florence warmly in spite of sensing uneasiness between them. Amelia couldn't make up her mind if Florence was just quiet and nervous or quietly arrogant. She had tried to begin conversations on novels she had been reading, but discovered that Florence's reading in her view was very restricted and unadventurous.

Later at night in their bedroom, Amelia sighed deeply while she brushed out her hair. George noted the sigh and enquired, hoping it would only require a short response before he could return to the papers he was reading.

'You know, George, it may be unkind, but I think we have to acknowledge that our son is a bit of a stuffed shirt and Florence lacks personality. She is so quiet!'

'What would you rather Amelia? Someone quiet with whom you will hopefully be able to build a relationship or someone who is fiery and who will challenge you?'

'I know. I realise I am being churlish.'

Amelia turned to meet George's gaze.

'This garden, this house, we built it! I could not think of us moving somewhere else even if it were somewhere close. I know in a way I should be grateful that she shows little interest in the garden otherwise all that has been built up could be changed in a matter of months! I don't mind that she will take over running of the house and that is as it should be but....'

'I know. The garden, your garden,' said George. 'Amelia you cannot have forgotten how you felt when we stayed with my parents.'

'Indeed not, but it was smaller. George, am I behaving like your mother?'

'No, Amelia but you need to be careful. Let Florence see your generosity of spirit.'

'Oh George, you are right. I want Ted to be happy and settled. I want Garraiblagh to continue, to be appreciated. If I fail at this I fail with everything.'

George looked at his wife.

'Amelia, my love, you have faced many things, you will find a way I'm sure of protecting our legacy.'

Having no daughter of her own Amelia hoped that Florence's family would be agreeable to the wedding reception being held at Garraiblagh.

Florence's parents, Mr and Mrs Aitken, drove up the drive in their fashionable landau. Mrs Aitken had decided that the drive would be more comfortable and reliable in the horse drawn carriage than their new horseless carriage.

She noted the bluebells in the grass beneath the trees.

'Really, wild flowers! Don't they have proper borders? Really, it is more like a jungle!'

'Now m'dear, don't be difficult,' said her long suffering husband.

'Mother, please remember that Mrs Henderson is very fond of plants and the Hendersons created this garden from a wilderness,' pleaded Florence.

'Well, my dear, that may be so, but I hardly think they created it, surely their gardeners have done that.'

'I have seen Mrs Henderson working in the rose garden, trimming flowers and taking cuttings and she spends a good deal of time in the conservatory.'

Mrs Aitken raised her eyebrow. Her ample chest raised too in a form of confirmation that suggested solid citizens did not involve themselves in such things.

Amelia and George greeted the Aitkens and Florence and brought them into the drawing room. Mrs Aitken was determined not to be overwhelmed by anything.

'It must be so inconvenient living so far outside the city. Mrs Henderson. There's so little here.'

Amelia smiled. She was determined not to be riled by any comments and murmured a few reassuring but non-committal remarks while trying not to stare with fascination at Mrs Aitken's hat. It was a concoction of satin over–decorated with flowers, lace and ribbons.

Mrs Aitken felt that she had now achieved some superiority and opened her mouth to advance another point when the tea was brought in and the party sat down in front of the fire.

It was hard for Amelia to find anything on which she could truly agree with Mrs Aitken.

She realised that if they wanted to help with the wedding she would have to curb her annoyance and bring Mrs Aitken around to her ideas.

She was glad that they had decided to invite the Aitkens for the weekend. At least, Amelia sighed, the woman wouldn't find anything lacking in the comfort of their home.

Dinner was a tense affair. George did his best to find common ground with Mr Aiken and he in turn worked to present a positive and agreeable relationship, but Cyril Aitken was a banker who had rarely been beyond the counties of Antrim and Down.

Amelia found herself tiring in the onslaught of observations from Mrs Aitken.

'Our dear Queen has extensive gardens at Osborne and I understand on good authority she takes a very particular interest in the plants that are grown there. I understand that the Queen and Prince Albert and their children grew vegetables as part of their summers there,' said Amelia.

For the first time Mrs Aitken appeared to be without words.

'In fact it is our proud boast that we have a cutting of one of Her Majesty's Osborne myrtles here at Garraiblagh given to our Mr Black by the Queen's Head Gardener.. It is now a substantial shrub. It is the same myrtle that her daughter, the Princess Victoria had in her bouquet at her wedding and most recently, Her Majesty's youngest daughter, Beatrice also had myrtle in her bouquet. It would please us so much if Florence had some in her bridal bouquet. Our head gardener, Mr Black who knows many of the royal gardens would be only too happy to create the wedding flowers...'

Mrs Aitken knew that she was out done. She concentrated instead on the thought of being able to tell her friends about this rare royal plant that her daughter would have in her bouquet on her wedding day. Having a royal flower in her daughter's bouquet would be a triumph. She made a mental note to ensure Mr Aitken informed his client, the Belfast Newsletter, who would be reporting the wedding.

As agreed the garden and glasshouses at Garraiblagh provided the flowers for Florence's bridal bouquet. Stephanotis and orange blossom, gardenia, rose and carnation with, following tradition, sprigs of myrtle and as part of the wedding settlement the reception was also held there. The marquee set up on the lawn for the reception was decorated with swags and garlands of flowers and greenery.

The gardeners found themselves working over the usual, long hours in order to carry out their normal work, prepare the fruit and vegetables for the wedding feast and work on the constructions of the garlands. Straw for the garlands was brought into the main shed in barrow loads from the farm for the task of binding and covering with moss in preparation for the introduction of the flowers .

Florence understood her role as the wife of an influential linen producer and ship owner. She accepted that she had been bred for that as carefully as the prize camellias that were grown at Garraiblagh. She managed the house capably and took her mother-in-law's advice, in spite of the fact that she had been heavily influenced by an overbearing and snobbish mother, more interested in city life than country.

Florence, having grown up in an imposing town house on Derryvolgie Avenue off the Malone in Belfast, found the size of the gardens and the estate daunting and its distance from Belfast even more so. She missed the carriages on the quiet residential roads around Malone and the Lisburn Road. Her father, now retired, had headed a firm of accountants and was now a director of one of Ireland's leading banks in Belfast. They had not travelled widely; in fact they had not travelled at all, preferring the society of Belfast, only leaving it to spend summers at their house in Bangor.

Florence understood the walled vegetable garden. It had a purpose. It was part of the running of the house. Dressing the vases in the drawing room and morning room was one of her regular activities. In this she was in control, she knew what to do. Flowers were brought to the house for her to make her selection each day.

'You have an eye for colour my dear!' said Amelia, hoping to draw Florence out of herself.

Florence jumped. She had been remembering having tea with friends in Belfast and the inconsequential chat about the newest fashions and gossip.

'Oh! Thank you, Mrs Henderson. I enjoy arranging the colours, but I don't know much about the names of the plants. Today one of the gardeners brought in a flower I hadn't seen before. What is it?'

Amelia took the stem and smiled at Florence.

'This is a dahlia. It has an interesting history. It was first found in Mexico and only arrived in Europe about a century ago. There are evidently medicinal properties to the plant. I love the colours and the shape of the flowers. Aren't they wonderful?'

Florence plucked up her courage.

'Have you always known about flowers Mrs Henderson?'

'I've always loved plants. I spent much of my childhood in India and other places. Then when I was sent back to Scotland to live with my uncle and aunt we lived in a town house with very little garden, but the Botanic Gardens were close by.'

To her credit, Florence made up her mind, she could not be

defeated by a garden. She would take a walk, collect some flowers and stamp her new ownership as mistress of the house. Florence was strolling through the formal gardens, trug and secateurs in her hand, looking for flowers when Amelia caught up with her.

'There is a cutting garden beyond the conservatory. You might wish to obtain blooms from there. Mr Black and his gardeners have ensured that a wide range of flowers for all seasons are grown there.'

Florence looked confused.

'I'm sorry, I did not realise.'

There was no hint of sarcasm in her response and Amelia could see that Florence was unnerved.

'Don't worry Florence. You will soon get used to everything,' said Amelia, patting her daughter-in-law on the arm, before hurrying off.

Florence walked on to the hedged area close to the pond, put down the trug and seated herself on the love seat. Eyes closed she let the tears roll down her face. She had not realised it would be so difficult to live at Garraiblagh and the garden seemed to be against her. She felt like a stranger in it.

Nevertheless, Florence liked the parterres. They were neatly planted like the flower beds in the Botanic gardens in Belfast. But, and here she found it difficult to even explain it to herself, there was an air of sensuality in the way the plants blossomed so confidently, their scent intoxicating. There were areas of wildness which she found unsettling and when she ventured into the kitchen garden there was an earthiness and ripeness. The garden seemed almost human.

She had once strayed into the glasshouses and had been intrigued, stopping for a moment to watch one of the gardeners carefully using a rabbit paw brush on the peach blossom. When asked what he was doing he explained that he was pollinating the flower. This left Florence horrified. She stayed away from the glasshouses after that.

Plants and their procreation was something she felt very uncomfortable about.

Rory had said his farewells to the other gardeners in the glasshouse at Kew. He had made his decision. He stood at the entrance to the gardens and took one last look. He was going home to Garraiblagh. The lure of it was too much. It might not be the largest of estates but there was something else, something undefinable about Garraiblagh. It had made him. He had enjoyed his time at Kew, being in the company of other, knowledgeable gardeners working together and discussing new ideas. Rory had gained the respect of senior members of staff. There was a definite career for him if not at Kew then in some grand English garden, but the long letters between him and his father and his aunt Morag convinced Rory that his future was in Ireland. It was true Rory wanted to be home, but there was some uncertainty in his mood. For how long would he want to be working for an estate however pleasant the owners were? He had seen changes in how horticulture was developing in England and he wanted to be creating his own future, his own business, he had heard of others accomplishing this. But discussions about that could wait until he was home. And Alice would join him he hoped. He had fallen for the daughter of a gardener at Kew.

1895

January was icy. Foxes camouflaged against the ginger brown winter bracken, smelled the air as the search for a mate took them through the wild grasses and into the quiet and ordered gardens of Garraiblagh, breaking the silence with their late night howls. The witch hazel flowers with their spidery yellow and orange flowers and exotic scent spread colour beyond the lower lawn and the side of the house closest to the drive. Then as winter began to fade away the first flowers could be seen. Snowdrops and crocus. Wild primrose and lesser celandine covered the hedgerows and dog violets appeared in the green of the mossy banks.

In the big house there was excitement and trepidation. Florence was heavily pregnant and felt the first pains while clipping back a plant in the conservatory. Amelia heard her cry and the fall of the secateurs. Ted had been called home. He and Amelia waited anxiously throughout the evening as the midwife was joined by Dr Semple. Amelia's memories of the loss of Timothy remained very vivid.

Daisy was born early in the morning after a long labour which left Florence exhausted. Amelia lifted up her granddaughter, wrapped in blankets and took her to the window of the bedroom to be shown the garden. The sun was just beginning to light the garden and the pinks and reds and shadows of the trees. Amelia was never sure whether it was her imagination or not, but Daisy stopped crying and seemed to focus on the light and the colours.

Alice, heavily pregnant, washed and swept, cooked and cleaned and even helped harvest in the kitchen garden right up to her due date. Alice was sitting among the roses reading when she felt the first pains. It was as though she and the garden had come to an understanding.

Frank Black was born to Rory and Alice just as the big house was adjusting to the arrival of Daisy. In the gardener's house there was celebration. Rory kissed his wife and then followed the path he had walked so many times, towards the standing stone with his

Aunt Morag when he was younger. Through her he had learned that the old ways were not to be scoffed at and he knew there were others locally who believed in the power of the stone.

Touching the stone with his hand he thanked the earth for his son and placed a posy of primrose flowers at its base, promising a new spray of flowers for Beltaine[19]. The oak tree branches creaked and the still bare branches seemed to thrust their new buds into the sunlight. There was hope and promise of all new things. There was no one more pleased than James Black. Not only that he had a healthy grandson but that his daughter-in-law had survived. The very same morning he laid flowers on Janet's grave and through tears of gratitude told her all about the momentous events.

Mrs Murray, who had died many years ago, had left a legacy of recipes of herbs that could be used to ease childbirth which Amelia now championed. Both new mothers. Alice and Florence made use of the potions and to Amelia's delight both prospered.

Garraiblagh summer 1896

It was a beautiful June day, blue sky, white clouds. Amelia and George had suggested afternoon tea on the lawn and Ted and Florence had quickly agreed to the idea. The wicker chairs and tables were brought out and young Daisy sat on the blanket laid out close to her parents and grandparents. Blackie, the spaniel had his ball and was chasing round after it.

Amelia smiled. She reflected on the past year, the birth of her grand-daughter and the development of the garden. She was pleased to see Florence looking a little more relaxed. The sunlight which had been highlighting the herbaceous border nearby clouded over a little.

She thought of the Black family and the arrival of Rory so close to Daisy. It seemed as though nature was smiling on all at Garraiblagh.

19 Gaelic May Day Festival dating from pre-Christian times.

Now, perhaps she could afford to enjoy the contentment of what had been created.

She half heard George laughing as he spoke to Blackie

'Alright, boy, I'll throw the ball for you.'

She turned to watch the two begin their favourite game and saw George throw the ball and get no further. She let out a gasp as she saw her husband fall to the ground. Lifting up her skirts she ran to him, sinking to her knees with her arm around him. Ted and Florence followed with Ted, shouting for the doctor to be called.

George was dead as he hit the ground. He was only sixty years old. Amelia lay, her arms about her husband where he had fallen on the grass. Her crying was a keening. Ted gently lifted his mother to her feet while Florence went ahead to the house to advise the other staff. George's body lay on the bed that he and Amelia had shared. Amelia grew silent as tears streamed down her face.

'It was his heart, Amelia,' Dr Semple said gently. 'It may be little comfort to you but it was quick and he died at home surrounded by his family.'

Amelia wanted George. She ached for her husband. The awful silence, the knowing that there would be no responses to conversations engulfed her. She had wanted so many more years with him.

They had built everything together. Arguing, agreeing, deciding things, coping with the tragedy of Timothy and celebrating so many achievements. They'd balanced each other and now, he was gone. George had believed in her garden and Garraiblagh had been created out of their love. Amelia steeled herself to sit in the summer house and let the memories echo around her.

Amelia was supported by Ted at the graveside. Florence close by felt again the strong connection between mother and son. James Black, slightly stooped with age and using his favourite stick for support, stood back and watched in sadness as Amelia laid the flowers on the grave.

George Henderson had joined his baby son beneath the earth in the sun dappled shade. James Black could see the cycle of life. Nature gave and it took according to its rhythm. George's headstone had now been put in place alongside Timothy's in the woodland glade. Decorated and sculpted with a pattern of hawthorn, willow and celandine around its edge in traditional symbolism, showing that George as a man who had lived a full life. The pale stone stood out in the glade, close to Timothy's grave and its sculpted decoration of rosebuds for a life cut short.

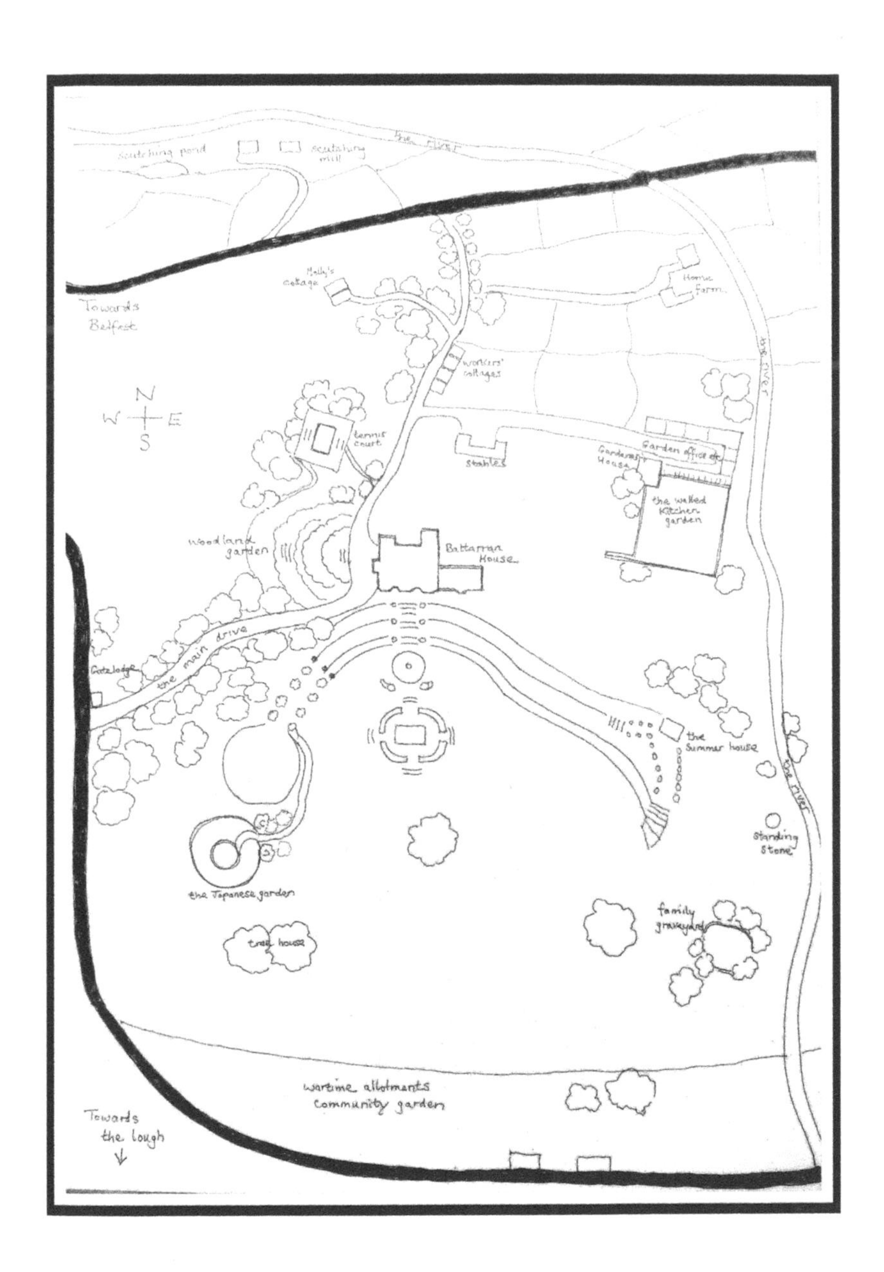

Garraiblagh estate 1900

PART THREE

Growth and War

'Garden as though you will live forever'
William Kent

Garraiblagh house 1910

Chapter Seventeen

1898

AMELIA, REMAINED LIVING at Garraiblagh. Florence though deeply affected by the death of her father-in -law found the close contact with her mother-in-law challenging. Amelia was not overbearing or unkind, but Florence still felt ill-educated and inadequate in her presence.

At first in her grief, Amelia did not realise that she was distant with Florence. Then as the initial grief lessened Amelia realised that if she didn't inspire Florence with the same enthusiasm she had for the garden, the garden, like life itself, would not prosper and neither would the relationships of all involved. She wanted to find a common interest, something that she and her daughter-in-law could develop.

'The garden is looking so well. We have added to the planting beneath the limes and I notice your flower arrangements Florence have been full of the beautiful roses and agapanthus.'

Florence nodded slightly but was wary, waiting for what came next.

'Florence, my dear, I know that you are busy, but I wonder if I could prevail upon you to accompany me to the Royal Horticultural Society Great Spring show in London. George used to come with me and I do not want to go on my own. We will have time for shopping. The show is at the Temple Gardens close to the Embankment so it is not out in the sticks.

Florence responded but without enthusiasm. She had never been to London or indeed outside the narrow confines of the north of Ireland. Besides, Daisy had only just turned three. She was caught between her duty to her husband's widowed mother and a strong disinclination to traipse around a place looking at flowers. Though she had to admit that the possibility of visiting Harrods and particularly Liberty's newly opened Eastern Bazaar was tempting.

Amelia's enthusiasm and Florence's desire to support her mother-in-law led to arrangements being made for their travel in early May. Taking the steam ship from Belfast to Heysham and then the Midland railway to London tired Florence more than the well-travelled Amelia, in spite of the age difference. Florence needed a day to recover from the journey which to her had seemed to the ends of the known world.

Florence was amazed by the tents crowded into the grounds at the Temple Gardens, five marquees full of exhibits of every sort of plant imaginable. The show was full of interested spectators and knowledgeable growers, while police constables patrolled quietly in their smart blue uniforms and helmets: so different from the dark green of the Royal Irish Constabulary and their flat caps.

Florence was surprised at the fragrance from all the blooms filling the air. A particular display of a new form of rose and carnations reminded her of a scent that Ted had bought her recently. She finally began to understand the seductiveness of plants. Welsh poppies, aquilegia, orchids of purple and pale violet sat potted up on their various stands and society women with wide brimmed hats, almost as decorated with flowers as the displays, promenaded through the area.

But the model gardens had been a revelation.

'Mama, is that the Duke and Duchess of Westminster? It never occurred to me that gardens could be held in such esteem.'

Amelia, like a spider weaving her web, drew her daughter-in-law slowly into the world of gardens.

'My dear, look at those roses, aren't they exquisite? Such a delicate shade of pink!'

Florence leant forward and read the label. 'Florence! The rose is named Florence!'

Amelia smiled. Not for the world would she let it be known that she had read the rose growers catalogues before leaving home. Everything was going according to plan.

'Without doubt there must be 'Florence' roses at Garraiblagh!' Amelia declared to Florence's immense delight.

The seed was sown. Florence could hardly contain her excitement. She began to view the exhibition of plants carefully. In her mind she saw Garraiblagh as a garden in which the newest and most intriguing plants would have their place and perhaps even the Garraiblagh name.

Florence's roses, a dusky shade of deep pink with an exquisite scent, were carefully positioned at the bottom of the steps onto the main terrace. From there they could be seen easily by all in the house and any visitors approaching the long windows. They became one of the opening conversations at social events

Other roses which had become well-established found themselves being removed to less prominent positions to sulk. Roses were taken by Mathew the gardener to bloom in his mother's cottage garden and were given all the attention and cosseting of a long lost child.

A sundial with its carved Italian marble plinth intricately decorated with flowers and hearts, a wedding present to Ted and Florence, was placed at the centre of a new enclosed spiral made from oak hedging very closely trimmed. This was Florence's favourite place. It was hidden and sheltered. It did not require her to acknowledge the huge expanse of the rest of the garden or to be aware of the gardeners busy in their work. It was where she could sit and dream.

Bright green sundews[20] with their red edged claw traps brought in from the peat bogs and growing in pots of spaghnum moss lay in wait for unsuspecting insects that might dare to attack the delicate fruit and flowers grown there and quietly feasted on them. The glasshouses required sensitive observation and regular ventilation. Cleland, having been trained by Willie McGonigle, had been assigned to working the winding mechanism, watering and spraying to just the required level, becoming in effect a conductor of an orchestra of tools and equipment.

The new leaves on the old oak fluttered above the standing stone. The local people revered it and spoke of it in whispered conversations. The old ways never fully forgotten. It was a special place. Not owned by money or power. At the old festivals of Lammas[21], Beltaine[22], Samhain[23] and Imbolc[24] offerings were left. Flowers

20 carniverous plant.

21 Also known as Lugnasadh. British and Gaelic festival marking the beginning of the harvest on 1 August

22 Gaelic May Day Festival dating from pre-Christian times.

23 Gaelic festival marking the end of the harvest and beginning of winter on 31 October.

24 Gaelic traditional festival marking the beginning of spring on 1 February.

laid on the stone, sometimes an occasional daisy chain hung lovingly over it. A different rhythm emanated from the stone, one which acknowledged a longer sense of time, unhurried. The wild parts of the gardens in Garraiblagh also had their rhythms, marking the seasons with their flowers, seeds. The local rector disapproved. Feeling moved at these pagan festivals to deliver long sermons on worshipping pagan symbols. It had little effect.

Amelia found herself struggling to hold the unwieldy plant upright and then laughed to herself, imagining what anyone would say seeing this woman standing in the middle of a flower bed dancing with a huge plant.

'Here, let me help you, Mrs Henderson.' Amelia looked up to see James Black hurrying towards her. 'It must have been that wind last night. The other plants held it up at first and it wasn't noticed by the lads when they did their rounds of the garden.'

'Oh thank you! I would hate to lose it. It is exquisite isn't it?'

'It's going to take both of us. If you could hold the main stem I'll re–attach it to its supports.'

Amelia felt absurdly young and carefree standing in the flower-bed, as though she was now part of the natural world and not the world with so many social rules.

'Do you always carry twine around with you?' Amelia asked.

'Always,' James smiled and added 'and my pocket knife. The habit of a gardener.'

For the first time Amelia felt as though they were having a real conversation between friends.

'Very well, I shall stand here and await your instructions!' Amelia giggled.

James' hand shook. Why should he feel discomforted? Just

silliness and he walked quietly over to Amelia and the plant. As he looked at the flowers on the rare plant, he also noticed Amelia and thought, not for the first time, he admitted to himself, that she was still a very beautiful woman.

Amelia could detect the faint tang of tobacco and noticed the pipe in his tweed jacket pocket. His eyes, which had been half hidden by the brim of his hat, became very noticeable as he reached up to tie the twine onto the plant. Amelia had never noticed the actual colour of his eyes and wondered why she had never noticed such an intense blue. She felt as though she was in a dream. Recovering herself she queried

'Are you able to restore it?'

'Aye, it looked worse than it was. I'll keep an eye on it over the next few days an' tell Rory to do the same. Just hold that please, Mrs Henderson.'

Amelia adjusted her grip. James' hand brushed against hers and a tingle of electricity passed between them. Both startled, looked into each other's eyes.

'Thank you, that seems to have fixed it.'

James held out his hand to help her onto the grass. She noticed the firmness of his grip. It made her feel connected in a way that she had not since George had died.'

Amelia felt overtaken as though she was not in charge of her actions any more. Before she could stop herself she said: 'Mr Black, we have known each other now for almost thirty years, I think we should be able to call each other by our Christian names. I am Amelia.'

'Well, no I....' mumbled James, looking around in case they were overheard.

'May I call you James?'

James was in danger of losing his composure. He had never called an employer by their Christian name, man or woman, in his life. He stood like an embarrassed schoolboy.

'I see I have discomforted you. I'm sorry, I'm being rude. I...' said Amelia.

'No, no, it's alright, Mrs Henderson...Amelia. I'm too old fashioned for the modern age, I'm afraid. What about the staff?'

'Just for the two of us. When others are around, it's Mrs Henderson and Mr Black. Is that acceptable to you, James?'

'That's fine with me Amelia.'

Amelia smiled. 'Thank you.' She felt she had gained a valued friend.

They began to walk together along the path.

Amelia pointed out the dierama with their delicate pink flowers on long arching stems and the purple headed allium.

'I love this border, James. I know I originally had doubts about it, but you were right. I was too restrained in my thoughts on the colours that could be achieved and the way in which it moves from season to season. There is always some wonderful scent or colour to notice. It is one of my favourite places.'

'I'm glad you feel that way about it, Amelia. It seemed to me that the planting should reflect the enthusiasm of a new garden and not be held back by traditional values of planting.'

'Does that mean that you approve of Miss Jekyll's planting designs?' asked Amelia.

James stopped and turned towards her. Fixing her with his blue eyes he grinned, 'Perhaps not wholly, Amelia'.

Their walk had taken them to the lower lawn and James and Amelia noticed the under-gardener leaning on his hoe for a moment as he too saw the couple.

'I should be going, Mrs Henderson.' James removed his hat, replaced it and moved off towards the walled garden.

Amelia suddenly felt alone. 'This is stupid. I live here with my son and daughter-in-law, my grand-daughter. I am not lonely.'

She reached her room, the sanctuary she often sought when she needed to consider problems. She threw her hat down on the bed and walked over to the window. There it was, the garden that almost thirty years ago she and George had created with James Black's expertise. She knew, had always known, it wasn't only the professional expertise and knowledge that James Black had given that brought about its reality, it was not only James' love of the garden but his quiet diplomacy and respect for her. They had hardly ever had a cross word in all those years. It was quite remarkable. Amelia began to remember conversations she had had with James Black over the years. Now, what was happening?

The sound of tuneless whistling came from behind the hedging near the Japanese garden. Ignatius the gardener was reliving his trip to the music hall in Belfast. Mathew joined in, equally lacking in tunefulness. The flowers didn't appear to mind. They both enjoyed collecting the seeds and dividing the bulbs of the larger plants. They placed the seeds inside the envelopes they had brought with them and in careful copperplate copied out the full names of the plants from the labels standing close to them. Even after so many years working in the soil they still stood in awe as the seeds they had collected began to show their first green shoots and they knew they had to be exact in copying out the name and variety of each plant they worked on. A mistake might not be noticed immediately but the Blacks, father and son, would notice soon enough.

Ned loved the early morning light when the dew was on the ground and there were still the remnants of mist across the garden.

He could think of no better place to work. He stopped, just in time to see a heron pierce the water's surface on the lower pond and emerge with a struggling fish before lifting off in its rather awkward flight. As it did so it squawked at Ned for disturbing him.

'Right, that is the first item to be dealt with. A new net for the pond.'

The sunken garden and pond were quiet. Although quite close to the house they were shielded by the terracing and the wind did not disturb the area. The intricate fountain at one end was in the form of a head and Ned always felt that it was laughing at him.

'Well, how're ye the day?' Ned asked of the gargoyle. 'Ye should hae bin keepin' a tighter eye on the fish in the pond, ye boy ye. I seen the heron now three times tha' for'night. There'll be a death, mark me words. Damn the bit. Ye can say wha' ye like, but I feel it in me bones.'

The stone head looked back at the gardener without comment. Ned turned to the weeding of the flowerbed, thrusting the small fork in between the leaves of the schizostylis.

The autumn sunlight cheered the garden and the fiery red of the last of the crocosmia danced at the back of the borders with the dark blue of the echinops. Rory stood; assessing which clumps of plant would be divided and moved, cuttings taken, seed gathered.

In the kitchen garden Sam McBride was taking blackcurrant cuttings while Ollie Butler collected the last of the autumn fruiting raspberries.

Davy Taggart, the new apprentice gardener opened the apple store door and manoeuvred the wheelbarrow with its special sectioned boxes for carrying apples, through the entrance with a deft turn of his arms before standing it on its feet. He enjoyed this task. The scent of the apples reminded him of home and the fruit his father kept to make cider. It was a cool and dark in the store but his eyes adjusted soon enough and anyway he knew which apples he was looking for. Mrs Johnston, the cook, had ordered bramleys as she was going to be making apple tarts.

A sound, indefinable, but threatening broke the silence. An apple rolled down from one of the shelves. Davy stood frozen to the spot.

'Is anyone there?'

There was no reply. The sound came again. Something, someone in pain. In agony? Davy wasn't sure but he wasn't staying. Davy left the wheelbarrow, grabbed some apples and headed for the door, running headlong into Rory Black.

'Watch what you're doing, boy! Why haven't ye got the apples in their sections?'

'I'm not going bak in tha' place on me own. Ye can fire me, sir!'

Rory looked at the boy whose face had lost all its usual colour and who appeared to be genuinely terrified.

'Let me see,' said Rory, steering the boy back the way he had come.

As Rory entered the store house the sound came again. It made his hair stand on end.

Davy looked up at him.

'Tha's wha' I heerd.'

This time there was a snorting sound and apples tumbled down at the back of the store.

'Get a lamp, Davy an' ask one of the others to join us. Quick now.'

Davy wasted no time and was back with a breathless Jack Butler.

'What's to do?'

'I'm not sure, Jack.'

'Give me the lamp, but stand well back. Jack can ye pass me the hoe there.'

Rory edged closer to the source of the sounds. More apples tumbled down and began rolling towards him.

'It's an animal I think — but it's big!'

'How would it get in here, it's always shut?' queried Jack.

Rory held the lamp high. Black and white striped hair appeared.

'It's a badger! An' he's none too happy.'

Going closer, Rory was aware the badger was warning him off, but it was also clear the animal could not or would not move from where it was.

'Watch yersel, sir. Them boys can bite ye bad.'

'It's caught in something.'

'Netting — The netting for the currant bushes.'

'Tell the men to stay away from this area and bring me a couple of long handled brushes.'

James and Jack quietly moved wooden boxes away from the entrance. They needed a clear exit for the badger when he was ready.

Carefully the two men worked their way round to the back of the store, keeping their brooms in front of them.

'When I say so, push the broom from behind and try to force the badger forwards.'

Jack nodded.

The badger did not agree with the use of brooms and decided with some heavy snuffling and growling that the best thing was to make a run for it. James and Jack breathed a sigh of relief as they watched it exit the shed and make for the woods.

'The door must have blown open or somethin' an' the badger got in, smellin' the apples. No one noticed he was trapped an' then found himself in an even worse situation. It's as well Mrs Johnson needed apples when she did,' said Rory. 'Well, I think we deserve a cup of tea for that. Davy, take the apples up to Mrs Johnson and see if she has anything she can send down for the heroes. I reckon we deserve a treat.'

Chapter Eighteen

1899

THERE WAS A BREAK in the rain at last, followed by a silence. Only the dripping of rain drops falling from the trees onto the summer house roof made a sound. Cabbage white butterflies, in the slightly increased heat, flapped drunkenly as though still disorientated by the weather.

Hazelnut clusters littered the ground near the edge of the lawn close to the adjoining field and its mix of hawthorn and hazel. Some of the nuts, still covered in their intricate pixie cap covering, had been nibbled by mice. There was little movement except for the graceful bowing branches and the dancing leaves below a grey sky painted in wide bands of smoky white cloud..

With the passing years the garden gathered its strength, beginning to cultivate its own personality, occasionally abandoning the gardeners' orders as a sport[25] or sucker invaded or a trailing vine overcame the neatness and separation of imposed order. Birds obligingly dropped stray seeds and, hidden behind imposing verbascum and agapanthus, grew into giants. The plants and trees kept a silent pact to help each other. A carefully placed thorn, a sharp prick or scratch often made the removal less important and one that could await another day.

Convolvulus preyed, when it could, on the unsuspecting choice seedlings, strangling them quietly in the background. The unseen and unnoticed elements of the garden operated in the twilight undergrowth waiting their opportunity.

Small red heads with shiny black noses tested the air and tentative steps were taken, following their russet furred parents out into the gardens across the lawn then back to home, running and jumping until they fell into a heap closely watched by their mother. Gardeners began to notice where the creatures enjoyed spending time. They knew hunters from further afield would take delight in removing the foxes. The gardeners kept their secret.

The old oak tree at the edge of the land acted as a further symbol of strength and timelessness, suggesting the house and gardens had been on site for centuries. It stood sentinel, watching the changes in the humans and the plants. In the summer it gave shade to the solitary reader, anyone with thoughts to consider. Its energy pulsing through the trunk and into the individual. It now looked out across the area that had been fields and saw paths, flower beds, areas hidden from view by the planting of hedges and climbers but the old oak could see above it all and what it saw in those hidden areas it kept to itself.

25 Part of a plant that shows difference from the main plant.

It had begun with Amelia noticing James Black slicing into an agapanthus clump and, then intrigued, asking him to show her how to propagate plants by division. Now here she was confidently and carefully labelling and placing root cuttings of oriental poppies in pots. She had always been intrigued by the propagation of plant varieties, but recently having been to the latest Royal Horticultural Society show her interest had deepened. She felt she needed to be doing more practical work in the garden, but not the work of weed pulling, something more adventurous possibly, she thought to herself. Something that would be different.

She smiled and sighed. James had shown her how to take cuttings and then how to work on the more complicated methods of grafting and developing new varieties. He had explained that many new forms were not worth bothering with, but occasionally and sometimes by accident, there was a real find. It was, she realised, the closest she would get to plant hunting in exotic places. Now Amelia regularly joined James in the greenhouse, as the pupil, learning the various techniques.

James looked over at her, standing at her bench in the greenhouse. Amelia turned from her work towards him.

'What I realise, James, is that there is never going to be enough space for all these plants to be placed here in the gardens at Garraiblagh. It has made me wonder.'

James had now become used to Amelia using his name and slowly he was relishing the use of hers. He wasn't sure what was happening, but there was something changing, a curious connection that was intimate, even when they were apart. Part of that allowed Amelia to talk to him in the way she was doing now, as though continuing a conversation, informal and without a polite start and end to it. And for James it meant that he began to relax into his Scots language more when with her.

James responded by turning his head and laying down the knife he was using.

'Aye, it has made ye wonder what in particular?'

'There are now plant nurseries being started up in various parts of the country, some specialising in particular plants, some not. Could we, here at Garraiblagh, create a plant nursery?'

'Are ye thinking of using part o' the gardens at Garraiblagh?'

'No, not that. I don't want the gardens to become public or to take away from their beauty. I would prefer the nursery to be somewhere else, but not far.'

'It would mean working very differently, but it's an interestin' idea, Amelia. Have ye spoken to Master Ted about the idea?'

'Not yet. I would prefer to present him with a much more definite plan. That's where you come in, James.'

James thought back to the conversation he and Rory had had about the future when Rory had returned from Kew. It seemed as though the subject was not going to go away. He thought that he had persuaded Rory to continue in the garden at Garraiblagh and, with his marriage and then the birth of Frank, it had indeed taken Rory's mind off things.

He would talk to Rory.

'Well, father, I'm curious. What has caused this urgent meeting?' I assume it's not to do with the runnin' of the garden or ye would have spoken to me earlier.'

James handed his son a whiskey and sat down in front of the fire. Now that Rory was here he wasn't sure how he should discuss the idea. James reached out and used the poker on the fire, watching it suddenly leap into life. He sat back. He realised that he needed to revive things between himself and his son. By dampening Rory's enthusiasm for the future he was keeping him, holding him in check and he had never responded well to that himself.

'Ye mind the conversation ye an' I had when ye returned from Kew — your ideas about the future?'

'I do. I also remember how ye squashed them with as many practical points as ye could muster, father.'

'Aye, I did. Two things have happened since then to make me think it's something that should now be considered, at least for ye. I realise that for me Garraiblagh has been me creation as much as anyone's an' I have nae wanted to let it go. It's also where your mother an' I were happiest and where ye grew up. I love the place, but I ken things are changing. It will soon be a new century. That is the first thing. The second is that I was speaking to Amelia... Mrs Henderson today an' she has raised the idea o' creating a plant nursery.'

Rory sat back, not immediately responding to his father. He found himself unsure. The stumble over Mrs Henderson's name and his father's explanation of his love for Garraiblagh. He put that to one side.

'A plant nursery at Garraiblagh?'

'No, separate to Garraiblagh, but close by. It is an idea that has some merit, but she's not discussed it with Master Ted.'

'But you're discussing it wi' me?'

'Aye, it would tak mair discussion, but I wonder if there is no' an opportunity for ye here, for us to have something ootside Garraiblagh — an' for ye — something ye would have control over.'

'How would I or we have control over it if Mrs Henderson owns it, father?'

'Aye, now there's the thing,' said James, lighting his pipe. 'I'm thinking she might have us as partners, rather than as employees.'

'What about money?'

'I have me savings. It amounts to something.'

Rory sat forward, turning the glass in his hands.

'Of course, a plant nursery would rely on the knowledge an' expertise of those running it. It wouldn't be like a private garden. It would be on a commercial basis designed to turn a profit!'

James nodded. 'An' I think Mrs Henderson is fully aware o' that. But, I dinnae think that it would necessarily be something tha' would happen quickly.'

Amelia and Florence's trips to London for the Royal Horticultural Society Shows had become an annual excursion. They returned from their latest trip full of ideas for a Japanese garden. They had been to see Gilbert and Sullivan's Mikado Operetta while in London. Humming merrily, they had returned to Garraiblagh, intent on creating their own Japanese garden which would then become the stage for a great event — a Gilbert and Sullivan evening and a tour of the new Japanese garden.

Ted listened patiently to their ideas and retreated behind his copy of the new Financial Times.

'I think you will need to consult James Black on this idea. It may sound manageable, but I would like to hear his views before taking it further.'

Florence was quiet, saying simply, 'You are right, Ted.'

Amelia would not be silenced.

'Ted, it can be done! It just requires the gardeners to take some time and create it.'

'Mother, what you are asking is not just a case of 'taking some time,' It is a major project!'

'Mr Black will have work organised for the men and remember we still need the garden to continue to run efficiently, particularly the walled garden, if we are to continue to eat! We're not going to be left buying our produce from those stall holders at St George's market!'

'Very well, I will speak to James.'

'Mother, you are very good at convincing people to your way of thinking, I know to my cost!' and he smiled at Amelia. 'If you ask James then I will see him about the details and practicalities to ensure that he has not been browbeaten into this!'

'That's unfair Ted. I've never browbeaten James into anything, I'm sure. I'll go and find him.'

Ted smiled at his mother's departure and considered this recent use of the name 'James.'

'Florence, I am really glad that you and my mother are getting on well but be aware that she is very strong willed and likes to get her way in everything. She's tried to bully poor James Black for decades. He's just too smart for her.'

'Oh, I know, Ted. I do realise that!'

Ted laughed and held out his arms to his wife. Florence held out her hands in response and Ted grasped her, turning her so that she lost her balance and landed on his lap.

'It must be the thought of gardening that makes me want to kiss you.' With a slow kiss Ted encircled his wife with his arms.

'What do you think Mr Black will say?' asked Florence.

'If I know James Black he will listen carefully and astutely work out the reality, curbing my mother's excesses when it comes to the plan and ......'

'And what?'

'And James will consider which plants he may be able to obtain that are rare and beautiful, probably plants he has been thinking about for some time. I know he still meets up with his old plant hunting cronies on occasion.'

Amelia found James Black, smoking his pipe and considering the new planting arrangement of perennials in the herbaceous border. She stopped before reaching him. He seemed to merge with the colours of the garden. It wasn't just the shade of his tweed jacket merging with the leaves it was something more subtle, a tranquility and yet a strength. This was a man who had spent his entire life around plants and gardens. It was almost as if he was part of the garden now.

'James!'

He turned his head and rose stiffly from the bench he had been sitting on.

'Aye, Good morning, Amelia,' he said gravely.

'James,' and then Amelia realised that she didn't know what to say next or rather, faced with his full gaze, she had lost her words.

James waited. 'James, I need your advice and support.'

'Me advice?' Amelia could see there was a hint of humour playing around his mouth.

'Perhaps we could sit here and I'll explain.'

Amelia arranged her skirts and sat waiting for James to join her.

'Florence and I have seen something that we would like to replicate here at Garraiblagh.'

'Tell me more,' said James.

'We would like to create a Japanese garden.'

Amelia waited for a response.

James tamped down the tobacco in his pipe.

'Oh, aye, Japanese, eh? So ye would want a pond with a central island?

'Exactly!'

'An'a wee wooden bridge to cross it?'

'Yes. Can it be done?'

'Where had ye in mind, Amelia?'

I was thinking that the lower part of the grounds that we have until now left as wild meadow and woodland.'

James nodded. 'It would be possible technically, but it would take some work — the digging out o' the pond area, the construction of the island and the planting...Well, there's nae time like the present! Shall we go and see the area?' said James.

Amelia was surprised at his enthusiasm and how easily she and James were able to walk in step with each other. The discussion of the plants that could be used and the colour palette kept the conversation focused on the possible work at hand.

Out of his jacket pocket James took his battered notebook and pencil and began to draw. Then hesitating, he removed his jacket and laid it on the grass.

'We are going to be a wee time here an' it's tiring to stand. I ken it's no' a rug, but if ye would allow me, please sit on me jacket, Amelia.'

Amelia nodded agreement and took James' hand to help her down onto the grass. There it was again, that feeling as she held his hand. Not for the first time she cursed the impracticable nature of her clothes with their heavy fabrics, stays and bustle.

James sat down on the grass beside her and held out his notebook for her to see. He drew with clear confident lines as though he could see the finished project in detail. As he drew he mentioned possible shapes, connections, difficulties, solutions. Amelia found herself straying from the drawings and plans he was making to another study, a careful study of James' profile. His thick eyelashes, his ginger beard, the strong chin and mouth.

'What do ye think about the possibility of a magnolia stellata here just at the top o' the incline. The pale smoothness o' the flowers would create a very attractive foil for a Japanese lantern?'

James looked up to see what Amelia thought of the idea and stopped. Their eyes met. He was transfixed by the blue of her eyes returning his gaze.

The huge wooden crate arrived, well tied down on the cart. The old cart horse raised his head and whinnied as he came to a halt on the drive. Florence and Abigail saw the cart arrive and hurried to see it.

'Call Mr Black and let him know that the crate has arrived,' Florence instructed one of the maids.

James and Rory had gathered several gardeners to help lift the crate from the cart. Getting the carefully packaged lantern off the cart would be one thing. Getting it down to the woodland area would be another.

The large stone lantern looked magical in its setting just on the edge of the island, close to the bridge. James and Rory looked at the moss covering part of it. It was dry and yellowing and some had been rubbed off. James touched it with his hand.

'I remember reading that the moss can be revived by applying a mixture o' water and rice wine.'

'Where are we going to get rice wine, father?' said Rory with a grimace.

'Aye, a good question. I'm just wondering what we can use in its place.'

'Well, we are not using any of the whisky Aunt Morag and Uncle Freddy gave us!'

'Och no! I would nae suggest that. I was thinking mare aboot a bottle o' white wine.'

Amelia spoke to Patrick Russell the butler. An inexpensive bottle of wine was procured from the cellar and with deep misgiving from Mr Russell, given to Rory.

Down at the Japanese bridge two gardeners were standing, resting their elbows on the lacquered wooden bridge rail.

'Kenny, I want ye and Paddy to mix half this bottle wi' a watering can full o' rainwater and carefully spray the lantern all over.'

The two gardeners took the open wine bottle reverently and

walked off towards the lantern with the watering can.

'We could just try a wee sip o' the wine, Paddy.'

'Squashed grapes! It looks like..... while like piss.'

'This is what the folk in the big house have wi' their dinners!'

'If it's good enough for them in the big house then it's good enough for us, boy.'

Both men took it in turn to have a slug of the wine. Neither were accustomed to it.

'Let's water the lantern,' said Paddy, but as they began, Kenny started giggling.

'Watering a lantern wi' wine. Whatever next?!'

And both men began laughing as they danced around the lantern spraying it liberally with the mixture.

'Here hand thon over, Kenny or we'll never get it done an' then there'll be some handlin' if it's not.'

The entrance to the newly created area was guarded by the beautiful magnolia stellata and a pagoda dogwood tree both laden with creamy scented flowers. A cherry tree and exquisitely coloured maple led down a slight incline, bordered by mossy rocks to the brightly painted red Japanese style wooden bridge which reached across a small, shallow pond to a tiny island.

A simple rock garden had been created to give a sense of age and serenity while water lilies floated delicately in the dark water with violet and mauve Japanese water irises lighting up the damp bank.

Amelia and Florence were delighted with the result. They made their way down the gravel and onto the bridge. Amelia was amazed at the smoothness of the lacquered wood and its warmth in the mild sunshine. In front of them, to the side of the end of the bridge, stood the stone lantern.

'I'm glad we did go to the trouble of bringing the lantern over from Japan,' said Amelia.

'I think the gardeners may not be quite so enthusiastic. It was such a heavy and cumbersome object for them to manoeuvre!'

'I know,' Amelia sighed, 'but it would have been incomplete if we had not.'

As Ted had suspected James saw the construction of the new Japanese garden as an opportunity to include some plants that he had coveted for some time. A Japanese wineberry planted against the wall of the kitchen garden sprawled in the sheltered position. Its sweet bright red and crimson berries drawing anyone close by.

Increasingly James involved Rory in the discussions relating to new planting, ordering of seeds and plants. It was understood that his son would take over his role when he was no longer able to manage though James would remain available as a consultant for the garden when required.

Chapter Nineteen

1900 – 1902

THE LETTER FROM THE BOTANIC GARDENS at Glasnevin in Dublin arrived in the early post. Amelia read its contents and then recounted it to her son and daughter-in-law.

'The director would like me to attend an event they are holding to honour a number of gardens in Ireland that have shown themselves to be outstanding.'

'That is certainly a great honour mother, but I wouldn't be able to go with you on that date.'

'I can go on my own!'

'Mother, it is a long train ride and then a lengthy trip out to Glasnevin. I don't think it would be advisable.'

'Ted, I am a grandmother who saw more of the world before she was twenty than many a man. This is important. I would like to see Garraiblagh honoured.'

Ted huffed. 'Well, in that case would it be appropriate for James Black to accompany you to the event. He was after all a part of its creation. It would be fitting.'

Amelia hesitated.

'If you do not think it appropriate, mother...' responded Ted.

'No, it is not that. It is a good idea. I should have thought of it. It was selfish of me.'

'Very well, I will speak to James and ask if he would accompany you to the event. If he is happy with the arrangements Russell can book accommodation for both of you in the Shelbourne.'

James Black listened to Ted Henderson.

'I would be happy to accompany Mrs Henderson.'

'It is only right that you are there Mr Black. It is the garden that is to be honoured and without you there would be no garden. The family recognise this.'

Ted looked directly at the older man. James could see that the young Master Ted had inherited his father's ability to understand the sensitivities of those working for and with the family. James had great respect for Amelia, but she was too close to the garden, too determined and sometimes did not see how others might feel.

Florence was learning to enjoy the garden and to feel less intimidated by some of its wildness. She knew that she would never have the passionate devotion to the garden that Amelia had. She would not have considered creating such a garden herself, however beautiful but, she had come to realise its importance and its absorbing beauty. She enjoyed the controlled beauty of the plants in the herbaceous borders and the cutting garden. Collecting the blooms for the arrangement in the vases in the house was a job that she relished. She now enjoyed the notoriety that having such a garden as Garraiblagh with its mixture of rare and unusual plants gave. However she still felt rather overwhelmed by its size. Since visiting the Royal Horticultural Society shows Florence had become a subscriber to several of the gardening journals. From this she discovered that she was not alone and that other ladies found gardening within the confines of the conservatory a rather more appropriate activity. Palms in pots provided the screening with just a suggestion of abandoned and dangerous tropicality. While red, orange and blue abutilons spread their delicate flowers and branches out to provide colour and structure. The staging in the conservatory was at waist height, built so that Florence did not have to bend and therefore find herself painfully reminded of her position by her corset. She could use a small copper trowel for the work and a pair of gloves and an attractive apron was all that was required to complete the picture. Much to her surprise Florence found herself fascinated by the colour, shape and scent of the pelargoniums while the jasmine and gardenia provided stronger background scents. Often in the afternoons after she had dealt with the household issues and organised the social calendar for the week she brought her watercolour book to the conservatory and made detailed drawings and paintings of the flowers.

Florence then had the idea of transferring the illustrations of the pelargoniums to embroidery and began work on a linen tablecloth.

Ted began to appreciate Florence's art work more and more and on one visit to Manchester to discuss business he noticed on his ride through the city tiny plants in the windows of some of the old weaving cottages. While he had never had the same passion for plants as his mother, there was something about the regularity of the almost geometric petals and the colour combinations that intrigued him. For Florence's birthday he organised a special event. He discussed his idea with his mother who then assisted.

For several days the sound of construction came from the garden and Florence saw gardeners moving bricks and carrying wood in various lengths over their wheelbarrows. Queries made to Ted were responded to with very off hand comments.

'They must be working on some trellis or some such.'

On the morning of Florence's birthday Ted advised his wife to wear her outdoor clothes, but told her nothing else.

A parade of Ted and Florence, followed by Amelia made their

way down the path and past the border full of the pinks and icy blue purples of filipendula and eryngium to the edge of the walled garden.

'Are we going in?' queried Florence.

'No, we are just going to follow the wall round for a little and then you'll see.'

They stopped at what seemed to be a strange site. A large piece of what looked like heavy fabric was hanging over the wall. Florence was puzzled. She could not understand the need for a heavy curtain against the high stone wall.

Ted, with a broad smile on his face asked Florence to close her eyes and to count to twenty.

'Now open your eyes.'

A deep brick alcove had been constructed at the end of the kitchen garden wall and within it five levels of wooden shelving had been built and carefully painted in black.

On each shelf small clay pots full of small round petalled plants a little like a child's drawing of a flower. The colours took Florence's breath away. She moved closer to look at them in more detail. Each perfectly formed flower had a yellow centre with a white surround but then the colours changed. There were purples, blues of different shades and hues, a ginger colour, yellow, magenta, rose, gold and cream.

'Do you like it?'

'I have never seen anything as beautiful! They are delightful! Like little faces staring out. What glorious colours and patterns.'

Florence for once lost her composure and flung her arms around Ted.

'This is your very own theatre, an auricula theatre,' Florence kissed Ted.

'Oh, thank you my love. But tell me why does there need to be a curtain?'

'I'm told that the flowers do not mind cold but they do not like rain so the curtain is there to shield them. Is that not right, Rory?'

'Yes, sir, that's right enough.'

'I had the idea when I was over visiting the mills in Lancashire and I thought about the connection between the weavers who brought them over to Britain. It seemed appropriate to have such plants in our garden, but they were just so pretty I thought of you.'

1902

Ted was, as usual, reading the newspapers that he had delivered on Saturdays, it was a time to relax and focus on the wider world as well as that of commerce and, in particular, linen and shipping,

'I see the White Star Line are to launch their new steam powered liner next Thursday. Harland and Wolff are doing well. As long as they keep building ships everything will be fine. I just wish this war with the Boers could be resolved. It doesn't make for good reading.' Ted sighed.

Florence nodded in response, knowing that Ted was not seeking her opinion on world affairs.

The sun at that moment came through the window and highlighted his wife concentrating hard on a new piece of embroidered linen. He looked at Florence as though he hadn't really seen her before. He watched her in the sunlight, her blond hair carefully pinned up. There was a slight frown on her face as she sought to thread a needle with a new colour. The shape and colour of the pattern she was working on attracted him.

'What is that pattern you are working on, Florence? It's unusual.'

Florence put down her work and smiled uncertainly at her husband. She couldn't remember a time when he had ever asked about her embroidery. She felt a little unsure of herself, but held out the white linen cloth, spreading it over her knees.

'It's a pattern I have made myself. I draw the plants in the conservatory and then make note of the colours and adapt them to my embroidery stitches.'

Ted laid down his precious paper and walked over to the chair that Florence was sitting on. Taking a seat on a nearby stool he took one end of the linen, tracing his fingers over the carefully embroidered work.

'This is a regal pelargonium. The late Queen grew them at Sandringham,' Florence explained. 'They really are quite beautiful with their velvety petals and deep colours.'

Ted looked more closely.

'I wonder. I'd never thought about embroidered decoration before. What if patterns made from some of our plants could be used in our linen products? Would you work with our designers, my love? I know it is asking a lot, but I think it could work.'

Florence put down her embroidery in surprise and the shock showed on her face.

'Of course, you may not feel you have time. I shouldn't have mentioned it.'

Florence looked at her husband. Perhaps this would help her feel more included, more involved. From the first day of her marriage she had noticed how George and Amelia had worked easily together. Their conversations meant something. She was in a way, jealous of that.

'Oh, I would love to, Ted,' said Florence smiling 'Yes, yes, I would.'

Ted, looking at his wife began to suspect that there were hidden depths to her and he realised that he had not spent enough time with her. Perhaps he didn't really know her.

Florence woke the next morning wondering whether she had really had the conversation with Ted. Still in a daze at breakfast Florence stopped midway through buttering her toast, put down her knife and looked at her husband.

'Did you really suggest I work with the designers?' 'Yes, the more I think about it the better the idea seems.'

Florence and Amelia pored over the latest gardening articles. The connection between the two women had developed and now Florence found it easier to spend time with Amelia than with her own mother.

Florence's mother rarely visited, making it plain that she saw Garraiblagh as being too close to the ends of the Earth. Florence was instead expected to drive into Belfast with young Daisy however. Florence found it increasingly easy to explain to her mother that she was too busy with social and business functions. She knew also that her mother would not approve of her work in designing for the linen pieces.

The new century and the death of the old Queen were bringing changes everywhere and the garden reflected this. The garden was being re-structured in some areas. Japanese anemones, Welsh poppies, Michaelmas daisies lifted their heads above the waving grasses of the new area and through them ran young Daisy often followed by young Frank Black, Rory's son. The relationship between Daisy and Frank had grown. Daisy, fearless and following in her grandmother's footsteps roamed the estate.

The formal aspects of the garden were being softened, just as Florence and Ted's relationship was softening, becoming less rigid in its boundaries. Plants mixed and merged in a different colour palette. Longer stemmed astilbe and candelabra primrose mixed with longer grasses, drawing the eye into the dappled woodland area.

Chapter Twenty

1903

As Ned the gardener weeded, the robin watched from the post, offering encouragement in the warm late winter sunlight.

'There's a worm for ye, ye'd better tak it quickly.'

The robin lent his head to one side, considering. A sudden fluttering movement and Ned looked up to see the robin in a sparrow hawk's talons. Life and death so speedily exchanged. Ned considered the poor robin and went back to his weeding. Nature could be ruthless. When he next looked up another robin had taken the place of the first and was once again suggesting that the hunt for worms and insects be continued apace. Life goes on, muttered Ned.

Frank knelt down in the deep snow. The scarf was tied around his neck but it still got in the way as he used his gloved hands to gather the snow together. He was free for a while. His mother had shooed him out of the house and his father was busy talking to the gardeners in the glasshouse. He knew his grandfather was around and was fairly sure he would be carrying out his usual checks on the most delicate of the plants and those weren't down here near the Japanese garden. He threw one snowball from the bridge, hitting the Japanese lantern with a solid thud. Ebony, the black spaniel, snuffled up to him and wagged her tail.

'Hello girl, your ears are covered in ice balls. Here let me.'

Frank was busily removing some of the frozen ice from Ebony's ears and paws when a snowball hit him on the back. 'Daisy! I might have known it was ye! You're not a bad shot for a girl.'

Daisy appeared from behind the tree, smiling.

'Is your father around? What about your grandfather?'

'Naw, neither of them is around here.'

'Good,' said Daisy.

Frank looked at her suspiciously, 'Why?'

'I think I've just broken a branch on mother's favourite philadelphus with a snowball but I'm more concerned that your father or grandfather will hear about it. Perhaps they'll just think it was the heavy snow.'

'I wouldn't be too sure about that,' commented Frank, knowing from his own experience that both men seemed to have eyes that could see everything.

Chapter Twenty-one

Garraiblagh September 1910

PADDY MURRAY AND IAN JAMESON did most things together. They had been born within a couple of days of each other and now at nine, they were as close as any brothers. Their fathers worked at the scutching mill to the north of Garraiblagh.

Exploring the known world, as they saw it, took them into the gardens at Garraiblagh.

Paddy had been up to the estate a number of times with his uncle who brought the bread from the local bakery. His eagle eyes had noticed the enticing fruit hanging from the apple trees.

'They've got plenty a' apples up yonder. Them'uns don't need aw them apples. I reckon we could fin' a way in.'

Ian was not so sure but he went along with Paddy's idea, as he usually did.

'Sure, it'll be airy an' who's goin' to notice a few wee apples?'

'If we get caught we'll be in for big trouble from the big man Black, an' our fathers.'

Paddy saw this raid on the apple trees as an adventure. They would be outwitting the enemy.

A large rhododendron had thoughtfully been grown close to the wall of the kitchen garden. Its low branches offered the ideal route up the wall. Initially the boys found it difficult to get any purchase on the flaking bark, but they persisted and reached the top. Once there it looked a much longer way down than they had thought. They surveyed the walled garden from their viewpoint on the top of the wall. Cleverly they had picked the time of day when there would not be any gardeners. They knew it wouldn't take much to arouse the suspicions of one of them, possibly even one of the Hendersons themselves. A pile of grass and weeds had been pushed up against the wall nearby along with some manure and soil, a compost heap in the making.

Ian and Paddy looked at each other. 'It's our ony chance.'

The apples were too inviting. Taking the apples and placing them in their turned up jumpers they stopped.

'How're we goin' to get out carryin' aw of these? We can't climb the wall agin. We'll have to find a gate.'

Over in the corner was the small wooden door that led onto the back lane. By chance it had been left ajar. The two boys squeezed through and crouched down under the windows of the sheds before running carefully down the track for a few yards. Once they'd passed the home farm they stopped. Ian picked the largest apple and bit into it. Instantly spitting it out. Paddy laughed 'Damn the bit. It's a cooker!'

'I hope they're not aw like thon!'

'Ian! Wheest!'

'Wha' is it!'

'Look at yer trews, ye eejit. You're clabbered,' whispered Paddy.

Ian turned to look and as he did so apples began to fall out of his jumper.

'Yer trews are covered in red shitty stuff.' Ian put a hand down to touch. His hand felt sticky and greasy and when he saw it, it was covered in red too.

'Aw na! They'll kill us.'

'That's if aul Black doesn't see ye first,' said Paddy comfortingly.

'There must've been some shite o' top o' the wa'.'

'Turn roun' yersel, Paddy.' Ian laughed. 'Aye, yer red too!'

'Wha's worse — being caught by aul' Black or our Ma an' Da?'

'I don't have ony other trews.'

'Right,' said Paddy. 'Put them apples doon.'

Paddy began to undo his trousers.

'What ye doin, ye slabber?'

'I'm turnin' em inside out. At least it won't be so obvious.'

'Ye look like Harry the tramp, ye messer!'

Both boys turned their trousers inside out and then, picking up their haul, walked carefully, but rather gingerly home.

'I see that young Murray and Jameson have been up at the scrumpin.' said Rory.

'Aye, I ken,' James Black acknowledged as he took another draw of his pipe.

'I don't think we'll be seeing them again in a hurry. I have a feeling their parents will be dealing wi' that.'

'How so?'

'I smeared red oxide on the top of the wall and their trews will be covered with it. It doesn't come off.'

Chapter Twenty-two

1911

DAISY OPENED WIDE the door to the dining room.

'I thought I'd find you both here still.'

Florence raised an eyebrow. 'How very fortuitous for you, dear.'

'Mother, father! It is such beautiful weather this summer I was just wondering...'

'Wondering what, dear?' Florence queried spreading butter on her toast, as though continuing to do so would lessen any request Daisy might have. Florence was also aware that Ted had raised his newspaper without comment.

'There is so little to do! I was wondering whether we could build a tennis court. It would be so useful and we could have such fun.' Then as though as an innocent after thought, 'The Scotts have built one.'

Ted listening from behind his paper queried why this would be important.

'Tennis is so fashionable and I've been reading Mrs Lambert

Chamber's book on Tennis for Ladies.'

'I really do not think that that sort of exercise is appropriate! What about croquet?' said Florence.

'But mother, the King and Queen watch the women's tennis at Wimbledon and there is nothing inappropriate! I refuse to just sit and read or play the piano or play boring croquet!'

'Your mother and I will discuss it, now leave us in peace, Daisy.'

Daisy made her withdrawal as skilfully as any army general, making his initial foray to test defences.

After some further skirmishes, Rory Black was consulted and soon the preparation for a tennis court was underway on the grass area behind the house and just off the path to the walled garden.

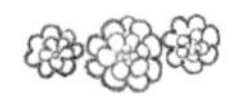

Autumn was early. The leaves changing colour and sycamore keys were spiralling to the ground. The last two days the wind had blown many of the drier leaves off the branches. The scent of wood smoke drifted across the lawn from the kitchen garden where cuttings and leaves were already being burnt on a bonfire: the low sun almost blinding Jack Butler who had carefully wound his scarf around his neck and placed the ends over his chest before buttoning up his jacket. He was a careful, methodical man, certainly not one to be given a task that required speed, but he could be relied upon to ensure the basic tidying of the garden was done. He raked the leaves in a slow and careful way, whistling to himself. He liked this time of year. He had always seen this part of the year as exciting, as though something different was about to happen. Perhaps that was due to his grandmother who had always told stories late on in the cottage in front of the fire, stories of ancient people. A rustling in a pile of leaves close by alerted him to the presence of a robin and a blackbird, searching the leaves for food.

The blackberries had produced fruit slightly early, the hot weather pushing them forward. Cook had sent Bridget, the scullery maid out to collect berries for jam making. Some would be for the master's afternoon teas, but most of it would be for the kitchen staff and gardeners. It wasn't often that Bridget was able to escape from the kitchen. She felt a sense of importance.

'What're ye doin' the day, young Bridget? Shouldn't ye be in the kitchen wi' Mrs Johnson?' shouted Ollie Butler as he wheeled a barrow full of manure along the path opposite her.

'None o' yer business, Ollie Butler. I'm on 'portant work for Mrs Johnson,' responded Bridget throwing her head up and looking away.

It was clear when Bridget returned that she had sampled a number of blackberries as well as filling the deep baskets she had. The smell of blackberries cooking in the preserving wafted through the door and out into the yard.

'Now young Bridget do ye think ye can tak' these jars down to the garden bothy with those fresh scones, wi'out eatin' ony?'

At dusk as the moon came into view and a stillness fell, a different set of blackberry pickers worked their way along the edge of the back field to the bushes. Several foxes were pulling the blackberries off the stems, licking their chops as they bent again and again until their white fronts became stained with the purple juice, the young cubs running in and out of the gaps. Food came where they could find it, as autumn made itself known, with stormy weather lashing the shrubs and the trees creaked and groaned.

The dog fox lifted his head and sniffed. He felt his fur beginning to change, to thicken to his winter coat. Would it be a hard winter? He and his vixen would need to make the sett secure.

Chapter Twenty-three

Belfast 1912

TED WAS PROUD that linen from the family mills had been included in the Titanic's furnishings. He and Florence had met with other manufacturers and producers in Belfast to celebrate the fact that many of Belfast's finest materials would be evident on the majestic liner. It felt as though a little of Garraiblagh was on board. There was a buzz in the city. The huge hulk of the new liner could be seen easily now with its four huge funnels and there was a pride that a ship was being built that would show the world what the craftsmen of Belfast could do.

The second of April brought the sea trials for the huge ship.

'I've brought back my telescope from the office, Florence. I thought we could watch the Titanic going through its paces out in the lough. The sea trials have to be completed before it is able to sail out to Southampton after the send-off later tonight.'

Ted and Florence arranged that all the family members and staff within the house and garden should meet on the lawn late afternoon and raise a toast in champagne to the great ship as it returned from its sea trials. Rory Black put his eye to the telescope and examined the ship in the harbour. He had never been one for sea trips and he hadn't relished the short voyages to and from Ireland and England. He knew he preferred dry land. He then helped his father to the telescope and gave him his arm to the nearest bench afterwards to sit down.'

'One of Alice's cousins, David, lives down outside Southampton. He works at a nursery there and he wrote telling us about the preparations for the Titanic's maiden voyage to America,' explained Rory.

'What's he got to do wi' the Titanic?' queried James.

'The nursery is to supply flowers an' plants for the ship. Hundreds, thousands o' them.'

'Why do they need so many?'

'David has said they want plants in pots for the general areas an' fresh flowers for the first class cabins every day! They also need flowers for table top decorations for the dinners an' even for tables at breakfast.'

'How on earth are they going to manage that number of flowers, and more to the point, how are they going tae keep them in top condition?' asked James.

'They are goin' tae use white roses an' carnations, also freesias an' they want daffodils tae an' they'll keep them in cool rooms. I'm glad we're not havin' to cater for such numbers here at Garraiblagh!'

'I'm sure it's a grand contract for the nursery though. They'll be supplyin' flowers for all the voyages if they do well this time.' said James.

'Probably,' said Rory, 'though Alice's cousin isn't happy down in Southampton. He reckons he could do better in America and he's got himself a third class berth on the Titanic's maiden voyage. Boy! Is he excited!?'

The news on the 15th April sent Florence and Ted reeling.

'The Titanic has sunk! I-I can't believe it! There were almost two and a half thousand people on that boat, passengers and crew, Florence,' said Ted.

'Do we know how many have survived?' asked Florence.

'It does not look good, my love. Tommie Andrews was drowned! Such a good man and Captain Smith, they don't know yet how many people have managed to survive.'

'Oh, Ted, Tommie Andrews! His poor family and all those other people! It seems so short a time since we were all there at the docks, waving them off. Everyone was so happy, so proud.'

In the garden, news of the sinking of the Titanic had reached the gardener's house. Rory was holding a distraught Alice in his arms.

'Davy only wanted to find a better life for himself, Rory. To see America. And now? Auntie Ann and Uncle Billy will be beside themselves over in Southampton.'

'Alice love,' said Rory as he caressed his wife. 'We'll have to wait for more news but it's not good. It looks as though there were few survivors.'

Alice sank to the floor, crying.

If this could happen what else could?

Daisy could not believe that there could be any more rain to fall. For days now she had been watching the heavy rain laden clouds and then seeing the destruction of the flowers and delicate stemmed plants in the garden.

She was however determined that the weather would not put her off her trip into Belfast. She had told her mother that she was going to buy some lace and silks from Anderson McAuley and hoped that her mother would not then either suggest that she accompany her or give her a list embroidery threads and needles that she wanted for she had other plans

In Belfast Daisy found the hall with a little difficulty down a narrow street a short distance from the Royal Avenue. There was nothing to suggest that it was the right place, but then, she considered, it probably was not a good idea to advertise too widely. She shook out her umbrella, took hold of the large metal doorknob in her gloved hand and walked in nervously.

The sound of raised and excited voices echoed in the dusty hall. Dust motes like a strange form of confetti were held in the early afternoon sunlight coming through the high windows. Women's hats bobbed up and down as murmurs of agreement filled the air.

'Ladies, we must fight on. They will be made to take us seriously,' said a loud voice.

A number of speakers followed and Daisy had the opportunity to look at the women, old and young who filled the room. As the women began to sing their anthem, "Shout, shout up with your song," there was laughter and excitement. Some women linked arms and began to sway to and fro. Daisy squeezed in at the back of the hall, sang in agreement, 'March, march.'

In her head the sound of the anthem echoed. She felt buoyed up by being in the presence of such powerful women as she joined the queue of the 'sisters' who began to filter out of the cramped hall. Once out she took a deep breath and then, noticing that it was beginning to rain, unfurled her umbrella and began hurrying towards the tram stop. Hurrying with her umbrella down to avoid the rain she suddenly heard a cry.

'Ow! Be careful!'

Daisy stopped short and raised the offending umbrella. Tall young women, a little older than her, stared at her as she rearranged her hat.

'I'm so sorry! It was entirely my fault, I wasn't looking!' said Daisy.

'Did I see you in the meeting?' asked the young woman.

'Yes, it was wonderful, wasn't it?'

'I'm Molly Baker,' said the woman, extending her hand.

Daisy responded 'I am Daisy Henderson. It's good to meet you, Molly. Have you been to many of the meetings?' They shook hands.

'Two, but I hope to attend others. If you are going to go as well perhaps we could meet for a cup of tea and go together?'

'I'd like that,' said Daisy. 'I don't know anyone else who is involved.'

'They certainly are exciting times, but I feel it's going to take a lot to convince men that there is a need for change,' said Molly.

'Not just men either,' commented Daisy. 'My mother and her friends are horrified at the idea.'

'Well, they're going to have a shock,' giggled Molly.

While she waited for the tram, watching the rain drops fall from the umbrella, Daisy announced to herself. 'Well, Daisy, this is what you wanted. Times are changing.'

The rain now falling heavily began to lower Daisy's spirits and the enthusiasm she had built up being with the group of women. It was easy to feel confident when surrounded by other like-minded females. She had told her mother that she would be back for tea. Her mother did not approve of the 'awful' suffragettes. But then her mother did not approve of any change to women's lives and why should she? She lived comfortably in a large house with servants. She did not have to deal with what Daisy saw as the 'real world'.

'Well,' thought Daisy to herself, 'that is going to have to change. Mrs Pankhurst is right.'

The tram arrived and once seated, looking out of the window at the city, women from the mills were hurrying along the pavement, heads bent against the rain and tired from long hours at work. She wondered were some of them her father's employees and shifted uncomfortably in her seat. It convinced her of the rightness of the suffragette movement. It was about much more than making the lives of privileged women less boring. More importantly it was about stopping the dreadful exploitation of poor women.

Daisy contemplated her reflection in the dressing table mirror and slouched back, as far as her stays would allow. She was dressed for afternoon tea, wearing her powder blue dress and favourite cameo at her neck.

The face staring back at Daisy described a young girl with brown hair, pinned up in the latest style, large brown eyes which looked slightly exasperated and a mouth, Daisy realised dispassionately, that had a rather too forceful set to it, most often seen when attending one of her mother's soirées. It was not the vision of the pale and compliant beauty that attracted husbands.

'And I don't care!' she said aloud to herself as she stood up and pulled at the material of the dress' skirt.

'I want to do something with my life. I will not sit quietly taking tea and waiting for a husband to be found for me who doesn't care what I think.'

Daisy's parents had both agreed that their daughter should attend the Ladies College. Their expectation was that she would be able to converse intelligently and knowledgeably, up to a point, and therefore attract a better match. Daisy, however, had different ideas. One of the young teachers who had recently started teaching the year before Daisy left, had continued her education at Trinity College in Dublin before teaching. One of the first female graduates. Daisy was impressed and inspired.

She looked out of the window and across the rose garden and lawn. Young Ollie Butler was clipping the ornamental rose bushes. They were beautiful. Shades of pink, yellow, crimson and white. There was no doubt about their beauty, but did they have any choice in how they would grow? They were for show too. Was everything just for show? she wondered.

She thought of yesterday's meeting and the powerful words uttered by the suffragette leader. There was nothing showy about that. The women had purpose. They wanted their lives to have meaning. Then the bedroom door opened and her mother appeared.

'Ah, my dear, you're ready. Our dinner guests will be here in a moment. Do try to remember not to drift off into one of your dreams!' She looked at Daisy's dress. 'We really will have to get you some new outfits. That one looks so, so..' as she sought the word, 'ordinary and it looks far too relaxed and comfortable.'

Daisy sighed as her mother left the room in a swish of expensive perfume. She knew well that anything her mother was thinking of would be full of stays and would limit her movement.

'I feel like that rose being clipped and trained!' she whispered to herself angrily and threw her hairbrush across the room.

Large vases of flowers lit the entrance hall and drawing room of Garraiblagh. Florence had asked Daisy to take charge of the floral decorations and had been somewhat surprised when her daughter had agreed.

'I'm so glad you're taking an interest in the evening, darling. The flowers are beautiful'.

It was not until the dinner itself that the awful truth became clear. Amelia, on her son's arm stopped briefly at the entrance to the room and gave a quick gasp.

'Are you quite well, Mama?'

'Nothing to concern you, Ted.' A brief smile lit up her face.

The table was lit with candles which glowed in the reflections from the ornate Victorian silverware which contrasted with the newly decorated room itself, in pale green and rose pink. Along the centre of the deeply polished table were floral decorations, quite different from the pale pink, rose and salmon colours of the flowers in the hall. The flowers in the dining room were a combination of greens, purples and whites. The scent from the white gardenias was spellbinding.

Florence had been pleased when Mrs Gillespie had remarked on the unusual beauty of the floral colour combination. However it was Mrs Crawford's remarks that had set light to the evening in as cold and as calculating a way as the suffragettes fire-bombing of a government building the night before. Mrs Crawford's eyes widened and then narrowed as she entered the dining room and took her seat at the table. While the other guests moved to their places, her deep, piercing blue eyes looked around the room and focused on the floral decorations. With a slight inclination of her head and a stretching of her mouth into the closest that could be described as a smile, she sat and waited her moment.

The conversation ranged from the weather to the recent catastrophe of the Titanic and to the Home Rule crisis. Mrs Crawford regaled the party with her experience of signing the Ulster Covenant and meeting Mr Carson. Then she saw her opportunity. The cool smile was manufactured and her eyes hooded in pleasure.

'I see that those awful Suffragettes have been causing trouble again. They really do give such a poor impression of womanhood.'

She knew that this was guaranteed to invite Daisy's mother's views.

'I do so agree. Such an unladylike obsession with rights'.

Mrs Gillespie nodded her small cherry–faced head in agreement and a small potato rolled off the plate in agreement.

'I see that they have started wearing sashes when they march and hold their meetings,' said Mrs Crawford. 'An unusual colour combination.'

'Really?' responded Florence, being drawn closer into the trap. 'What are they?'

Mrs Crawford lifted her eyes for the first time and at the same time, raised her elegantly gloved hand in a slight gesture.

'Actually the colours of your floral decorations almost exactly match! How strange.'

Daisy felt her parents' eyes focused on her. She was in a quandary. Her courage wavering– to speak out or remain silent.

'Daisy?' queried Florence.

'I think they...' Daisy began.

'Daisy has been very involved in her French lessons recently, haven't you, my dear?' said Florence.

The tone of her mother's voice was one of controlled anger, but also an appeal to her better nature. Daisy did not have the heart to break free at this point. Mrs Crawford's happiness in finding this vulnerability in the Henderson household was cut short as Daisy, in her most boring voice, regaled the table at length with her knowledge of French verbs.

One of the young men, Tom Guthrie, a new recruit to her father's firm as an engineer, watched Daisy, a smile hovering around his mouth. This made Daisy more embarrassed than the comments made by Mrs Crawford. She looked at him and saw, not a look of derision, but possibly one of shared ideas, a knowing look.

'They are wonderful colours,' said Tom to Daisy.

'Humph,' said her father.

'They are indeed, Mr Guthrie,' said Daisy's grandmother, looking approvingly at the young man. 'Well done, Daisy. Heaven knows we need colour in this troubled world to lift our spirits.'

Daisy doubted that her grandmother grasped the significance and was just being kind.

'Don't you agree, Ted,' said Amelia.

'Humph,' repeated Daisy's father.

Daisy sat in the kitchen garden, away from the anger and disturbance she had caused at the previous evening's dinner. She bent to pick up a parsley stalk and considered the horror with which her mother would have responded to such an action, her daughter sitting in the garden picking herbs like a common flower girl. To Daisy's mother the gardeners picked the produce and brought it to the kitchen. Daisy did not know her place. She looked around her, taking in the orderly rows. She hoped that she might see Frank Black. Frank was her ally from childhood. While they came from different social backgrounds, both Daisy and Frank had to manage the expectations of forceful parents and grandparents.

She admitted to herself that she did feel a little guilty about her mother who had, with white knuckled determination, managed to continue with the evening. She had even managed to field the unpleasant comments from Mrs Crawford. But as soon as the guests had left, Daisy's mother had given her a look that she knew well from experience did not bode well. She had then informed Daisy and Ted that she was retiring to bed with a headache brought on by the stress of the evening. Ted announced that he would have a further cigar and called the butler to bring him a bottle of whiskey. The door of the study was closed firmly.

Daisy's head had been full of the meeting she had attended and what she could do to highlight the suffragettes concerns, her concerns. She knew it had been a risk but, she considered, a worthwhile one. The idea had come to her during a walk through the garden. She loved the garden and was used to its formal nature, but she had begun to notice small changes and additions that had occurred, beyond the carefully planned and organised. Daisy realised that she enjoyed that aspect of anarchy and wanted to recreate it for herself.

She had been relaxing with Emmeline Pankhurst's new book,

hidden from view inside a copy of a more appropriate book, in case her mother walked past when the thought of the colours that the suffragettes used in their banners — violet/purple, for dignity, white for purity, green for hope had come to her. Flowers of these colours must surely be here in the garden? She had never considered it before.

Daisy began to look around her with different eyes. It wasn't long before she was able to pick out white peonies and roses, purple delphiniums and lobelia, green pittosporum and fern leaves that would be perfect for what she had in mind.

Her mother had been impressed, believing that she had, for once, convinced her daughter of the importance of her role and status as the eligible daughter of a rich mill and shipping line owner.

Daisy walked from the kitchen garden, past the rose garden and the herbaceous border where the flowers she'd used in the decorations were relaxing in the sun, oblivious of the impact they had had. Daisy stopped. Her parents had told her they would meet with her at eleven. She felt the timing was probably to give her parents the opportunity to consider the situation and what they could do with this headstrong seventeen year old daughter. Looking at the plants Daisy commented to herself, 'I will just have to put up with whatever they say. What else can they do?'

On the spur of the moment she picked a bright crimson rose and walked to the morning room to face the music.

Daisy opened the door and moving over to her mother who was sitting in the sunlight from the window presented her with the rose. 'I'm sorry for the discomfort the colours caused you and father, but I can't be sorry that I believe in a life for women, one that gives them equal rights to men. Women should be able to make a life for themselves, pursue a career, a life beyond marriage.'

'Beyond marriage?' exclaimed Florence.

Daisy's father looked at her.

'We've been considering the situation, Margaret,' interrupted her father.

Daisy knew the conversation was serious when her proper name was used, but she could think of nothing to say in response.

'We have spoken to Mrs Tweed at the Ladies College and she has told us that Trinity College in Dublin now has appropriately chaperoned lodgings where young ladies can stay in Dublin and attend lectures at the university. Perhaps if you are busy in your academic studies in Dublin you will be less open to those suffragettes and their exploits here in Belfast. Mrs Tweed has reminded us that the daughters of some of the best families are now attending university.'

'Oh! Yes! Yes, father! Thank you!'

'There's nothing to be thankful for. It's for your own good. We don't wish to be embarrassed further.'

Her father's piercing blue eyes boring into her. Daisy was still amazed at her parents' proposal and while glad of it did not believe that that would be the last argument she would have with them.

September 1912

James and Rory were aware that there had been whispered conversations among the gardeners on the burning issue of Home Rule and the signing of the Ulster Covenant[26].

'We're going to have to say something, Father. I've held off so far, but it's becoming more difficult,' said Rory.

'Aye, they need a reminder, son. There will be nae damned politics in my garden.'

26 A petition signed in 1912 expressing opposition to Home Rule for Ireland.

The bothy was full. Some of the men standing, some leaning against the wall, all wondering what they had all been called in for. There was a low hum of conversation.

As Rory and James walked in and there was silence. Usually there would be light-hearted banter and a feeling of comradeship, but the looks on the faces of the head gardeners stopped all thought of that.

James began 'Ye men all know that we have a strict rule in this garden — nae politics, nae religion. This garden is a place where the only thing I care about from my men is that they are good gardeners and hard workers, nothing else. Ye are aware that the workers in the shipyards and other places are being given time to attend meetings and there is to be a day when those who want to can attend meetings. As gardeners in this garden you are free to attend, but I do not want it brought into the garden in any way. Any man breaking the rule will pack his bags the same day without a good reference. Is that clear tae ye all?'

There was a nodding of heads. No one would openly confront James Black or his son and James and Rory knew that. They also knew that this speech, the reminder, would not solve the problem. If anger and bigotry made their way into the garden it would destroy it and for both James and Rory, the only solid reality was the garden.

Chapter Twenty-four

August 1913

DAISY'S MOUTH BECAME a straight line. She would not give up. It might only be a small element of support but who knew what could happen. Taking sprigs of white heather, purple Michaelmas daisies and rosemary sprigs she wove together small corsages of the Suffragette colours. It felt as though the garden was complicit in her actions and she felt supported. She would hand these out at the next protest.

Daisy's grandmother had raised an eyebrow when she'd heard her grand-daughter explaining to her mother where she was going.

'I'll be going out later myself, Florence. I can collect Daisy from town on my way back.'

Daisy's face flushed.

'Thank you, Grandmama. That's very kind of you.'

Amelia could see that the smile that accompanied Daisy's gratitude was somewhat less than fulsome and smiled to herself.

Daisy hurried as best she could along the cobbled footpath. She had managed to convince her mother that she would be meeting a friend for lunch in town and would be visiting the bookshop. But now she was already late as the carriage dropped her off outside Anderson McAuleys. She then had to wait for the carriage and a new automobile to drive off into the distance before she crossed the street past the front gates of the new City Hall to the north corner of Donegal Place.

Molly stood at the corner. Her curly red hair creating a frame for her dark purple, flower decorated hat. She was tapping her foot.

'Where have you been, Daisy?'

'I know, I'm so sorry! Nothing is ever simple! My grandmother has now insisted that she will meet me in town later and bring me home!'

'Anyway, I have remembered the corsages? Shall we take the tram to Ormeau?'

Walking along the avenue from the red sandstone gates of Ormeau Park and the tram stop, Molly and Daisy saw several of their friends from the last meeting.

While waiting for Mrs Sheehy Skeffington to speak to the assembled crowd from a dais, surrounded by women of all ages Daisy handed out her corsages, happy to see women pinning them onto their coats and jackets with pride.

It was towards the end of the speeches that Daisy saw with astonishment that her grandmother was seated on a bench with two other women.

'I thought I might see you here, Daisy. Introduce me to your young friend.' said Amelia smiling.

'You may both come with me in the car and we'll have afternoon tea together before returning home.'

Daisy noticed her grandmother was now looking at the few remaining posies that Daisy had in her hands.

'I collected the plants from the garden, Grandmama and then bound them with some ribbon that I purchased in Robinson and

Cleavers when I was last in town. They've been very popular!' added Daisy defiantly, waiting for some admonition.

'I'm sure they have. I'm glad to see that Garraiblagh has been assisting.'

Taken aback, Daisy noticed that her grandmother was finding it hard to keep laughter at bay.

'You are not the first one in the family, my dear, to push against the boundaries and I doubt that you will be the last. Well done.'

Amelia regarded her grandmother with pride.

An early frost came out of nowhere, surprising the gardeners with their normally watchful gaze. The pear trees at the delicate stage of producing blossom were hit hard. All the new buds were killed off, leaving a barren pear-less year.

Colin, Ned and Andy pushed their wheelbarrows along the path back towards the bothy, the sounds louder in the cold air.

'It's a full moon the night, a strange wan though,' said Colin looking at the sky.

'Aye, a blood moon. They gi' me the shivers. Nothin' good comes o' a blood moon. The animals don't like it. No sign o' the foxes the night,' said Ned, spitting on the ground to reinforce the point.

'It' s freezing!' shivered Andy.

'Haud yer wheest! If ye don't lak it, turn yer han' tae somethin' else,' said Colin.

'I've a mind to an' aw! I heard there's good money to be made in the city,' said Andy.

'Damn the bit, let me tell ye ... I'd rather be here shovelling shite on the roses, gettin' wet and caul, pullin' thorns out o' me fingers than spendin' a minute down the docks o' the shipyards!' announced Colin.

Andy looked at him.

'That's the nub o' it, boy. Ye won't be plaised till ye've gone an' tried it for yoursel,' said Colin to Andy.

'Ye'll wear yersel out tryin to tell thon wan onythin,' said Ned. 'Sure he thinks Belfast streets are paved wi' gold!'

'There's a deal of opportunities in the city, boys. I'm tellin'ye!' asserted Andy.

Colin stopped the wheelbarrow. 'Me father an' brother are still in the yards. I haven't visited them in a brave while, but they don't look too well on it an' both o' them have had injuries — things fallin' on them an' gettin' ill an' they daren't take time off. Now... I'm happy enough here an' I'm larnin'. I've spoken to Mr Black about doin' a spell in the Botanic Gardens, larn more an' then increase me job prospects. I don't want to live in that bothy much longer wi ye boys an' I want to ask Bridget to marry me. There's ony so long a man can wait!'

The older gardener laughed. 'These plants are getting in yer head, lad.'

Chapter Twenty-five

1914

IT HAD BEEN A GLORIOUSLY WARM SPRING and the flower scent and colour was overwhelming. Working in the garden had been all Frank Black had ever wanted, preferring the sound of the rake and the hoe to the noise and chatter of people trying to make conversation.

His eyes followed the horizon around. It was too beautiful for there to be a war, surely? He watched as another frigate joined the grey steel filling Belfast Lough. Warships of every size crowded the water. The angular steel shapes of the ships and the gun emplacements he could see across on the southern shore were so different from the gardens, the plants that he tended, the natural rhythm and cycle of life, sustaining and comforting and reassuring. Out of the corner of his eye he noticed a movement. A small black and white cat was making its way carefully through the herbaceous border to an ash tree where several finches and wagtails were enjoying themselves. Frank's deep voice became lighter as he called the cat over.

'Cass, away from there!'

The cat lowered her body and looked at him before deciding to continue. Frank strode over and caught her.

'No, ye don't.'

The cat squirmed and wriggled to be let down, but then realised the uselessness of that and lay back, enjoying being placated.

As he continued to stroke the thick fur of the cat, Frank's mind drifted to the thought of joining up. He felt sure it would come to that in the end. It wasn't just the pressure he sensed when he wandered down into the city and saw the recruitment hoardings; he knew also that the Hendersons were encouraging their younger staff to 'do the right thing.' Their view was replicated in the papers and in dinner party conversations. The war would not last long they all said. The older staff would be able to manage for that short time.

Frank didn't want to go. His world was the garden at Garraiblagh. It wasn't Ireland and it wasn't Britain. He knew what it was like when he had to uproot a plant and place it somewhere else against its will. The plant never thrived. Frank felt his roots were so deeply embedded he could not imagine anything different.

He was shaken from his thoughts by a high pitched squeal of agony. Frank placed the cat on the ground and walked towards the kitchen garden. A small rabbit was caught in one of the traps laid out to prevent the plants being eaten. Frank felt sick. He disapproved of the traps and believed there were other ways of protecting the plants. As he came closer he could see the terror and agony in the animal's face. Its body was in spasm, its heart beginning to give out as it knew its fate. Frank knelt down beside it and held its body. He could not undo the trap. It was too tightly wound around the struggling rabbit. He could not let the suffering continue. Reaching for a nearby stone he caressed the rabbit gently.

'Is this what war will be like?' Frank asked the rabbit.

'God help us all if it is!' With a blow, he crushed its skull.

Winter Garraiblagh 1914

Florence's skirts swished against the newspaper she was carrying in front of her as she entered the drawing room where Amelia was sitting, reading the latest edition of the Gardening Journal.

'You seem in a hurry, Florence, what have you found?'

'There is an article about the ways in which we can support our soldiers from home. They're setting up collection points for sphagnum moss and they need people to go out and collect it in their areas. Do you know what it looks like, Mrs Henderson?'

'I don't, Florence. So I think we should speak to James Black or Rory. What is the moss needed for, Florence?'

'They're making packs for dressings using the moss. It's very absorbent and has antiseptic qualities. Now that Daisy has joined the Red Cross and is working through her first aid training, I think I should be doing something. I'm hopeless at knitting. It can't be too difficult to pick some moss.'

Amelia kept her thoughts to herself and suggested that they drive over to the scutching mill the next day.

Amelia made her way to the peach house. It had become second nature for Amelia to guess where James was. They had been careful since their return from the visit to the Botanic Gardens in Dublin, but the time they were able to spend together was precious. As Amelia opened the door of the greenhouse James saw her and shook his head, an almost imperceptible movement, but a signal noticed by Amelia. One of the young gardeners was working at the far end.

'Mr Black we need to understand where spaghnum moss can be collected. Mrs Florence and I would like to see if it is possible to collect some,' Amelia showed James the article.

'Well, there is spaghnum moss over by the scutching mill. We collect it for the pots in the conservatory, but it can be wet work!'

'Nevertheless could you accompany us and show us?'

'Aye, certainly, Mrs Henderson.' He smiled and handed the paper back to Amelia, touching her hand as he did so.

The small group, James, Amelia and Florence, took the cart along the back lane, past the farm and over the road to the mill buildings. Amelia had always had a soft spot for the old place since it had enabled them to purchase Garraiblagh.

James showed the two women to where the moss was growing in the boggiest ground. Florence had worn galoshes, as had Amelia, but the look of horror on her face was comical to Amelia.

Florence bent down and pulled at a lump of moss and then another. The intense cold and wet soon became too much for her.

'I thought it would be like cutting flowers or gathering herbs!' Florence said in anguish as she removed her gloves and rubbed her hands together. " I did not realise it would be like this.'

Amelia looked at her daughter-in-law. 'My dear, we are not all meant to be the same. Daisy is young and practical. It is an adventure for her, especially when she goes to France.'

'France! She hasn't said anything about that,' said Florence forgetting her frozen fingers.

Amelia wished she'd bitten her tongue. She had assumed Daisy had mentioned the fact to her mother, but she obviously hadn't. This morning was not turning out well.

'The Red Cross are training women to go to France to help with the casualties,' explained Amelia as calmly as she could.

Florence sat down heavily on the low wall.

'But she's a lady, not a servant.'

'She is a young woman of the twentieth century. Things are changing Florence.'

James, listening to the discussion in the background felt he should intervene. 'I thought it might be a good idea to bring a picnic and now might be an appropriate time to have it don't you think, ladies?' He placed the picnic basket in front of Amelia who began to hand out its contents. As they ate the sandwiches, James was the first to break the silence.

'I have been thinking about the gathering of the sphagnum moss,' said James. 'We usually get two of the younger apprentice gardeners to collect small amounts for us for use in some plant decorations. I think it would be appropriate if I had three of the men come up to gather moss on a weekly basis. They can then bring it down to the gardens and we can set up a washing and packing station. Might I suggest, Mrs Henderson,' James said, looking at Florence, 'that you could oversee this and ensure the moss is sent on to Belfast?'

Amelia mouthed the words 'Thank you' to James.

'Oh, that is a very sensible idea, Mr Black. I will contact Belfast and explain what we will do,' said Florence. Shall we leave now, Mrs Henderson, as that has been decided?'

'Why don't you take the horse and cart Florence and I'll stay behind. I need to collect some herbs and I'm sure Mr Black will accompany me home.'

'Are you sure, it's a long way?' queried Florence.

'Perfectly sure, my dear and now that you know what you will be doing, it is probably best to write to the Red Cross and get it started.'

'Yes, you're right. You are sure?'

'Absolutely sure.'

Amelia turned to James.

'I would like to see if there is any pennyroyal. Would you help me please?'

As the horse and cart made its way down the track to the road and towards the perimeter wall of Garraiblagh estate, Amelia sighed.

'Thank you James. I wasn't sure what I was going to do to stop Florence losing face and I didn't want to suggest it was too much for her.' Amelia took James' hand. 'What would I do without you!'

'Ye don't have to, my love,' and taking her to the other side of the old garden wall he drew her to him and kissed her. Amelia leant her head on James' chest.

'I wonder at myself sometimes,' she said. 'I have a granddaughter who is about to take herself into the dangers of war, you have a grandson who will be leaving soon for the Front. No one knows what will happen and here I am with you, snatching time, feeling wonderful when I should be the elderly grandmother; sitting, knitting and reflecting on times gone by.'

'Nae, ye'll never be elderly, Amelia,' said James as he moved a strand of hair from her face and laughed, 'I'm afraid I have interfered wi' your hat and your hair. Amelia, ye an' I both believe in the power of nature an' the beauty of this world. Ye know I used to believe that it was the God of the Bible that we should worship, but I dinnae now. I believe in the earth, the trees and the plants an' we are of them and fae them. Our love is part of that cycle.'

James bent down, picked up a daisy and placed it in Amelia's hair and kissed her.

Chapter Twenty-six

1915

THE MORNING WAS MISTY and there was a chill in the early summer air. This was the only chance that Mary would have to get something to give Frank. She knew that her mistress would not require her services for some time and there it was, the deep velvet petals of a new rose. Her sewing scissors made short work of the stem and as she lifted the stem clear of the bush she saw a man standing still facing towards the lough. For a moment Mary was taken aback. In his soldier's uniform he somehow didn't look like her Frank. Quickly without thinking she moved hurriedly over to the figure.

'Frank?' she said softly.

'Aye.' The man turned nervously towards her.

'This is for ye.'

It was rare that the two had a chance to be together. Snatched conversations were often the only contact, but both sensed, hoped there was a deeper connection.

Leaning down to look into Mary's face, Frank took the flower, inhaling the scent of the deep red velvet petals and then, winced as a sharp thorn ripped his finger as he put the flower in beneath his newly acquired uniform jacket.

'Mary, I will write. I just don't know where I'll be.'

'Stay safe, Frank Black, just stay safe and come home to us.'

Her hand reached up to his uniformed chest and straightened the buttons. Frank caught her hand and held it over his heart.

'I will be thinking of ye, Mary. Never doubt that.'

For Frank it was a long speech. Mary looked up at him. His blue eyes fixed on her.

'I'll be waitin', Frank.'

Mary, already hurrying back to the house to hide her tears, seemed as close to being a ghost as was possible. Everything seemed unreal to Frank.

He took one last look around the garden and on impulse picked up some broad bean pods. The fresh scent calmed him and he placed the beans in his pocket. There was a pulsing strength in his hands, a reassurance of the land he knew and the connection he would bring with him. Something made him move to the pea plants and carefully he removed some of the pods, thrusting them into his pocket as well. It was as though he was taking the garden with him.

Frank knew that there had been arguments between his parents about the war, but in the end there was a sort of inevitability about it all.

The Hendersons had come out to see the men off. Frank hardly heard the short speech Master Ted made from the steps of the terrace and he only vaguely heard the accompanying clapping at the end of it. He saw Mary anxiously holding the edge of her apron with both hands as though if she didn't she would lose control and run through the crowd of people to hug him and beg him to stay.

'Well, this is the chance yer lookin' fer, boy,' Colin reminded Andy. 'I just hope ye won't regret it.'

'Sure, it'll be an adventure,' laughed Andy 'and we'll be home soon.' He blew a kiss to Bridget the kitchen maid like a conquering hero.

Jack Butler moved to stand beside his son, Ollie. 'Well we'd better be off, son.'

Father and son had discussed joining up and had decided it was the right thing to do. Jack did not want his son to go without him. Mrs Butler had not wanted either to go.

Ollie gave his mother a hug and Jack put his arms round his wife, now wiping tears away from her eyes.

'Wheest, love, we'll be home soon enough.'

'An' I'll be waiting here wi' Bouncer.' Ollie reached down to pat the dog and Mrs Butler turned her head away in tears. 'Write soon, both o' youse.'

And for Frank Black like all the others, the long walk away from everything he knew and loved had begun.

The train drew to a halt. Packed with new recruits and their baggage. It had been a tiring and airless journey from Belfast. A loud order was barked out and Frank and his comrades stood to attention. They would walk the last mile from the small station halt at Ballykinlar to the barracks for their period of basic training. Frank realised that he was staring at the famous Mourne mountains, which from Garraiblagh had been on a distant horizon. 'So this is where the mountains of Mourne sweep down to the sea,' he said to himself.

As he marched he noticed the greens of the hedges now in leaf, the whitethorn blossom and the coconut scented gorse. Wild pink roses scrambled over the ancient walls of the small roadside cottages and red campion was dotted everywhere, so many jostling for position, lining the narrow road as the soldiers passed.

An elderly man leant on a shepherd's crook at the edge of a field. 'Good luck to ye boys!' He shouted, waving his crook.

Time away from the barracks was limited and Frank grabbed

the first opportunity to take a train from Ballykinlar to Newcastle. Train times from the new station at Ballykinlar didn't always work in with time off. He stepped from the platform and out through the booking office into the bright daylight. Looking to his left he saw the glimmering water and waves crashing against the shore and directly in front of him were the mountains. 'Mary would enjoy a visit here. I'll bring her here when I get back,' he thought. As Frank sauntered along the Main Street he remembered the plant nursery his father had often mentioned. Following directions he turned off along a tree lined road, past houses and small gardens. He found the nursery, close to the corner of the Tollymore Road and the Bryansford Avenue and Road with its acres of open ground filled with flowers and plants. It drew Frank like a magnet. He walked through the gate and was amazed by the roses of all different colours. As he stood admiring the field a man came over to him.

'I see you're admiring our roses? he said to Frank.

'They are grand. Ye have a brave display here.'

'You've come at the right time for the roses. The daffodils are o'er, more's the pity. We have some rare ones here.' The gardener looked at Frank. 'You're aff to war then? I'm glad I'm wi' me plants. They don't fight much 'cept when I'm trying to cut them back!'

Frank grinned. They stood admiring the scene.

'It's a scythe ye'll be needin' in France, lad, to deal wi' thon Germans. Good luck tae ye.' They shook hands.

On his way back to the barracks, instead of continuing to the station close to the camp, Frank got off the train at Dundrum. He wanted the two mile walk back to Ballykinlar and a little more time away from his roistering comrades and talk of the war. Soon he saw the old man who had wished them luck when they had first arrived, puffing on his pipe and stroking his dog.

'You have good looking cabbages there,' Frank said.

'Aye, lad. I use seaweed on my vegetable beds. It always brings them up a treat.'

The old man's garden had an unusual combination of plants. Pink hellebore stood nestled against the cottage wall

'Rats don't like the roots, y'see. The skitters. I always think it's a bit of extra protection close to the cottage! Them an' Henry.'

'Henry?'

At that moment Henry appeared round the corner. A large marmalade cat with a torn ear and more battle scars than Frank ever wanted to have.

'Would ye like a cup of tea, lad?'

'I would. Thank ye.'

'Come over here an' set yourself down while I mak it.'

A small clump of geraniums with unusual blue flowers caught Frank's eye.

The old man brought out the cups and set them down.

'What are those flowers?'

'Geraniums but they are unusual aren't they? I got them in a sale in Newcastle. I think they may have come from one of the big houses.'

'Would ye like a piece of them?'

'I would certainly. I'll send them to me father.'

'I served mesel y'know?' said the old man.

'Oh?'

'Aye, the Boer war. The Boers were tough. The Germans will be too. Don't believe what they tell you, son. It won't be over by Christmas. Prepare yersel and keep yer wits about ye'.'

Frank thanked the old man in spite of his chilling warning and, taking the small parcel of damp roots, began his walk. Just finding and thinking about plants for a few hours had lifted his spirits. These geranium roots would soon be on their way to his father. He realised he had taken on his grandfather's plant hunting genes.

The old man watched the young recruit walking down the road

from beneath his bushy eyebrows.

'Come, Meg,' he said to the dog. 'Let's get that bacon in the pan. I wouldn't want to be thon young bucko for all the tea in China. May God watch o'er them!'

France 1915

The garden called to him in both his dreams and nightmares. Sometimes Frank felt that if he just closed his eyes for long enough he could merge with the soil in his hand and be beyond it all.

The trench, was on the outskirts of an old French village and was deep and clayed. He remembered the days it had taken them to dig it. It was an awful parody of the smaller trenches he would have dug in the garden for the potatoes. This trench was full of a different manure and inhabited by human plants, some alive, some withered by war and some dead.

The earth at home that had nurtured the plants he'd worked with had in France become earth that devoured half decomposed bodies of horses, humans, rats along with excrement and vomit: all thrown into the maw of the ever changing landscape. This world only had one season, the killing season. It was April and he could see no sign of spring.

His hands that had revelled in the soil, feeling the crumbling earth, dry and humus rich, between his fingers had become mired in this mud-packed hell.

The bean seeds in his damp uniform pocket that soothed him in the darkness were now becoming mouldy. Something in his gardener's heart brought him to realise that this was the time to give them the opportunity for life in the most unlikely place. In a sheltered spot at the base of the planking he scraped away the soil and planted the pea and bean seeds. It felt good. Peas climbing the barbed wire. It seemed advisable to plant vegetables that would have edible blossom, rather than vegetables that would have roots reaching into the mire. To even think what the mud was made of made Frank sick. The bean flowers at least might have the chance of reaching towards the sun, away from the earthly abyss.

He found himself checking on their progress, surprised to see shoots, half expecting them to be killed off as quickly as everything else. As the weeks passed he found himself in his spare moments concentrating more and more on the delicate twining tendrils, prepared to attach themselves to anything, pulling themselves upwards towards the light and the sky and away from the earthly horrors. A fleeting beauty, with a strong will to live, even here. Their urge for life sustained him and gave him hope.

One of his comrades began to help. Others noticed and also sought seeds from home. It became a habit to go to the 'garden' after a skirmish. It grew. Often silent, the soldiers would attend to the plants making use of anything, including spent artillery shell casings as pots.

One day Frank and his platoon walked through an orchard and into an abandoned French village. For Frank it was a surreal experience as he noticed the pottagers of fennel, artichokes and rhubarb interspersed with thyme and sage, cabbages and the beans. The scent of roses both spicy and sweet hung in the air. All abandoned with no one to harvest them. It was as though they had wandered into paradise in the midst of hell. The ache for Garraiblagh was so great that Frank felt sick. The flowers triggered strong emotions in many of the others. Sweet William, Forget me nots, cornflower, were carefully collected and pressed and sent back home to loved ones. In some way it felt by sending these flowers they were saying that life in the trenches was not that bad, there was still nature and with it hope. Only the soldiers knew the reality.

Field Hospital France 1915

Back at the dressing station there was more order. White aproned nurses hurried along duckboards between huts, keeping their feet out of the mud.

Daisy finished scrubbing the operating table. She had been in France for six months now. Her parents had had to give into her demands. University could wait and there were other young women from similar backgrounds volunteering their services. Walking outside she gazed across the camp.

A patch of muddy ground near the woods had been made into a flower garden tended by soldiers of all ranks. Daisy recognised the scented Sweet William and the delicate forget-me-nots and cornflower. She had seen forget-me-nots being picked and added to letters sent home by men who were feeling lost and bewildered. Some cabbages and carrots were also being cultivated. She wasn't sure how she felt about these gardens. On the one hand it provided an element of reassurance, a connection with home. On the other hand it suggested an element of permanence, of acceptance she did not want to contemplate. What had happened to the war that would be over by Christmas?

The small plots of cultivated ground played tricks with her thoughts. She knew only too well that this was nothing more than a war zone. Sometimes though, seeing the plants made her feel connected to what was so far away back home, but at other times it made her feel as though she was caught in some terrifying limbo, where reality had split open and was allowing her to see both heaven and hell.

She found her eyes drawn to a daisy flower blooming unexpectedly. It had managed to stay just out of reach of the mule's hooves, poor animals on their way to slaughter as surely as if they were sent to an abattoir. Daisy knelt down and brushed some mud off the small flower.

Suddenly tears began to fall.

Tom Guthrie had been in her mind. She carried the card that he had sent several weeks ago. She had heard nothing recently and knew only that he was now flying. She imagined that every plane she saw was him looking down on her. She also knew how many airmen she had helped to nurse after disastrous take offs or landings and those that had never made it as far as the end of the runway. More were injured in accidents than in combat as far as Daisy could discern. What a stupid waste!

A small area outside the window of the hospital had been converted into an official vegetable garden and for this the army had sent seeds to all the units back from the front line trenches. 'Good for morale,' they said. The rows stood to attention as the seedlings were beginning to appear, but they lacked the gentleness of the more haphazard plot full of forget-me-nots, sweet Williams. Everything seemed to have a military aspect now, even plants. Daisy felt an anger growing inside her. For some reason she thought of her childhood companion Frank Black and his love of gardening, of the gardens at Garraiblagh and all the gardeners there, and their care of the gardens, a genuine care. This garden seemed more like propaganda, 'official' gardening. Everything was propaganda. She smiled wryly as she looked at a large ungainly and rather plump turnip she had nicknamed 'the general'.

Closer to the wood a small patch of earth had been cleared and a few rotten tunnel posts had been placed around to mark the edge. An empty shell casing stood in the middle, filled with soil and bright blossoms. Amongst them Daisy noticed stones and small pebbles and sticks had been laid out in patterns. She knelt down out of curiosity and picked one up. The name of a soldier had been scratched on the surface. She picked up another, which had another name and date. The third just had one word 'hell'.

Frontline gardening

Frank and the others moved their feet forward, one painful step after another. The bright sunshine of the early summer contrasted with the dark mud and broken trees. Poppies and cornflowers were growing haphazardly, a nightmarish parody of Garraiblagh's garden back home. The colours, reds, yellows, blues were almost too bright for Frank's eyes. Cabbage plants, unharvested and then thrown into the air through the tremendous force of the explosions to land in odd places, had also begun to flower in forlorn hope to fulfil their purpose.

Frank's training as a gardener meant that he could not help but focus on the various plants going to seed, almost as soon as they were sown, as though they too recognised how short, how unnatural their lives were in this place of death, impotent to change things. He picked some of the flowers as he passed, placing them carefully in his pocket book. He would send them to Mary in his next letter.

As the days and weeks dragged on Frank and his comrades worked at the small garden they had created in the furthest section of the trench away from the front line. It began to take on an importance that none of them could have foreseen. The dampness of the trenches suited the celery seeds and they grew quietly, close to the Jerusalem artichoke, salsify and beans and peas. After each foray out from the trench the small group of men hurried back to check on the plants. Any ready for harvesting were added to the rations they had.

No one mentioned the future they might or might not have. The plants believed in a future and that gave hope.

So the plants were cosseted and spoken to. They heard many a whispered confession and hidden dread. The reminder of a world they might not see again. Some plants were even given names of loved ones back home and a few, the less polite nicknames when it reminded them of a commanding officer or sergeant.

Chapter Twenty-seven

France Midsummer 1916

FRANK WAS USED TO THE COLD, the wet and even the deep mud, but the heat of summer in the trenches was almost worse with the flies and rats. He could normally keep himself sane with mental pictures of the gardens back home at Garraiblagh. He developed a routine where he forced himself to imagine Cass the cat sedately making her way down the paths past the onions and the cabbages in the kitchen garden, the roses against the south wall, their colour and, if he really concentrated, their scent. Each time he would try and see a different part of the garden. Mary had sent him her photograph and with it a short stem of forget-me-nots and this he kept close to his heart at all times.

He kept watch as the seedlings began to produce flowers. The plants kept him grounded. Some aspects of life in the trenches, like the night-time cutting of grass, where there was still some, he understood. The grass cutting was to ensure the sight-lines for firing at the enemy positions was not hampered. It played havoc with his memories of cutting grass in the most peaceful of conditions.

Burying his nose in the broad bean flowers and their exquisite scent was one way of lessening the impact of the smells brought by the hot weather. Decomposing bodies and swarms of flies created a black veil over the landscape, while further away the stumps of trees looked like wind-whitened bones.

Frank was gently tying a pea stem to a piece of broken stick when he suddenly recoiled. A large bloated bluebottle chose to land on his hand. Swiping at it he shivered, seeing it as an omen.

Midsummer and the sun was beating down on the wooden huts of the field hospital. Daisy stepped out of Hut 3 with a heavy yawn. She and Wenna, her colleague, had just finished cleaning the ward ready for the next influx of injured.

The normally dark shaded wards were now exposed to a bright light and though it brought with it the welcome faint scent of pine from the wooden structure. It was also merciless light. The faces of the wounded men were pale where bandages and bloodied injuries were not present. It was as though the real fallout from the battles was being placed under a spotlight.

Finding a chair, carefully positioned in a little shade, she sat down. The weight of her clothes, the heavy serviceable materials and the corset, even though lighter than the old steel boned ones, made her feel trapped. Her mother would have been horrified at her sitting outside without a hat and becoming quite tanned. She thought how many old attitudes had changed in the last couple of years.

The windows of the huts had been opened to provide some ventilation in the stifling heat. This helped to let out some of the smell of putrefaction. The carbolic caught the nose and so too did the gangrenous tissue with its own pungent scent. Daisy looked at the whitethorn tree nestled against the closest hut. Its blossom still looked beautiful, clean and unsullied. The tree reminded her of home and walks across the fields in spring, seeing first the blackthorn, then whitethorn and then the elder blossom. She recalled being told that it wasn't lucky to bring whitethorn blossom indoors. Apparently its scent was similar to the first stages of decomposing flesh. Now Daisy knew this was not an old wives tale. Daisy promised herself there would be no whitethorn in any garden of hers in the future. She shocked herself. For the first time since arriving in France she was thinking of the future. Normally she didn't allow herself that luxury. She'd had a letter from her parents not long ago which described the everyday life at home. The life they described seemed unreal. Daisy realised she had not heard from Molly in some time and reflected on the way in which their lives had separated since the beginning of the war. She had come to France, Molly had married Edmund, her childhood sweetheart. Daisy had been surprised at the time to hear that Molly had married but then she did not know anything about Edmund's views on women's rights.

The sound of bees and the warmth made Daisy's eyelids heavy. All the tension of the last weeks began to leave her body as she relaxed into sleep. She didn't know how long she had been asleep when she heard someone calling her name.

'Daisy! Wake up!' Wenna was standing in front of her, smiling. Wanna from Cornwall where her father ran a fishing fleet, shared a hut with Daisy. She woke with a start, unsure where she was. The bright sunlight shaded by the figure in front of her.

'Here, have this cup of tea! There's word that the casualties are on the way.'

'Oh, thanks Wenna. That's the deepest sleep I've had in ages! I hope nobody saw me.'

Wenna sat down beside her. 'Midsummer! Before the war I would have been collecting flowers to put under my pillow and everyone would have been enjoying themselves. I don't know if it will ever be the same. My mother told me in her last letter that the village is silent. The men from the local estate joined up together. Now most of them are ......’

Wenna turned her face away and picked up a daisy flower and paused.

‘Did you as a child take a petal at a time — ‘he loves me, he loves me not’? I have a new rhyme — ‘tomorrow, this year, next year, never’. When will this war end?’

Wenna’s shoulders were racked with silent sobs. Daisy had not seen this side of Wenna before and she realised that they had kept a distance from each other because it was easier to deal with the awfulness that way.

Daisy held Wenna’s hand and waited for the sobs to diminish.

‘Oh Wenna.’ Daisy realised that the exhaustion she felt was not just physical. She could not formulate the words of comfort she wanted to help her colleague. All she could do was hold her.

Daisy had developed a routine in which she focused on the garden at home willing her mind to recreate her usual routines, to manufacture a vision so powerful it took her away from the horror she experienced on a daily basis.

She even thought of her mother’s staid dinner parties with some affection.

Tom Guthrie was in her mind day and night. His last letter had said very little. She knew the censors would stop anything that might give his whereabouts away. He’d signed the letter off with his usual drawing of an aeroplane. She had no idea when or if she’d [illegible] again.

The first of the trucks arrived. Bodies were quickly laid out on [illegible] boards as Matron categorised and ordered. The red stripes to [illegible] those in danger of immediate haemorrhaging being hurried through to the small operating hut.

‘Nurse Henderson, four for your hut.’

Daisy moved, her skirt hem catching in the splintered duckboard making her pause for a moment as she unhooked it.

It was the accent she noticed first.

'Please, can I have some water, miss?'

The sound of home. Then she looked.

'Frank?, Frank Black?' There was agony in the dark blue eyes and a flicker of recognition.

'It's Daisy, Daisy Henderson.'

Frank's eyes closed again.

Daisy had to hold back an urge to embrace him.

A voice interrupted.

'This soldier is for Hut Three.'

'Yes, my hut. Bring him in please.'

Garraiblagh 1916

Rory carried the basket of vegetables and fruit up to the back door of the house, then scraping his boots, he entered the kitchen. He enjoyed coming up to deliver the produce from the garden. He didn't have to do it as would have been the case in his father's earlier days, but it gave him a chance to talk to people other than the gardeners.

'Well, Rory, what have you got for us?' asked Mrs Johnson. 'By the way I'll need some mange tout peas for Saturday. Master Ted and Mrs Florence are having a do and it's going to be a fancy menu.'

'I'll make a note of that,' said Rory as he pulled out a chair and sat down.

'I suppose ye'd like a cup of tae while ye're here?' said Mrs Johnson taking the hint.

'That, Mrs Johnson, would be grand!'

'Well, I'll tak the weight off me feet for a wee moment as well.

Have ye heard anythin' from young Frank? Mary walks around as though she's in a daze most days, not that she doesn't do her work mind, she does. She keeps his latest letter in her pocket.'

'These wars aren't for us, Mrs Johnson they're for the high and mighty. I sometimes wish Frank hadn't been persuaded. If ever there was a boy who didn't know what a fight was, it's Frank. This will be the last war, mark my words. They're all saying it. They won't have men rushing to enlist next time!'

'I hope ye're right. Me brother's son is somewhere. I can't get me tongue round it an' the number o' folk that rush to look at the lists is terrible.' She shook her head and moved to the sideboard, 'Have a bit o' me fruit cake, it's new outta the oven. The young Miss is out in France too. Who would have thought that she would have gone out to be a nurse,' Mrs Johnson drank her tea. 'I heerd there were fierce rows when she toul', 'toul'' mark ye, her parents that is what she intended to do. Maggie, says she could hear the arguments when she was up doin' the bedrooms. It was fierce loud.'

Rory was relishing his slice of cake. He knew that once Mrs Johnson began she was difficult to stop.

'Me father thinks she's like her grandmother. He says Mrs Amelia was always fiery an' determined, but he held that he always found her to be fair an' willin' to admit it if she made a mistake.' 'Aye, well. If this war goes on much longer we'll see the changes. I'm lucky I've still got aw the staff I need, but it must be wile difficult for youse in the garden wi' the young wans away.'

'We can only do our best!' said Rory. 'The family know we can't work miracles, but it's brave an' sad to see some parts of the garden beginnin tae look un-cared for, Mrs Johnson. Father is findin' it hard. He minds every change in the plants like they are his children.'

Frank ad lapsed into unconsciousness with the aid of morphine after the operation. Daisy was grateful for that. It felt easier to examine and wash his semi-naked body without his eyes on her embarrassed and watching for a possible reaction. Frank, whom she had known all her life and who had mischievously helped her to collect the flowers she needed for her great Suffragette revolt, was now so different from the tall, strong young man she had last seen in Garraiblagh. Daisy had seen too many injured soldiers who did not know what lay ahead. In Frank's case his lower right leg had been amputated.

Then, from the change in Frank's breathing and the slight movement of his head, Daisy knew that he was wakening. Unable to leave it any longer, Daisy took a deep breath, looked around her and straightened her uniform, stroking her red and roughened hands down her apron.

'Frank?' she began and took his hand.

'I thought it was you, Daisy. I wasn't dreaming.' He noticed her anguished look. 'I know, Daisy, the doctor told me.' he whispered.

She paused, not sure how to continue.

The lyrics of the new song floated through the window 'Roses are blooming in Picardy' was being played on a gramophone somewhere close by.

Frank made a wry grimace. 'Roses. The thought of them and other plants in our garden back home has been keeping me going.'

'Frank, you've come through the operation. Just think about getting better now!'

She realised it was trite, but she knew also that if his mood did not pick up it could be as dangerous as any post-operative complication. The will to survive, to get better was essential to any wounded soldier.

Frank looked at her. He knew he needed to tell her, but the words came slowly.

'Just after the war started, when I hoped ......stay an' work the garden not enlist, ...near the delphiniums, ye know, just close to the conservatory .... I heard this terrible screaming .....Unearthly. A rabbit ......in a snare ...one of Jobson's.... Ye know how he hates anythin' to mess up his vegetables.....Had to kill it. It was injured .. dying.....couldn't save it. Beautiful plants, I had to kill. If I ... what good would ..... Three legged rabbit? No chance!'

Tears rolled down Frank's cheeks.

The plea in his voice was there as he searched Daisy's face. She smiled weakly and continued to wash him. She thought of the times when she and Frank had played in the garden: each one backing up the other when trouble was brewing from parents or adults in general; the daughter of the house and the head gardener's son. She knew that this situation was awkward. The military code would allow no fraternisation, lifelong friends or not. For Daisy, as a nurse, she had become quite accustomed to seeing men's nakedness and their vulnerability. As she washed down his body in a business-like manner Frank closed his eyes and groaned.

She hoped he was more pained by embarrassment than the loss of his leg

'Daisy, get another nurse, for pity's sake!' he said angrily.

'Frank, I've washed and bandaged so many men. It's my job. I can't ask anyone else. You'll get me into trouble.'

In an attempt to change the subject Daisy began to recount what she had heard from her mother in a letter. 'Garraiblagh seem to be managing the spaghnum moss parcels for Belfast. I think your grandfather has been helping make sure mother can do her part managing the spaghnum but it has left the garden short, allowing men to go and collect it. They've started to plough up the bottom lawn to grow more vegetables. I don't think your father is too impressed.'

'He won't be.'

Frank made a desperate effort to rise above what was being

done to him.

'Have ye heard anything from Tom?'

Daisy shook her head.

'Not recently. I often wonder if it's Tom when I see one of our aircraft overhead.'

Frank reached out and caught Daisy's hand.

'Don't say anythin' to your father about me when ye next write home, Daisy. I want to tell them myself.'

Daisy nodded. 'What about Mary?

'I'll write when I can think clearly. I still have me hands don't I?

Daisy smiled.

'You do, Frank Black, indeed you do. All the rest of you is in fine working order. You survived.'

London June 1916

The amputation would mean an eventual return home to Belfast for Frank Black. An ambulance train took Frank and the other soldiers to the coast at Calais. It was an uncomfortable crossing, not only because of the weather, but Frank's leg continued to hurt him. Once in Dover the casualties were move onto the train that would take them to London. By the time he was transferred to an ambulance for the final part of his journey Frank was exhausted and biting back the agony. The journey had greatly aggravated his stump.

The slow beginning of Frank's recovery came during his time in London. An old mansion had been converted into a makeshift convalescent hospital. The interior furnishings had been removed and stored. Iron beds and basic mattresses had been placed in all the main rooms.

Leaning on the crutch, Frank hobbled down the steps into a walled garden. The sound of birds and the bees making their way from flower to flower calmed him.

As Frank stood breathing in the garden, the scent of old roses against the stone walls, he noticed another soldier with bandages around his head, carefully and brutally cutting all the rose heads off a large rambling plant. Deep blood red petals dropped to the ground. When all the flowers had been decapitated the man fell to his knees, his hands and wrists bloodied from the thorn scratches, deep sobs of agony coming from him. Frank did not move to him, did not make any gesture. There was nothing to say, nothing to be done. Frank was simply glad his own mind had been left intact.

The war had done so much to people and this petty act brought it home to him that the internal war for many would be lifelong. He recalled the red rose that Mary had given him and wondered about her. He had not written in the last few weeks, fearful of putting anything in a letter which might seem as though he was expecting anything in return from her.

It had not occurred to Frank that he would require further surgery. His memory of the field hospital and the horror and agony of having his lower leg amputated made him blanch, but on the other hand for any type of progress to be made; further surgery would have to be undertaken. He desperately wanted to be able to walk again.

Doctors had warned him that the process would be slower than he hoped. There would be a transfer to a new hospital set up at Roehampton to work with servicemen who had lost limbs. Then came the dreaded surgery. Cutting off excess skin and bone to make it easier to manage the stump and prepare it for connection to a metal limb. The field hospital surgery had saved his life, but now they had to save the rest of his leg and make it possible for him to walk on it without great pain.

There would be months of recuperation. He knew there were hundreds of others like him, many worse off than him with no legs.

The time spent at Roehampton moved slowly. He read the

newspapers and saw the lists of injured and dead being posted each day. Frank received letters from his parents and from Mary. He knew they tried to keep the tone of their letters light, but word that both Ollie Butler and Andy Baker had been killed in France brought him low. In reading one of the day's notices Frank came upon a short piece that had been posted by the nearby Kew Gardens. One of their under-gardeners had been killed in France. He had never been to Kew but his father had worked there and spoke warmly of it.

'Nurse, how far is it from here to Kew Gardens?'

'About three miles. I live just beside the entrance.'

'Is it difficult to get there?' The implication in Frank's query was left to hang there.

The nurse looked at him. 'Do you mean, could you get there using crutches?'

'Aye.'

'Someone would have to take you. Your stump is healing but it's still delicate. Let me enquire. I may know a way.'

The nurse came back to Frank a couple of days later. 'I think I may have fixed it, Frank, as long as you're prepared to be a part of a group.'

'Of course. What sort of group?'

'Kew Gardens is now a base for servicemen who have suffered shell shock. With your background in gardening and the shock you have sustained, Kew could be just the ticket. The doctor is willing to make a case for you to join the group. It would mean travelling there by ambulance two days a week and spending the day there. You would be provided with a wheelchair.'

To see Kew! Frank's spirits lifted. That would be something. He felt a sense of purpose course through him. It was a sensation of pleasure that had become so alien.

What Frank saw on arrival at Kew the following week, when he was wheeled down the main drive, amazed him. Women, wearing jodhpurs and leggings with wide brimmed hats were gardening and carrying out the work that he and his colleagues back at Garraiblagh would never have considered fit for a woman.

Frank was set to work in the glasshouses where he worked alongside the women gardeners. The more Frank saw of the women the more he realised that physical strength was not the main prerequisite for all garden work. They wheeled barrows, lifted sacks, and dug, but they also excelled at the essential tasks of propagation and planting which didn't require the same level of physical strength. The positive change in Frank's mood was noticed, and after further discussion, it was agreed that he would spend more time at Kew. He discovered other soldiers, wounded and sent home for convalescence with whom he could talk. It was also helping him to think about his plans for the future. But above all, being in a garden again, restored his faith in life and himself.

Once the everyday tasks of looking after the stump had become second nature Frank realised that he was ready to move on, to return home. The weight of the new leg was the worst thing. If he walked across a lawn it sank in further than his own leg and could easily become stuck in mud. He would have to decide how to manage this and how that would affect what he wanted to do next.

Garraiblagh in the snow

The snow began that year of 1917. It fell thickly. From the drawing room window Amelia and Florence watched the flakes twirl and float in dizzying profusion. The silence that the snow brought took any words the two women had and melted them before they had a chance to speak.

The topiary trees were changing shape, clothed in heavy, muffled white. They now looked more like large snowmen standing in conversation on the lawn.

An elderly Amelia wrapped up in her fur stole, woollen coat and hat walked with the aid of a walking stick onto the path aided by Florence. She would not be defeated by the weather. Not when her grand-daughter was still facing danger in France. Daisy's letters home could not disguise the awfulness of her situation. Being out in the garden, even in the snow, made it easier for Amelia to think positively. Indoors there was always a ticking clock somewhere and she felt confined by that artificial linear time. Amelia was not a religious person. She attended church, but really that was out of a sense of obligation and to meet her neighbours, than to listen to tedious sermons that were very little more than badly constructed essays.

In the garden, in her Garraiblagh, she could feel the pulse of the real world.

It was cold, but at the same time Amelia felt protected by her surroundings. Very little in the natural world frightened Amelia. It was human-kind that worried her.

As they walked slowly back to the door, she noticed the Christmas roses sheltering beneath the leafless lime trees and then remembered their other name, black hellebores. It somehow seemed to match the times that something that looked so pure could have a darker side. The white flowers surrounded by their dark green leaves looked so delicate and yet they were strong and bold under the weight of the snow. She hoped Daisy had been likewise able to maintain her strength of spirit. The skeletal shapes of the allium were changed into frozen ornaments by the chill and tiny icicles hung from the dark green ivy of the walls. What must it be like in France, in winter, and in war!

Amelia could only imagine what this generation of young people were having to contend with. No one could have imagined that this was what the younger generation would inherit. The years of her youth were a virtual paradise in comparison.

Chapter Twenty-eight

1917

MOLLY READ THE LETTER that Daisy had sent. She thought about it. It would cost £5 a year for two years. What did she have to lose? She would have to find accommodation, but wasn't there a cousin down in Dublin that her mother had spoken of?

It was almost six months now since Edmund had been killed. They'd had so little time together as man and wife before he had gone off to war. Her heart ached at the thought she would never see him again but at other times it almost felt as though he had never been, that he was just a figment of her imagination.

Molly remembered the heat of the awful summer day when the telegram had arrived. She had gone down to the allotments near the Botanic Gardens as usual and had been busy among the cabbages, checking for caterpillars. She could remember the coolness of the huge leaves and the drops of moisture at their hearts. Since Edmund left, she and her family had decided to help the war effort by growing food and had taken an allotment bordering the Lagan. Many of her friends had also done this after seeing the posters encouraging women to grow food in the allotments while the men went off to fight.

She found the work in the garden helped her cope when she thought about Edmund. Weeding and watering and tying up plants concentrated her mind in a way no housework or knitting did. Gardening gave her a hope in a future life.

Molly had straightened from checking the cabbages, and held her hand against the small of her back to untangle the muscles. Looking around at the heat haze hovering over the colourful allotments she smelled the scent of the sweet peas her mother had planted. It was a glorious day!

And then, Molly had seen her mother approaching from the gardens entrance waving. Her mother had walked quickly towards her with something in her hand. Molly waited. Molly didn't actually think she could move any more. Her eyes were fixated on the yellow paper in her mother's hand.

'Molly love, a telegram arrived for you'. Not caring that her hands were covered in soil, Molly took the paper. She felt its thinness. How could something so important be on such paper?

'I didn't want to leave it until you came home.'

The words 'deeply regret to...' merged into one another as tears rolled down her face.

Molly remembered sinking to her knees among the cabbages, still holding the paper and keening. Her mother's arms around her, stroking her hair like a child as they both rocked back and forth in agony.

From that time, although she had first heard the news while in the allotment, gardening remained a sanctuary from the harsh world. No awkward questions, just practical tasks. The other allotment holders knew and spoke kindly words, but they did not intrude. Many suffered in the same way and they were held by a communal grief. Molly threw herself into the allotments. She was elected onto the management committee by an overwhelming majority. It was through her drive and enthusiasm that the Botanic allotments won an award presented by the Duchess of Abercorn.

She had put up a barrier to human contact to protect herself. A large part of her was angry. Why this stupid war, why? If we'd got the vote before the war we could have stopped this madness of stupid men,' she said to the weeds as she punched the fork violently into the soil.

The train rattled along the rails. Molly had brought food with her to keep her going on the journey. On her lap lay a copy of Beeton's Everyday Gardening 1909 with its red cover and gold lettering, a gift from her parents. She sat in her compartment looking like any other young woman, but Molly knew that underneath it all she felt different and she was at the start of a huge adventure and a new life.

She had tried on her new gardening uniform for college and she felt rather good in it. The long boots and leggings with the crimson and grey 'aviation' skirt, hessian apron and large, wide brimmed hat suited her. It was yet another aspect of social change. She had rather lost sight of her suffragette involvement because of the many pressures of war and losing Edmund. Now some of those thoughts were once again bubbling to the surface. Gardening was a new profession for women and she was going to make the most of the course she had been accepted onto. She was glad that she would be staying with relatives in Dublin only a short tram ride from the gardening school.

Belfast March 1917

Frank reached Belfast in the early morning. One of the mornings when the cold rises gently up from the water. He tucked his chin deep into his army greatcoat.

There was one place he needed to go before he saw his family and faced the questions they would have for him. He needed to go into the garden at Garraiblagh on his own. It was in the garden that he had said his goodbyes and now he needed to tell the garden he was back.

He asked the car to stop close to the bottom of the drive and got out.

'Frank!'

Startled, Frank looked round to see Mr Butler coming out of the gate lodge with Bouncer at his heels. He was shocked by how much the man had changed.

It's good to see you Jack.'

Frank looked at the older man. 'I heard about Ollie. I'm so sorry.'

Mr Butler looked down determinedly at the ground and nodded. 'I hoped that if the two of us enlisted together I'd be able to look after him. Maeve hasn't got over it and I doubt she will.'

Frank walked slowly up the drive, aware that Mr Butler was watching him and his strange gait. Then as he reached the bend from the main roadway, he walked through the wood where the violets and primroses carpeted the ground to the lower garden. At first he thought he'd gone the wrong way, then he remembered Daisy's news in France that the lower lawn had been ploughed up to grow more vegetables. It was as though the garden had suffered injuries from the war as well. He moved on towards the rose garden.

Greeting the plants like old friends, he stroked leaves and branches as he went. Cass, the black and white cat, now a little battle scarred like himself, walked up to him, curling herself around his leg.

Frank remembered the rabbit and the very spot he had killed it. His leg hurt, the stump ached badly and sometimes spasmed. Walking was painful and tiring. It had taken time for Frank to realise that part of what he had to get used to was the fatigue from wearing the heavy contraption. Carefully and with some difficulty, Frank lowered himself down onto the lawn; the ground still cool and with the smell of new mown grass. He breathed in the scent and stroked the earth. The realisation came to him that the ground was not moving to the echoes of bombs, tunnels and the sound of spades, rats or the agonised cries, both human and animal. Just stillness; though the ground was wet with dew, it didn't matter. It was fresh, live, and fecund. An early bee was humming in the nearby honeysuckle blossom that scented the air. For a moment he was thrown back into the awful day he had left for war, collecting the bean seeds in his pocket. Images arose, unbidden,

He lay till the birdsong diminished and an evening chill began to touch his face. The battle scarred cat lay on his legs, guarding him from further nightmares. Frank reached out his hand and stroked its fur.

'So, Cass, I must move on from here and find my future. I can't garden in Garraiblagh.'

This was the first time Frank had truly relaxed since France. He wanted no more than to be a part of the earth. Reaching in his pocket, he felt the seeds that he had taken from one of the deserted gardens before he'd left France and carefully he planted them in the edge of the border.

Though the day was darkening into dusk, it was as though none of that mattered as long as he could make his way through the plants and trees. Swinging his body on his good leg and then transferring to his new aluminium prosthetic, which still felt heavy and unwieldy, it crushed the daisies underfoot. He knew what he would do. He knew as long as he stayed close to the soil he would be alright. It was time to talk to his father and grandfather.

An urgent shout came from the edge of the top lawn.

'Frank!' Mary was running towards him.

She stopped short just in front of him. 'I thought it was ye. You're walking great, sure!'

Mary went to embrace him. 'Yes, but don't jump into my arms however much I want you to! We're likely to both fall over like a couple of skittles.'

Nevertheless Mary reached over and gently kissed him. His eyes were still the blue of the hills, but there was now a sadness in them.

'Mary!' He balanced carefully on the sloping ground, pulled her into his arms and kissed her properly.

'Now I'm really home!'

Amelia and Florence were coming out of the house towards them and someone was calling for James and Rory and Alice. Soon the couple were surrounded, only parting to let through Rory and Alice and then James, now moving more slowly with a limp.

'It's so good tae have ye home, son!'

The gardener's house 1917

Alice had left food in the oven. She knew the men needed time to talk. 'I'm going to go down to see Morag and Freddy for a wee while.'

'Well, son, how does it feel tae be back?' asked Rory.

'It's all I ever wanted. But I have this yoke aroun' me I'm no' in one piece,' Frank tapped his new leg. 'I've had time, too much time, lying idle, wondering what I can do, should do'.

James looked over at his son and grandson. Rory wanted to respond, to offer a solution but saw his father, James, gently shake his head.

'Go on,' said Rory. 'What have ye been thinkin'.'

Frank started 'I've never wanted to work at anythin' else, but gardening. Watchin' the gardeners at Kew made me think. I can't do the heavy work as I used to, but I can manage other things.'

'Aye, good,' said Rory, intrigued. James watched and waited.

'I want to start a plant nursery.'

'A nursery? Here at Garraiblagh?'

'No, somewhere else.'

'Move away from Garraiblagh?'

'Things are changin', father. This war has shown me that. I don't want to be taking orders and bein' at anyone's beck an' call anymore. Garraiblagh always brought me a sense of peace and purpose, but now with the friends I've lost, the things I've seen....' He fell silent. He looked at his father and grandfather. I hope to marry Mary too.'

Rory smiled and nodded. 'That's great, son. A wise move. Mary is a great girl an' she's fair set on ye.' James walked over and patted Frank on the shoulder and reached for his best Islay malt.

'Your grandfather will tell ye I've been thinking along the same lines myself. Father, you're already married. Bigamy's still illegal I think!, quipped Frank.

'Wha?, No, I mean the nursery!'

They laughed as James poured the whisky. Our family has been this garden, helping to grow it for the last seventy years. Perhaps we need to start our own garden.' James looked over at his son and grandson. His own connection was as much to Amelia as to the garden. A different situation to his grandson's, more complicated than the tendrils of a passion flower.

Frank looked from his father to his grandfather. Rory sat back in his chair nursing his glass of whisky. 'I know where there is land for sale. Old Smith's smallholding. His sons were killed at Vimy and then his wife died, of a broken heart I think. God help him. His heart's not in it any more either, poor man.'

Frank sat forward. 'I will get a pension of sorts because of my leg, but I don't know how I would be able to work out the rest of the money.'

James and Rory looked at each other .

'When your father had just returned from his training' in Kew,' said James, we discussed the same idea. I had a conversation wi' Mrs Amelia that suggested she would be interested in starting up a plant nursery away from Garraiblagh, but what with one thing and another the conversation didn't go any further.'

'It looks as though the times right now,' said Rory, looking at his father.

'Well, I still have my savings,' said James. Mrs Henderson may invest as a partner so we need to look at this in earnest now.'

'I thought of specialising in Irish plants, What do you think?' asked Frank.

'Irish! There'd be some raised eyebrows at that,' joked his father.

'I served with men from all parts of Ireland an' Scotland an' England for that matter. This independence will be sorted an' anyway, I'm talkin' about plants not politics!'

'Some may disagree with ye on that, son, but I think it's a brave idea,' said Rory. 'A new business — Blacks Nurseries.'

'Well, it will take time to work out', added James.

'I've been thinking about the plants we could grow. Fuchsias and Irish roses, spring squills and anemones'

'Even some of the larger shrubs, the rhododendrons and olearia,' added Rory.

I wouldn't feel happy fae us all to abandon Garraiblagh an' the Hendersons straight away wi' the war still on,' said Rory.

'I agree, Rory. But let's not get ahead of ourselves,' said James. 'Listen to youse two. Frank's just back from war and ye are talkin' nurseries. Let's enjoy our dram. Here's tae ye, Frank boy!'

James and Rory raised their glasses to Frank. 'That is good whisky!' said Rory. 'Only the best Islay malt fae my grandson.'

said James.

'Now, tae business,' said James. 'I wonder if we could assist Frank by helping to purchase the small holding initially. Then, Rory, you could talk to Ted Henderson about beginning to hand over to a new head gardener with you remaining as a consultant just to oversee things initially.' They toasted Frank and Mary and Black's Nurseries.

Chapter Twenty-nine

Post-Armistice Garraiblagh 1918

On November 11, the sound of the church bells and hooters could be heard from every direction: a moment in time when the victors could celebrate.

But then came the reckoning. The slow return of those who had left and the acceptance that others, many others, would not be returning.

Old habits die hard. The peace negotiations might have started, but skirmishes still took place on the front. It was an uneasy time.

Garraiblagh had changed in so many ways. Four gardeners had left to go to war. Only two had returned.

It was still a shock for those working in the estate to see young Frank Black with his slow ungainly gait when they remembered the active young man who wheeled the barrows, dug the beds and rows and climbed the trees.

The rain had been falling for days. The work of the previous week; the dead-heading, tying back and checking over of the large cabbage roses had been the main victims of the incessant rain. A carpet of pink and white petals lay on the wet grass. Ned hadn't yet been able to tidy up the area as he moved through the flowerbeds, trimming back and staking other plants where the weight of the rain was close to breaking stems. His heavy waterproofs were useful for keeping the rain off, but the nature of the fabric meant that the rain also ran in rivulets down his arm and onto his wrists and down from his hood onto his face. He had to wipe his face every few minutes to ensure that he could see what he was doing. A robin watched from the back of the bed, its beady eyes intent on any worms Ned might dislodge in his work.

'It's alright for ye!' he said to the robin as he shook the rain off him. 'I'm gettin' worms for ye. What are ye goin' to do for me? Sweet Fanny Adams. I thought when the war ended that people would stop their fightin'. Damn the bit. Instead they're still at it. If it's not France and Germany, it's here! This independence an' Home Rule will split us apart. I'm glad I'm in this garden, mind ye. Better here than down in the south,' he mused to the robin.

Garraiblagh March 1919

Returning from France Daisy had felt as though she wasn't attached to reality. She had arrived in Belfast at midday on one of the last hospital trains from Kingstown, through Dublin, Drogheda and Dundalk. It had made its way slowly, as though it also was exhausted by the war. It stopped regularly at crowded stations full of relatives and friends awaiting the disembarkation of their wounded, moving them closer to relatives who could care for them or to hospitals where their stay might or might not end in discharge.

Now that Daisy was nearing the end of her time in uniform she felt oddly tired. She wasn't sure how or what to think anymore. She was now more concerned at the dreadful flu epidemic that had found its way from France to Ireland. Now there was the prospect of war in Ireland. Was there no end to the horror? John Finlay, the chauffeur at Garraiblagh collected her. He had been under strict instructions by Ted Henderson not to worry Daisy if she asked any questions about the family, just to tell her they were waiting at home for her.

Daisy gazed out of the window of the Model T. There was always that sense of coming home — knowing all the turns in the road, counting the bends, watching for the different cottages and landmarks along the way, each bringing her closer to home.

And now she was there. The gateposts marking the entrance as they had always done. The car slowed down and stopped for the gates to be opened. Daisy was shocked to see Jack Butler. The first of the changes she thought. She wound down the window and leant out.

'Jack! How are you and Mrs Butler?'

'Oh we're not so bad, I'm fair glad to see ye home, Miss Daisy.'

Daisy knew that her parents had given Jack and his wife the gate lodge when he'd returned from France, minus a leg and a hand. The death of Ollie their son had hit everyone on the estate.

She sat back in the seat and reflected. She had worked with so many men who'd suffered similar or worse injuries. She tried to think, to grasp the uneasy feeling floating around in her head. Yes, that was what it was. She had thought of Garraiblagh as separate, away from the awfulness of war and here it was, staring her in the face. Nothing and nowhere was untouched. What would the future hold for them all?

Daisy opened the car door and got out. She put her hand on the old Jack's shoulder.

'I was so sorry to hear about Oliver,' said Daisy.

Jack leant heavily on the ancient crook and looked at the ground.

'I don't like thinkin' o' him buried so far away, Miss Daisy, but he's wi' his friends, so many o' them. I still think he's goin' to come aroun' the corner, whistling a new tune he's larned. It's while quiet without him and Bouncer misses him for-by.' At the sound of his name the raggedy collie dog wagged his tail. 'We were worried,' explained Jack. 'We didn't want to leave Garraiblagh, but wi' me injuries I thought it would be the workhouse for us. I know the government has given pensions, but where would we have gone? Our friends are here, Miss Daisy.'

Getting back into the car Daisy wondered what other changes she would find. The drive through the trees was the same as always. Pale yellow and pink rhododendrons now jostled their way along the edges. They made the driveway a little darker but at this time of year the colour of the flowers and the scent made it more beautiful.

Soon the sound of car tyres crunched on the gravel at the house. The two big Labradors,Tiger and Fred, bounded down the steps of the house and across the gravel, barking delightedly.

Her mother threw open her arms.

'Darling, it is so good to have you back!'

Her father, hugged her, adding gruffly, 'Thank God, Daisy Thank God!.'

With tears in her eyes Daisy asked about her grandmother.

'She's not well, Daisy. It is the influenza. Doctor Brown is very worried about her.'

'I'll go and see her at once.'

Amelia's room looked out onto the garden, her favourite part and she had been propped up in bed so that she could see the new growth and the colours.

'Grandmama!,' Daisy smiled and had to make an effort not to look shocked at how her grandmother had aged.

'Daisy! I hoped I'd see you again.'

Daisy rushed to hug her grandmother and smelled the delicate rose scent of Attar of Roses that her grandmother always wore.

'You'll be fine. Rest is what you need.'

'I am not going to be fine, dear. Don't flannel me. I'm not one of your young soldiers. Can you sit me up a little more so that I can really see the garden? I know my eyes are not good, but you can tell me what is in flower and how everything looks.'

Sitting with her arm around her grandmother's frail form Daisy began. And as she described the different flowers and the shapes of the trees and bushes she realised that she was slowly unwinding. The knots in every part of her body were relaxing. The sound of the names and the descriptions of the colours occupied her mind. Within a short while Daisy noticed that her grandmother had fallen asleep.

Later in the evening, taking a walk in the garden she realised that she was tracing the route that she had described to her grandmother only a few hours before. She thought about it. She was still able to be a part of it — the luxurious growth and colour and the energy but her grandmother could only relate to it from a distance, see the outlines and the slightly misted colours. The garden that Amelia had dreamt of and that she had created was beginning to let her go. How would it react to her passing?

Later as more lights twinkled on the far side of the lough, Daisy realised that Belfast had expanded during the war. The perfume of night-scented stock filled the air and moths fluttered from honeysuckle flower to clematis in their hunt for nectar while the last of the birds made their way homeward to their newly constructed nests. Picking some stems of stock Daisy left the garden and returned to her grandmother's room.

Amelia lay, hardly breathing. Daisy sat reading Pride and Prejudice, noticing an occasional smile on her grandmother's pale face. Daisy knew that it would not be long. Life was ebbing from Amelia Henderson. The nurse bathed Amelia 's forehead and straightened the bedding. Daisy had seen this so many times before. Life then death and she hoped, for the sake of all the friends she had lost, some sort of rebirth.

A loud rap at the front door woke Daisy, who had been snoozing through the night in a chair beside her grandmother's bed. She could hear the urgent sound of a conversation,

'I'm here to see Mrs Henderson.'

'Good morning Mr Black. I'm afraid the family can't be disturbed. Mrs Henderson is very ill.'

'I know that. I need to see her,' said James sharply.

'I'll see if the master can speak to you.'

Ted came down the stairs, his mouth set firmly.

'What is it James? My mother is near the end.'

'I need to see her, Master Ted!'

'James, she's drifting in and out of consciousness and this flu — I don't want to be responsible for you coming into contact with it!' said Ted. 'I can't let you risk it.'

'I need to see her,' James repeated, his voice harsh with emotion. 'I'll take the risk, it's not as though I will be long for this life!'

There was something in the old man's eyes that Ted didn't quite understand, couldn't identify. He was considering how best to make it absolutely clear that his mother could not be disturbed when Daisy came down the stairs, dressed in her nursing uniform.

'Hello, Mr Black, have you come to see Grandmother?'

Daisy saw the look of hope in James' eyes and then the stern face of her father.

'Father, Granny has been asking for Mr Black.'

Daisy brought James into the bedroom and moved over to her grandmother's bed. James hung back, glancing out of the window and noticing how the view took in so much of the beauty of the place.

'Mr Black is here, Granny.'

Amelia opened her eyes and with difficulty, smiled.

'James, is that you?'

The warmth that could be heard even in the fragile voice was enough for Daisy and she quietly left the room.

'Amelia!' James reached out to take her hand in his. 'How are ye my love? I never wanted to see ye like this!'

Breathing with difficulty, Amelia responded.

'Nor I, James. I am dying, I know.'

James brought his chair closer to the edge of her bed and leant towards her.

'I'm too auld tae waste time arguing the point with ye. I have missed you, Amelia!'

Amelia looked at the large white haired man with the gentle eyes.

'So much hidden,' she whispered. 'Perhaps we should have shocked them all, but I wasn't brave enough. I didn't think our families would understand.'

'Hush,' James said softly as he touched her face, stroking her cheek. 'We have known each other in a way it would have been difficult for others to understand.'

'And now we will part.'

'And you still believe in God? Even after the commandments we have broken?'

'Yes. Who do you think brought us together to create this wonderful garden?'

'We did. He's nae getting the credit.' said James flatly with a smile. 'This is not the end, James, I feel that.' said Amelia tightening her grip on James hand. 'Our souls will live on in the garden. I don't think I'll ever the leave the garden. I don't think either of us will. I don't want to leave.'

James leant forward and kissed Amelia on the lips just as the door opened and Daisy reappeared.

' I have your water, Granny.'

Daisy stopped. James moved back from the bed, still holding Amelia's hand, kissing it he left the room.

Amelia caught her grand–daughter's eye.

'Love is a wonderful gift, Daisy!'

Daisy looked at her grandmother uncertain how to respond.

'It remains my secret, Daisy. You do not need to know more.'

'Your secret is safe with me, Grandmama.'

Dublin June 1919

The appointment of Constance Markievicz as Minister of Labour in the new Dáil Éireann had given hope to Molly and the other women on the gardening course. It seemed to augur well for the role of women in a future Ireland. But with yet more violence and blood-shed beginning to escalate across the country Molly was relieved that her course was coming to an end. She wanted to be back home. She just had to decide where her future would be. She didn't want to leave Ireland and hoped she wouldn't be forced to.

Molly's time at the Irish School of Gardening for Women at Terenure in Dublin had given her the skills and knowledge that she had wanted and she intended to obtain a job as a gardener. Lectures had surprised her. There had been practical sessions, but also botany and chemistry and visits to the Botanic Gardens at Glasnevin.

She knew one friend who had just obtained an assistant gardener's post in the west and envied her, but at the same time she missed her family and friends in the North. Things were becoming complicated and uncertain around Dublin and beyond. And she knew she needed distance between Connor and herself.

Molly reflected on Connor's pleading that she stay in Dublin, look for work there and also become part of the struggle for a new nation. There was a part of Molly that considered it, it would be a logical continuation of her suffragette work in a way and although Connor was exciting and full of ideas there was also a part of Molly that was naturally cautious.

She had left him saying that she would think about it. She wasn't even sure what 'it' was.

As the train pulled out from Amiens Street station[27] Molly began to relax. She had almost missed her tram, saying goodbye to her cousins. She had made it clear that she did not want them to see her off at the train. She had become very close to them during her time at the gardening school and it was yet another change, a wrench from what had been a happy experience. Molly watched as Dublin disappeared into the distance and decided to disregard the urge to eat the sandwiches and other foods that her cousins had given her by reading the newspaper she had bought. She was relieved she had missed the recent train strike but was wary of the violence that was beginning to spread, especially after the general strike in Belfast. She leafed through the Belfast Newsletter in order to reacquaint herself with the goings on at home, though her parents had been writing regularly to let her know about the major events.

Then she saw it, an advertisement in the paper, 'An assistant head gardener required for Garraiblagh estate.'

It would be putting her training to use, there might be accommodation and she knew Daisy Henderson. She read the advertisement through to herself again and immediately self-doubts set in.

'There will be much more experienced gardeners applying. What would they think of a woman?' Her new confidence began to wilt. 'This is not going to be easy.' It had been some time since she had seen Daisy Henderson, she would be home from France now. Molly wondered how she could enlist Daisy's help. She would know how

27 renamed Connolly Street Station in 1966.

her application might be received by Mr and Mrs Henderson. In a moment of courage she wrote to Daisy.

The train drew in to Great Victoria Street Station in Belfast and Molly could see her parents waiting on the platform. For the moment she would just enjoy being home.

'Slowly analysing and defining what she saw around her in the garden she began to draw. A sense of peace descended on her as she began to see that she was connecting with the garden around her in a way that she had never done before'.

PART FOUR

Post–war

'Gardening is the work of a lifetime — you never finish'
Oscar de la Renta

Chapter Thirty

1919

THE DAYS SINCE AMELIA'S DEATH had been hard for everyone, particularly for Daisy, who had hoped she would have years more with her grandmother. Death had taken even those far from the Front. She knew the future had to be faced, but somehow her mind recoiled and would not focus. She felt tired. Molly's letter lifted her mood. She read the letter with excitement. 'Perfect' she announced to herself. 'Just perfect but it will require some persuasion of mother and father!'

Daisy did not think Frank's father, Rory Black, the head gardener, would be too difficult to persuade and besides she knew Frank's father had a soft spot for her since she had nursed Frank in France.

'There's no time like the present! 'Carpe diem! It is a new world!' and she strode determinedly through the house to the morning room where her parents were having coffee.

'Mother, father, I've had a lovely letter from Molly Taggart, a great friend of mine. Her husband was killed at the Somme. It has been a very difficult time for her. While her parents are supportive,

Molly has been living on a widow's pension.'

'Yes, dear?' Mrs Henderson queried. She had learned that only a very few words were required as a prompt and to show they were listening. The formality of Daisy's greeting suggested their daughter had a scheme afoot.

Daisy's parents waited. The pause was noticeable and both understood that this meant something they might not want to hear.

'Molly worked hard in the Botanic allotments during the war. She won prizes. She has spent the last two years in Dublin training to become a gardener. She has qualifications in horticulture. Molly has great courage I think you'll agree.'

Mr Henderson moved uncomfortably in his wing backed chair and focused more intently on his daughter. Ted Henderson had had to revise his thoughts on women and their abilities, not only because of Daisy but because of the women in his linen mills who had taken on roles that would normally have been the preserve of men and done them well.

'Yes, Daisy? And?' he enquired, glancing over at his wife. She did not look as though she had been forewarned of anything.

'Well, a gardener is needed here. Molly is fully trained and she received a prize from the Duchess of Abercorn when she managed the Botanic allotments. At that Daisy glanced at her mother.

Florence sat up. 'The Duchess of Abercorn?'

Daisy nodded her head and continued her argument.

'Frank's father is getting older in any case and needs to train up a successor. Molly has no children.' She added for good measure.

'How would Molly's father feel about this, Daisy?' queried her father.

'Father, she's a married woman — a widow! She has to take decisions for her future and she's strong! Strong as an ox!'

' An ox! A woman working among men?' Florence tut tutted.

'Mother! I was working among men in France!'

'I know that, dear, but this would be in a garden! What would she wear? A woman couldn't be expected to dig and weed!' An almost visible shiver ran down her mother's back.

'Mother you know very well that there are a number of women gardeners. What about Gertrude Jekyll?' Her mother shook her head.

Daisy sighed and was about to make further arguments, but thought better of it. It was her father and Rory Black who needed to be convinced. She would have to work on them further.

Molly arrived for the interview at Garraiblagh wearing her College gardening clothes. She had wondered what to wear and thought the best way to show that she was serious was to be seen as any other gardener would be. Her leather hemmed skirt and gardening jacket were woollen and warm. She hadn't quite realised how warm they would be as she sat in the hall waiting for her interview and hoped her heat-reddened face would not give the wrong impression. The hall clock ticked remorselessly and, to take her mind off the impending interview, she looked at the floral arrangements around her. She considered what flowers she would want to grow to bring more interest to the indoor flower arrangements.

The door to the morning room opened and a middle aged man in a suit appeared. As he closed the door behind Molly he paused, looking at her. She had seen the initial look of surprise in the hall which had now turned to one of quiet amusement.

This first look of amusement made Molly feel even more uncomfortable and her clothes were not helping.

'Perhaps this was not such a good idea,' she said to herself.

She took her place on the high backed chair opposite Mr Henderson who was sitting behind a rather grand desk. She smoothed her hands over her skirt. She had thought wearing these clothes would make her appear more professional, but now it felt like fancy dress.

Rory sat to the side of the desk, noted her work clothes and silently approved.

Mr Henderson opened the interview.

'Mrs Taggart we need a gardener who will command the respect of the gardeners and not only maintain Garraiblagh as a garden with a high reputation in horticultural circles throughout these islands, but maintain its ability to provide produce for the estate and flowers for the house.'

Molly nodded her head.

'So Mrs Taggart, I would be grateful if you could outline your skills and experience to Mr Black and myself,' said Ted Henderson.

'I trained in the management of soils and manures and the cultivation of flowers, fruit and vegetables at College in Dublin, sir.'

'What did you learn in relation to work in conservatories and hothouses generally?' asked Rory.

'That was covered as part of the general course, but I also attended lectures in greenhouse management at the Botanic Gardens in Glasnevin. It was there that I also took classes in plant pathology. The second year of my course became more specialist and at the end of it I sat the Royal Horticultural Society examination and passed with a commendation.'

Rory Black had been listening carefully to Molly's responses.

'That is all well and good. I can see that you can apply yourself to study, but what about the practicalities of gardening. The gardeners start at six in the morning during the summer months and work for twelve hours.'

'I am used to being up early in the garden. It was part of our training and spending the day outside. Working in all weathers is something I am fully used to.'

'What of your knowledge and practice of gardening beyond your course?' Rory asked.

'Before the war I became interested in gardening and joined the Women's Farm and Garden Association. Then when war broke out I worked in the allotments beside the Lagan at Botanic until 1917. My skill led to me being asked to lead the allotment work at an early stage in the war.'

Ted listened to Molly's responses, knowing from Rory's expression that he was warming to this woman. He then asked his own question about her time during the war.

'My husband was killed on the Somme, sir, and with no children I had time to become more involved in war work. It helped me cope with ...my husband's death.'

Molly dropped her head and cleared her throat. Then raising her head again she looked directly at Ted Henderson and awaited his next question.

Rory Black, nodded. His admiration for this young woman was clear in the murmured agreement he gave to her replies.

Rory was surprised at the depth of her knowledge but he had one final query to put to her

'Do ye foresee any difficulties managin' men? Men who would not be used to taking orders from a woman?'

'At college we were taught to rely on our skills and knowledge and I believe if I am confident in my work and the directions I give to the men, then they will appreciate that it does not matter whether it is a man or a woman giving them their orders.' Molly said. 'I had to work with men on the allotments at Botanic. There were no particular difficulties. In fact we worked together so well we won prizes.'

Molly noticed that she was holding her hands together so tightly they were hurting.

'Thank you. Please wait in the library while we discuss your application, Mrs Taggart,' said Ted.

The maid showed Molly into the library and, realising that her legs were shaking, she sat down. Molly had known it would be difficult but not to be given a chance! She thought of all the confident responses she had made to the questions and groaned.

'What have I done? They're sure to think I am over–confident, and perhaps I should not have worn these heavy clothes!'

'Well, Rory, what do you think? It will be you and the gardeners who would be working with her. Could you work with her, Rory? Could you see her taking over from you when the time comes?'

'She'll hae to prove herself, Master Ted, but the world is changin' an' we know what the war taught us. She has courage an' from her history she has had plenty of practical experience an' knowledge. I would suggest we give her a six month trial.'

'I agree. I think she deserves at least that from us,' concluded Ted.

Through the window Molly could see one of the gardeners working at the topiary. She wondered to herself if they had thought of creating some informal planting around the base of the topiaries pieces rather than the more traditional and formal planting. At that moment Rory came through the door. Without thinking Molly turned and put her thoughts to him.

'Aye, well, that is somethin' that ye can deal wi' as one of your first tasks, Mrs Taggart,' said Rory smiling. 'Congratulations, ye have the job on an initial six month trial, if that's acceptable?' Molly stuttered 'Oh!Oh! Thank you. Y-yes it is. Thank you.'

'Come back to the study then an' Mr Henderson will provide more information.'

Ted Henderson rose to welcome Molly back into the room and he and Rory began to go through the practical details.

'Accommodation can also be offered in one of the farm cottages.

We do need the assistant head gardener to be on hand, you understand.'

Mollie could feel her heart beating. This was what she had hoped for and now she was nervous.

'I understand completely the need for the gardener to be based here and I am happy for that, Mr Henderson.'

After the details of her new role were finalised the two men shook hands with Molly and she left them.

'I hope the men take to her, Rory, for her sake and ours,' said Ted.

'I'll see to that Master Ted,' said Rory. 'It is possible for a woman to do the job. Frank wrote to me about the women gardeners at Kew when he was convalescing in London. He made a point of asking them about the work and the plants they were dealing with. They were very knowledgeable. I was also speaking to a woman a few months ago who was one of a number of women who were sent to France in 1917 as part of the Women's Army Auxiliary Corps, who had been given the specific task of gardening.'

'What were women doing gardening in France, Rory?'

'They were given the job of tending the graves in the military cemeteries.'

'Oh, I see. I know this is a changing world, Rory. It's just moving too fast for me.'

Daisy was waiting for Molly outside the house. Taking her excitedly by the arm, she took her friend down the steps and into the rose garden.

'Well?'

'I have the job and I start next week!.'

'Oh, Well done Molly. I'll find out which cottage it is and I'll get it ready for you! This is great news.'

Molly was so excited about the job she didn't consider any of the difficulties there might be. She knew for her time on the allotments in Belfast during the war and her training down in Dublin that women were capable gardeners. She was confident that she was up to the task.

As she arrived at the bothy beside the walled garden earlier than agreed. She noticed the blossom on some broad beans had begun to be infected with greenfly. She made a mental note to come back to them. Just at that moment she heard a voice and Rory Black appeared.

'Welcome Mrs Taggart, Good mornin'. A good day to start. If you're ready I'll introduce ye tae the men now.'

The sound of voices, of good humoured banter, could be heard as they walked closer. Molly suddenly became nervous.

'Mr Black' came the chorus.

'Mornin' men. This is Mrs Taggart who I've been tellin' ye about. She is the new assistant head gardener. She will be takin' over the day to day runnin' o' the gardens.'

Molly could not fail to hear the sudden silence or to see the stony faces.

'I am sure ye'll welcome Mrs Taggart an' give her every assistance. I expect nothin' less. I'll leave ye to get acquainted. Mrs Taggart, over tae ye.'

Rory left Molly alone, facing the men. Old Ned spat black tobacco juice onto the ground as was his habit and leant heavily on his spade. Molly had had her speech prepared about new beginnings after the war and what a great job they had all done caring for the garden during those difficult years. She stumbled through it, beginning to wither under the passive stares of the men. At the end there was a silence. Ned spat again. The men stared at her.

'Wha's the Duchess of Abercorn like, Mrs Taggart?' piped up Colin.

'Did ye meet yon Countess Markievitz in Dublin?' asked another.

Molly was surprised at their knowledge of her. Someone had been helping to make her case to the gardeners.

'So what would ye say we treat them black fly on the broad beans wi'?' asked a more hostile Ned.

Molly turned to face Ned.

'I'm sure an experienced gardener like you will have your favourite, but I like to use a pyrethrum spray, but only if we can't remove them using water and a damp cloth.'

Ned nodded. 'Aye, aye,' mumbled Ned as he conceded the point.

Any thought of university had gone for the time being as far as Daisy was concerned. When she thought back to before the war it seemed a world away. She knew her place was guaranteed at Trinity but after France she felt she couldn't go back to academic study. Her mind was no longer suited to that life. She needed time to re-orient herself to normal everyday life. The garden was helping. But losing her grandmother had hit her hard so soon after returning home and she still wondered about the relationship her mother had had with James Black.

Her grandmother's will had been straightforward. One element had delighted Daisy. It was the gift to her of her grandmother's garden diary. She had only seen the diary occasionally when her grandmother was making notes about some new plant, she had never been allowed to read it. The bequest came with the proviso that it should not be shared with anyone.

Daisy looked out across the garden from her bedroom window. It was one of those days when the heat haze had started early and the sky was completely blue. Bees flitted from plant to plant below her and the only sound was the distant one of grass being mowed:

a perfect time to look in more detail at her grandmother's diary. Grabbing her sun hat she hurried down the stairs and out of the French windows in the drawing room.

Walking past the deep purple blue of the delphiniums suddenly triggered the memory of the dinner party when she had arranged the flowers in the colours of the suffragettes. Daisy giggled to herself. It was at that party that she had met Tom and in the following weeks and months they had become closer. Daisy and Tom discussed the war at length and both felt that the small nations needed protection from German aggression until finally over lunch in November 1914 they entered a pact to join up. That afternoon Tom enlisted in the Royal Flying Corps and Daisy joined the Red Cross.

But now, as she stood looking across the terraces towards Belfast Lough and the Mourne mountains beyond, she wasn't sure what she felt. The war had changed her.

The garden had also changed. Plants and shrubs were running wild, as though caught on a bad day, slightly dishevelled. Her parents and Rory Black along with two gardeners had tried to manage as before, but the garden seemed to have its own mind.

Daisy walked to the stone bench at the end of the herbaceous border beside the delicate Japanese anemones. She opened her grandmother's book and drew her hand across the first page. She had only skimmed through the diary until now. There was an energy there, as though Amelia was still present. There were her grandmother's thoughts as a young woman like Daisy about the land, the ideas she'd had for planting but Daisy was drawn more to Amelia's illustrations than words.

Daisy noticed a coloured drawing of the summer house. Her grandmother had made notes of the varieties of climbing rose used, but then Daisy noticed that she had also made notes of a more personal nature, describing passionate encounters with her husband in that very summer house. Taken aback Daisy lifted her head from the book, trying to come to a new understanding of her grandmother. She was beginning to grasp the nature of the garden and her grandmother's connection to it. Everything in the garden had felt strictly controlled in its planting but here was her grandmother, very definitely not controlled!

'You loved my grandfather that is obvious. But what was the relationship with James Black?' Daisy asked herself out loud as she stood up. Somehow it seemed more appropriate to read her grandmother's diary in the summer house where her grandmother kept her drawings.

Taking a stem of one of the old crimson Bourbon roses she sniffed the delicious scent, twisted it in her hand, looking carefully at its structure, the play of light on the petals and the changes of tone across the leaves and walked through the rose arbour to the summer house. The door creaked open and light flooded in causing dust motes to rise in the air. There was still a slight scent of her grandmother's perfume mixed with the old wood of the building. It felt comforting. Daisy sat down, looking out of the window.

Sometimes she had accompanied her grandmother to the summer house and on special occasions they would have afternoon tea brought out to them. Daisy could almost taste the strawberry jam on the scones. She also remembered the times when her grandmother had shown her how to paint flowers and how much she'd enjoyed it.

She felt an impulse to start painting again. She had always been rather good at drawing although she had rejected it in her suffragette days, believing it to be only a 'ladylike' occupation, approved of by people like her mother. Daisy had seen the work of war artists. Art did not have to be safe but she would leave the painting of war and people to others. She would concentrate on plants and gardens. Her old art materials must be somewhere. She looked round the interior and noticed the old wooden box in the corner of the room. Opening it she checked her watercolour paints and brushes and some unused sheets of watercolour paper. That's it, she thought. She would take over the summer house and use it as her studio.

Slowly analysing and defining what she saw around her in the garden she began to draw. A sense of peace descended on her as she began to see that she was connecting with the garden around her in a way that she had never done before. In the past it had been a place of beauty, of escape, but now she was connected to the garden in a deeper sense.

As she drew she thought about her grandmother. She had always felt close to her and there were the times when Amelia had supported her against her parents' wishes. Daisy remembered her shock at seeing James Black kissing her grandmother in a way that suggested it was not unusual for them and then her grandmother's words to her. 'It remains my secret, Daisy.' Amelia hadn't tried to justify anything. Daisy, for her part had not said anything to her parents nor would she.

The garden and her art began to work its magic, giving Daisy some sense of place and continuity. It had its own rhythms and routines that continued regardless of the humans. She had recently found herself drawing individual flowers and plants and working on larger scale paintings of the garden landscape.

She took out the letter that she had received from Tom that morning. She could hardly believe that he was finally on his way home. She would go into Belfast and meet Tom at the docks. Daisy had only recently learnt to drive. Her father had eventually agreed to her being taught by the chauffeur using the roads on the estate and nearby. She had gained her father's final approval by driving him into Belfast for a meeting. Since then she had made sure that she gained every opportunity to expand her driving skills. She was thrilled at the sense of empowerment it gave her.

The morning had been fresher than she had expected and in the car she felt chilled. The early morning mist made the water and the huge sheds from which passengers disembarked, appear surreal. But the docks were far from surreal, they were a hive of activity as luggage was carried off the steamer and placed on trolleys by porters.

'Tom!'

He was thinner than she had last seen him. She threw herself into his arms and he hugged her close.

'Daisy, it is so good to finally have you in my arms.'

'Come on, the car is waiting.' Daisy took Tom's arm and pulled him towards the entrance.

'Where's Mr Finlay? Is he not driving us?'asked Tom.

Daisy shook her head and laughed. 'I have learnt to drive she declared with pride.!'

'I am going to be driven by a woman?' joked Tom. 'I'm not sure about this. Can we get a taxi?'

'Ha ha, I think you will be very impressed.'

Tom got into the passenger seat and watched with admiration as Daisy manoeuvred the car out onto the road.

'Well I have to say I am impressed, Daisy. If you continue like this I'll have to teach you how to fly a plane. I've heard of some women learning to fly.'

Later, walking in the garden at Garraiblagh Tom stopped, looking out across the lough.

'Daisy, I know I've hardly arrived back, but we need to talk about the future. You know I love you and I want us to marry. But first there's something I must do. I need your help, if you can give it.'

'What do you mean, Tom?'

'It means waiting before we marry.'

'But why, what has happened?'

'It's not that something has happened particularly it's more that

I need to feel I'm doing something to repair the damage.'

'Go on,' said Daisy 'the damage caused by the war?'

'Yes, flying over France, the miles of dead and broken ground, bodies, trenches, deserted and abandoned villages. I can't get those images out of my mind.'

Tom turned and picked up a daisy, twirling its stem between his fingers. He paused for a moment looking at the flower. 'Do you know there's something so right about a daisy. It sounds stupid I know but I found it was the little things that really got to me when I was waiting on the airfield for the next sortie. You really will think I'm mad, but I actually made a daisy chain once while I waited.'

Daisy looked at him. 'I can understand.' She decided not to say any more and instead prompted him to continue with what he needed to say.

'People are still trying to get home,' Tom said. 'If there is even a home for them to return to. Everything has been thrown into confusion and there are so many national interests at play.'

'So, what do you mean to do, Tom?'

'I have the opportunity to join the British delegation to the Paris Peace Talks. It would mean working in Paris for a few months at least.'

Daisy knew Tom was right and she sensed that if they were going to meet the future together as a couple they would have to deal with the past in their own ways as well.

Later that evening Ted and Tom retired to the study after dinner. Each man had questions of the other but first the lighting of the cigars allowed for thoughts to be better considered. Ted watched the young man and waited. Tom, taking his cue, spoke directly.

'I want to marry Daisy, sir. I think you know that but I would like us to wait. The war is still causing changes. There are still so many things to be agreed. I want to feel I am a part of that repair work. I've secured a position with the British delegation at the

Paris Peace talks.'

'Are you suggesting that you and Daisy would live abroad?'

'No. I want us to live here when we marry: after I'm finished in Paris. Is it possible that there would be a place for me to return to the business?'

Ted relaxed.

'Tom, I have always hoped that you and Daisy would marry. That has been our dearest wish. As for your view on the holding off the wedding, if Daisy is agreeable then so are we. I do have one request of you. When you talk of living here and being involved in the business, I would hope that you and Daisy would live here at Garraiblagh. Her mother and I are getting older and I want to make sure the estate my parents brought into being will continue. Marrying Daisy would also mean marrying the estate, Tom.' Both men drew on their cigars. Ted continued, 'I hope to retire and take a step back from business so that Florence and I can travel. The war made me realise that you can't take the future for granted. And now I don't know what may happen with this boundary issue in Ireland. It's all becoming so complicated.'

Florence had learned much during the war. She surprised herself. Outward appearance meant less to her now she had seen the world change for women. She was relieved that her daughter would never have to follow the restricted life that she had been brought up to. But it didn't stop her worrying about Daisy's future. Florence stood at the table in the window and rearranged the flowers in the vase. Daisy laughed.

'Mother! I do not think there are any more different ways for the flowers to be arranged. What is it that's bothering you?'

'Do not laugh at me, Daisy! I've tried very hard not to interfere and to ask what you intend to do and what the situation is with you and Tom, but I can't hold off any longer.'

'Very well, mother. Tom and I want to marry.'

'Oh, I am so glad, my dear!'

'But,' said Daisy, as she held up her hand to stay further comments from her mother, 'we have to wait while Tom is in Paris. He is to join the British delegation at the Peace Talks.'

'What will you do while Tom is working in Paris?'

'I've been thinking about that. I can't quietly sit about and wait for Tom to return. It is a new world now and too much happened in France. I want a career of my own which I can carry on even as a married woman. It is you, Mama, who has given me an idea. You know that I have always admired your art work and I think, I hope, that I have some of that talent. I have been drawing since Grandma died.' This time it was Florence's turn to laugh.

'Oh, my dear! I think that's perfect. I had always dabbled with paint and pencils, but it was only when your father suggested I make more of it and in a sense, make a job out of it in linen design, that I realised what a difference it made. Your father, I think, began to see me in a different light. If it hadn't been for your grandmother, whom I initially found so fearsome, I would never have considered drawing the plants around me. Garraiblagh and the gardens have a way of seducing one! But perhaps that is not an appropriate word to use.'

'I think it is, Mama. This estate and its gardens hold us all, the staff and the tenants as well as the family in good times and bad.'

Florence considered the conversation with her daughter. Life was precious. There had been so many deaths and so much change. She was still so scared of losing Daisy.

Chapter Thirty-one

1920

IT WAS CLEAR TO FRANK and his father that ever since Amelia Henderson's death, James had not been the same. His health had deteriorated and his mobility also was getting worse. He had been so enthusiastic about the setting up of the new nursery, advising and even physically assisting with some of the preparations and planting. Now it was almost as if he was willing the end to come, and had slipped into a world of his own. Rory and Frank tried to think how they could raise his spirits and in the end it was Alice who suggested a wheelchair tour of Garraiblagh. James refused all thoughts of a wheelchair. 'If I go back to Garraiblagh it will be on my own two legs!' he declared.

With the Hendersons permission, Rory and Frank accompanied James around the garden at Garraiblagh. James' spirits rose as he was walked slowly around, noticing his favourite plants, pointing out ones which needed attention and reminiscing about plants they had hunted for and brought back from India and other places. Being among the plants seemed to give James some peace. They noticed the gardeners gathering at the end of the path ahead of them. As they came down each man came forward to shake James' hand.

'It's an honour to have ye here amongst us again, Mr Black,' said Colin. 'We hope we're keepin' well, sir,' said Jack.

'It's good to see you all, men,' responded James. 'Ye have the place looking well, I have to say.'

'Mr Rory and Mrs Taggart keep us at it,' joked Davy, looking at Rory and Molly. They laughed and gradually drifted away to their work.

James asked to be allowed to sit by himself amidst the roses for a while. In his mind's eye he could see all the old hands gathered in front of him for his introductory speech fifty years ago. His friend, Freddy McPhee, Billy McGonigle, Ignatius O'Kane, Paddy Cleland, Kenny Jones, Tommy valley, William James, Mathew Armstrong, Johnson White and Willie McAlpin. He could still name them all. Most were no longer alive. And of course Amelia Henderson, standing at his side.

Ted and Florence had laid on afternoon tea for the three men and in the past, James would have looked forward to such an event however he remained quiet throughout. At one point Daisy caught James staring at her grandmother's portrait with a faraway smile. She fancied he was talking to Amelia.

James died peacefully in his sleep exactly a year after Amelia died. Letters from well-wishers and gardening contacts he had made around the world flooded in to the family. James was buried in the local churchyard. Rory and Frank followed James' request and planted one of the roses which he had created and named 'Amelia Henderson' on his grave, along with his favourite flower, the Scottish primrose.

The day that Daisy received the offer of a place at the Slade School of Art in London she began to pack. She wanted to begin this new chapter of her life as soon as possible, and there was, in the back of her head, the idea that Tom might at some stage be due some leave from Paris and at least be able to travel to London.

The move to London did not hold the fear for Daisy that it might have done had she gone to study there when she first left school. She walked through the streets, took the trams and the underground in her stride. Her time in France had done that for her. However the Slade School of Art itself was rather more intimidating and the first few months there were gruelling as she worked to perfect her drawing technique. The focus on life drawing with head and figure painting did hone her skills, but she knew that she wanted to paint nature, its plants and landscapes. Following a letter from Frank Black, she took his advice and went to Kew. In spite of her training at the Slade she spent most of the day sketching the plants, rather than the visitors.

Tom wrote long, amusing letters, describing the various officials and dignitaries he saw and with whom he worked, but underlying the humour there was seriousness about the complexity of the work being carried out. Then he wrote that he had been offered a post with the League of Nations.

'I'm coming to London before I start in Geneva. Please meet me? I need to explain.'

Daisy was very unsure how she felt. Was he ending their relationship? What was happening?

She waited for Tom at Victoria station as agreed, unsure how she felt and steeling herself to take any bad news as well as she could. It seemed to her that sitting watching the world go by that the ghosts of all the servicemen and women, who had passed through there on the way to France and back again, echoed in the coldness. She shivered.

Daisy realised how easily her eyes found Tom, amongst all the travellers getting off the boat train from Folkstone. Amidst the smoke and steam she saw him, hat pulled forward and his coat open as usual. She wanted him as badly as when she had first met him.

At dinner in the restaurant Tom talked of Paris and the personalities involved in the peace talks. She watched him as he moved his hands to describe what was happening. The excitement in his eyes was undeniable.

'You're quiet, Daisy?'

'Tom, tell me about this job with the League of Nations.'

Tom settled his hands on the table, watching Daisy.

'They need people to work in the different departments of the League. It helps that I have French and German and that my background in engineering is useful for reading maps and surveys.'

Tom took her hand.

'Daisy?'

' I can see that this is what you want, Tom. Perhaps you would prefer to reconsider our understanding? I would not want you to feel that I would hold you to that.'

Tom dropped her hand and moved back as though he'd been punched.

'Is that what you would wish?'

'No, but if you would, I would understand.'

Daisy, I love you.' Tom grasped both her hands. 'I want us to marry. Oh, I've handled this very badly. I was so excited about the work I didn't think it through.'

'You still want us to marry?'

'Of course! This post would keep me in Paris and Geneva for another year. Then I would be free to return. Would you be able to wait for me, my love?'

'Yes, Tom, I would, but will you want to return?'

'I give you my solemn promise, Daisy. At the end of the year I will return and we will be married. To that end I think we should make it official. Tomorrow we will buy an engagement ring and inform the families of our plans. I wonder if I will be able to get hold of my brother and book him for the end of the year. I'd like Patrick to be best man but he's due to travel to the Far East on medical duties.'

'Well, if we are already planning the wedding and you have your brother for best man I will have to decide on bridesmaids. I would like Molly to be matron of honour and perhaps Wenna would be a bridesmaid although it's a long way to travel from Cornwall to Belfast.

In London Daisy was also closer to Tom, whenever he obtained leave from the League of Nations. Her work grew, focusing on the development of her own style and technique. She was fascinated by the artists who painted flowers and landscapes. Redon's vases of flowers, the subtlety and size of Monet's water lilies, Klimt's jewel like combinations of pattern and colour, Mary Cassatt and then Mondrian's bright and stylised work.

On trips back home to Garraiblagh Daisy drew and painted and noticed aspects of her home that she had not seen before. She had already decided, with her parent's agreement that she could use the summer house as her studio and found when she returned home that, shelving and storage space had been built. A heater had also been installed for the colder times of the year.

While Daisy was sitting underneath the oak tree one day completing a water colour, Molly walked past.

'You look engrossed, Daisy!'

'Molly! Yes, I am. I've been thinking.'

'I want to make a garden! One for painting.'

Molly sat down beside her, taking off her hat and gloves and laying down her secateurs.

'You may not have noticed this, Daisy, but we're sitting in a series of very beautiful gardens!'

'I know it sounds odd, but since I've been drawing all the plants and views here I want something new.'

Molly looked around her and then commented, 'Mind you, I've been thinking for a while that some of Gertrude Jekyll's ideas would fit in well here. Perhaps there could be two aspects to your new garden, one formal and full of roses and another, wilder, more naturalistic but with lots of interesting plants so that you can do broader views and also more detailed pictures?'

Daisy put down her brush. 'Of course it is a beautiful garden, I know. But I think it needs some different shapes, a tunnel of roses or wisteria perhaps? I've also been experimenting painting wild garden areas with sweeps of coloured planting and dappled shade.'

Molly nodded in agreement. 'We can go and see the roses in Dickson's nursery. I've been thinking that there is room for a proper rose garden and there are so many new varieties as well as the old. We could work on some geometric shapes to place them in and I know Frank has been trailing some new varieties in his nursery. He's doing so well now. I know Kew have already asked him to take part in a new exhibition there.'

'I'm delighted for him. How are you getting on with the gardeners, Molly? It seems so long since you got the job.'

'They're fine now, Daisy. Initially there was a little unease at a woman taking over as assistant head gardener, but Rory was very helpful and I think they now see that I know my stuff.'

'Good. If you're free tomorrow evening, perhaps we could work out the plan to go down to Dickson's?'

'Definitely. Why don't you come round to the cottage and we can spend the evening catching up properly.'

The tweed jacketed figure of Rory Black was making his way along the path from the gate. Molly waited and went on cleaning the trowel.

'Good morning Mr Black! What can I do for you?' said Molly. 'I was just going to stop for a cup of tea, would you like one?'

Rory smiled at Molly.

'That would be very kind, thank you, Mrs Taggart.'

Molly watched Rory as he slowly drank his tea. He was usually quiet but today he seemed somehow different. She waited to see what he would say. Then, looking out of the window, a figure walking slowly past with a wheel barrow caught his attention.

'Is that young Ian Jameson?'

'Yes, it is, do you know him?'

'Aye, I knew him when he was a young lad' and Rory laughed. 'I'm surprised he's back here looking for a job!'

'Is there something I should know?'

'Nay, just a harmless childhood prank.'

Molly looked quizzically at him.

'I've just taken him on. He's been working in the Botanic Gardens in Belfast, but he was keen to move closer to home. I gather he's been walking out with Jessie, the parlour maid.'

'Well, I never! When he was a lad, he an' his friend, Paddy, came scrumping for apples an' they got quite a shock!'

'What happened?'

Rory recounted the episode.

'So, I shouldn't mention apples too often, not that I'm sure I'll be able to after what you've told me!'

'What happened to his friend Paddy? Do you know, Mr Black?'

'Aye, tragic. All the family died of the Spanish flu.' Rory stared into his tea.

'Oh, that's awful!' They sat in silence. 'How's the nursery going, Mr Black?'

'Well, we are getting a brave bit of interest from both sides of the new border and further afield. We're looking to take on someone else.'

'I hope you're not thinking of poaching anyone from here?

'I'll nae do that to ye Mrs Taggart. I'd have Master Ted and Miss Daisy to reckon with tae!'

Molly refilled their cups.

'I'm glad I work in a garden,' said Molly, relaxing in her chair. 'The world certainly hasn't settled down much after the war, has it?'

'Aye, well, at least we're not at Chatsworth,' said Rory.

'Why, what is happening there?'

'The Duke of Devonshire ordered the Great Conservatory to be blown up.'

'But that's one of Paxton's!'

'Aye, but the Duke evidently believed it was tae extravagant for these times. They had had difficulty heating it during the war and a brave few plants died.'

'At least our conservatory isn't going to suffer the same fate. At least I hope not.'

'Not as long as we're here, Mrs Taggart.'

Daisy walked down the sunken lane, following the wisps of lazy wood smoke and the sweet scent of apple wood to Molly's cottage. A mass of cottage garden plants overflowed through the wooden fence and made it difficult to close the gate. Molly heard Daisy approach and waved from the door.

'I suppose this is exactly what a gardener's garden is like! The plants have taken over the place while you are busy elsewhere.'

'Ha–ha! You're right. By the time I get home in the evenings I really don't have the energy to do anything here! What an awful admission. Come inside and have some tea.'

'How are you, Molly?' said Daisy as she watched her friend prepare the tea.

'Busy..... and enjoying it,' responded Molly as the kettle hissed on the stove.

'When ` I first trained I was so busy, so confident about the way forward, breaking new ground and finding a place for myself in the world after Edmund's death, I didn't think much beyond that. Then there was a time when I wondered if I was just hiding.'

'Hiding?'

'Yes, spending time doing something that I loved, but also focusing on nature, on gardening — not politics, not finding work that really matters. Staying safe. Plants don't ask awkward questions — at least not usually!'

'Go on?'

'Well, Edmund died in a war that I don't think he understood, who did? It made me angry that his innocent way of seeing things could be used, manipulated for the profit of others. It still makes me angry. If you ever notice a plant that has been pruned too closely it's probably because I've allowed myself to think too much. I wonder now, looking back whether we would have had much in common at the end of the war if he had survived and that makes me feel guilty. I suppose that must sound very harsh.... but I've had a lot of time to consider it while I work with the plants.'

'I can understand that, Molly.'

'I think what I have found about gardening is that I know I am part of something larger .... There are the seasons for planting and harvesting, the seasons for dying and quiet stillness. I think Edmund would have understood it this way. I know that I can only begin to make sense or manage what has happened by concentrating on the plants around me.....That does not mean I am religious. I left that behind.'

Daisy leant forward. The fire in the grate crackled. Looking at Molly she placed her cup and saucer on the small side table.

'When I was in France I thought I'd never know anything else. The mud, the gore, the cries from men so damaged I couldn't imagine their pain. My only way of coping was to think of Garraiblagh. Sometimes I felt guilty too.'

'Oh, why?'

'Guilty that I had a place like Garraiblagh to think about, somewhere that I could take my mind to when what I was seeing around me was so hideous, but then I began to listen to some of the soldiers. It was the everyday, simple, home things that they craved for and which comforted them. I remember one man who had been caught by a shell. There wasn't much left of him. The doctor patched him up, fed him morphine and I sat with him when I could. The smell of gangrene was everywhere. He wasn't conscious a lot of the time but on one occasion, when was he was near the end, he could smell roses and lilacs and he talked of his garden and seemed to imagine himself walking through it. For that short time he was peaceful.'

Daisy had withdrawn into her thoughts and her voice began to trail off.

Molly took her hand as Daisy continued.

'Then there were the gardens made by some of the men. I didn't see the ones they created in the trenches but I saw the small spaces they pulled together at the first aid centres. I know gardens are important Molly and what you do is important. If we lose touch with the earth I think we are doomed.'

The two women sat silently looking out into the fire, conjuring up their individual devils.

'We will make the painting garden, Daisy.'

Molly drew back the curtains and looked out of the window onto the flowerbed beneath where peonies flowers were being weighed down by the rain. It was one of those mornings, a greyed brightness with rain, but a clarity that almost hurt the eyes. She shook her shoulders as though to rid herself of thoughts and watched the rain drops trace their way down the window pane blurring the trees in the distance.

Daisy's visit had made her think. Not that what was bothering her was anything new. She realised that what she had said about Edmund was the first time she had openly voiced it to anyone.

Molly stroked her cat, Florry, who was also at the window watching for birds and being distracted by a bee making its way to some snapdragons.

'Well, Florry, the bees are out so the temperature must be reasonable, even if it's wet! It almost seems pointless to put on clothes when I'm probably going to get soaked, but I need to think and better out there than in here.'

Dressed and ready, Molly walked down the gravel path, enjoying the sound of its crunch beneath her feet, feeling the rain on her face. She kept her head down without consciously knowing where she was going.

The lawn was littered with the flower petals blown from the plants by the wind and rain. She reached the edge of the wood and then walked in under the cover of the trees. She stopped. The heady scent of the rhododendron and azaleas hit her. Looking up and around she was surrounded by reds, yellows, mauves and purples. She breathed in the scent, held in the moisture of the air like an insect caught in amber. Memories came flooding back. Her time in Dublin had been revealing. She'd learned so much about gardening and almost herself that she was still trying to understand.

Through one of her classmates, Deirdre, she had met Connor. Connor with the dark eyes, unruly curly hair and a deep love for his country, or what he wanted his country to become. Molly had felt the effects of one war and was clear she did not want to experience another and the death of another loved one. She had her own views on the pointless nature of war that Connor didn't share. But, she admitted, she had been flattered by his attention and had relished his friendship. They had met up a couple of times since she'd returned to Belfast. Connor, aware that tensions were high in both cities had suggested meeting in Newcastle where they had spent the day walking along the promenade and the lower paths of the Mourne mountains. Molly knew Connor wanted to be much more than a friend and, she had toyed with the idea. However the discussions with Daisy had clarified the issue for her.

A feather fluttered down landing on the ground in front of her, a fluffy white underbelly feather from one of the wood pigeons cooing in the tree tops.

'A time for truth,' she thought as she picked up the feather.

She did not want to marry again and she would have to tell Connor. Gardening was her love. It gave her a power and freedom, an occupation that she had only dreamt of in her suffragette days. Freed from the war and conventions of femininity, Molly felt more able to be herself in Garraiblagh and it felt good. She had learnt a lot. She knew now she did not want to become a wife again.

'Well, some women may have got the vote, but there's still a lot to do to ensure the rest of us get it. It's why I joined the Women's National Land Service Corps. We did well getting the land army going, but we in peace time we still need support to get women back on the land,' she mused.

Chapter Thirty-two

1922

TOM JUST MANAGED to board the train from Paris, his head still full of memoranda and discussion. He had been delighted to move on to work at the League of Nations after the Peace talks had finished. At the time it had felt important, a way of changing the world, but now he wasn't so sure.

Sitting back watching the Normandy countryside go past, he reflected on the people with whom he had worked. So many different nationalities, many of whom he now counted as his friends. Letters from Daisy and her father had warned him of the trouble at home, the impossible task of creating a boundary. He'd had enough of boundaries. The thought of more division in Ireland saddened him. At one point he had wondered if returning to Ireland had been the right thing and whether it might have been better to try and convince Daisy that they should move abroad to start a new life. However he realised that she would not willingly leave Garraiblagh and he had to admit that the place and the people had a hold over him as well. They would stay, but he was not going to compromise. He would tolerate no divisions in the workplace, no matter what.

Tom slept for most of the Calais to Dover sailing and by the time he disembarked from the boat train in London, he was exhausted. He'd already decided that he would stay in London before travelling over to Belfast. He wanted to be at his best when he met Daisy. It had been months since their last meeting and this next one was important with much to discuss.

Daisy was waiting for Tom at the docks. She had driven her new Austin down. In some ways it reminded her of their reunion after the war. She drove Tom through the gates of Garraiblagh and then stopped just beyond the gatehouse, placing the car just off the drive.'

'Why are we stopping here?'

'Wait and see,' said Daisy, 'and taking hold of Tom's hand drew him down a narrow woodland track. The glade of dappled sunlight had led to the old green door. The surrounding red brickwork was warm and sensuous as she leant back against it, feeling Tom's body against hers, urgent and seeking. Old traditions and manners had vanished in the hell of war as far as Daisy was concerned and Tom, her Tom, was back for good. Daisy held on to Tom's hand as she led him along the new paths and into her rose garden and painting garden.

She took him first to her painting garden. Drifts of colour spread across the ground in wild profusion and at the edge was the old standing stone around which Daisy had hung garlands of wild flowers. Near the old oak tree blue petalled meconopsis, seductively scented azaleas, astilbes and candelabra primula led into the small spinney and beyond the meadow was full of wild flowers, wanton and prolific. Tom dropped Daisy's hand and stood looking around him.

'It's magical, Daisy! I always thought of gardens as rather ordered and careful places. Pretty, yes, but not seductive and beautiful.'

Daisy took his hand and drew him towards her. 'I've been waiting for you for so long. The garden knows it. I love you Tom.' Daisy touched his face with her hand and kissed him. Tom's arms encircled her and then he was kissing her with a hunger she delighted in.

Daisy pulled away, breathless. 'Come with me.' And she led Tom to the summer house.

She opened the door aware of Tom's excitement. Cushions had been spread on the floor and a rug thrown across them. Tom lifted Daisy into his arms and carried her to the cushions.

'I want you, Daisy, I've wanted you for so long.'

'And I my love!'

Later, lazily rising from the cushions, Daisy tried without much success to straighten her dishevelled clothes. 'I've just remembered!'

'What?'

'I left a bottle of wine cooling at the edge of the stream and I've made a picnic!'

Tom rested his arm on the floor and brushed his hair out of his eyes.

'You are a very forward young woman my love! Wine chilling! Cushions on the floor!'

'I have been living in London remember, Among bohemian art students!'

Tom laughed. 'Yes, I had forgotten that. Well, show me the feast you have prepared and I'll see if I can keep my hands off you long enough to eat it!'

The garden was on its best behaviour. It had played its part and was excited for the future. The hypnotic scent from the roses and the quiet sound of a warm breeze through the grasses and leaves lulled the couple into sleep again.

As they lay in the grass later, looking up into a cloudless blue sky Tom watched a ladybird crawl over his hand and drop down onto some clover.

How could the world be so changed? He could still lie on the grass, hear the bees and see beauty all around in the natural world. The ground seemed so solid, and yet, looking at the sky Tom was back in his plane, flying over the remains of a battlefield — horses, humans, trees piled on a pock marked earth that was no longer solid. The contrast between sky and earth was stark.

Daisy felt the change in Tom. Deciding not to say anything, she put her hand on his shoulder and waited.

'I just had an awful memory of flying a particular mission. Daisy, how do we stop this horror happening again?'

For a long time they stayed lying there. Tom fell asleep once more. Daisy collected a sketchbook from the summer house, sat down and began to draw him. He awoke when a bee landed on his wrist.

'How long have I been asleep?'

'Not long and in any case I think you needed it.'

'Come on, I'll show you some of my paintings. We didn't seem to have time to look at them earlier, I can't imagine why,' she chuckled.

'I was being led astray by a Bohemian artist!'

Daisy walked back into the summer house. The warmth from the sun's rays through the windows highlighted the scent of turpentine and oil paint mixed with the smell of warm timber.

Two large canvases faced Tom. He was stunned. He realised that he had not actually seen much of Daisy's art work.

'Daisy, these are wonderful!'

Tom looked at the canvas on the left. It felt almost as though he had walked into one of the herbaceous borders. The colours and the shapes of the plants seemed to surround him. The right hand canvas featured a pond with water lilies.

Daisy, watching his eyes moving to the second canvas commented 'An unashamed copying of an idea from Mr Monet, but I like to think I have put my own twist on it.'

Tom crossed the studio and took Daisy in his arms. 'Daisy, how lucky am I to have such a talented fiancée! I am so proud!'

'So you like my garden and my studio, Tom?' she asked mischievously as she drew him to her once more. He needed no encouragement.

The wedding was arranged to take place in the local church with the reception in the grounds of Garraiblagh.

'Have you decided which flowers you want in your bouquet, Daisy, time is getting short!' queried Molly.

'I know I should be able to decide easily but there is so much choice. I don't want an old fashioned bouquet and, to add to everything I would like a small floral headdress. I know the fashion is for a lace cloche hat, but I would prefer flowers, perhaps as a circlet. Mother is keen for me to have a long veil and train so I'll ask for it to be embroidered with flowers at the edges. This is a lot of work Molly, I know!'

'It is, but it's much better that Garraiblagh provides the flowers for the church and the reception as well as for your bouquet. It would say very little for the garden if we couldn't do that. I'd never live it down!'

'I know you will create a beautiful bouquet for me, Molly. I have seen some bouquets which are really just like large stalks of lilies and others where it looks as though someone has gone into a florist, picked a lot of different flowers and thrown them together. I certainly do not want that.'

'And you definitely won't be having that if it means I have to throw away the bouquet myself,' said Molly.

'Now, have another cup of tea and a slice of that particularly nice lemon cake and let's get down to it.'

Between Daisy and Molly they sketched out drawings and shapes for the wedding flowers.

'I do like these!' announced Daisy, looking at a picture in a magazine, 'they're just what I want.'

Molly slid the picture over to her side of the table and looked at it.

'This would work well. Let's see which flowers it needs in more detail.'

'Roses and peonies for the larger elements with gardenia, stephanotis and lily of the valley, so mostly creamy whites with some very, very pale pink. Beautiful!' said Molly.

'Could the circlet for my head be made with tiny rosebuds and some greenery?'

'Yes, I think we can do that too.'

'Oh Molly, thank you!' and Daisy reached out to take hold of her friend's hand.

The wedding

Florence was in her element and set about showing Daisy pictures of the most fashionable dresses and trousseaus. In the end the simple lines of a white silk crepe dress with a long veil decorated around the edge with tiny white embroidered flowers was the choice agreed by Daisy and her mother. Her wedding gown was beautiful.

The garden was looking its best with the wide borders full of colour and scent.

Daisy had been happy to see Molly and Tom's brother, Patrick, chatting away together at the reception and mentioned it to Tom.

'Do not start any match making, Daisy. Apart from anything else you know that Patrick has his heart set on working in the Far East. He's probably not very good husband material.'

Tom had promised to show Daisy some of the places that he had frequented in Paris during his time there before they motored down to the south of France.

Molly saw the sports car rounding the bend towards her cottage and laughed, shaking her head. 'I don't believe it! You were on your honeymoon, Daisy!' The back of the car was full of interesting looking plants.

'And we had a wonderful time, Molly, but I couldn't resist buying some plants while we were there. You've no idea how difficult it was keeping them in good condition all the way home though.'

'Why don't you come in and tell me what you bought then we can take the plants over to the garden and sort them out.'

'A cup of tea would be wonderful! I have lavenders, irises and a jasmine. I brought home a bougainvillaea and I've put it straight into the conservatory. I'm hoping the others will manage in the garden?' Molly nodded adding that she would have to find a very sheltered position for the lavender.'

'Well, 1925 is going to be a momentous year,' Daisy said as she finished her breakfast coffee.

Why is that, love?' asked Tom rather absent mindedly.

'Because, my love, we are going to have a baby!'

Daisy concentrated on her art work. She had originally decided to complete three oil paintings of the Wild Garden over the first six months of the year. She hoped that at least one would be accepted by the Belfast Art Society for their exhibition in October. She hoped that by finishing them in the first six months of the year it would not clash with the baby's birth. In the end the idea of oil paintings had to be changed to watercolours of smaller areas of the garden. Daisy found that the smell of turpentine was making her feel sick.

Molly had the gardeners out watering the garden on a daily basis and even then the effect of the exceptionally dry weather could be seen to be having an impact. There was little time for conversation between Daisy and Molly except when Molly passed the summer house studio as Daisy worked.

She found the heat almost unbearable by the beginning of July and even walking down to the studio became irksome. So it was with relief that Daisy called Tom from the tennis court where he was playing a game with Patrick, his brother who had just returned from Singapore for a short break. Daisy had felt relaxed in the last few weeks knowing that there was a doctor, even if her brother in law, close at hand.

Daisy and Tom decided on the advice of the doctor that the birth would take place in the cottage hospital. Tom waited anxiously in the tiled corridor of the maternity unit, jumping every time he saw a nurse come towards him. The pregnancy had been without incident and Daisy had been finishing one of her large canvases, a painting of a rose, when the pains started.

Eventually a nurse came up to him, smiling.

'Come this way Mr Guthrie. Your wife is ready to see you now.'

'And the baby?' A sudden twist of fear pulled in his stomach.

'The baby is fine. A healthy little girl.'

'Could we call her Rose. Tom? I think she's just so perfect.'

'Let's show Rose the garden. The couple took Rose out in the pram on a tour of the garden with Daisy pointing out the various plants and Tom, watching the mowing machine told his baby daughter about the mowing machine and its mechanical parts.

Tom laughed. 'If Rose ever remembers any of the conversations we've had with her at this stage in her life she will be the most knowledgeable baby there is. Her first word might be 'delphinium'.'

'I remember my mother telling me that after I was born Grandma held me in her arms and took me to the window of the bedroom to show me the garden. Obviously I don't remember any of that, but I think there was something that connected me to the place, to the garden. It sounds stupid I know, but I want her to love Garraiblagh, for there to be continuity.'

Chapter Thirty-three

1926 — 1932

THINGS WERE CHANGING in the garden and outside. Molly enjoyed the teaching aspect of the role of head gardener. She had gained a reputation as someone who taught well and who had good connections for those who wished to move on to other places to further their careers. She limited her apprentices to one every two years reasoning that when an apprentice progressed and possibly moved on there was less disruption to the gardeners as a whole.

Paddy Wilson the new boy was certainly going to be entertaining. He was Belfast born and bred and sometimes she struggled to make out the strong Belfast dialect. She knew the others did too and it had already caused some hilarity at confused messages and instructions being delivered to the wrong person. But he was a good worker.

Rory and Frank's nursery was going from strength to strength. The land they had was only three miles down the road and Molly often took to her bicycle and rode down to see the latest plants and to get the newest horticultural gossip.

Frank's idea of concentrating on Irish plants was paying off. He and Rory had worked hard to produce good specimen plants and had also managed to create several new cultivars. On the birth of Rose Guthrie the Blacks had named a new rose, Rose Guthrie. Tom and Daisy had been delighted and had planted the shrub rose close to the summer house where the rose created by James Black and named after Amelia was planted. James Black's 'Amelia Henderson' rose was a deep. While 'Rose Guthrie' was a rosette shaped rose of the palest pink.

1927

'I do think it is the most beautiful flower, don't you? Himalayan Blue Poppy,' said Daisy admiring the new meconopsis that Molly had obtained. 'It's amazing to think that these poppies originate in the Himalayas. Perhaps we should have named Rose, Poppy.'

Tom laughed. 'I don't think she's going to be a Poppy somehow.'

'Blue poppy, meconopsis it sounds a little like Dumas's black tulip. As though wars might be fought over it. It certainly caused a sensation at the RHS spring show last year. I'm so glad that Molly and I were able to travel over to it and it's one of the advantages to having a mother and father here, even if they are only here part time. They are talking about moving to France full time you know,' said Daisy.

'Yes, your father was talking to me about it. They really do seem keen to do it. I don't think we've pushed them out of Garraiblagh, have we?'

'No, I don't,' said Daisy. 'Remember they wanted us to take on Garraiblagh when we married. No, I think they just want to travel and see more of France in particular.'

1931

Daisy breezed through the door into the kitchen.

'Good morning Mrs Johnson. I have something for you.'

Mrs Johnson turned from the range where she had been stirring a pot. Putting it aside she looked over at Daisy.

Daisy handed over the book. 'I got this from a friend of mine in New York. She says it's the newest thing, very fashionable.'

Mrs Johnson picked up the book and looked at it. Vegetable Cookery by Mrs Lucas.

'A book on cookin' vegetables, Mrs Guthrie? Am I not cookin' the food to your satisfaction? I was readin' about this. I don't hold with this American way of using the vegetables when they are only half grown! It's wasteful, that's what it is and there's hardly a mouthful in each vegetable! Mrs Taggart and me were havin' a conversation about it the other day. She says she thinks it's wrong to pick the vegetables before their prime.'

She could see that Daisy was about to contradict her and held fast.

Mrs Johnston liked Daisy and she, along with the rest of the household had admired her for becoming a nurse in the war. Mrs Johnson could see the resemblance to Mrs Amelia. But she was not going to be peeling baby carrots and leeks for anyone.

'I thought you might like to have it, just as reference, obviously.' Daisy saw Mrs Johnson's eyebrow raise as she turned the pages of the book, as though she was likely to find some unsavoury images hidden within it. Daisy knew when she was beaten. Smiling broadly she changed the subject.

'The Inglis and Smiths are coming to dinner. 'Mrs Taggart has informed me that the first tips of asparagus are ready. Could we have a soufflé with them, Mrs Johnson?'

'Aye, of course, Mrs Guthrie and I thought a rhubarb sorbet?'

'Wonderful — and with some of those exquisite biscuits you make?' said Daisy, knowing that whatever her hope of seeing tiny, newly grown vegetables presented on exquisite platters for dinner parties, it wasn't going to happen.

October 1932

Tom's journey to and from the mill and the shipyards left him feeling on edge.

'It feels as though I live in two different worlds,' he sighed as he and Daisy sat beside the lily pond watching Rose trying to reach the goldfish, her hands outstretched.

'When I'm in town there's a very ugly atmosphere and we are part of the problem I know that. I am trying our best. I'm having as many arguments with fellow mill owners as I am with workers. I swore when I returned here after working in the League of Nations that I would not stand any division. I take workers on who can do the jobs, I don't care what religion they are. But now it's about pay. I am paying what I can. I can do no more. Coming back to Garraiblagh I am in a place of peace. But I don't know how all this is going to end. Will these people turn up at our gates one day?'

Daisy took his hand

'If we didn't live here and you hadn't come back to take on the business we would be free of this. Is that what you're thinking?'

'I belong here, Daisy but I am not sure how much more of the business I can manage. I'm still an engineer by training and, well, we'll see how it goes. I don't want to let your father down, or you.'

Over the next few months tensions increased. Riots broke out again in Belfast. This time Catholics and Protestants were on the same side against the employers.

'Tom, what are you doing with the gun?'

'Daisy, things are pretty crazy in town. I need to make sure I can protect our family. From now on I'm bringing the revolver into the bedroom.'

'Are things that bad?'

'I just don't know but I don't want to find out. We're a bit more isolated here but...'

There was no moon. It was one of the blackest nights Tom had experienced. He wasn't sleeping well and when he did sleep his dreams became nightmares. He thought he'd gone through the worst he could imagine during the war but this tension, the business, the politics, religion. It was not the post-war world he had hoped for.

Even in the dark Tom knew that someone was trying to get in through the window. Tom raised the revolver and fired. The sound was deafening. The figure fell from the window sill.

'Oh God Tom you've killed him,' screamed Daisy.

Tom raced to the window but could not see anything. Taking the gun with him he ran down the stairs and out through the door to the area beneath the bedroom window.

There on the ground lay the body. The body of Daisy's ancient teddy bear shot through the heart.

Molly came round the corner from the back of the house just in time to see Tom lift up the bear and start laughing with relief.

Chapter Thirty-four

January 1935

THE SNOWDROPS WERE EARLY. One minute there were only leaves and grass creating mulch under the trees on the drive and then suddenly small green spikes, white topped and dew covered leading the eye towards the bright white petals and green stems of full snowdrops.

The lunar eclipse was bringing change.

Paddy Wilson looked around him. He'd come to love the place. It would be a wrench leaving the gardens at Garraiblagh, but needs must he thought. The offer from the Botanic Gardens in Belfast meant that he could continue his interest in greenhouse plants and at the same time rent a small place in the city and marry. At twenty-three years old he felt he'd been gardening all his life, and in a sense he had. His father had been a jobbing gardener and Paddy had picked up his love of plants early on.

'So, your last day then Paddy?' said Molly. 'I'll be sorry to see you go, but I know it's an offer you can't refuse.'

'Thanks Mrs Taggart. I've enjoyed workin' here, but ye know

Cathleen has her family out near Milltown an' havin' family nearby when ye hope t' raise your own is wile helpful.'

'Well, remember Paddy, if you ever change your mind...'

'I will, Mrs Taggart. I'd best be off.'

Paddy's departure left Molly one gardener down. Working in estates was becoming less sought after with more municipal parks and gardens and even larger private gardens opening up all requiring gardeners. She knew that she could advertise for a more experienced gardener to fill the position but, she thought to herself, 'I do enjoy teaching. Perhaps it would be better to recruit another apprentice gardener?'

Eileen Boyle buttoned up her coat and tightened the belt and adjusted her beret. With school finished she had started work at what she considered to be the very adult age of fourteen. Working in the kitchen at Garraiblagh she was bringing home money.

'I'm away now, Ma. I'll see ye later.' She shouted up to her mother still in bed. Eileen cycled along the lanes towards Garraiblagh. The whitethorn was out and the hedgerows looked as though they were covered in intricate white lace, like the lace her grandmother made. She knew the plants in the hedgerow and liked to see the different plants change through the seasons. Eileen knew she'd been lucky to get a job so close to home. Her mother had lost heart after the death of her husband in an accident on the farm ten years ago. Two of her older brothers had found the atmosphere at home so bad they had looked for work elsewhere: one going as far as Dublin. Her eldest brother ran the farm but his heart wasn't in it. It barely made ends meet. Despite the situation at home Eileen was content and now proud to be bringing some money home.

She considered her family as she cycled. She wasn't sure how her great-grandmother Bridie would have felt about her getting a job at Garraiblagh. Eileen had been told Bridie hadn't believed in bowing and scraping to people just because they had a big house and she'd heard that Bridie had had a couple of run-ins with the family in her day. Bridie had only died a few years ago and while she was still at the farm she ruled everything.

It was six o'clock when Eileen leant the bicycle against the kitchen wall and walked in.

'Mornin', Mrs Johnston.' She wrapped the large white apron around her and began to scrub the kitchen table. She worked a long day, made longer by the bicycle journey home, but she didn't mind being outside, whatever the weather. When she got any free moments, Eileen wandered down to the kitchen garden. She was intrigued by Mrs Taggart, the head gardener. The gardeners all followed her instructions to the letter and respected her. She knew that from the conversations the gardeners had with Mrs Johnson when they brought fruit or vegetables up to the kitchen.

Eileen had been considering how to pluck up the courage to speak to Mrs Taggart outside the kitchen when the opportunity just happened.

'Mrs Taggart?'

'Hello, Eileen! said Molly, smiling at the young girl.

'How did ye become a gardener?'

'I trained in Dublin, but I also had done a lot of practical gardening before then. Why do you ask?'

'I'd like to become a gardener.'

'But you're working in the kitchen. Is that not where you want to be?'

Molly bit her tongue. She wished she hadn't said that. What an assumption to make, as though everyone had a choice in what they worked at.

'If you're really interested in gardening Eileen I'll give you a book to read. That would be the first step. Come round to the garden office on your way home this evening and I'll look out the book for you.'

'Ye have had a smile on ye face all day like the cat that has go the cream, Eileen! What are ye at?' asked Mrs Johnson. Eileen looked at the cook, suddenly serious. 'Nothin', nothin', Mrs Johnson.'

'I'm nae complaining, ye know. It's nice tae have a body happy in their work!'

Eileen knocked on the bothy door, suddenly feeling uncertain. She could see a light on in the building and heard a conversation. She wondered whether she should just leave. Perhaps it was a stupid idea. Suddenly the door flew open and a man, one of the gardeners Eileen presumed, hurried out. Eileen knocked on the open door. 'Come in, Eileen, come in. I have the book here.'

Molly was curious. Despite the fact that she taught apprentice gardeners in the garden she had never been asked to take on a girl. Eileen asking about gardening had made her consider things. She realised that while she had trained and been one of a group of female gardeners leading the way earlier in the century, for many not much had changed.

'When you finish the book come back to me and we can talk again and I'll show you around the garden, let you see the sort of work that is involved.' said Molly.

'Thank you Mrs Taggart, thank you!' said Eileen. 'It's just a book, Eileen, just the beginning. We'll talk more when you come back.' Eileen said goodbye to Molly and left with the book carefully wrapped up in her bicycle basket.

A week later Molly was walking back to her cottage when she heard the sound of bicycle tyres on the lane.

'Mrs Taggart!'

Molly turned to see Eileen dismounting from her bike and walking it towards her.

'Mrs Taggart, I'm sorry to disturb you but I've finished the book and wanted to return it.'

'Well, Eileen what did you think?'

'I think I'd like to train to be a gardener, Mrs Taggart. Can you help me?'

'Being a gardener involves long hours and a lot of hard work, some of it quite physical, Eileen.'

'I can do it Mrs Taggart, I know I can. I help out at home in the fields. I know what it's like to work hard. My brothers didn't make it easy for me being a girl.'

Molly looked at the young girl. 'Very well, I'll take you on as an apprentice if your family are agreeable.' She would have to stand by her principles of equality for women and realised that she had become rather forgetful of those principles over the years.

Eileen arrived on her bicycle ready for work in the garden. Mrs Johnson had been a little annoyed to lose a good worker and for a short while there was a certain frostiness in relations when Molly came into the kitchen with the fruit and vegetables. Eileen's mother agreed to her daughter's change in work with little comment. Molly had told the other gardeners that Eileen would be starting in the garden. They did not comment, but the expressions on their faces told her what she needed to know. They did not believe a young girl could manage. It made Molly wonder how they saw her. Had they, over the years forgotten she was a woman? She thought wryly that probably was the case.

Initially Molly kept Eileen working with her, partly to see how much she could handle physically and also to start her instruction. If she was going to have a female apprentice then she was going to make sure she did well.

Eileen took to the garden work as though she'd been born to it. Having older brothers also meant that she was not fazed by working with the men though Molly kept a close eye on how they treated Eileen.

Daisy spent much of the week in the studio. Her paintings were now much sought after. Her style had changed since the early flower and garden paintings she made after her return from London. She now painted and drew in pastels with a confidence that allowed her to create images of gardens and garden life as well as more detailed studies of flowers and general still lives. She submitted her work in the annual

Collectors also came to visit her in the summer house studio and gallery, the summer house itself becoming well–known among fellow artists and dealers. Daisy was reaching a point in her career where she could ask large sums of money for her work and she was being invited to exhibit both locally and further afield.

Rose was not impressed. 'Do you have to go over to London again, Mum? It's only another exhibition.'

'I will only be gone a couple of days, Rose and Mrs Johnson and Daddy will be here.'

'Couldn't I come with you?' pleaded Rose. Daisy hesitated. Perhaps Rose did miss out. There was school, but was her daughter unhappy?

'I'll think about it, Rose.'

'You always say that and then nothing happens. You don't mean it.'

'I will think about it and I'll talk to your father.'

Daisy tackled Tom about it that evening after dinner. 'Tom. Do we, do I, not spend enough time with Rose?'

'What brought this on, Daisy?'

'Rose asked me if she could come with me to London, you know the exhibition I have work hanging in next week.'

'Well, I suppose sometimes she may feel a little left out. Your painting is fairly full time.'

'I suppose so, but I try to get her involved. I set up the little easel so that she could work beside me in the studio.'

Mm, I don't think she is a budding painter somehow. She prefers the social life. I'm no better, Daisy. When I suggest she helps me with something she looks as though I've just suggested she will never be allowed to eat cake again.'

'Why don't you take her. She's ten now and would manage the trip well enough.'

The trip was a success. Daisy's work was well reviewed and from Rose's point of view, it was everything she hoped a trip to London would be. Daisy took her shopping for a special dress to wear to the exhibition opening and an opportunity to spend time going around the large London shops left Rose breathless with excitement. 'Why can't we live in London, Mum. There's so much to do.'

Instead of Rose settling down after her trip to London it seemed to just increase her desire to be anywhere rather than home. The phrase, 'It's so boring here' echoed through the summer months while Daisy and Tom gritted their teeth and arranged for Rose's friends to come and play tennis with her.

And the summer at Garraiblagh was glorious. The garden was at its best and there seemed to be a permanent shimmering heat haze over the lough in the distance. Peonies and roses in deep reds and crimsons jostled with delphiniums and hollyhocks in the borders. The trees behind deep were green, their leaves hardly moving in the sun. It was a summer for relaxing and for once Daisy and Tom took time off from their work, inviting friends for the weekend and having afternoon tea on the lawn.

Everything in the garden seemed calm and settled, the only sound being croquet mallets echoing across the grass. The garden was a place where time could stand still, where humans and plants could bask in a sense of permanence.

Rose stroked the tabby cat lying on her lap. She had gone to Molly's cottage as she often did.

'Aunt Molly, why do you like gardening?'

'Gosh, that's a question! Have a biscuit while I think about it.'

Molly pushed the biscuit tin towards Rose. Rose looked in and picked out one of the chocolate coated shortbreads. She looked at Rose's serious face, brown hair in plaits tied with ribbons, a carefully chosen summer dress and cardigan. Not for the first time Molly considered the differences between Rose and her mother, Daisy. Knowing Rose, this was not the real question or rather, not the main issue.

'I think I feel at home in the garden. I love plants — their colours, the scents, and the differences, there's always something new and there's a pattern to things. It is reassuring in a way I suppose.'

Rose's head was bent as she carefully stroked Tiger the cat, and then she lifted her head, picked up the glass of orange squash, but apparently thinking better of it replaced it on the table.

'Have you ever lived in a city?'

'Yes,' said Molly, 'when I was I was younger I lived in Belfast and when I was training I lived in Dublin. Why do you ask?'

'I was just wondering...'

Molly stopped herself from saying anything further and instead, offered Rose the biscuit tin again and waited. The biscuit was chosen and nibbled.

'You know your mother named you Rose after her favourite

flower.'

'But it's a flower! Everything is about flowers or plants or gardens! My friend Sarah lives in Belfast. Her mother doesn't talk about painting and plants all the time. Her mother takes her out into town for ice cream and things.'

'Is she the girl who sometimes comes to stay?' asked Molly, playing for time as she wondered what was going to come next.

'Yes, she does come to stay but she doesn't really like it here. She says it's too quiet.' Rose took a bite of biscuit and added, 'I don't think I'm a person who likes the quiet either. I think I'm a city person.'

'Have you told your mother?'

'No, not really. She wouldn't listen anyway or she'd just tell me 'there are lots of things to do here and I should be grateful.'

Molly smothered a smile as Rose mimicked her mother's voice so well.

'I know you're not my 'real' aunt but you are really.' Rose looked at Molly pleadingly. 'Please could you talk to Mummy?'

'What about, Rose?'

'Tell her I want to, tell her I.....,'

'Tell her you want what?'

'I want to go away to school, to be with others of my own age. I want to have fun.'

'Some people don't like going away to school, you know. How do you know it would be fun?'

'It would be.'

'And if it wasn't?'

'I would make sure it was fun,' said Rose determinedly.

'I'll talk to your mother, Rose but you know I can't guarantee anything.'

'I know, but please talk to her.'

Rose hesitated for a moment as she opened the wooden gate

onto the lane from Molly's cottage. She looked back at Molly who was standing in the doorway, holding Tiger.

'Do you know, Auntie Molly, I sometimes think there's a ghost here in the garden.'

Before Molly could ask anything Rose has skipped off along the lane, waving to her from a distance.

Molly poured herself another cup of tea.

'Well! I think I need a biscuit!' she said to Tiger.

'I need to speak to Daisy. A ghost eh? It's odd but I have often wondered too. Either a ghost or a malicious fairy. The tools keep getting moved. What about you, Tiger?'

Tiger stretched and lay back on the cushion.

'Have ye seen Philip? He's not back,' said Matt, coming in from the garden.

'Where was he goin', Matt?' asked Colin, only half listening as he busily oiled the hedge cutters. He was used to Matt getting into a bit of a state about things. Matt always seemed to need to know where everyone was, to make sure they were alright. A bit like a human sheepdog Colin thought.

'He went down into Belfast to see his parents yesterday. He was worried about them,' said Matt rather impatiently.

Colin shook his head. 'Mrs Taggart won't be best pleased if he misses work. Let's hope he gets back before mornin'.'

'That's just it, Colin. Ye know Philip, he's not wan' to be late. It's not like him.'

Philip dragged himself further into the hedgerow. It was cold or at least he felt cold. He knew he shouldn't have taken the short cut from his parents' house, but he'd been worried about being late back to Garraiblagh. At least his mother had liked her geranium. He'd been cultivating it for the last few months, feeding it and potting it on and he'd told her that there weren't too many others like it around. Philip tried to concentrate on his mother's face, her happiness at seeing him and the pleasure at the plant. He pulled himself to a sitting position with difficulty. There was a stab of pain from his ribs and he could feel the warmth of blood running down his face. Sickness suddenly overcame him and he vomited into the hedgerow. Philip started to shake as he thought of the men who'd surrounded him, closed in on him as they saw that he wasn't one of them. He'd hoped he could visit his parents quietly. He'd heard about the riots and the deaths but his need to make sure his parents were alright was too strong.

'Aye, it's not like him,' said Matt. 'Somethin's happened. I think we should tell Mrs Taggart.'

Colin reluctantly accompanied Matt to find Molly.

'I think you're right Matt. It is unlike Philip.' said Molly. 'The rioting down in Belfast has been bad. I just hope he hasn't got caught up in it. What time was he due back, do you know?'

Matt answered quickly. 'He shoulda been back this two hour, Mrs Taggart.'

'It's still light. I'm going to ask Mrs Guthrie if I can borrow the car. I think the best thing will be to drive down towards Belfast and see if he's on the road somewhere. If things are bad he may have had to walk.'

Molly arrived back at the lane behind the gardener's cottage in the car. To Matt and Colin's surprise Mrs Daisy was driving.

'Right, let's go. Something tells me time is of the essence.'

'Wha? Ye wan' us to get in, Mrs?' asked Matt as he and Colin stood looking worriedly at the car.

'Of course,' said Molly

'Mrs Daisy are ye alright wi' that wheel there?' asked Colin. 'An' have ye a way for stoppin' this yoke?'

'It's perfectly safe Colin I assure you. I've driven a car many times.' said Daisy suppressing a laugh.

'Well now ...' began Colin.

'If you two don't get in we'll go ourselves,' said Molly.

'Alright, alright, Mrs. We're comin'.'

It took several minutes to guide the two men into the back seat where they sat holding on grimly to the back of the front seat.

The car turned on to the road towards Belfast. Driving slowly the four people looked out for Philip. They were coming close to the outskirts of the city when Colin called out.

'Over yonder! It's him, I'm sure o' it.'

Daisy drove the car over to the high-banked road edge. The two men scrambled clumsily out of the car. Matt ran to Philip's side. 'He's alive!'

Daisy, putting into action her nursing training from the war checked him quickly. 'I think he may have broken ribs. Quick, let's get him into the car and out of here. We don't know when he was injured. There could be people close by.'

As Colin and Matt arranged Philip between them on the back seat as Molly directed Daisy in turning the car.

Back at Garraiblagh Daisy directed the men to bring Philip into the house where he was put to bed and the doctor called.

'Broken ribs and a nasty gash on the head. He really shouldn't be going anywhere for a while. It looks as though he's been lucky. Although I'm sure that's not how he feels at the moment. If he'd been left for much longer before you found him it would have been a very different story. I'll leave him in your capable hands, Mrs Guthrie.'

Watching the doctor drive off Daisy turned to Molly. 'It's times like this I realise that Garraiblagh is not separate from the rest of the world, no matter how much I might like it to be.'.

Chapter Thirty-five

1936 — 1938

SUNLIGHT WAS STREAMING through the drawing room window when Daisy flopped down on the couch. The brightness of the day outside seemed at variance with the downcast look on her face. Tom, happily reading with his feet up looked over but kept on reading. She would tell him soon enough if it was important.

Daisy sat forward, resting her forearms on her thighs, her hands clasped. 'I think you're right, Tom it's time to look at our finances. I've been selfish assuming everything could just go on as it always has.'

Tom sat up. After their last discussion on the business he wasn't sure what the next step would be. At least Daisy had been thinking about it.

'Let's talk about it then,' said Tom, eager to seize the opportunity. 'The home farm and its herd are good, the scutching mill is really only making a slight profit. Your work is selling, your paintings and your botanical illustrations though that can't be seen as a regular income. Then of course there are the mills and the ships.'

'You want to talk about the business as well?'

Daisy waited for Tom to continue. 'It has to be a part of it. I would like to sell our shipping interests and, this may be more difficult, Daisy. I think we need to look at the number of people we have working in the house and garden.'

'Oh dear, I can understand the need to change the business Tom, but change things in the garden. Why?'

'The war changed so much and then the Depression. Trade hasn't really come back. The estate is a big overhead. The garden is changing, Daisy, you know that. It changed because of the war and your grandmother's death. It changed afterwards too. We don't entertain in the way your grandparents or even your parents did. And as far as I know, you are not asking Molly to ensure you have corsages for all the dances we don't attend!'

'No, that's true, I suppose I hadn't really thought about it too much or hadn't really wanted to.'

'Mr Finlay the chauffeur went some time ago and we haven't had a butler since the war. The garden has.....' Daisy could feel herself becoming agitated. Yes, she'd wanted the discussion about the business and the estate. But the garden; it wasn't just a piece of land to her, it was a living being.

Daisy tried to sound calm. 'I think we need to consider the garden carefully Tom. The garden provides us with much of our food as much as anything.'

'That's true but a lot of the garden doesn't provide us with food. It's beautiful but it doesn't pay the bills, Daisy.'

'It is its very beauty that I use to create my art work, Tom. Don't forget that. My work is known as far away as London for its association with Garraiblagh.' Daisy didn't know how much more of this conversation she could take. She had started it but now she didn't know where it was going to end.

'I love the garden too, Daisy but we need to consider its future.'

'You mean leave Garraiblagh altogether, Tom?'

'No, but can we garden it differently?'

'I'll talk to Molly,' said Daisy. She wasn't sure what she would say. She wasn't even sure she wanted to have any conversation with Molly. She was angry with Tom for raising the issue of the garden.

'It's odd, synchronicity perhaps,' said Molly. 'I've been thinking about the garden and how it's changed, even since the time I started here. Styles have changed in garden design. The kitchen garden is still a hive of activity though we're not growing as many exotic plants as we did before. The huge Victorian feasts involving goodness knows how many courses no longer happen. There are new varieties of fruit and vegetables coming out which is interesting and there are still modern–day plant huntings bringing back new varieties. Garraiblagh is still a private garden and I assume you and Tom want out to stay that way?'

'Yes, why? Do you have an idea?'

'It's just something I've been thinking about for the last while. You know young Eileen our only female gardener?'

Yes,' laughed Daisy. 'I don't think Mrs Johnston has ever quite forgiven you for taking her away from the kitchen!'

'I know — well, anyway, Eileen has proved herself to be very skilled. She is working towards the National certificate in Elementary Horticulture and I think she will continue with the RHS qualification. Taking Eileen on in the garden has made me think again about women and horticulture. And within The Women Farm and Garden Association we've also been having discussions about horticultural training for women. It's now quite difficult to find gardens to train in but there are some private gardens where women gardeners can be taken on. They pay for their board and training and complete the RHS examinations.'

Daisy listened intently. 'Are you thinking that we could provide training for women gardeners here at Garraiblagh?'

Well, it might be an idea. It could certainly be a way of helping the garden pay for itself. Some places charge one hundred guineas a year!'

'That sounds interesting Molly but how would we work the accommodation and meals?' Perhaps the living accommodation over the stables where the chauffeur and the stable hands lived could be revamped? And, dare I say it. Perhaps Mrs Johnson would relish cooking for some more people, if she had help? There would be one proviso that I would make though.'

'What would that be, Molly?'

'That for every three students who were fee paying we would take one female student who could not afford the fees.'

1937

Daisy felt numb as she watched the raindrops run down the window panes. It was cool in the dining room and quiet. She had wanted somewhere to be quiet, on her own. Tom had left yesterday shortly after they had received the telegram. He would manage the arrangements from France.

Her parents, Ted and Florence were both dead. Killed in a car accident in the south of France. The news was still circling around in her head. She didn't want to think about it deeply. She'd dealt with a lot of death, but this was different in its unexpected nature. She'd only had a letter from them a few days ago, full of their travels and a forthcoming trip to the medieval city of Carcasonne. Daisy pressed her forehead against the glass and let the tears roll down her face. She could hear the wind swirling through the trees on the drive. A pale moon was still high in the early morning sky.

Her parents had longed for some hot weather and they had been having such a good time in France. Daisy shivered. It wasn't a cold day, but the wind was certainly suggesting more bad weather to come. A flash of white on the lawn showed the snowdrops beginning to flower. She tried hard to focus on their beauty but couldn't.

Ted and Florence were buried in the family plot. Daisy tried hard to banish the repeated thought during the funeral that this was where she and Tom would end up. Ironically this grim reality was one of the few certainties in life.

The butterfly landed on the drawing paper in front of her, its wings pulsing as though it had landed on a flower instead of the image of one that Daisy was creating. She took it as a great compliment. Its slight noise brought her back to the present and she looked up. There was another butterfly hovering above a mauve coloured wallflower, weaving its way up the plant and then on to the top of the border, landing on a buddleia. Daisy half closed her eyes and then used her hand to shield her eyes, as though trying to see beyond the garden and the present to the future. Things happening in the outside world were ominous. She had a sudden picture of her parents, a glimpse of them smiling, words they had written, the adventures in France they had described. Muffled voices hung in the still air. A shout from a gruff voice broke the quiet. She dropped her paper on the seat beside her and stood up. Willow, the spaniel had disturbed a leveret sheltering under the leaves of a gunnera plant and was determined to chase it.

'Come here, Willow, bad dog!' Daisy shouted. Her voice sounding louder than she'd meant to. No more death, she thought. Daisy knew the war had left its mark in many ways and the death of her parents was still raw. She still had mixed feelings about her parents' will which had left money for the preservation and upkeep of the gardens and the estate. This became part of a fund that her grandparents had created. Money that Daisy hadn't known about and it made her feel guilty that her parents' deaths had secured the garden's future at least for the foreseeable future.

July 1938

A deep shimmering heat haze lay over the lough where several yachts floated with sails aloft like butterflies. The sound of the lawn mower confirmed that the tennis court would soon be rolled ready for the weekend. Daisy could see Maud the maid bringing the tray of tea out to the lawn.

This exquisite weather made Daisy lazy. What more was there to do than relax and read at the wicker table and chairs set in the arbour. The scent of carnations and pink centred roses filled the air. Daisy had often wondered how the scents from the garden could be bottled.

Lounging in her wide brimmed hat Daisy watched the game of croquet. The sound of the mallets against the balls had that satisfying sound. She could see Tom was struggling to beat Rose and her friends. Daisy chuckled to herself.

Croquet, inconsequential, superficial, like the conversations increasingly taking place at dinner parties and even in some newspapers. Conversations that felt as though they went so far, hovered over a precipice and then withdrew to safety. Poppies had appeared in the field in this hot summer beyond the formal garden and Daisy's mind was pulled, unwillingly, into thoughts of war. They'd said the last one would be the war to end all wars. She remembered the daisy she'd wept over at the dressing station in France. So many had been lost in the last war but now there was increasing talk in the newspapers of Herr Hitler, the German chancellor. Daisy had heard that gas masks were being distributed in England. It felt suffocating. There was an inevitability to it all which she didn't want to accept.

Putting down her book, she got up and walked across the lawn to the herbaceous border. The sound of the bees was almost deafening. The blue and purple delphiniums and pinky rose of the peonies, with their bright vital colours and large shapes, seemed so sure of themselves, so confident of their future. She was glad that they had decided to add the lupins. Their spikes ranged through almost every colour and jostled for position among the other tall plants. Daisy touched them as if hoping their strength and colour would transmit to her and reassure her. Their colours and shapes given an added strength from the brick wall behind them. Daisy relaxed, her shoulders lowering as she tuned in to the hypnotic sound of bees moving from flower to flower.

Simon the cat stretched his body and honed his claws on the bark of the wooden upright of the arbour. His routine scratching had left gouges in the wood. Now he watched the birds as only a cat can, crouched amidst the philadelphus in their huge stone pots.

Willow, the black spaniel, had a daily patrol around the gardens, checking the new scents around the gates, laying down his own markers for unknown predators and rivals. Chasing Simon the cat was an added bonus which Simon himself enjoyed. Willow kept a selection of tennis balls and bones in his favourite hide out in case of need. Lying on the lawn he raised his nose to the air and smelled the human and animal scents and beyond that, the tantalising smell of food being prepared. Nose down and long ears flapping, he unwittingly carried the seeds of many plants to new places. When burrs covered his ears and coat he angrily pulled at them with his claws. The ground received these new intruders, interested to see how they would fit in.

Burdocks found their way into the herbaceous borders, ingratiating themselves, pretending to be inconsequential. Hoping not to be seen by a keen eyed gardener, they settled themselves and then became more demanding. By the time their burrs were full size, they had pushed other less robust plants out of the way.

There was a silent ongoing battle between the wild and the cultivated plants. The dandelions caught in the gentle wind spread their seeds across the garden, lodging, but only briefly, in the well weeded flowerbeds. Since the decision had been made to reduce the number of gardeners there had been fewer eyes ready to pounce on an unwary weed.

Clapping echoed from the lawn and Tom threw the mallet on the ground as he lowered himself into the deckchair.

'Beaten again! I'm going to have to improve!' laughed Tom.

'We beat Daddy again! Can we have a biscuit Mummy?'

'Rose, dear, would you take the baskets and go and collect raspberries please.'

'Can't Ned or Colin do it? We want to play a game of tennis.'

'No, they're busy and you are quite capable of picking raspberries. Off you go.'

Daisy shouted after her, 'Remember the sooner they're picked, the sooner Mrs Jessop can make the jelly.'

'Oh yes, with ice cream? And can I choose the mould? Please, a biscuit now, and then we'll be able to pick raspberries so much better.'

'Very well, there's lemon barley water there as well. You must be thirsty.'

The children ran to the biscuits leaving Daisy and Tom.

'Well, darling, how's your book?'

Daisy grimaced. 'Actually Tom, I haven't read much of it. It's odd. Everything here is so settled. It's sunny. We're having afternoon tea in the garden. Everything seems safe and secure in our wee world and yet there is trouble coming, isn't there? I haven't really wanted to admit it, either to myself, or you. The headlines are full of war in Spain and in Europe generally. It seems that each day something is happening that brings us closer to war. We need something to brighten us all up. We haven't had a Garraiblagh fête since before the war. They were fun! I was talking to Mrs Maitland in the shop the other day and she was voicing the same feelings. What do you think?'

'Well,' responded Tom, 'the economic situation isn't that positive at the moment. We're in the lucky position that I'm able to do some consulting and you are selling your paintings and teaching the occasional class. Without the kitchen garden and your family's legacy it would be hard to manage everything. I'm glad we've been able to keep the home farm on under our control — at least for the present.'

'I know it's difficult but I just think people need a lift, something to take their minds off the news,' said Daisy

'What are you suggesting, Daisy?'

'Well, we could do teas and a tour of the gardens, sell some plants, have a fruit and veg and flower competition, include jams and cakes. I could sell some of my smaller watercolours from the summer house studio.'

'You have been doing quite a lot of thinking, haven't you!'

' Well....'

'What are you both talking about? Did I hear you talking about a fête?' said Rose, carrying a basket of raspberries.

'Well, Rose, I might have guessed you would hear. Yes! Your father and I were just discussing having one.'

Rose threw herself down on the rug. Now aged twelve she longed for excitement and complained loudly of being bored much of the time.' I could be in charge of games and we could have a children's section for growing vegetables or plants.'

'I thought you didn't like plants and gardens?'

'This would be different. I don't have to grow them. I would just be organising things,' she said airily. 'I just remembered, I saw another fête where they had someone reading palms or we could do tea leaves!'

'No tour of the house though, Daisy!' warned Tom.

'No, I know Grandmama and grandfather did that at one time but no, there won't be any house tours. It is the garden which is the most important part.'

'Yes, always the garden!!!' moaned Rose.

Later as the moon shone down the family of foxes who had the den near the old oak decided on their own raspberry picking expedition taking many that Rose had left behind in her hurry.

The smell from the kitchen was mouth-watering. Mrs Jessop had early strawberries in the copper preserving pan and was just testing for jam.

Tray upon tray of scones sat on the scrubbed wooden table to cool down.

'These are wonderful, Mrs Jessop, Thank you! I hope Rose hasn't been bothering you too much?'

'No, ma'am, She has come up with a novel wee game though,' and Mrs Jessop laughed.

'What's that?'

'Ha-ha, it involves making a jelly in the large rabbit mould an' gettin' the people to guess its weight. Between times she's been very good. She's helped me mak' coconut fudge an' peppermint creams. Though some of them'll never get to the fete!'

Rose sat with her friend, Jane wrapping small items for the tub. They had decided on a position close to the terrace which they felt would attract children.

Daisy and Tom watched as Rose spoke animatedly to everyone who approached her sweet stall. She and Jane were confidently managing both the tub and the sweet stall.

'Just look at that, Tom. She loves meeting people. At times like this I feel bad that she has no brothers and sisters.'

'It couldn't be helped, Daisy and being the only child has meant that she's had a good deal of attention! Too much in fact.'

'I don't think she sees it like that, Tom'.

'I can't believe that Mrs Jack, Tom!'

'What happened?'

'Molly found her taking a pair of scissors to an astrantia plant. I know she admired it, but really!!'

'You know what Molly is like. She can be quite ferocious. She suggested that Mrs Jack might like to give a donation and pointed her also in the direction of the plant stand, reminding her at the same time that these were private grounds.'

'Mrs Jack certainly won't be welcome at Garraiblagh again. If she had asked nicely I might have given her a root. There were good 'Irish' cuttings[28] on sale at the plant stall and it isn't as though the Jacks lack money.

28 Rooted shoots. Held to be of good quality.

PART FIVE

WWII and after

'Many things grow in a garden that were never sown there'
Spanish proverb

Garraiblagh House 1945

Chapter Thirty-six

1939

THE SOUND OF WOOD PIGEONS in the fir trees was clear through the open window of the breakfast room. Tom came in with his newspaper.

'Mm that smells good,' as he poured a cup of coffee while Daisy ate her bacon and eggs.

'Oh, a letter from Wenna!' exclaimed Daisy hurriedly opening it while balancing the toast in her other hand. Daisy opened the paper and scanned it quickly.

'She says that everything is becoming very tense over there and they're not even in London!' Reading further down the letter Daisy commented 'Tom, Wenna says that shelters are being built and I read in the paper that conscription had been brought in even though the country is not yet at war!'

'If Wenna is feeling the effect of things down in Cornwall then events are moving rapidly.'

'Damn it! I'm sure Molly will want to be involved if the Women's Land army is re-formed over here,' said Daisy. 'Food is going to be critical once more.'

The colours in the garden had taken on that early evening muted tone. The sweet, vanilla rose scent of stock flowers just by the French windows mixed with the white phlox and pinks still creating a seductive scent.

'It is still so warm,' said Daisy as she opened the French windows wider and looked out across the lawn. Tom left his chair and stood behind her.

'Not so warm when you open the windows!'

The strange, shadowy outlines of the topiary stretched across the lower lawn in the dusk and birds late to return to their nests rustled in the dense foliage.

Tom was right. Daisy shivered and rubbed her arms to warm them. He put his arm round her, knowing as he did so that it was not just the cool summer evening air from which he wanted to protect her. He was too old for active service, approaching fifty, but he would have to consider what he could do. The thought of a second war weighed heavily on both of them.

While he headed the Henderson mill Tom had managed to extricate himself in the last couple of years from some of the more mundane issues. He believed engineers would be critical to the home war effort. The gardens and estate at Garraiblagh would probably undergo further changes. Garraiblagh had been a refuge from the world outside. He wondered how many more changes the place could absorb.

Daisy sat on the old bench. The situation with Hitler was now leading irrevocably to war. She herself had been seventeen, almost eighteen when the Great War had started like everyone else. She had hoped that there would never be another. Rose was only twelve thankfully, but decisions would have to be made about her education. Daisy didn't share the government's optimism that Northern Ireland would be too far removed for the Germans. She certainly did not want Rose away at some school in England or even Belfast which could easily be a target. It might be wise though to consider the idea of being a weekly border at school near Armagh. There were relations close by and Rose would be home at weekends.

The vegetable garden's routine continued in much the same way as it always had. Colin found the everyday chores soothing. Pruning the currant bushes with their elusive scent, was always something that he enjoyed. Getting the cut just right and shaping the plant was almost like sculpting. He cut and then stood back to reflect on his work. In the distance he could see others busily working. Only the noise of a spade, a hoe and a barrow were causing any sound.

He thought back to his early days at Garraiblagh when he'd worked on the home farm. He'd been glad that he was needed to milk the cows rather than go to war though he had felt guilty when only Frank and Jack had survived. Oliver and Andy did not come back and frank lost a leg. Oliver's father never talked about the war but Colin often wondered if old Jack resented his survival.

He remembered vividly the day he had approached Rory Black, looking for a position as an under gardener. Since then his life had revolved around the garden and his family. His work was hard, physically demanding but, with the renewed uneasiness of war he was glad of his position. He didn't speculate about what was happening further afield. He reckoned most folk in the area wanted no part of another war. There wouldn't be the same crowds of young men joining up.

Eileen had surprised even Molly by her enthusiasm and commitment to gardening. She was a quick learner and soon Molly found herself giving Eileen tasks that normally would have been given to much more experienced gardeners. Eileen for her part was relishing the work in the open air. She didn't mind working with the men and her good humour and conscientiousness was respected. After further discussion with Daisy it had been agreed that the old stables would be renovated

While Hitler continued to threaten and Chamberlain tried to appease, it felt as though the only thing keeping everyone sane was the routine of the garden. And there was plenty to be done. Molly had been keeping in touch with the Land Army organisation. Initially she had not felt able to do anything on top of her work as head gardener. She spoke to her gardeners, 'We may not know what is going to happen next week or next year with this war but we've got to believe there's a future and if we don't get these carrots and beans planted there will be more trouble than Herr Hitler to contend with, believe me!'

Despite the focus on the garden, the young gardeners began to talk among themselves about joining up. Eileen asked Brian 'Are ye going to join up?'

'Nay fear! Me father was in the last war. I know wha' it done to him. It's not my war.'

'It's no' the same this time. I fancy the RAF,' said Brian. 'Flyin' planes like Mr Guthrie did. It'll keep us out o' the trenches.'

'Rather ye than me, Brian!'

'What about ye, young Eileen?' asked Brian.

'Me? I've begin thinkin' about it. Mrs Taggart has spoken o' the Women's Land Army. I reckon if I need to leave here that's what I'll do.'

The older men knew that war was not the exciting adventure some believed. They had first-hand knowledge of its impact. This new generation of the Henderson/Guthrie family was not going to promote the idea of joining up to their workers as their forbears had done.

Daisy and Rose walked across the field from the scutching mill, carrying the flowers and plants in the trugs. In the sky, dark against the sunlight, were two planes.

Rose held her hand up to her face to shield her eyes. Are they German?'

'No, we'd have heard,' said Daisy sounding more confident than she felt. But, she thought to herself, 'How would we know? How safe are we actually?' She was still unsure about Rose being away at school during the week in Armagh, but then she had to balance that with the knowledge that for Rose the garden and the estate did not provide her with company of her own age.

Daisy remembered France in the last war and the occasions when the dressing station had had to be moved back because of artillery bombardments coming too close. Remembering the tremors in the earth from not so distant battle, her mouth became dry. Images flashed in front of her. So many years ago, a generation ago and here we are again. How could this have happened?

She looked at Rose, a little younger than she had been but, thank God, not old enough to take part, yet. No one was daring to claim this war would be over by Christmas.

Daisy shook herself free of the mind numbing thoughts.

'Come on,' she said to Rose, putting her arm around her daughter's shoulders, 'we'll leave these in the apple store and I'll work on them later. Do you want to help me with the hand cream recipe?'

Rose hesitated. 'As long as I'll be ready in time, Jane is coming over to play tennis.'

Daisy thought back to the Garraiblagh fête they had had three years ago. She was glad they'd made the effort. It had gone well. At the time there were mixed feelings about the expense and the sense of frivolity, but now, looking into a bleak future it was a memory of fun and laughter they could hold on to.

Chapter Thirty-seven

1940

TOM BECAME MORE CLOSELY involved with the mill again as the linen was now being used to make parachute harnesses and canvasses for the Royal Navy. It was something Tom could use his engineering expertise on and still stay at home to look after Daisy and Rose and Garraiblagh. He hoped it would not be for too long.

By early 1940 Brian had left the garden to join the RAF. The same work was still needed to maintain the gardens, both flower and vegetable. In October Molly sat down with Colin, Matt, Davy and Eileen to discuss the way forward.

'There's no way around it, we're not going to be able to manage the grounds the way we would want to,' said Molly.

'That's clear enough, Mrs,' said Matt. 'None of us is getting ony younger an' we're working while hours as it is.'

'I know and we appreciate that, Matt,' said Molly 'I've been thinking that we should make a list of all the work we do and then see how we can manage. I'll have to talk to Mr and Mrs Guthrie, but I'm sure they will be understanding. Mrs Guthrie has always been keen to help out in the garden anyway.

'I was readin' about this 'Dig for Victory' in the paper last week,' said Colin. I reckon we're goin' to be as important as ony soldier or airman if wha' they're sayin' is true.'

'You're right, Colin. I got some information through from the ministry just yesterday, talking about the need to grow as much as possible and to cultivate areas that would have been lawns.'

'Damn the bit! Digging up that lovely lawn,' said Matt. 'Me father laid that wi' auld Sam John Scott fifty year ago.'

'I know, I know, Matt. We all feel this, but we'll need food,' said Molly.

'The mare I think 'bout this, the mare I realise that this is a brave lump o' a job for us 'uns!' said Colin.

'Right, let's divide the things we do into the different seasons and divide up the fruit and veg from the flowers and the lawns and the ponds.'

The list, when finished looked as much as like a military campaign as anything.

Composting and feeding the ground was common to all the areas.

They agreed between them that the perennial plants in the flower garden could be left to expand without too much injury. Any gaps that occurred in the flower beds would be filled with vegetable plants appropriate to the season.

The fruit trees and the soft fruit and bushes would still need pruning and netting, but they were an important source of vitamins and could be bottled and stored.

The greenhouses would be essential to maintaining a supply of vegetables and fruit as they had always been, but the conservatory, it was suggested, could be left to Mrs Guthrie.

Molly also suggested that the rose arbour should be left to Mrs Guthrie as well. There was a shifting on their seats from Colin and Matt, uneasy that Molly would be suggesting too much to the

Guthries and also, a little more worryingly, perhaps making it clear that fewer gardeners were needed.

Potatoes would be increased as basic food which could be shared or sold locally as would the brassicas and the legumes. The more time consuming vegetables which required blanching or special attention to achieve a harvest would have to wait, hopefully to be worked on later, but not immediately critical. Asparagus and seakale would remain as vegetables that covered a difficult time of year for other food.

Rhubarb could be left to its own devices and still supply a useful source of food at an important time of the year. They would deal with possible division next year if there was still a war.

Molly would walk the gardens and mark the rare and unusual plants. These would be given attention. There would be no annual planting of bulbs and the annuals that were usually propagated in early spring for the parterres would be left. Instead lettuces and herbs would be the new 'annuals'.

Molly, Eileen and the two men looked at their plan and over a cup of tea and a slice of the rich fruit cake that Mrs Jessop had made for them, congratulated themselves on a job well done.

'I'll speak to Mr and Mrs Guthrie tomorrow, but I think this is the best way forward. I hope to this war doesn't last as long as the last one!'

'Damnable Germans!' spat Colin. 'Sorry Mrs, but they can't take a beatin' an' stay bate!'

Molly met with Daisy and Tom in the drawing room. Daisy noticed the file under Molly's arm, 'That looks serious, Molly?'

'Yes, it is Daisy. We need to look at the management of the gardens and the grounds generally to produce more food and, to add to everything elsewhere there is talk of building air raid shelters in people's gardens.'

1940

George the ginger and white cat sat on the terrace and pondered. While cleaning his fur thoroughly he watched the small finches congregating on the bird bath where a small amount of seed had been left for them. He knew the gardens in a way that none of the humans could ever hope to.

Each morning he appeared from his bed in the upper floor of the stable and made his way down the rickety, wooden stairs. The stables still had the scent of horses though there hadn't been any for a number of years now. Rats found their way in and George dealt with them in his professional way. He had a vague recollection of his early life and knew that some would say he'd already used up his first life. The memory of the farm worker coming up the ladder in his heavy boots with an old sack and grabbing his brothers and sisters, roughly throwing them in before tying a rope around the top was still with him. He knew it wasn't good and his mother had grabbed him, holding him in her mouth and had dragged him away into a dark corner, where they had survived.

He sniffed the air as he did every day. He knew where the fox and the badger moved during the night on their way to hunt. Hopping across a puddle and shaking his paw to remove the remains of a small amount of water, he disappeared through a hole, accommodatingly supplied for him in the wooden gate of the walled garden. George took in the panorama.

Some cabbage white butterflies were flitting across the young brassicas in an absent minded way. George knew from past experience that catching the cabbage whites got him tasty morsels from the gardeners. He prowled across to the carrots and half hidden in the ferny fronds and waited. A spring and his large furry white paws caught a butterfly. He felt pleased at an early kill and moved on.

He enjoyed the herb garden. The fennel leaves were good for pawing and pulling at and he enjoyed rubbing his chin against the mints. A blackbird pecking at a strawberry caught George's eye and, although he didn't catch it, he felt that he had shown his authority.

Taking a last look around the vegetable garden he lowered his body and wiggled through a gap into the herbaceous border. This was an area that George loved. He was no different than a lion in the jungle. Weaving his way behind the agapanthus plants he peered through the kniphofia with their orange and yellow poker shapes, not unlike his own and batted at them with his paws. He settled down to watch and to listen. He didn't mind if it was human or animal talk though he particularly enjoyed listening to humans. They chattered just like birds.

It was a beautiful day and later, he would sun himself on his favourite bed of lavender.

George felt that he was needed in the garden. He had status. He moved around the side of the bench to check, opening his mouth in a silent miaow, as he stared at two of his favourite humans.

'Georgie! My wee boy. I saw you got that cabbage white. You're such a good boy!' Daisy lifted George up and cuddled him. George tolerated this for a few moments only to pass himself like any polite human would; then demanded to be released and to go about his business.

'Of course I'll help in the garden as much as you want me to, Molly,' said Daisy. 'I can't just sit around. The new civilian handbook has information on the Women's Voluntary Association. I believe I could help by being involved with them.'

'Daisy, you were pretty busy in the last war if you remember,' said Molly drily, 'and you were twenty years younger. More than that!'

' I know, we both were. I suppose you will be involved in the Land Army in some way?'

'Yes, I've been meaning to speak to you about that. I do want to join them, but at the moment the government seems to be reluctant to start up the Women's Land Army over here. I think they believe that there's no need while there are still men around, but that won't last forever. Don't worry though, Daisy, I can manage the garden. I'm lucky I have the gardeners though I have a feeling Eileen wants to join the Land Army. We'll see when the time comes.'

Rose and her friends helped with the hay making, but spent most of their time throwing themselves into the gathered hay, provoking a stern warning from the farmer. When she woke the next morning to see a rash along her arms and legs, she ran to her mother. Daisy initially thought of measles and then remembered her daughter jumping in the hay and the prickles she'd received from this. At least one panic was over!

As before, it didn't seem possible that anything bad could happen when the sun shone and everything was continuing to grow. So it took them some time to agree to build the Anderson shelters[29].

'Their bombers won't get this far, I heard? Mrs Taggart,' said Davy, who did not like to have to work harder than necessary. 'More likely to be invaded by sea, they say. Do we need to go about disruptin' everything?'

'I don't think we can be sure of anything, Davy and we don't want to take any chances.'

The Anderson shelters needed to be a little distant from the house, but not too far and space was needed for all the family and staff.

Colin was given the task of camouflaging them with plants.

'I reckon marrow plants would do the job fornest the shelters, Missus. They'll soon be crawlin' all o'er the place an' they'll last into

29 Air raid shelter used in private gardens.

the autumn. If it goes on into winter we'll have to think of something else to camouflage them. Firs from the wood maybe.'

Daisy was just finishing a sketch of the building of the Anderson shelters for her garden diary when Tom came in full of excitement.

'Have you read this, Daisy? We have to try it.'

'What are we going to try, Tom?' asked Daisy, still engrossed in getting the detail right in the picture.

'Look, it's becoming more and more difficult to get tobacco for my pipe. This article is suggesting that it can be grown here! I'm going to have a word with Molly. We could grow some in one of the greenhouses.'

It was true and in time the huge tobacco leaves were left to dry in the conservatory, their smell mixing strangely with the pelargoniums and gardenias.

'It's lucky it's been a good summer, Tom, and that we've had cover for them. I don't think growing tobacco is going to become the next sensation,' commented Molly. Tom wasn't convinced as he looked forward to his first pipeful.

Balancing the dried tobacco leaves on the front of the bicycle Tom made his way down the drive and on the few miles to Mr Creighton's tobacconist shop in the village.

'Thanks for cutting it for me, Mr Creighton.'

'It's a pity it can't be sold,' said Mr Creighton. 'I'll be interested to see what you think of it when you come to smoke it!'

A very pleased Tom slowly made his way back to Garraiblagh.

The smell was hardly the normal aroma of the carefully blended tobacco that Tom usually bought, but he was determined to enjoy it.

'That is really quite disgusting, Tom'

'But it is something, Daisy! I'll get used to it!' said Tom with a smile.

'But I won't! I hope this war doesn't last long if for no other reason than to stop that foul smell!'

'I'm calling it Garraiblagh original blend. Could we make our own pipes do you think?'

Chapter Thirty-eight

Belfast Blitz 1941

It had been a beautiful Easter. People had taken advantage of the good weather to go on outings and to have picnics. By Tuesday people were back at work.

That night the world was turned upside down. The sound was something Belfast would never forget. Huge aircraft engines growling, heavy and dark, becoming unbearable as the noise moved closer overhead. The sky had been made even darker by dozens of huge bombers flying overhead. The moonlight gave it an additionally eerie quality. People waited and prayed. There weren't enough shelters and many hoped it just wasn't happening. Surely the fighter planes from Aldergrove would be scrambled. They knew the small number of barrage balloons would not protect them. A smoke screen hung over the docks. The bombers would aim for the docks wouldn't they?

In the end it happened too fast. It had been too unbelievable. First magnesium flares dropped, held in the sky like a hundred grey umbrellas, their parachutes providing them with a safe landing. They lit the dark and narrow streets surrounding the mills and the docks.

The Germans were thorough. The bombs and the incendiary devices within them descended. Crazy colours bloomed in the sky. It was as though all the colours of a garden had thrown themselves into the sky, crazily illuminating the darkened buildings. The bombs began to impact and where they fell were darker areas of red.

Terrified people looked out at their city under siege and retreated to whatever meagre shelter they could find as the huge vibrations of the bombs shuddered through their bodies.

After the raid Sean McLister stood in the rubble of his home, staring at the street in bewilderment. There were no houses. He couldn't hear anything. The sound in his heart was so deafening it felt as though there was going to be a second explosion. Annie, his wife, scrambled out of the debris behind him onto Vere Street. Picking up Dolly, the dog and a bag of clothes they ran for their lives. It seemed to them that running uphill away from the fires and the smoke, which made it hard to breathe, was the only thing to do. They were not alone. It seemed that most of Belfast was doing the same thing. Women covered in dust and dirt, shawls wrapped round themselves, one woman holding a dead baby tight to her body. Toddlers screamed, holding on to the coats and skirts of adults.

From Garraiblagh, standing above the city and protected by the trees and hills Daisy and Tom stood watching, gripping each other's hands tightly, and feeling like audience members at a horror film. The vibrations as the bombs landed in the city were felt at Garraiblagh. For both of them the memories of France came flooding back. They were both shaking uncontrollably. Willow lay in the corner of the room, whimpering.

'Oh God, Tom!' Tom put his arm around Daisy's shoulder hugging her close. Tears streamed from her eyes.

'Not again, not again!'

Rose was screaming. Flying down the stairs in her nightie she ran to her parents, a terrified cat in her arms scrambling to find a hiding place. They could see clearly the area that had been targeted. Belfast was illuminated like a gruesome stage set showing the dark and broken outlines of buildings. At the edge of the city there was what looked like a grey lava flow, moving outwards slowly and then forming streams that moved uphill. For a while neither of them could make sense of what they saw. Then in a moment of awful realisation Daisy whispered in shock.

'It's people, Tom! Hundreds of them. They'll be here before long.'

Daisy and Tom found blankets and went to the bottom of the garden and across the field to the road. Molly ran, catching up with them as they entered the field. Mrs Jessop came hurrying down still with her rag curls in place and a heavy coat over her nightdress. Daisy saw her. 'Mrs Jessop could you go up to the kitchen and put as many kettles and pots on the stove to boil so that we have some tea. We'll start bringing them up.'

They saw huddled groups of grey people so covered in the dust of the buildings that they were like wraiths. Some moved on up the road as though following an ancient path, heading anywhere away from the horror. Others stopped, looked back at Belfast, unable to move.

Soon the ground floor of the house was full of huddled groups of people. Matt and Colin had come from the cottages to help and cups were being found to hold tea. Willow, the spaniel, and Rose were sent upstairs out of the way as a variety of cats and dogs also made their way into the hall with owners trying to quieten them.

That night no one slept.

People were nervous, not only because they were in the big house but because they worried the Germans would follow them to Garraiblagh.

'What are we going to do, Tom?'

'We'll think about that later, Daisy. Let's get people somewhere to at least sit.'

'How are you managing, Mrs Jessop?' said Daisy as she came into the kitchen with another tray of cups.

'I know I haven't asked ye, Ma'am, but I'm going to mak' some soup. I got Matt an' Colin to do some night-time diggin' for me an' we have carrots an' all sorts an' that's what it's goin' to be — an all-sorts soup. The childer out there are exhausted, but more than that, half the people out there don't look as though they've had a square meal in a while long time. Ye can sack me now if ye want, but I did it for the best!'

Mrs Jessop stood with her arms crossed over her chest defiantly, with tears running down her cheeks.

'Of course you did the right thing. Don't be silly, I would never sack you,' and Daisy hugged the elderly woman. 'I'm going to ask Matt to go up to the farm to get some milk.'

Daisy, Tom and Molly moved through the rooms. Daisy was providing first aid where she could.

'Quite a few people have left now that its light,' said Molly. 'The ones I spoke to have said they're going to try and move on to family and friends outside the Belfast area.'

Tom nodded 'I've heard the same from some but there are a lot of others who don't want to go back into Belfast and I can't say I blame them. There are fires still raging by the look of things and I can't get through to anyone. I don't know what state the mills will be in.'

'I've heard people say that they never want to spend another night in a house again and that they'd rather live outside,' said Daisy.

'We need to look at the numbers we have,' said Tom. 'I'm thinking we could use the bottom fields and the stone buildings down there to create a makeshift camp at least. What do you think?'

Daisy and Molly looked at him.

'Yes, there's a water supply to the old carriage house. There are two floors to that and we're not storing anything in there at the moment that couldn't be moved,' said Molly.

'What about heat? I know it's been warm but when you're shocked you're easily chilled,' said Daisy.

'Well, that also means cooking. We're not going to be able to keep up the cooking in the house and what about beds?'

'We need to get hold of the civil defence people and ask for camp beds and bedding. Cooking may need to be outside,' said Tom.

'Food we can deal with for the moment but we will need to see about supplements — tea, bread, things like that. I'm sure some people left with nothing, never thinking they'd need to be out of their homes.'

'I'll go into town and speak to them,' said Tom.

'You can't go now Tom, you have no idea what is happening and by the look of it if you did manage to get to see anyone in the civil defence unit they would be up to their eyes just trying to manage what's happening on the ground there. From their point of view the fact that a good number of people have taken themselves out of Belfast means there are people they don't immediately need to worry about,' said Daisy, drawing on her experience in France.

Daisy opened the garden door while Molly unlocked the barn and the sheds. It might not be much but it would be shelter of a sort until things became clearer. Daisy had spoken to the people who were unable to get to relatives or too frightened to find out how things were with their old homes she asked for people to volunteer for a working party. The working party brought with them whatever brushes, buckets and mops they could find and worked all day on cleaning the buildings for use.

By June, the bottom part of the estate had become a functioning makeshift camp for those who had run, terrified from the burning city: refugees in their own country. Some, those that did return during the day, 'the ditchers' they were called, returned each evening to Garraiblagh. There was no going back to the city as far as anyone was concerned. The carnage was too great and now mistrustful of government reassurance that the air cover for Belfast would be better. They camped out or stayed in the barn. Cold and damp was better than a bomb. Brick buildings, however small, now seemed dangerous to many. They still ached for the ones they could not find beneath the rubble. The makeshift mortuaries were overflowing.

Daisy and Tom met with Molly to discuss the situation.

'We can't force them back. What would that be like? We force them back to be potentially blown to smithereens?' said Tom. Daisy agreed.

'But what do we do?' asked Molly.

It became clear that for some there was nowhere else. People needed shelter and food. Tom and Daisy agreed that they would make the bottom acre a place for those who had become refugees.

'There is a separate entrance from the bottom road into the two lower fields. We haven't been using them recently. We could set up allotments for the families,' suggested Molly.

Trees from the bottom wood were felled for firewood. The lower lawn was dug up sooner than expected for vegetables. Matt and Colin found themselves being aided by people who wanted to help in the kitchen garden but didn't know a plant from a weed. 'Ye know, Matt, I'll never gurn agin 'bout havin' ony us tae do the work or 'bout not havin' much in the way o' money!'

'Yer right there, boy. I've had to stop one boyo diggin' up the kale and toul' some weans off for walking around with the rhubarb leaves on their heads!' said Matt.

'I haven't seen the boss since the mornin''. She's been down wi' the master an' mistress in the lower field.'

'Aye, it's bad enough havin' yer man bombin' us, but I'm beginning to think we'd have been better placed in the army!'

'Damn the bit. We're well out o' it here. Sure it's a bit o' craic, boy. Come on let's get that new bed dug wi' them boys from the Falls.'

Those families and individuals who had settled after the first bombing, began to take charge. Food was in short supply. The house vegetable garden provided some, but was quickly overwhelmed by the need. Those beginning to find their feet helped others. Sean and Annie were among the first. The allotments drew people together. While it would take time to grow things, swapping seed and seedlings, eating round a fire, swapping stories and singing songs, they cursed the Germans and forgot about their differences. During daylight hours some people forced themselves to walk back the miles into Belfast to forage in the rubble of their old homes, bringing back things that made sense to them. Memories, broken plants, photographs, ornaments as well as more practical items, like bedding, clothes and kitchen utensils. Daisy helped where she could and was shocked to find how little the people had had to begin with. Their clothes were wretched, the work of poverty not the Blitz. She never dreamed that war would come to Garraiblagh like this. War was meant to be somewhere else, not here in the estate, in the garden. War was throwing up more than memories. It was also throwing a light on what life was like for many in her own country. She had been shocked by the absolute poverty of the people who had had nowhere to go but come to Garraiblagh. Daisy realised that she and others had, through their ignorance, allowed this state of affairs. She felt ashamed. She had once fought for female suffrage.

What needed to be fought for now was more than the downfall of Hitler, it was a new way of living for all and she vowed she would be working for that.

Pavement pieces blown apart by the bombs became crazy paving, marking out the different vegetable beds. Sean spent much of his time tending his small area, feeling the soil as he slowly planted. Bricks and mortar meant little to him now. There was no home, but there was reassurance in the earth. Pets that had been abandoned by their now dead or terrified owners went feral and began to find their way into the edge of the estate. Their old homes no longer existed and they too had to find new ways to survive.

In Garraiblagh the foxes and other animals who counted the area as their home drew back into the shadows and watched, waiting.

Sean found himself frequently wandering through the formal gardens, touching the leaves and the flowers. His hearing had remained badly affected after the bombing and conversation was difficult with so many missed words in what seemed to be the underwater echo chamber of his head. The plants didn't ask anything of him. They in their own way seemed to sense Sean's agony. The scent of lavender and chamomile wrapped their warm, calming scents around him.

One decision he had made was that he would never live in a town or city again. He had been watching Colin and Matt in the garden and saw their frustration. It wasn't that they had no feeling for what everyone was going through but the garden had had a rhythm and they were calmed by it. The disrupted rhythm jarred their nerves. Plants were being broken, trampled on. Molly knew that things were becoming difficult. She would have to keep the main gardens secure from the people in the bottom field. She didn't like doing it but if nothing was done it might end in those people being told to move on, to find somewhere else and at the moment that was the last thing they needed.

Daisy caught Tom as he was finishing breakfast and about to drive into Belfast to check on the mills.

'We could take evacuee children. We have the room, Tom. I know we're not that far out of Belfast, but better than being close to the docks and their parents can visit them easily.'

'Daisy, don't be ridiculous! snapped Tom. 'We are still managing what happened in the Blitz. There are people still living in the bottom fields. Everything is topsy–turvy. Have you really looked at what is happening? Have you spoken to any of the staff and Molly?'

'What about Molly?' asked Daisy.

'Molly is shattered. She's been working all the hours God sends, keeping Matt and Colin and the others on an even keel and helping set up the allotment area and what about our daughter? Where is she to figure in all this?'

Daisy had the grace to look embarrassed. She sank down on the chair.

'It's just that...' Daisy began. 'We've lived this gilded existence for so long Tom. A few miles away, many of these people had nothing.'

'I know, Daisy but we've got to be realistic. We have people of whom we know nothing or very little about, who've suffered awful horror, and are now living basically at the bottom of the garden. Have you thought? We don't know anything about them. Are we putting our daughter, Molly, Mrs Jessop and the others at risk?'

Tom looked at Daisy, forcing her to look back at him.

'And then you want to bring in other children to that? Sometimes you can be as single–minded as your grandmother!'

Tom banged the door closed and trying hard to keep his temper he walked into the garden. He took the path through the pleached lime trees, pulling leaves off as he went. He reached the Japanese bridge and began to walk across it to the island. The sound of his hard steps on the old wooden planks made him stop and he turned to look down into the pond. The creamy white of the water lilies contrasted with the darkness of the water. He had never looked that closely at the flowers and slowly his breathing began to return to normal. He realised that he often experienced plants and flowers in a detached way, through Daisy's artwork. The garden provided fruit and vegetables and it was a beautiful place in which to sit or play, but until this moment he had never fully realised the strength of the garden and the plants and trees. He had seen the people who had ended up at Garraiblagh and were living in the bottom field, seen how they sometimes wandered into the gardens, touched the plants and sat among them. They never did any serious damage.

The garden had a spirit, a way of holding people and bringing out the best in even people who probably had never been in a garden. He would have to trust what was happening in Garraiblagh. The estate could not be their private refuge any longer and nor should he want it to be. That much was clear. At that moment he heard steps on the path to the bridge and looked up. It was Daisy.

'I'm sorry, Tom...'

Tom held up his hand. 'So am I, my love. I always saw that my job was to protect you and Rose and this place, but I know that that has to change. I can't be King Canute holding back the tide.'

The two children, Joe Quinn and Philip O'Brien, arrived at ten o'clock on the Monday. It was agreed with the coordinator Miss Scott that the two would attend the local country school. Bicycles were provided. The two boys stood on the gravel drive and watched Miss Scott disappear down the drive in her car. There was a heavy and uncomfortable silence. Daisy, usually so confident found herself unable to say anything, and began to think that Tom might have been right.

Philip was thin and tall with dark curly hair and green eyes stared at the house. Joe, shorter and plumper than Philip, with wavy red hair, fingered his gas mask case and looked around for something, anything that seemed ordinary. His eyes lit on Willow, the spaniel who had come to see what was happening.

'Ye're covered in burrs, boy!' Squatting down he began to stroke the dog while he removed the seed heads. He had made a friend and he would stick with Willow if the humans weren't alright. Daisy breathed an inward sigh of relief, glad that there was something at least one of the boys could connect to.

'I had a dog, Bouncer. He was the best ball-catcher in our street an' he could play hide an' seek too.'

'Where is he?' asked Daisy, too enthusiastically, clutching at the first possibility of starting a conversation. She immediately regretted it as she saw the young boy's face dissolve in tears.

'He was killed in the bombing, Mrs. The Jerries got him.'

Willow licked Joe on the hand and the boy buried his head in the dog's fur.

'When you're unpacked you boys can go and explore. Willow can go with you. He knows the way'.

'Do them 'uns own aw this?' said Joe to Philip in a whisper. 'Boyso, I wonder how many people live here?'

'This is like a palace.'

The boys saw a girl, just a bit older than them, come over. 'This is Rose,' said Daisy introducing her to the two boys. 'Rose can help you find your way around too.'

The two boys and Rose regarded each other suspiciously. 'Come on, I'll take you down to the pond. There's a bridge to an island and a hut on it.' The boys began to follow her.

'You know there's a ghost here' said Rose confidently. 'I've seen it. So you two better watch out.' The boys stared at Rose wide–eyed.

That night, although the two boys were exhausted, they couldn't sleep. Philip and Joe sat up in bed. They'd both heard the noise.

'Could be the ghost the wee girl was sayin' about?' said Michael.

'Or a wild animal?' suggested Joe. Joe plucked up courage and went to the window.

'Mind the blackout, Joe!'

Joe drew the heavy curtains carefully. It was pitch black.

Joe screwed up his eyes to try to see out into the darkness.

'This is scary. I can't see nathin'. There's no houses just grass an' shapes, maybe trees or somethin'. If there's somethin 'out there, we've had it.'

'Well, at least it's not the Jerries!' said Philip.

'Aye, ye're right there, boy. We've landed here alright but what about them'uns back home?'

Breakfast was a revelation to Philip and Joe.

The children had never had milk straight from a cow and seeing the cows and where the milk came from had been a bit of a shock.

'This bread's not like the loaves we get at home.' Joe sniffed it suspiciously.

For the next few days, towards the end of the school holidays, Joe and Michael investigated the garden and the farm.

'Well, have you seen the ghost yet?' asked Rose. The boys shook their heads.

'You will,' said Rose. 'I suppose I'll know if it gets you by the screams I hear!'

'There is no ghost,' asserted Philip .

'Isn't there?' said Rose with a shrug and left them, feeling she had got them sufficiently worried.

'We need a look–out tower to watch for ony more Jerries.' said Michael. 'How do we know they won't bomb us again?'

'They only bomb cities. Big McFadden said!'

'If we build our hut in the woods,' said Joe, 'it'll never be noticed sure.'

'It would be brilliant if we could build it high up.'

The boys made their way down the drive and then turned off into the depth of the woodland.

Michael saw the tree first. 'This'n'll do.'

The low branches gave easy footholds for the boys and then the open crown of the tree provided a perfect space for a tree house. Climbing up a further branch the boys were amazed to see down towards Belfast and across the lough.

Tom was allowed to visit the boys' lookout. Excitedly they told him what they had done and how they were watching the sky for enemy aircraft.

'Do you know, I think I know what might help,' said Tom. The boys waited.

'Naw, what, Mr Guthrie?'

'A pair of binoculars and I think I have an old pair for such important watchers.'

Even the mock banana sandwiches made by Mrs Jessop the cook with parsnip and banana essence tasted good in the open air as they scoured the horizon for any sign of Germans.

The binoculars soon became indispensable to the boys and after an argument; they came to an agreement to share them equally. One or other always being seen with the binoculars around his neck.

The makeshift shelters in the old stone buildings in the bottom field below the gardens had become home to those that had fled the Blitz, Sean and Annie McLister among them.

'The Johnstons have moved back into the town and the Doyles

are movin' to Magherafelt to live with family.' Annie told Sean as they tidied their camp beds and straightened their belongings.

'I can't go back to Belfast, Annie. I won't,' said Sean, his head down, intent on folding the jumper, anything to prevent eye contact with his wife. He and Annie did not usually argue and he didn't know how it would end if this couldn't be resolved. Sean wasn't sure he could explain how terrified he was of being back in the city. He worried that Annie would think he was a coward. Annie listened to the silence. She knew she was edging towards dangerous territory, but she had got to the point where being back in a home of her own, with or without Hitler dropping bombs, would be preferable to the sort of communal living they had at the moment.

'Well, what are we going to do? Neither your family or mine have room to spare,' asked Annie.

'I'll think o' somethin,' said Sean.

'What though, Sean? I'm gettin' worried.'

'I'm not sure. I have a notion or two, but I don't want to say, not yet. It may not come to anythin'.'

Annie sighed. She knew Sean when he dug his heels in about something and she couldn't blame him. 'Don't take too long with your notion.'

Annie poured water out of the kettle she had been boiling on the primus stove and into the teapot.

She tried a different tack. 'Don't get me wrong, boy. It's not all bad since we've been here at Garraiblagh. Mr and Mrs Guthrie may be posh, but they've been very good to us. But we can't stay here when the winter comes. The government says they'll get us housin',' said Annie.

'And ye believe them, do ye Annie an' us Catholics an' how far down the list do ye think we'll be! But ye're right about being here and it's to do wi' this place that I have my notion.'

Dolly, the dog, lay down beside the couple with a worried look and put out her paw. Sean lent down to stroke her.

'It's alright girl, Annie an' me'll work it out,' and Dolly wagged her tail. 'No time like the present,' said Sean and he stood up, put on his cap, straightened his jacket and set off up the field towards the gardens and the house.

Sean had grown to love the gardens and over the last couple of months he had, with the aid of old Colin the gardener and a book he had borrowed, learnt many of the names of the plants, at least in the herbaceous borders and he understood the basic nature of gardening.

'Well, Da,' he said to himself. 'I'm glad I watched you working in the allotment and grandad's farm. I'm going to need yer help!'

Sean saw Tom Guthrie coming out of the first greenhouse beyond the house. Tom waved to Sean as he lit his pipe.

'Mornin', Mr Guthrie. I wonder if I could have a wee word wi' ye, sir.'

Tom drew on his pipe and looked at Sean. He'd come to respect him over the last months, had watched as Sean and his wife had worked, helping others, comforting, sharing, doing what they could for others who had also been badly hit by the Blitz. Tom knew that Sean and Annie had lost close relatives, but more than that he had watched Sean and had seen the tell-tale signs of stress, of shell shock, signs he had seen in France during the last war.

'Let's sit down over here, lad,' said Tom pointing to a bench close to the conservatory entrance.

Sean was glad that he would be talking to Mr Guthrie in the open, in the garden, where he felt at ease. Sean took off his cap and began unconsciously to turn it round and round in his hands.

'How can I help, Sean?'

Taking a deep breath Sean began and when he had finished, Sean watched for a reaction from Tom. Tom drew again on his pipe and then knocked it out on the stone edging of the step.

'It's a difficult time but one thing is clear, here at Garraiblagh we need to grow as much food as we can. We've been able to grow a bit more than we need and have been able to share it around the area, but we're low again with everyone down in the bottom field. Mrs Taggart has become involved with the Women's Land Army and my wife is helping with the Women's Institute, as well as continuing with her own work. We have two evacuees and our own daughter. We've just lost two of our gardeners to the RAF and our cook housekeeper, Mrs Jessop, has had to leave to look after her elderly mother. So, Sean, we're up a creek without a paddle and you're offering help. You're asking at the right time. And yes, there's a place for you here.'

Tom looked at Sean then added with a smile, 'Can I ask, do you think your wife might be interested in the position of cook housekeeper?'

Sean replied excitedly 'Annie? Yes! Annie is a very good cook and she's always keen to learn. I'm sure she would have a right good go, sir.'

'We have a cottage at the home farm that you can have. I'm sure that it would feel good to be back in a house,' said Tom.

Sean walked back down through the gardens with a proprietorial air, whistling and looking over his shoulder to check nobody was having a laugh at him having the cheek to believe he could get a job at this fancy place. But it was true. His grandfather had always said 'If ye don't ask, ye don't git!' He would be working here, ensuring the plants grew, that food was grown. The lough in the distance glistened and the sky was a perfect cornflower blue.

Annie waved as she saw Sean return, holding tight to a heavy metal basin of wet laundry.

'Put that down and let me kiss you. We're not going back!' said Sean before lifting Annie into his arms and twirling her around. 'My notion paid off big time, Annie! We're not going back! We're staying here and I've got us jobs and somewhere to live!'

He twirled Annie around again until they both overbalanced onto the grass laughing while Dolly barked and wagged her tail.

'Don't ye take a han' out o' me, Sean McLister. This is no time for one o' yer games!'

Annie knew by the look in Sean's eyes that this was no practical joke.

Sean walked back up into the garden still full of excitement.

'I'll be joining ye an' Matt in the garden, Colin. Mr Guthrie has said.'

'Ye don't say. Well, I'll be damned. A city slicker like ye doin' a day's work? Never heard o' such a thing. Good luck to ye son.'

'Thanks. I'll go an' tell Matt.'

Colin hesitated. 'Ye might be better just leavin' that to Mr Guthrie an' Mrs Taggart.'

Sean looked at Colin. 'Aye, aye, maybe so.' He didn't say anything else.

Sean left Colin and wandered back down towards the camp. The excitement he had felt had dropped away.

'Do ye know that we have a new gardener?' asked Matt.

'Aye, I did!'

'When did ye hear? Mrs Taggart's after telling me it's that Sean boy.'

'Houl yer wheest, Matt. He's here to garden. He's a good worker. Ye know that.'

'An' what about our folk lookin' for jobs. He's one of them'uns.'

'The garden is no place for that sort a talk. He's a good lad. If the Guthries or Mrs Taggart hear ye talkin' like that ye'll be out on yer ear. I don't want to fall out wi' ye o'er this, Matt!'

Matt walked through the vegetable garden wheeling the empty wheelbarrow, ready to dig the carrots and cabbages needed for the kitchen. He took out the fork ready to loosen the carrots with their thick green fronds and noticed holes. The vegetables had obviously been ripped out. Counting six or seven holes, he looked around the other vegetable beds. Onions were missing too and a cabbage. He raised his hand to his head and scratched.

After consulting with Molly, Colin, Matt and Sean kept watch over the vegetable beds the next few days.

'I'm startin' to think I dreamt it. Perhaps it was just a one off, someone got in an' took some an' scarpered.'

'Disturbed by who?' said Colin. 'It's away off the main road.'

'Perhaps it was a giant rabbit,' said Sean.

The other two looked at him, unsure if he was joking.

'We'll give it another night.'

'Watch out for the giant rabbits, boys,' said Sean, managing to get away before Matt threw a clod of earth at him.

'He's a smart Alec, thon boy,' said Matt.

'He works wile hard,' nodded Colin, drawing on his pipe.

'Aye he does,' admitted Matt.'I'm right glad o' that. Since Eileen went off to that Land Army it's been difficult.'

'For a girl she did a wile amount o' work too,' said Colin.

Life had been a bit easier since Sean had started work and, mused Colin. Sean's wife made a right good cup o' tea and a treacle scone.

Matt watched from the bothy at the top of the garden. Through the old gate half hidden by the clematis, two small figures crept as Joe and Michael made their way purposefully towards the carrots, pulling out several each from the soft ground. The two boys then made their way to the turnips and the cabbages. Matt quietly followed the boys, struggling to carry their prizes, down across the lawn and into the wood. He kept out of sight, pulling back at one point because Joe stopped to pick up a carrot that had fallen out of his arms. The boys reached their tree house where Joe handed the vegetables up to Philip. Carefully moving closer to the tree-house, Matt listened to a whispered conversation between the two boys.

Matt made his way back to his cottage where Maura, his wife, had been waiting up for him.

'Well, did ye catch yer thief?'

'Ohh, Maura, do ye know who it was. It fair makes me heart break. It was them two wee boys. They were takin' the vegetables. I heard them talkin'. They're takin' them to give their families in Belfast!' Not for themselves, but their families.'

'Och the wee souls. This war is evil, turnin' good folk into thieves.'

The next morning Matt arrived at the bothy. Sean and Colin were already there.

'Well,' said Sean, 'Did you see any rabbits?'

'Naw, just humans.'

Molly opened the door to see the three quieter than she had ever seen before. Matt told Molly about the boys.

'They're takin' food for their families. They're worried that their families don't have enough.'

'Oh dear,' said Molly, 'We should have thought of that. I'll talk to Mr and Mrs Guthrie.'

Daisy and Tom were in the dining room with the boys as they finished breakfast.

'It's really important that you're thinking of your families. Perhaps you would like to help them even more?' suggested Daisy.

The boys looked up at Daisy. It wasn't what they had expected.

'What if you two and Rose each have your own gardens. You can grow extra vegetables to give to your families and Matt and

Colin and Sean will help you. Your fathers are helping to fight the war and this way you can also help by growing food.'

The look on the boys' faces was enough.

'What do ye want to grow?' queried Molly. Michael and Joe looked at each other, uncertainly.

'Peas,' said Joe.

'Anything else?' asked Molly.

Philip considered, 'Carrots, spuds and 'nunions.'

Joe nodded. 'What about cabbage?' asked Molly. 'Aye, s'pose so,' said Philip.

'What do your mothers and fathers eat usually at home?' asked Molly again, trying to get the boys to consider their choices.

'Onythin' they can get for the pot, Mrs,' said Joe and Michael nodded in agreement.

'Well, we'll have to get the beds ready to grow the vegetables you want. Matt and Colin will help you. I'll leave you all to it,' said Molly and she turned towards the upper lawn and the conservatory.

Joe looked worried. 'Bed, who's going to bed?'

'Vegetable beds, lad,' said Colin, laughing. 'That's what ye call the place that ye plant the vegetables.'

Matt handed the two boys a spade each. 'Right, here youse. First things first, we'll need to get some manure. So collect your wheelbarrow.'

Philip screwed up his nose. 'This stinks Mr Maynes,' he said to Colin. Joe held his nose, pretending to choke. 'It would make ye boke!'

'Is that what's in the vegetables we eat?' asked Philip.

'They need this to grow,' added Colin.

'Look at those worms. They're whoppers!' said Joe.

'Aye,' said Matt 'an' we need them in the soil to help as well.'

Matt and Joe showed the boys how to dig and then watched them, impressed at their concentration.

“Here, no need to dig that deep, you two,’ said Matt. ‘Youse aren’t goin’ to Australia!’

‘But I’d like to, Mr Simpson,’ said Philip. ‘There are kangaroos there.’

After a while Colin and matt called a halt.

‘Right lads, it’s time for something to eat.’

Both boys dropped the spades, ready to get some food.

‘Not so fast! Ye can’t leave the spades like that.’

Both boys looked puzzled.

‘They need cleaning and oiling.’

The boys looked shocked. ‘They get washed more than we do!’ said Joe.

‘So when can we plant the carrots?’ asked Philip .

‘Well, it’s no’ as aisy as that,’ said Colin. ‘Ye have to plant the seeds first.’ Colin shook some seeds out of a seed packet he had in his pocket.

‘Ye’re havin’ us on! These wee things! They’re not like the carrots in the big garden.’ exclaimed Joe.

‘No, but ye need the seeds to grow into carrots.’

‘We’ll prepare a bed for the carrots this afternoon. They don’t like as much manure when they’re growing.’

‘I’m glad o’ that,’ said Philip.

Over the next few days the boys dutifully planted the seeds of the various vegetables, being shown how to plant the different sized seeds at the correct depth.

‘My mother likes flowers. Can I grow some to gie her?’ asked Joe shyly.

‘Me, too,’ said Philip. ‘Aye,’that’s a good idea, said Matt. ‘What about some Sweet William. The women like them. They have a nice smell.’

‘Who’s William?’ asked Joe.

The laughter could be heard all over the garden.

Molly met with Matt and Colin at the end of the week.

'Well, they've started. We'll see how they go. Thank you both for helping them.' she said.

'I remember when I were a nipper I could nae understand how the seed changed into the plant. I reckon they're goin' to get a quare shock when they see what them seeds can do!'

'Where are the carrots and the cabbage,' asked Philip the next week.

'They're no magic seeds boys. It'll take a while,' said Colin.

'How long?' demanded Joe.

'Depends what we're growing.'

The disappointed boys left the garden. Matt and Colin expressed their concerns to Molly.

'I agree, it could be a problem,' said Molly. 'They might lose interest and if they do, they might back to stealing. Let me see, what would be .... I know, mustard and cress! They can grow that quickly and even have it to put in their egg sandwiches. I'll bring some blotting paper down from the cottage and I think there were some seeds in the hardware shop the last time I was there.'

Colin nodded. 'What about lettuces an' radishes. They grow faster. Matt an' I will get them on to them too.'

Once the boys began to see the seeds developing into seedlings and then plants they were hooked.

Hoeing and raking became a careful job as they carefully avoided their precious plants. Occasionally the hoe and the rake became anti–aircraft guns when a plane flew overhead and the boys became lost in a world of fighting the Jerries.

The first time the boys picked vegetables to take down to their families they could hardly contain their impatience to deliver them. As time went on both boys became proficient at gathering tomatoes from the greenhouse and assisting the gardeners more knowledgeably.

The old Chinese glass chimes hung in the wooden arbour. The painted pattern on the long, thin strips of glass were still, for the most part, bright and unchanged and made a delicate tinkling sound when the breeze caught them. It was a time for thinking.

Daisy sat down with her paints and sketchbook. She felt out of practice. It seemed such a while since she had painted or drawn, other than in her garden diary. There always seemed to be something that needed her attention and she found it difficult to concentrate when in the world outside things were changing on a daily basis.

Molly and the gardeners did their best to save as much vegetable seed as they could. Every surface in the sheds and greenhouses was covered with seed, drying, ready to be stored. The increase in vegetable gardening generally had made seed scarcer. Molly had found that it was difficult to get seed by the pound weight recently at the hardware store in the next village. There was relief when the Americans began to send seed over to Britain through the British War Relief Society.

Molly breezed through the door of the kitchen at Garraiblagh where Annie and Daisy were busy labelling their harvest of jars of bottled fruit and pickled vegetables.

'The Americans have sent over nine tons vegetable seeds to Britain as part of war relief. It is to be used in home gardens, so there will be a lot more digging up of lawns. I heard that they have a lot of cauliflower seeds so we'd better get some recipes for cauliflower!'

'Cauliflower soup I suppose, very Austrian and a bit heavy. That would be one way. Cauliflower cheese, but we'll have to watch the rations, or cauliflower in white sauce, Mrs Guthrie,' suggested Annie, who had been studying all the cookery books in the kitchen.

'I just hope you don't find a sandwich filling made from it, that's all,' said Molly.

'So, you need lessons in how to throw snowballs do you?'

'We're not bad,' said Joe.

'No, we're pretty good,' said Philip unthinking. 'It's just that we hit Matt on the neck and' the snow was goin' down his neck.'

'Well, I have a job for the two of you.'

'What is it, Miss?'

'Wait and see.'

Molly brought the boys round to the tool shed and collected two hooks on long handles.

'What're we goin' to do?'

'Wait and see.'

Molly led the two boys round to the trees bordering the front lawn.

'The trees have so much snow on them some of the branches might break. I want you to take the hooks and lift them over the thinner branches like this and shake them gently. I want the snow to fall off and onto the ground.'

The boys began work immediately, not realising that most of the snow would land on them. They shivered until they had finished their task.

'Where are the boys? I haven't seen them recently,' asked Daisy.

'Molly has them working in the garden, pulling snow off the branches of the witch hazel and other trees,' said Annie.

Daisy went out of the house and round to the front, throwing on her coat as she did so. The sky was reddening with the beginning of the early evening. She stopped for a moment to take in the garden. Snow had covered many of the plants, leaving ghostly shapes, difficult to recognise. The sun's failing light was tipping the edge of the lower lawns.

Hearing laughter, she trod carefully along the path, feeling snow dropping into her shoes when she misjudged the depth.

'Hello boys, time for supper.'

The boys faces were rosy, the balaclavas matted with snow burrs.

'You've done well. Bring the hooks and we'll get them back to the tool shed later.'

Philip and Joe looked down at their hands as though only just noticing how cold they were.

The snow continued to fall for the rest of the week. Philip and Joe were warned not to interrupt Matt, Colin or Sean in the garden and in fact, not to use anyone for target practice with their snowballs.

Boredom was beginning to set in. There were only so many card games they could play. 'Ye know the way Miss Taylor told us in class the story of the Eskimos an' how they build their igloos?' said Joe, 'Well I think we could build one here. If the snow gets worse we can live in it an' make holes in the ice on the pond and go fishing.'

'That's a wheeker[30]!' said Philip.

30 An Ulster-Scots expression meaning an excellent or marvellous person or thing.

Chapter Thirty-nine

1942

THE SUMMER CAME EARLY and a welcome relief after the harsh winter. Miraculously the heavy blanket of snow had protected some plants from the worst of the freezing wind and soon the garden was green again.

'What's that?' asked Joe.

They had come along a path further from the house than usual.

'They're gravestones'

'Gravestones! Ye only get them in cemeteries! We used to visit our Granny Mercer in the City Cemetery'.

'It's a bit strange havin' dead people in your garden.'

'Maybe they're not dead!'

'Don't go near them, ye might fall in.'

'Wheest! I want to see what they say on them.'

Daisy was busily clearing up the breakfast things when Tom called to her. His voice sounded strained.

'Daisy, Singapore has fallen. Paddy is still out there.'

'Oh Tom! No! Surely being a doctor they'll have need of him there.'

'I'm going to contact the War Office and try to get information. I'm a close relative, a brother after all.'

Daisy could hear Tom dialing the operator and a number of conversations. His voice was becoming more and more agitated with each abortive call. Then, at last she heard Tom replace the receiver. There was no immediate movement.

'Tom, are you there?'

'Yes.'

'What is it?'

There was silence.

'Daisy, they think the Japs have taken him prisoner. He's not on the list of people who got out. My big gentle brother has been taken prisoner by the Japanese.'

Tom sat at the table with his head in his hands and Daisy wrapped him in a hug.

Philip was lying on the lawn, looking up into the sky, watching the clouds. He'd been down to the woods, but had left Joe to think on his own.

'Is God up there, Mr Guthrie?' Philip asked as he saw Tom walking past.

Tom lay down on the grass beside him, putting his hands behind his head. He had never dealt with such a straightforward query.

'I think perhaps he is everywhere.'

'Can the airmen in the spitfires an' the Lancasters see him? Up in the clouds'?

'I was in the air force in the last war. I remember friends coming back from a flight and telling us that they had seen angels. Perhaps they had. Maybe your father will see one.'

'Do ye think me dad can see me when he's in the air?'

Tom looked at Philip. The small boy was lying with his eyes focused on the blue sky. There was not a cloud in evidence, but for Tom it felt as though the sky was weighing down heavily on him.

'I think it depends how high up he might be, but your father will know that you're here always, Philip, because he can see much more from up there.'

'Can he see as much as God?'

'No, I don't think any human can do that but when you love people you can see them in your mind's eye even when you're very far away from them.'

Philip continued to stare at the blue distance but his jaw, which had been jutting out as though holding back tears, slackened and he sat up.

'Mr Guthrie, do ye think this war will ever finish?'

'Yes. It will,' said Tom with more confidence than he felt.

'I'm going to collect some stones an' make the shape of me name out of them here on the ground. Then when me Dad flies over he'll know I'm alright.'

'That's a good idea. Do you want any help?'

'No, I'll do it thanks.'

Tom knew that he had been dismissed and walked away, briefly looking back to see the slim frame of the young boy busily collecting stones and filling his pockets.

While the war continued outside the world of the garden continued its cycle. Vegetables jostled for position in the formal flower beds. The need for food had taken over from the usually clear differentiations. Cabbages grew among hollyhocks and carrots and onions sat comfortably between poppies and peonies.

The boys had become used to finding their way around the estate and now with their own pieces of garden, felt they had some ownership. Willow often walked with them but tended to become diverted by rabbits. Joe had become more adventurous and while the boys often went to their tree house it wasn't now out of fear of bombs dropping on buildings but to watch the animals that moved around the grounds. Philip and Joe had found a book in the library on tracking and were now quite expert at identifying the prints of hares, foxes and badgers.

The three children lay in the grass, now warm from the sun. Idly picking up a buttercup, Rose held it up to the boys' chins.

'Let's see if you like butter.'

'I like it alright, but I've only had it since coming here. Dripping was what I used to get,' said Joe.

Rose was still restless and went off to look for daisies. Picking the largest with thick stems, easy to create the slits in, she brought them back and began threading them.

Twisting the buttercup between her fingers, looking out into distance and to the lough, she went off to look for daisies. Picking the largest with thick stems, easy to create the slits in, she brought them back and began threading them. While Rose made her daisy chain, Joe rolled on his front and stared into the grass. It was a different world in there. Ants, beetles, worms and he wondered what it would be like to live underground and walk through a grass forest. A bronze coloured beetle moved quickly, ignoring the leaf that Joe had placed in front of it.

'Let's go an' do somethin', I'm bored,' said Philip.

Rose watched them argue while she finished her necklace.

'Naw. Stay here,' said Joe.

'Well, I'm goin' to. Ye stay here if ye want,' decided Philip.

'Let me finish this and I'll come with you,' added Rose.

'Alright!' said Joe not wanting to be left out.

'We could go down to the Japanese bridge and the island,' suggested Rose.

An aircraft flew over in the distance.

'Spitfire,' said Philip knowledgeably.

'What do you think is going to happen?' asked Rose.

'My father says we can beat Jerry easily an' then he'll be home. Mum got a letter from him, but he can't say where he is.'

Joe, not to be outdone, had run on ahead to the bridge.

There was a loud splash. Rose and Philip looked on in horror.

Joe appeared in the pond and carefully stood up, holding on to the sides of the wooden bridge as he dragged himself to the edge. As he dripped his way up the bank and out of the water, the other two stared, not sure whether to laugh or run.

'Ye edjit, look at ye!'

Though fully clothed in his shorts and jacket, Joe now had an extra layer — a layer of frogspawn, his hair covered with their jellied forms, his jumper and shorts and, as he took the jacket off to look, the pockets full of tiny tadpoles.

Rose eventually gave in to laughter and dropped down on the grass forgetting her superior age. 'You're the monster from the deep, Joe!'

Joe and Philip developed a routine to their lives. Every day after school they spent an hour checking their vegetables, sowing, harvesting and watching the gardeners. Then after their supper they had time to go down to their look out tree house. The weekends usually meant time to visit their families, bringing their vegetables and any other extras from the farm.

The most difficult time for them was when the weather was wet. While they played board games and cards boredom usually set in quickly and then the fights began. Daisy suggested that they take a look in the conservatory and see what they could find. Neither boy was very excited at the prospect of this.

'We're not wee girls! It's just flowers in there an' flowers with scent.'

Reluctantly the pair followed Daisy into the conservatory. They began to wonder why she didn't stop at the first plants to tell them something about them, but instead moved on past the brightly coloured abutilon and scented pelargoniums.

'What is thon, Mrs Guthrie?'

'Oh, that?' Said Daisy nonchalantly. 'You have to watch out with that plant.'

'Why,' asked Joe.

'It's carnivorous!'

'What's carnvos?' asked Philip curiously.

'It eats flies and other insects.'

'Wow, does it eat anything else?'

'Animals, people?'

'Not these, no!'

Instantly the two boys moved closer.

'It's called a sundew.'

'It doesn't sound card –iv–rous!'

'Just wait and see,' said Daisy.

Daisy picked up a dead fly and dropped it on the sundew. The boys held their breath and then whispered

'What's going to happen?'

'You'll see.'

Joe and Philip could hardly believe their eyes when the leaf pad of the sundew folded over, trapping the insect.

'That's like a lion's mouth closing! Brilliant.'

'And this is a pitcher plant.'

'Wow, it's got lots of different colours on it.'

'Yes, and that's what the insects think too! They are enticed to the top of those funnels and, then the surface is so slippery they fall in and the plant eats them.'

'Why are they in here?'

'Well, they protect the other plants from insects. It's better than using fly paper.'

'That's while clever, Mrs Guthrie.' The boys nodded sagely and continued to watch the plants.

'Can we get some more flies to feed it?'

'Yes, you can come in here any time it's wet and watch the plants work.'

'Where are the boys?' queried Tom. 'It's very quiet.'

'They've found a new activity. They're in the conservatory. It's become the place to go when it's raining. They go fly hunting.'

'Sounds worrying. Surely they haven't taken up house plant gardening?'

'Not exactly, come and see.'

Philip and Joe were engrossed, kneeling on two wicker chairs, they were feeding dead flies to the plants.

'I haven't shown them the sensitive plant[31] yet. I thought I'd leave that till I need another diversion!'

'Good idea,' Tom laughed. 'That plant will have no leaves left and it'll be anything but sensitive.'

---

31 Mimosa pudica

Daisy was the first to try the potion. She and Annie had been discussing the difficulty in getting anything that would take the whiteness away from their legs now that stockings were all but impossible to get, when she had come across a recipe for onion skin dye which would mimic stockings. They had tried to mixture of weak tea as well and Annie had even tried gravy browning but thought better of it when Willow started licking her legs and Sean asked what she was cooking.

Molly had joined the Women's Land Army and was now in charge of the local area. While it was exhausting working full time in the garden and overseeing the girls working on the farms and land nearby, she welcomed the opportunity to be doing something for the war effort.

By July she was busier than ever. Cycling around the area, was keeping her fit but irritable in the heat.

'This acorn coffee truly is disgusting!' said Tom. 'The only thing going for it is that we're able to use the acorns from our own trees but really....'

'It must be bad if you can't manage it, Tom.'

'Remember I became addicted to coffee when I was working in Paris. This can never be coffee!' 'I know it's ridiculous. There are so many really important issues and here am I complaining about the coffee.'

'Ha! I'm glad to hear you say that, Tom, because, tonight, we have carrot curry to eat and tomorrow we're trying a new sandwich filling — cabbage and carrot with chutney! So no comments!'

'I never want to see another carrot, I really don't! Even corned beef fritters sound better,' groaned Tom.

Chapter Forty

1943 — 1944

THE NOISE OF A STRANGE VEHICLE throwing up the gravel on the drive made Matt look up from his weeding on the terrace. An American jeep slew to a stop in front of the house. Matt looked on curiously as a young man in uniform jumped out of the vehicle. Another man waited in the jeep.

'Yanks!' grunted Matt and went back to his work.

'Ma'am, Sir. We're from the base that has been set up on the old farm site on the top road. We're here to introduce ourselves and let everyone in the neighbourhood know we're here.'

Tom and Daisy welcomed the young soldier into the house. 'Would you like some tea...lieutenant?' asked Daisy.

'Lieutenant Bob Smith, ma'am.'

'Yes, that would be kind of you.'

The young soldier walked over to the window of the drawing room. 'That's quite some garden you have there. My mother would love it.'

'Does she grow many plants?' asked Daisy.

'You could say that. She runs a plant nursery from our farm. My dad and she started it in the early thirties specialising in native plants and it's just sort of grown from there!'

Daisy wasn't sure whether to ask but was wondering whether his father was still on the farm too when Bob Smith added 'My father died three years ago. So now, it's just Moma and my sister and two workers holding the fort.'

Tom joined the conversation. 'Are you a plantsman too?'

"No, I'm an engineer by training. I like plants and I help out when I'm home but, no, I'm not a nurseryman.'

'That's my background too,' said Tom. 'I imagine you're putting your knowledge into action at the moment, Bob.'

Bob nodded but did not say more.

'Well, you're welcome to visit any time, Lieutenant,' said Tom.

'Thank you sir. I will.

Several weeks later the jeep drove up to the house. Colin was walking with Matt and Sean from the rose garden, wheelbarrows full of cuttings and old leaves. 'That's the same one I saw a few weeks ago. All neat in his uniform. Don't know why they have to be here,' said Matt.

'I hear they're arranging a party for the locals up in the village hall. My Doris is fair rarin' to go. She says they do a good feed an' the music is good too. I can see I'll have to go with her. I wouldn't let her near them boys wi'out me.' said Colin.

Sean laughed. 'Are you going to do the Lindy Hop then, Colin?'

'I will not indeed an' neither will Doris.'

Sean and Matt laughed.

'I think Annie an' I will go an' have a wee look. I'll eat at their food if nothing else.'

When they got to the village hall they realised that most of the people from the surrounding villages had also been curious about the American party. The place was packed and the music was bright and brash. Couples were already dancing and those that weren't were eyeing up food that they had not seen since before rationing.

Rose saw Bob and no one else. She watched excitedly from the sidelines with her parents and Molly. She was praying that he would come over. She had only met him once at Garraiblagh, but for her that was enough.

Bob left the group of American army officers and walked over to the Guthrie party.

'Hello, Mr and Mrs Guthrie, I'm so glad you could make it.'

'Hello Bob, you remember our friend Molly and our daughter Rose.' Bob smiled in acknowledgement of them.

'Would you mind if I asked your daughter for a dance, Mr Guthrie?'

'Not at all.'

Rose found herself being swept onto the dance floor, completely uncertain of the dance she was taking part in. Within a short space of time however, Rose had mastered the steps of several new dances and was obviously enjoying herself.

Bob became a frequent visitor to Garraiblagh.

'What's that plant over there?' queried Bob, pointing to the bright red spikes of flowers in the border.

'They're montbretia,' said Daisy.

'We have a plant known as the wild red Columbine which looks a little like it. I guess you have Columbine here?'

'Yes, but not in that colour of red. Your plant sounds wonderful. There must be a number of plants that we have in common. You may see more.'

Close to the woodland Bob pointed out another plant. 'Now I think I know what that is. It's a honeysuckle?

'Yes, smell the scent. It's rather wonderful,' said Daisy.

'We have trumpet honeysuckle where we live, it's a native plant, but there's no scent though the flowers are larger and redder,' explained Bob.

'Yes, I think I've come across it. There was a famous plant hunter from England in the seventeenth century and he brought back some trumpet honeysuckle from Virginia. It's amazing the way that plants have been found and then moved around the world. The head gardener in my grandmother's day, James Black, was a plant hunter and we can thank him for many of the unusual plants we have in the garden.'

'Perhaps we should exchange some plants, Connecticut to Garraiblagh and vice versa,' said Bob. 'I'll ask my mother to send over some bulbs and some seeds and make sure the wild red Columbine is among them. I think echinacea could be another one.'

'That would be very kind of you and your mother. I'll talk with Molly and we'll reciprocate with some of our native plant seeds.'

Bob laughed. 'Coming here certainly takes my mind off the war, Mrs Guthrie!'

'I think Bob is dependable but I wouldn't like to think of Rose going out with any of those other soldiers.'

'She certainly seems smitten and I haven't seen her look this happy in ages.'

'She's so young though. This is probably just a passing romance for him. He could be posted elsewhere at any moment and Rose will be devastated.'

'Well, we can't live her life for her. Remember what was happening when we were that age, Daisy.'

From their bedroom Tom and Daisy heard the jeep stop and voices quietly talking. Sleeping was never an option when they waited for Rose to return from a night out with Bob. The crunch of gravel suggested that the couple were walking round to the front of the house. Then there was silence.

'I think they must be walking on the lawn,' said Daisy.

'Perhaps,' said Tom. He was glad Rose was now back at Garraiblagh. He could try to fall asleep now. It felt intrusive to listen out for his daughter.

A bright moon lit the sky as Rose and Bob walked across the lawn to the summer house. The summer evening was still warm enough for Rose to be wearing her dress without any cardigan. The scent of roses was strong in the slight breeze. Bob stopped and took Rose's hand. She was so beautiful, her dark hair and blue eyes, and so young. He hadn't intended to become involved with anyone while he was in the army. And yet here he was, falling in love.

'I'm not sure when I'll be able to call round again Rose. We're very busy at the moment, but I'll write, I promise.'

Rose looked into his eyes. She had never felt this way and she felt as though she was floating on a cloud. Bob leant towards her and kissed her. She leant against him, savouring the moment.

'I must go, Rose. I'm sure your parents are wondering where you are,' and he smiled at her, moving a strand of hair that had fallen over her face.

Rose reached round and picked a rosebud from the bush close to her. 'Take this with you.'

Bob kissed her again and they walked back to the house. Rose stood on the drive listening to the jeep until she could no longer hear it before walking into the house.

Late June 1944

Rose hadn't heard anything from Bob Smith for several weeks. The letter came from America, addressed to the Guthrie family. Daisy opened it and read it out loud.

'My son, Bob, wrote to us so much about Garraiblagh and how you all made him feel welcome. It helped him to be able to spend time with you and to be in the garden. I think it reminded him of home and talking about plants took his mind off what he was involved in.

He sent me the bulbs that you so kindly gave him and they are blooming in our garden here in Connecticut. I am so sorry to tell you that our son did not survive the war. He was part of the D Day landings, helping to create a base for the troops following but he died there in France.'

Rose froze. Tears filled her eyes. 'He can't be dead. Why didn't he write to me. I should never have given him that rosebud out of the garden. This garden, I hate it.'

'Rose, don't be .....' started Daisy.

Tom stopped Daisy, and shook his head. 'Don't,' he whispered.

Rose ran from the room. 'I hate this place.'

'That poor boy.' said Daisy.

Chapter Forty-one

VE Day Garraiblagh

THEY GATHERED AROUND THE WIRELESS to hear the announcement at three o'clock made by Winston Churchill. 'It's over! At least in Europe!'

Tom and Daisy walked out to the front lawn, looking out across the lough and down towards the city. The sound of car horns and ships horns were almost deafening even from where they were.

'Mum, Dad, I'm going to make bunting to hang over the gates. We are going to have a party aren't we?' queried Rose.

'No, it's not over in the Far East, not until Uncle Paddy is home! I've given orders that the mills will be closed tomorrow so that the workers can celebrate, but the war's not over for us until Paddy or the others who are prisoners with him are home.'

Rose flounced out.

Daisy sighed. 'It's difficult to know how Rose will respond to anything these days. Bob's death really shook her I know. I just can't understand this need to party all the time now.'

'She is very brittle, Daisy and for whatever reason I don't think we're the best people to try and get through to her.'

Tom sat down on the wooden bench and focused on the lough in the distance. At the moment Paddy's the one I most worried about. I wish I knew where he was, how he is.'

'I know, my love.'

Tom turned to face her with tears running down his face. 'Half of me wants to celebrate and the other half can't think of anything else but Paddy. My brother and I don't know what's happened to him. The waiting has been hard!'

Daisy's arms encircled him and held him close. There was nothing to say.

It felt in many ways as though everything had changed and nothing had changed. Philip and Joe had gone home, now almost men. The place was so quiet without them.

'I'll miss they two, y'know. They did a good share of the work over the last years once they learned some sense. They were good boys,' said Colin to Molly as they sat in the bothy.

'And now they're away,' responded Molly. 'Well, I hope it's a good world they're going into.'

'They promised to come back an' visit but ye know what happens. We'll probably naw see them again, more's the pity. At least their families are back together again an' I heerd their fathers made it through the war.' said Matt.

"That's great. Young lads need their Das.' said Colin.

'I'm sure they'll never forget you two and what you taught them,' said Molly.

'Aye, well,' mumbled Colin and Matt.

Rose, now twenty, clearly wanted to spread her wings and sought every opportunity to be anywhere but Garraiblagh.

'Rose has gone up to Londonderry with Paul and Maggie. There's evidently going to be a celebration dance for the official surrender of the German U-boats. I do worry about her! She has to be out socialising all the time,' said Daisy.

'She's young and she's grown up in very strange times' said Tom. 'And I know, so did we, but our world was very different.'

Rationing was still in place and the gardens at Garraiblagh still focused on the food production more than the decorative flower gardens.

One of the gardeners, Brian, returned from the army, others did not, having found a world beyond Garraiblagh that they hadn't known about Brian, who had been one of the youngest gardeners noticed the changes and felt uneasy. The garden itself had changed. It had begun to think of itself differently. It was now less regulated. Gone was the constant trimming of box and yew. Branches were finding that they could reach out and create their own shapes.

'Well, I'll be glad to stop the extra Land Army work,' exclaimed Molly to Daisy who had gone round to her cottage with some newly baked scones.

'I think the wheels on your bicycle would have given out if the war had lasted any longer.' laughed Daisy.

'Herc, have some real coffee,' Molly said, relaxing back into her chair, proud of her recent purchase.

'Oh! How did you get that?' 'Don't ask!'

They drank their coffee in silence.

'It'll be strange to have Garraiblagh back,' mused Daisy.

'But what do you want to do with it?'

'What do you mean, Molly?'

'Well, things have changed yet again, haven't they? When I came here there was still a great deal of formality in the garden and in the gardening of the grounds. The people here and the garden itself were still recovering from the Great War.'

Daisy listened, thinking back over the years as Molly spoke.

'You made Garraiblagh well known in a different way before the war through the exhibitions of your drawings and paintings. There are now images of Garraiblagh in galleries and houses all over the place.'

'And my painting garden which you designed was central to that, Molly. And amazingly, with everything else that has happened, it is still there, though it needs some work.'

'Then the war came. Food was the priority. The flowers and shrubs, even the rare ones, had to look after themselves, although we did our best,' said Molly.

'I suppose just getting through each day, I didn't really think. I stopped painting really, apart from sketches for my garden diary. 'I couldn't have got through it without you, Molly, dear.'

The two held each other's hands tightly. As tears started to come, Molly spoke in matter of fact tones,

'None of us could think straight, Daisy. But I've been doing some thinking over the last few weeks. You know we'll soon be one gardener down. Brian has returned, but his heart isn't in it any more. He's seen a bit of the world and he's moving on. Colin should really be retiring. Matt is still working away. And Eileen, well, her time with the Land Army certainly changed things for her!' she laughed. 'She has settled into her new role as a farmer's wife. Sean's great. He really has found his niche in gardening and I think we'd literally have to drag him kicking and screaming from the garden.'

Daisy laughed. 'It's an ill wind that blows nobody any good. Out of that terrible time we have Sean and Annie and Annie to thank for these delicious scones!'

'Sean is working in the garden well beyond his working hours.

When I query it,' said Molly, 'he just shrugs and tells me he was just passing and saw a few weeds and thought he'd tidy up! I hope Annie doesn't think I've got him chained to the lawnmower or something.'

'I think Annie is almost as bad,' added Daisy 'but you're right, it is time to take stock. None of us is getting any younger. I'm fifty this birthday.'

'We're not that old, Daisy. I'm only two years older than you and I definitely don't feel my age, except when I've been trimming hedges. However I do think you and Tom need to consider what you want from the estate now.'

Chapter Forty-two

June 1946

THE OFFICIAL-LOOKING LETTER landed on the mat as Tom and Daisy were about to leave for Belfast. Tom held it gingerly. He was wary of official communications, feeling they usually meant problems.

'What is it?'

Tom scanned the letter.

'Patrick has been released. They're flying him and others back to the UK.'

'That's marvellous news!'

'Perhaps not so good. The language in this letter is couched in the usual impenetrable civil service speak but it sounds as though Patrick is in a bad way. It says that 'Dr Guthrie will possibly take some time to adjust to normal life.'

'Injured?'

'Not necessarily physically. We know what the Jap prisoner of war camps were like. I think the time in the prisoner of war camp has affected him more deeply than that. They want me as next of kin to meet him at a convalescent unit outside London where they can discuss his care.'

'He must come home to us Tom.'

'Let me go first and find out what the situation really is.'

Daisy was just starting on a new drawing in the conservatory when the phone rang.

'Tom?'

'Daisy, let me tell you first and then we can make a decision.'

'Tom, what do you mean?'

'Listen Daisy. I've spoken to the doctors. A psychiatrist is managing Patrick's care. Patrick, Paddy, can't speak.'

'Has something happened to his voice?.'

'No, it's more that he has seen so much he doesn't want to talk. Oh God, Daisy. He's so thin. I nearly didn't recognise him. You know what Paddy was like. Full of fun. Not now. It's as though he's hiding inside himself.'

Daisy could hear the strain in Tom's voice.

'His doctor says he may improve but then again he may not. He has given me details of the camp where Paddy was held. Evil bastards! Worse than the Nazis, much worse!'

Daisy heard the change in Tom's voice and then she heard the tears.

'My brother! How could they! He was a doctor for God's sake!'

Tom was shouting down the telephone by now.

'Bring him home Tom!

'This won't be easy, Daisy. It really won't.'

'Bring him home. We can manage.'

'I love you, Daisy.'

June 1946

George, the cat eyed the stranger who got out of the car. He didn't think that he'd ever seen anyone so thin. His whiskers twitched. Something wasn't right with this one. Rose, who had been playing tennis, ran up. 'Uncle Patrick!' and then she stood still, thinking better of it. Her tennis racket dropped to her side.

George watched as Tom helped Patrick into the house, giving him his arm and then he walked over to the drive and sniffed. There was something wrong. He followed the group of humans indoors.

Daisy held out her arms to her brother–in–law but he ignored her.

Tom moved Patrick to the old winged chair and Patrick sat down shakily. George, who had been watching from the window seat, turned and walked carefully over to Patrick, ignoring Tom and Daisy's strictures to move away.

With a backward glance at Tom, George jumped onto Patrick's lap. With an unconscious movement Patrick put a trembling hand on the cat's back and stroked it. George sat up straight and moved closer to Patrick's face. He leant his body forward and looked straight into Patrick's face as though searching for something. The others in the room looked on mesmerised as George purred loudly and pushed his head against Patrick's chin before settling down on his lap. It was clear that George was not going to move and he settled down to sleep. Patrick's hand lay on the cat's back and in so doing it became clear that at least that hand hadn't been badly injured.

George made a point of coming in through the front door each morning and proceeding straight upstairs to Patrick's room. A polite scratching and a miaow and the door would be opened silently. Sometime later, George would accompany his human patient downstairs and out to the garden.

This became the routine until Patrick hit one of his bad times. Memories overtook him, crying out in the night, whimpering like a child as he relived his captivity. George did not understand the door remaining closed. Determined he went to do what he felt it was his duty to do, to catch a bird and give it to Patrick as he obviously needed food. The old wisteria was tricky to scramble up at first, especially with a live blue tit in his mouth. Through the open window George pounced and landed heavily. The noise jogged Patrick out of his thoughts. Then George released the fluttering and struggling bird. The sudden movement of it released a thousand demons from Patrick's fractured mind. He was thrown back into the Japanese prisoner of war camp. Waving his arms around hysterically to defend himself, Paddy found sanctuary, hiding behind the old armchair while Daisy, running into the room managed to get the bird out of the window.

George was banished. But never one to admit defeat he watched and waited. George hadn't been told off before.

'Life is not getting any easier for Patrick, is it?' said Daisy. 'I saw him last week when the Murrays visited. He didn't want to be there. This world of humans is full of difficulties for him.'

'And difficult for the Murray girl. I remember she was besotted with him before the war and I think he liked her before he left for Singapore. What can we do?'

'He spends the day in the garden and I've noticed that he particularly enjoys thc area around the old summer house. George has taken him under his wing. I'm not sure what else we can do. It's probably a case of time. We can't force the pace.'

Patrick woke early every morning. The family could hear him crying out in the night. Going into his bedroom they would find him staring at the ceiling. He always looked exhausted.

He kept to the same clothes as much as possible. Tom had brought him some of his old trousers and jumpers, clothes he'd left at Garraiblagh before the war. He seemed not to notice what he was wearing. Tom sat with his brother, sometimes keeping up a one way conversation. At other times, just sitting and reading and while reading, Tom took covert glances over at his brother, trying in his imagination to understand what horrors Paddy was fighting.

George the cat seemed to be the only member of the household who had been able to establish a relationship with Patrick, but now he had been banished from Patrick's room because of the incident with the bird.

Patrick made his way downstairs and into the dining room. Daisy and Tom tried hard to tempt him with food but he seemed to have no appetite and had difficulty swallowing. The doctors said it was nothing physical but more to do with how he was starved in the prison camp. Picking up a piece of toast and adding some cheese to make it into a sandwich he walked out into the garden.

George was waiting, nonchalantly licking himself.

Nothing was said, but as Patrick made his way towards the roses the small, persistent cat followed. The scent of the roses wafted across the path and Patrick stopped to admire the colours, pinks, subtle yellows, creams and oranges, before moving on to the summer house. The garden comforted him with its softness.

The old wooden door opened easily. The smell of sun warmed wood and old plants was comforting. The chintz covered sun lounger was Patrick's preferred seat. From there he could lie back and look out of the windows across the lawns and watch for wildlife in the less formal parts of the gardens where the tall grasses swayed and the old oak tree provided shelter.

George moved towards Patrick and soundlessly miaowed his request to join him on the seat. Permission was given and George delicately landed on top of Patrick's legs.

As the months went on Patrick began to use a notebook to jot down changes in the seasons and the movement of animals and insects.

He noted the changes in the seasons through the different plants and colours and watched for the birds as they built their nests. George became his constant companion and confidante. He turned his head to Patrick as the man stroked his fur. He still seemed to be searching the man for signs. His paw moved to Patrick's hand and he bent his whiskers to stroke them along his hand.

Late spring and summer with the long days of warmth led Patrick to camp out in the summer house. He would take a flask of coffee and some sandwiches with him and settle down, leaving the summer house door slightly open. The scent of lavender wafted in to trigger memories perhaps of better times.

It was there that Patrick was able to relax and sleep, covered with the old blankets.

One night he heard a sound and noticed George's hackles rise as he jumped down to hide behind the couch. The moon was bright. Listening, Patrick heard the sound more clearly this time. It was a whine, a low howl. Patrick moved carefully towards the door. He didn't feel fearful. He realised that the natural world and its sounds weren't threatening. It was humans that were dangerous and this was not human. He could see something in the moonlight. Fur gleaming.

'Hello. What's wrong? Who are you?' said Patrick.

The whimper came again.

'It's alright I won't hurt you.'

Patrick turned to find the remnants of one of his ham sandwiches and placed it carefully on the doorstep. Crouching down, he sat on the floor and let his hand relax down onto the ground, close to the door. He waited. A small black nose then a bedraggled body limped in.

'Well, boy. This is the first time I will have used my medical training since Singapore.'

The fox allowed Patrick to touch him. He carefully felt the fox's sides and legs. The wet feel of blood. The leg had been badly cut. With absolute gentleness Patrick felt around the wound. It was clear that it would need more than he had in the summer house. Taking George out, he shut the wounded fox in the summer house and returned to the house. George waited by the summer house door like a sentry.

Returning with his battered old medical bag, Patrick saw the fox had not moved. His hands were steady and nimble, moving with skill and confidence to repair the fox. As he finished treating the animal, he slumped back in the chair and saw George silently watching him from a shelf. Patrick smiled at him. It was his first smile. He gave George a thumbs up with both hands and George smiled with his eyes.

Chapter Forty-three

Garraiblagh 1947 — 1958

THE SNOW KEPT FALLING. The silence only broken by the occasional fall from one of the fir trees as a rook took off and landed on another branch. Night had been disturbed by the barking of foxes looking for mates. For Daisy it sounded like lost souls searching for their loved ones.

'Perhaps we need a covering of snow to help us forget. Everything has been so focused on surviving and now this freezing cold.'

The Inglis bakery van made its way carefully along the drive. With a few slips and slides it managed to negotiate the snow covered grit.

Daisy threw open the kitchen window.

'Good morning, John, the usual please.'

Daisy wrapped her arms round her body, shivering.

'Morning Mrs Guthrie It's while bad the day.'

'Would you like a cup of tea?'

'Aye, I wouldn't say no to wan. I'm goin' to try to get up the road a stretch but the van is fierce caul'.'

'Come on in. The range is on and it's a bit warmer. How are your sons?'

'Oh, not bad. The eldest was de-mobbed last year an' he's for Canada. We're pleased for him, we are. He wants a fresh start an' who can blame him, but we might not see him again.'

'There's always the telephone these days. John.'

'I wouldn't know how to use it, missus. Letters will have to do.'

Daisy was about to make a comforting comment and then thought better of it.

The world was changing yet again even Garraiblagh and the garden. No more certainties and she and Tom were getting older. Rose was the one who would be meeting the challenges. Daisy had made the decision to restore some of the old planting in the garden having come across descriptions in her grandmother's diary.

1958

The old vegetable garden had been hit by part of a stray bomb towards the end of the war and pieces of shell casing could still be found when digging. The war seemed so long ago now. Matt had never worked away from Garraiblagh. He was now in his fifties, but he felt that if he stopped working in the garden, the world would cease to have any meaning. As long as he kept planting, life would continue. He remembered the first time he'd planted the raspberries and blackcurrants, even down to the month and the year.

The new council house he and his wife had been given helped. The damp stone of his old cottage hadn't been good for his back. There was enough room in the garden to grow potatoes and cabbage but he also kept an area for plants that had now become his passion. He'd first seen them in Garraiblagh and now, by carefully taking cuttings and propagating, he had grown them himself. By accident he had found the new variety and now he thought he had something unique. He was going to go over to Frank Black at his nursery and get his advice. New housing was springing up everywhere. Belfast was growing and the new housing estates were moving out towards Garraiblagh. The estate was no longer as isolated.

Summer

The heat was building slowly. From early in the morning the sun shone in cloudless blue skies. Windows were thrown open and the scent of the climbing roses invaded the bedrooms. Colours were everywhere. The black Morris Cowley car turned into the drive of Garraiblagh.

In the front passenger seat Rose opened her handbag and took out her powder compact. Pressing the powder puff over her face she turned to her husband. 'We won't say anything yet. Let's leave it for a while, Peter.'

Peter nodded his head, intent on his driving.

'What are you going to say, Mummy?' Said the small girl from the back seat.

'Nothing, dear. It's just grown up stuff.'

For Fleur the holidays started as they reached the gates of the drive at Garraiblagh. Through the dark leaved trees she waited for her first glimpse of the house. From then on it was like entering an everlasting summer. She was now eight and every summer for as long as she could remember she and her parents had made the trip to Garraiblagh from their home. Rose loved being at Garraiblagh more than going away on the other holidays that her parents seemed to enjoy where they stayed in hotels and went out for meals.

Opening the door to her bedroom which overlooked the lawn the sun shone in and the dust motes disturbed by the air movement floated like summer snow. She loved the smell of the old house. Fleur hurried to the window to check on the garden. Her map of the garden was clear, made up of memories and games. The path to the swamp led past the bamboos and behind them was one of the hideouts. The tree-house was further down in the meadow, where she set out her doll's tea set and Bruan, her teddy bear oversaw the picnics.

She knew every nook and cranny of her grandparents' estate and the first thing she did was to go to all the different places. Wood pigeons cooed in the fir trees as she ran down across the front terrace to the formal sunken pond with the strange little stone gargoyle at one end. The pond was carefully netted to keep the herons away and Fleur leant over to watch the huge orange and red goldfish slowly weave their way around, disappearing as they moved beneath the water lillies. The bamboos rustled their welcome to her and she trod carefully around the wild pond reminding herself that the water was deep. It was the place where huts and hide outs could be made and bamboos became fishing rods and anything could be imagined. On the tiny island in the pond, reached by the Japanese bridge, there was a stone with markings, difficult to make out but they were ancient according to Grandpa Tom. It made Fleur feel connected. In her dreams she imagined living at Garraiblagh forever and down at the wild pond she threw a penny in, wishing for that to become a reality.

Fuchsias with their tiny fairy hats lit up the sunken lane as Fleur collected them. A tapping sound stopped her in her tracks, delicate but persistent. Moving closer to the sound, Fleur imagined a leprechaun, working at a shoe. Holding her breath and leaning in to the undergrowth she saw a thrush with a snail shell in its beak hitting it against a stone. The thrush's dark eyes stared back at her. Fleur knelt down for a closer look, but the thrush, surprised by the human, flew off, leaving its work unfinished. A robin chattered at her as though chiding her for associating with a thrush.

The strawberry tree at the bottom of the lawn with its low hanging branches was the best to climb even though the ginger brown bark came off on your hands. From her vantage point Fleur could see the gate into the vegetable garden. But first she lay back against the tree trunk and surveyed her world. Her home was in a town. Houses built close together with small gardens and carefully erected fences. Here in Garraiblagh she never felt closed in, never felt lonely among the plants and it was the place that her grandmother told her stories about — the people who'd lived there, real and imaginary, the strange plants and their journeys from faraway place and the people who had found them.

Opening the gate Fleur stepped down into the carefully partitioned garden. Small box hedges surrounded the plants. She knelt down and picked some parsley, savouring its texture and taste. Everything was as it should be. The herbs, the peas, the beans, the cabbage. She checked off the different plants in her mind. She had a particular route she walked when she first came into the vegetable garden at the start of the holidays. In the distance were the tall fir and beech trees bordering the estate and then there was the deep red brick of the end wall on which cordons of pears were growing and ripening. Fleur picked a stalk of rhubarb. Its leaf like a huge umbrella shaded her from the sun and she sucked on the sour end as she went in search of her grandfather. The greenhouse door was warm to the touch, the white paintwork peeling a little. The bright brass knob was inviting her to turn it. Once open, she paused.

'Close the door. You'll let the heat out!' She could hear her Grandpa Tom shout. Fleur crept in quickly. She was standing on a tiled black and red floor. The greenhouse was hot and the scent of tomatoes and their bruised leaves filled the air. She breathed it in and saw her grandfather with his pipe and felt hat bent over the staging, concentrating. His old tweed jacket making him look very much like Mr Magregor. This was like Grandpa Tom's study. She held the door, ready to run.

'Granny says that lunch is ready.' There was a grunt and he nodded his head towards his grand-daughter. His hands neatly tied twine around the tomato plants stakes. His glasses lowered on his nose. 'Do you know how to pick tomatoes?'

Fleur shook her head 'No.'

She felt as though she was at school. 'Come over here and see. This is how you do it. Watch me and then you can try.'

Fleur reached out to the tomato plant.

'Remember, hold it at the join and only take it if it snaps off.'

The round yellow tomato was warm and smooth in her hand. The scent was something she would remember forever.

He watched closely and smiled. 'Now you have decide which ones you think are ripe enough to pick.' Fleur felt the awful responsibility, but knew that she wanted to collect these beautifully coloured fruits more than anything.

He watched his young granddaughter make her way carefully to the house carrying the red and yellow fruit in a trug[32]. Taking out his pipe and beginning to tamp down the tobacco he considered. It occurred to him that Fleur and he had something in common in the garden and perhaps, just perhaps, he could find a way of communicating with her which he had found to be more difficult with her daughter.

For the rest of the summer Fleur followed her grandfather around the garden. Naming plants, identifying seed and planting seedlings. Daisy watched, smiling at the young and old heads bent together in conversation. Tom knew that Fleur was somewhat lonely and knew that Rose was very caught up in her own world of fashion and dinner parties. Looking at Fleur she wondered what the future would hold for her only grand-daughter.

Later, on the old grass tennis court, shaded by the beech and

32 A wooden basket used for carrying flowers or other garden produce.

sycamores, Fleur would play tennis with Sam and Steven, Frank Black's grandchildren. They never bothered to bring rackets with them. Instead they opened the heavy wooden chest in the hall and reached into generations of sports equipment with the smell of cricket bats, balls, rackets in their presses and old deflated leather footballs.

The conservatory was Fleur's other favourite place. As soon as the door to the garden was closed the scents assailed her. Pelargoniums, jasmine, lilies and stephanotis. Somehow it made her feel safe. The scents seem to draw her into another world, one in which her imagination would, transport her back in time. With the slight echo as she walked across the tiles, the flies and bees buzzing, moisture dripping from the plant shelves, Fleur imagined ladies in long dresses, pinks and greens, satins and velvets, carefully admiring the blooms. The old cane chair was large enough for her to curl up on and read, sometimes accompanied by Felix, the black and white cat. Felix also enjoyed the conservatory, quietly sleeping, curled up in a pot if no lap or cushion was available.

Later, leaning out of the bedroom window she listened to the wood pigeons in the firs. She found their calls comforting. In a world like this nothing could go wrong. Nothing could change.

On her way downstairs again Fleur stopped at the stained glass window that lit up the turn in the stairs. It was one of her favourite places for just sitting and dreaming. She loved this window. It was made up of different coloured pieces and when the sun shone she could pick a colour and look through.

Fleur could make out voices, a conversation in the drawing room.

'New Zealand? Rose!'

'Mum, it's such a wonderful opportunity! Friends of ours emigrated last year. They say it is the best decision they've ever made. We're tired of this little country with its small mindedness!"

Fleur crept down to the drawing room door and listened. She

could hear her mother excitedly explaining more about New Zealand and her father telling everyone that he had found a good position in one of the large businesses out there. Then she heard her name being mentioned.

'What about Fleur,?' Granny was asking.

'She'll be fine. It will be an adventure! Children adjust,' came the response from her mother.

'Do you think you'll be able to come back over here?' queried Grandpa Tom, although it sounded to Rose as though he already knew the answer to that.

'Well, we'll have to see. We need to find our feet first and explore.'

'And Garraiblagh? We had assumed that you and Peter would take over eventually.'

'Mother, Surely you can't imagine me or us here. It's just not us.' Rose said 'here' as though it was something unpleasant.

Moving quietly back to the stairs she found herself staring through the coloured glass, hoping it would change what she'd heard. Nothing would be the same again.

She put on her gumboots, knotted the scarf and then tied the pixie hat around her chin. Her father and Grandpa Tom were waiting. It was the first time that she had been allowed to go with them to get the Christmas tree. Since the time of her great grandparents a tree from the estate had been cut for the house. In the past, grandpa had cut the tree himself, sometimes with the help of grandma. They had then pulled it up, balancing it precariously on a wheelbarrow. This year she knew that her grandfather was not well and it was likely to be the last Christmas they had at Garraiblagh before her father and mother took her to New Zealand.

The small plantation of firs to the north side of Garraiblagh provided both a windbreak and the Christmas tree. Walking through the gate into the field Fleur could hear the quietness fall. Birds fluttered off at the movement of humans and the trees waited. Fleur wondered if it would be possible to hide here among the trees when her parents got ready to leave. She could find an axe and make herself a tree-house and live on berries. She could have a camp-fire and cook on that as she'd been shown how to do in the Brownies.

Back at the house the tree was deposited in the drawing room and the hunt was on for the lights and the decorations. The lights, made up of a string of bulbs hidden inside different shapes were old but Fleur loved the individuality of them. She knew now that her wish would not come true. Her parents had made it clear that they would be moving to New Zealand in the New Year. For Fleur, not only had her parents removed her from the place she loved but they were now going to ruin her Christmas. Fleur watched as her mother helped with the decorations, wrapped presents and sang carols, seemingly oblivious to the sadness of those around her.

'Darling, you're being silly! It's just a garden! Think how exciting it will be to live in a large city with theatres and cinemas.'

Fleur was unimpressed.

'There are parks and we'll be able to go to the beach and there'll be lots of others of your age to play with!'

Fleur looked at her mother in her taffeta party dress with her hair newly permed and the smell of expensive scent lingering around her. She understood at that point that her father would never stand up to her mother even if he did understand.

'You don't care about anyone else, Mother, do you,' spat Fleur. The look in her eyes struck home, but only fleetingly.

Fleur hugged Grandma Daisy tight and closed her eyes to breathe in the light rose scent that she always wore. In a whisper Daisy knelt down to her granddaughter and stroked her hair.

'Fleur, I have something for you. Don't open it now. Keep it until you get to New Zealand. It will fit into your suitcase.'

Tom held out his arms to Fleur.

'I've made you a book.'

'Made it, Grandpa?'

Tom nodded not trusting himself to speak any more. Tom had not mentioned keeping it till later. Fleur tore off the paper covering. Inside was a book, of sorts. As she opened it she realised that it was more like a scrapbook or photograph album and this book held flowers that had been pressed, information on the history of the garden, the plants and pictures of all the people, both family and staff.

True to her word, Fleur did not open her present from her grandmother until she reached New Zealand. And when she did, in what would be her bedroom in the large townhouse, sadness mixed with love flooded in as she looked at the painting by her grandmother of Garraiblagh garden.

Japanese Garden 1950

'Settled in the chair he let his hand reach down below the seat. He had brought some scraps that he was going to leave for the birds but he was intrigued by the closeness of the fox and wanted to see if it would respond, hardly daring to hope that it would'.

Garraiblagh House 1960

PART SIX

Decline

'Many things grow in the garden that were never sown there.'
Spanish proverb

Chapter Forty-four

1960 — 1963

TOM, NOW SEVENTY FOUR, knew his eyesight was failing. Shapes merged one into another. He could still feel his way to the garden with the aid of a stick and old Duncan, his black spaniel but this also became more difficult with time. Daisy saw the depression that fell across Tom's face.

'But don't you see, Daisy?' and then he realised what he'd said. 'Of course you do see. I'm the one that can't! I don't want to be a burden.'

Since his retirement the vegetable garden had been his main focus. After so many years of working in Belfast and really only seeing the garden as a place to relax at weekends he had slowly become fascinated by the practical aspects of gardening and had used his engineering knowledge and skills to create mechanical solutions for watering plants and other things. Now he had to leave it to others, contenting himself with giving instructions on what he wanted to be planted and where and, since Fleur and her parents had left for New Zealand, he had missed having his young gardening companion. He wrote letters to her telling her about the garden and occasionally they spoke on the phone but the line was very bad. It was no substitute in any case and now with his failing eyesight letter writing wouldn't be possible.

The greenhouse was too far, but it was the place he understood. He lived in a world of darkness. Out in the greenhouse he could feel the light and the warmth more readily than when indoors. It helped him feel a part of the world. So much of his life had been vital, his engineering, his flying and his business management. Now he had to find his way in a world of darkness. A world he could not control.

Daisy, watching Tom's precarious path to the walled garden and the greenhouses, wondered to herself.

'Tom, what if we used the conservatory for the tomatoes, could we? You wouldn't have to walk as far and we could rig up staging.'

'What about your pelargoniums?'

'I can just move them around the windows at the front of the house.'

In the conservatory Tom taught himself to feel the edging of the new staging. The memory of the best places to set the trays, the compost and the pots focused his mind. With his hand in the compost it all suddenly felt tangible as though he wasn't in some limbo world. He could connect to the earth and the growing plants once more. Excitement gripped him as he filled the trays carefully and levelled them off. Using his fingers as a cover he sprinkled water on the seeds.

Coming back a week later he felt the trays, his fingers delicately searching for any cotyledon appearing. As they grew, the scent of the tomatoes confirmed the plants were growing. Every new sequence had to be tested with his fingers. Delicate flowers, tiny budding fruit. What was more difficult was checking for greenfly, but the stickiness and uneven surfaces alerted him.

The roses were a different challenge. They were Daisy's favourites and when he worked with them he felt close to her. Tom was wary of jagged thorns of the older roses and knew by the smaller but no less painful stems whether it was the climbing rose or the tea rose. If he concentrated he could tell whether it was a field rose or a cultivated variety.

Working carefully, he could cut and prune, but in the darker days of autumn and winter he had fewer guides and no scent. The winter months wore him down.

Daisy watched Tom from a distance. She knew he didn't lack courage, but she was worried.

There had to be a way to make a garden for Tom which allowed him to be independent. While Tom worked with the tomatoes and the roses, Daisy worked with Molly and Sean creating Tom's garden. Plants would be obtained that were full grown. Time was of the essence.

The obvious first step thought Daisy, would be to create a border, an enclosure. Plants would then have to be identifiable and at a height not to trip up her husband. Places to sit and feel the different textures and take in the scents. Scented plants and trees for the whole year, not just summer. Plants that would remind Tom he was still able to do things. The garden would have scent, sound and shape, be reassuring but also curious and provoking. Tom's garden would not be bland.

Box hedging created the perimeter and a deep trellis archway the entrance. A mixture of clematis armandii and lonicera twined around it.

Hamamelis and mahonia were included for winter, philadelphus, azaleas and daphne for spring, phlox, peony and dianthus for summer. At waist level were pots of herbs — lavender, rosemary, golden marjoram.

Feeling the stems and then the leaves Tom began to train himself to recognise the plants. At times when the utter separation from the world he had known threatened to overwhelm him he forced himself to concentrate on a flower head. Feeling the soft velvet, the shape and length, the central section, stamen.

One morning as Tom made his way into his garden he stopped. There it was! The distinctive smell of fox in his garden. Tom was glad the fox approved. In the cool, frosty morning he smelled the animal and feeling his way to his wooden seat in its hidden bower he heard a snuffling.

Settled in the chair he let his hand reach down below the seat. He had brought some scraps that he was going to leave for the birds but he was intrigued by the closeness of the fox and wanted to see if it would respond, hardly daring to hope that it would.

Tom was beginning to think that he was being foolish when he felt the sensation of fur brushing across his hand and then a gentle but determined pull at the scrap of meat in his hand.

'Oh hello Foxy, how do you do?'

Tom wanted so badly to reach out further and stroke it but knew that it would retreat if he did.

'I don't know anything about you, but I'll not hurt you.'

For the first time in many months Tom felt excitement.

The fox did not want to be seen and he could not see it. This seemed to give them both some confidence in the relationship.

Winter 1962 — 1963

The blizzard began, taking everyone's breath away with the cold winds. The fires in the rooms did not provide enough heat and there always seemed to be draughts. Daisy couldn't remember a time as cold as this. She wore so many layers of clothes she felt like a Russian doll.

The garden was being ravaged by the cold as well, but the

mahonia flowers in their lurid green yellow among the glossy, prickly leaves seemed immune and their scent mingled with the orange witch hazel.

Using a wheelchair Tom had been able to get around the ground floor of the house and Christmas had, in any case, been quiet. But now the weather really didn't help, Daisy thought.

By the time snowdrops began to show their heads in the grass and the woodland it was clear that Tom was fading. Standing at the window of the breakfast room she was entranced by their strength and beauty.

'Look, Tom, the snowdrops are out!' and then realised what she had said. She bit her lip at the stupid comment and turned to apologise to her husband.

Tom's head had slumped forward onto his shoulders. Duncan was whimpered, putting his paws on Tom's knee then barked. Tom didn't respond.

Chapter Forty-five

Garraiblagh Summer 1975

DAISY KNEW that at times she was forgetful. She had decided that it would be best if she kept a notebook in which she could write down all the important things, but she found she couldn't always make out her own writing or spelling. She walked slowly along the paths, touching and acknowledging the different plants as she went. This was her world, Garraiblagh, the garden. The bread van still delivered and the local grocer sent one of the lads round with the weekly shopping list. Daisy felt no urge to wander beyond the boundaries of the garden and felt that the garden protected her.

Sean called in every day, ostensibly to tend to the garden. But his real purpose was to check on Daisy Guthrie. He excused himself by saying he was just doing a bit of gardening and she accepted that with his friendship.

'Mrs Guthrie! There you are. I thought you'd probably be here. The roses are looking well.'

Sean leant over and picked one of the blooms. Daisy took the flower and gazed into the distance.

Sean wondered where she was. He had noticed Daisy's absences becoming more frequent.

'Mrs Guthrie?'

Daisy turned at that and smiled. 'Yes? Oh hello, Sean. Have you just arrived? We should have some tea.'

'I've brought a cake that Annie made for ye.'

'Oh, how nice. I'm sure Tom would like some too. I'm not sure where he is at the moment.'

Sean accompanied Daisy slowly back to the house and the kitchen, Daisy stopping at intervals to touch a plant or pick a blossom.

It was clear that someone was systematically digging out plants and not just any plants. Whoever it was had an understanding of the rarer ones and those that would be worth some money.

Sean drove home to Annie.

'Some bastard is thieving plants from Mrs G. It's disgusting. They must know she's become forgetful. And Annie, she is becoming much more forgetful.'

'That is beyond belief. Are you sure? Who would do that?'

'I'm going to find out. I didn't want to say anything until I was sure but I've been keeping note of the herbaceous border down near the rose arbour. They're clever, I'll give them that. They can't be seen from the house'.

'Have you told Mrs Guthrie?'

'No, I don't want to worry her if I don't have to. I'm goin' to get a couple o' the boys an' we will keep watch tonight an' for as long as it takes us.'

'Are you sure. Why don't ye talk to the police?'

'Look, they're plants. What do you think they'll do? We'll be watchin' and believe me it won't be the police they need to watch out for.'

Daisy looked down at the plant she had in her hand; the cool, slim stem and the succession of tiny purple blue flowers at its head. She had known this plant all her life, she knew that. She lifted the flower to see if there was any scent and a subtle perfume was drawn into her nostrils. In her mind she knew it was a purple blue, a colour she had mixed many times for her paintings but the words to describe it would not come.

Sean had driven round to Molly later in the day to discuss the situation.

'I'll go round early tomorrow to see her. I've been worried too, but to be honest I think I've been burying my head when it comes to Daisy's memory.'

Molly walked slowly down from the cottage, Bob, her old collie at her heels. It was the most glorious place to be. She'd loved the place from the first time she'd visited it.

She walked over the flagstones edged with creeping thyme and around to the front of the house with the lawn opposite.

'Hello, Daisy, what are you doing here? You must be cold.'

Daisy looked at the face in front of her and smiled. She had learnt that it was best to smile and be polite, while at the same time trying to work through the maze in her head to find the person's name.

As though her mind had been jogged out of a dream she looked around her to see that she was standing in an ocean of bluebells. Then she remembered and stated 'Bluebells' with a confidence she now felt and said the word again as though to pin it into her memory.

Molly, looked into Daisy's eyes and saw her old friend trying hard to find the reality expected of her without any awareness that she was standing in a long, pale pink nightie, her grey hair uncombed with morning dew glistening over her bare feet as she stood in the swathe of bluebells.

'I have some coffee. Let's go into the kitchen. I think there are some biscuits there as well.'

'Is it elevenses already?' Daisy smiled in anticipation.

'Almost,' lied Molly, swallowing down her own tears and fear at seeing Daisy reduced to this.

Molly met with Sean and Annie in the garden.

'We have to let the family know. None of us are getting any younger and something could happen. She needs someone with her,' said Molly. 'I keep a close eye on her. I've suggested we move in together but she won't hear of it.'

Sean sighed. 'We know and I hadn't said anything, but Jack and I found a guy who's been stealing plants from the herbaceous border — not just any plant — he knew what he was doing. They are the rare ones.'

'What happened,' queried Molly 'Why didn't you say?'

'It only happened a couple of nights ago. I'd wondered about plants being missing and then when I knew I was right I called Jack. And before you say anything there was no point calling the RUC, they have enough on their plate. They're hardly likely to prioritise some stolen plants.'

'I'll ring Rose tonight but...' sighed Molly.

'I know, that 'madam' won't be best pleased to be asked to do anything!' said Annie. 'She was always spoilt rotten.'

'There is Fleur though,' said Molly. 'I've kept in touch with her. I need to ring Rose first but I'll also phone Fleur, just in case her mother 'forgets' to mention it.' Molly raised an eyebrow.

'She cannot be taken from her garden! Do that and you might as well kill her.' Fleur slammed the door, following her mother into the kitchen.

'The garden has always been her sanctuary,' repeated Fleur.

'And what if she wanders off, wanders into the pond or she's found, or rather her body is found?' Rose leant across the table, focusing on her daughter, 'What then?'

'We have to be sensible,' said Rose.

'Do we? Then are you going to move back to Garraiblagh and look after her?' asked Fleur.

Rose made a moue of annoyance.

'Don't be silly, dear, you know that's not possible.'

'Well, I will. My grandmother is not going to be moved to a 'home'.'

'And how are you going to manage that?' queried Rose as though dealing with a young child.

'I don't know,' said Fleur quietly, ' but I have to do it.'

'Look what's happening over there. It's not a place for you and from what I've heard Garraiblagh is no longer miles from the city. Belfast has expanded and they're all busy murdering each other over there. Garraiblagh is in the middle of it all now!'

Fleur packed a suitcase and took the bus to the airport. She had sent her art materials on by post, hoping that they would arrive without damage.

Landing at Aldergrove, she found herself in a bizarre world of extreme security with police and soldiers carrying guns. Waiting just beyond the barriers were Sean and Annie. As soon as they saw her they waved and Fleur responded, tears threatening to flow.

The drive out of the airport, the ramps, the checks and the questions were never ending.

It seemed the army and police were everywhere. For the first time in her life Fleur felt real fear. 'Am I mad?' she wondered to herself, 'coming to look after Granny.' She hated to admit it, but perhaps her mother had been right.

'Are you alright, Fleur?' asked Annie.

'Yes, just shocked I suppose. It's like a war zone.'

'We forget. We're used to it and it's not like it's like this everywhere. Wait till you get back to Garraiblagh and settle in,' said Sean.

As they came close to the outskirts of Belfast Sean slowed the old car down.

'Looks like we're bein' diverted!'

In the distance Fleur could see army land rovers and what she realised was the sound of gunfire. She looked at Sean who calmly manoeuvred the car and turned it back.

'Where are we going now?' asked Fleur with panic beginning to rise in her.

'We're just takin' a wee detour down a road I know. It'll take a little longer, but that's ok.'

Fleur watched as the buildings passed and she saw the barbed wire and the sandbags.

The road to Garraiblagh was no longer through the countryside. It was one housing development after another and some of them didn't look very pleasant. It seemed an age before they finally approached a road she remembered and then came the turning and the gate posts of Garraiblagh. Her heart missed a beat. She strained her neck to look, to take in everything as the car began its way up what was now a pot–holed drive.

'Where will Granny be?' asked Fleur as she got out of the car. Lifting the suitcase out of the boot, Sean motioned to the house. 'She'll probably be in the kitchen. Molly is here to welcome you as well.'

Fleur walked into the warmth of the kitchen and the old Aga stove. This at least seemed the same.

'Fleur, my child, what a lovely surprise!'

'But Granny, you knew I was coming.'

'Did I, dear? Well, that's good.'

Fleur turned slightly and saw Molly.

'Auntie Molly!' They hugged.

'Hello, dear, long time no see. It's so good to have you here. We decided that you should go in your great-grandmother Amelia's old room, the one that looks out onto the front gardens. I hope that's alright?'

Fleur felt her grandmother's eyes on her and then noticed her reaching towards a large circular cake tin on the table.

'But let's all have a cup of tea and a piece of cake first. You're not against cake are you?' Molly laughed. 'Mrs Mullan sent over one of her special cakes.'

Molly took the top off the tin and Fleur finding herself reverting to her childhood actions, looked in and smelled the delicious aroma. The smell almost overwhelmed her. Closing her eyes she could remember the cakes her grandparents had had, tea on the lawn, in front of the fire. The circle of warmth that she had, she knew, never known with her mother.

'Coffee and walnut cake! Mm! Now I know I'm back.'

The evening breeze rustled in the leaves. Fleur had put on jumper, tiredness and the change in temperature had made her feel chilled. Garraiblagh. She was really here.

Fleur followed the old lane round and up through the trees to Molly's cottage. It had hardly changed. Opening the gate which Fleur realised still had a distinctive creak to it, she knocked on the door. She stood back from the top step, expecting to hear the slow steps coming towards the door as Molly made her way over the old stone floor to the door. To while away the few minutes Fleur turned and bent down to touch and then smell the lavender plants that Molly had in clay pots positioned around the front of the cottage and door.

Suddenly the door was flung open and a tall, dark curly haired young man stood in the doorway.

'Hello! I know who you are.' said the dark haired stranger. Fleur struggled to recover herself. 'I'm Kevin,' he smiled.

'Hello, I was looking for Molly.'

'Yes, come on in. She's inside. I said I would answer the door, her knees are a bit worse than usual today.'

'Come on in, Fleur,' shouted Molly's voice from inside the cottage.

'Let me introduce you. This is Kevin, his grandfather, Connor, was a great friend of mine many years ago.'

The summer heat continued 'This must be one of the best summers we've had,' commented Molly as she dead-headed some roses. Daisy sat close to her watching finches landing and taking off from the bird bath and nodded as though in agreement. Molly knew that her friend might be in another world completely but it felt reassuring just to talk.

'Where's Fleur? asked Daisy as though she had suddenly remembered someone she knew.

'I think she's down in the garden with Kevin. He's doing some potting on of plants and she's helping.'

Daisy appeared content with the answer. Molly, on the other hand, was not so sure. The attraction between the two young people had been instant. Anyone could see that. It was clear that Fleur was head over heels. Molly had a niggling doubt about Kevin.

Fleur had collected her art materials and decided to go down to the hammock she had, with Kevin's help, erected under the lime trees. She began work on a drawing, concentrating on the light and shade across the pond and the statue but her mind drifted to thoughts of the previous night. She smiled as she thought to herself that it was a good thing the house was so large. She and Kevin had made a flat of the top floor of the house, far from her grandmother or anyone where they could be together.

Fleur could think of nothing else. Kevin was in her head all the time. She found it difficult to concentrate on anything else.

The memory of Kevin's arms lifting her down onto the bed and then his hands as they began to explore her body sent waves of pleasure through her body even now. She imagined long summers into the future, she and Kevin together at Garraiblagh. She was now convinced she had made the right decision in coming back.

As she lay in the hammock she saw Kevin coming towards her, his dark figure cool against the colours of the hollyhocks and delphiniums in the border. He reached the hammock and smiled.

'It's too hot, I've got some cheese and bread and beer cooling in the river.'

Fleur needed no further encouragement. Taking his hand she leant against him as they walked to the wild area and the standing stone. Each could feel the energy between them. Lying against the old standing stone surrounded by poppies and meadowsweet they made love. As the sun beat down they lay in each other's arms, the trees and the grasses moving gently in the slight breeze.

Fleur hurried down to see Kevin, she now knew his routines as well as she did her own. He would be in the potting shed, and the dark cool space had on more than one occasion been a place to make love.

'Hi there,' she said as she wrapped her arms around him, smiling. 'I've brought you some sandwiches and some cake and,' she said, mischievously, 'in case you're hungry for something else — myself.'

Kevin put the pot of pelargoniums down on the bench beside him and lifted up a letter that looked newly opened.

'Fleur, I don't know how to tell you this. So I'll just say it. There's an opening for a gardener in Perthshire over in Scotland. I'm going to take it. There's a good probability that I'll be able to take over the garden eventually.'

Fleur listened, waiting for Kevin to mention her, holding her breath, hoping that he was just about to ask her...but he didn't.

'What about me, what about us?'

'Us? Fleur, it wouldn't work. It's been great, you're a great girl, but I can't get tied down and anyway he hesitated I don't love you enough to make it work.'

It felt as though she had been slapped in the face. Tears came to her eyes

'I'm sorry, Fleur. I shouldn't have let it go on.'

All she could think of was getting away, back to the house and her room.

She hadn't felt good for a few days and she'd put it down to Kevin leaving.

Kevin had packed up his belongings the next day and left without any further word.

'Molly? asked Daisy.

'No, it's Fleur, Granny.'

'Hello Fleur, are you getting our tea and cake.'

'Yes, Granny, you know I am.'

'Are we having tea and cake now?'

'I'm going to get it for you now, Granny, be patient. I'm getting the tea!' She banged the tea caddy down on the table.

Fleur saw the hurt in her grandmother's eyes.

'I'm sorry, Granny.'

Daisy grasped Fleur by the hand. 'Are we having the cake now?'

Fleur nodded and turned away. The tears kept coming.

The visit to the doctor was quick. Fleur was definitely pregnant, four months gone.

She certainly wasn't going to tell her mother and her grandmother would not understand. Molly was the only one, but she felt embarrassed, foolish that she had been so naive. Fleur sat in Molly's cottage, nursing one of her cats, holding a mug of coffee in her other hand.

Molly waited. She had wondered, but it was none of her business. She just hoped it wasn't what she imagined.

'My poor girl. I'm so sorry. I'll tell his grandfather. He would be so ashamed of him,' said Molly when she heard.

'No, I don't want him or his family to know, Molly. I'll manage.'

'You'll not manage alone. I feel responsible. That young man will not be welcome in my house again. I'll do everything I can to help, Fleur.'

Fleur had never seen Molly so angry and Fleur, although shocked, felt comforted by it.

Chapter Forty-six

1978

DAISY MOVED SLOWLY around her garden. She knew that time was getting shorter and she relished each day that she had to breathe in the beauty of the place. Each step, on a carefully plotted route of the garden was a chain of memories, held together by dancing daisies and swaying honeysuckle stems.

It had grown, and aged, as she had done. Favourite plants, cherished and lost, as in the human world. She had lost her beloved Tom and friends and for her it was the place where love had grown. The garden had held her at times which had been good and bad, anchoring her to life.

Daisy sat down on the bench in the rose arbour. A smile flitting across her face as she thought of the seasons and how they shifted from the spring of early snowdrops, the rare double varieties and daffodils, their yellows and purples through reds and oranges to autumn and lazy wood smoke, leaves raked and branches burnt. Winter and frost glazed paths with hanging stars on the late roses and the icicles hanging like tiny frosted necklaces from the ivy climbing the stone wall at the bottom of the walled garden.

She brought her mind back to the present, to summer and the scent of the pink and white twining roses around her, smiling at the recollection of their perfume as she and Tom had lain, so long ago, amidst the long grass. She touched and smelled the plants as she passed; the fire orange of the crocosmia, the spice of the carnations, the red ballet dancer fuchsia vital and untameable. Mint and thyme bruised and awoken by steps on the flagstones near them. The robin followed in her footsteps without fear. Daisy and the garden at one, their energies combined in the peaceful place. She closed her eyes to listen. As the bees soporific humming echoed in her mind, she left the physical world.

Fleur called to her grandmother through the French windows and then stopped herself from calling out again. Instead she walked out and down the steps; very aware of the extra weight she was carrying and fearful of a possible fall. She didn't want to startle her grandmother if she was sleeping out in the arbour. It was such a beautiful day.

Fleur found her on the old bench, surrounded by roses. At first she thought Daisy was asleep, but when she moved closer, gently calling her name, and then touched her hand, in which a small posy of flowers was gripped, she realised. Her grandmother was dead.

'Oh no, Granny' Fleur shouted as she slumped down beside her and threw her arms around her.

A small service in the nearby church was followed by a small private ceremony as Daisy was buried as she had asked, next to Tom and her grandparents in Garraiblagh. Molly, Sean, Annie and Fleur were joined by John Black, Frank Black's son and his elder son, Sam Black who'd just turned thirty. Tea and sandwiches were laid out in the drawing room at Garraiblagh. Conversation was stilted until Molly inevitably brought the conversation round to plants and gardens, the one subject that bound everyone together and that had been so important to Daisy. As discussion moved from the difficulties in running a plant nursery to the newest varieties on sale, Sam wandered over to Fleur, 'I'm sure we've met before.' Fleur looked at the red haired, bearded giant. She didn't feel in the mood for conversation. She shook her head, 'No, I don't think we have met though it's strange, you do seem familiar.' Sam smiled back. The laughter lines around his eyes were accentuated by his tanned skin.

'Oh, well, just strange. I'd better get back to the nursery now. It was good to meet you, Fleur.'

Chapter Forty-seven

1979

AUGUST BROUGHT WITH IT SOME SUNSHINE. The hot weather and her pregnancy made her feel tired. She was glad when the labour pains started. Sean and Annie drove Fleur and Molly to the hospital where the three awaited news.

'Have you phoned Rose to let her know about Fleur?' asked Annie.

'No,' said Molly, tight lipped. If Fleur wants to do that she can but her mother has been of little use to her so far.'

Molly burst into tears when she saw the tiny baby beside Fleur. 'Oh, she's beautiful!'

'She is indeed,' said Annie with Sean nodding in agreement.

'It's as well I've been doin' some knitting for the wee one,' said Annie.

'And it's good that you weren't relying on me for knitted garments. You know what my knitting's like!' laughed Molly.

Bryony wrapped in the shawl that Annie had crocheted for her, lay peacefully beside her in the kitchen of Garraiblagh. The kitchen

437

range, the old Aga, gave out a good heat and even though it was still only summer, the warmth was reassuring. The kitchen hadn't changed in decades. Fleur remembered the copper jelly and blancmange moulds that hung in the pantry along with the old soup tureens and huge serving dishes no longer part of everyday life. So much had changed and now her world had changed.

Molly walked slowly and with obvious pain, using her old cat-headed carved stick to lean on. She could only manage a slow shuffle these days and bit her tongue and winced as the pain in both knees shot through her.

'Molly, how wonderful to see you. Have a seat and I'll put the kettle on. Tea or coffee?'

The kettle spat as it was placed on top of the range. A comfortable sound.

Molly reflected, as she had done on more than one occasion, during her life what it would have been like if she and Edmund had had a child. Certainly simpler, more conventional, she thought to herself. What if she had taken Connor up on his suggestion? Certainly not conventional and possibly very problematic, but then I would never have had a career in gardening, never had the freedom I've had, she considered.

In Fleur, Molly could see the same strength and determination as she had known in Daisy and Amelia.

'Is your mother coming over?' Molly asked, but without much optimism.

Fleur shook her head. 'No, we argued about it. She is 'busy'. Mum says we should sell. I don't suppose my great-grandparents could have foreseen having no family in a position to take on the property when they first built the house and created the garden. It's going to be complicated. We don't want to have to sell or rather I don't and perhaps that's just as well from one point of view.'

'What's that?'

'We would have to look into what to do about the graves and access to them. Granny has now been added to the group. Who's going to want a newly dug grave on part of their land? Anyway I want to stay here for the moment.'

Molly looked at Fleur and decided that there would be no good time to say what she felt needed to be said.

'He won't come back you know.'

Fleur did not even attempt to misunderstand.

'I know,' but the voice was less certain than the words.

'His grandfather was a charismatic character, not a gardener, but a driven man with a dream, like Kevin, dangerous to be around.'

'Dangerous?' queried Fleur.

'In an emotional and romantic way mainly,' said Molly. 'In Connor's case he was a strong supporter of Irish independence and although he was fun to be around, the cause would have come first in the end.'

Molly's death, though expected was still a shock. According to Molly's wishes her ashes were scattered over the flowerbeds in Garraiblagh. Kevin did not appear for the funeral and there was no word from him. Patrick and Fleur, Sean and Annie were the only ones attending the service. Patrick, true to his style was accompanied by his dog, Jump. He left again soon afterwards, back to his hermit like existence with his animals, both tame and wild. Frank Black's son, now in his fifties attended the funeral and stayed for a short while reminiscing about Garraiblagh and his family's nursery.

The autumn weather began to take hold and there was a level of dampness in the old house that Fleur had not noticed before. Keeping the place warm was becoming difficult and she realised that while she could survive a bad winter she now had Bryony to think of and for the first time in a long while Fleur thought of the warmth of New Zealand.

It was a difficult phone call.

Things had been a little difficult since she'd announced her pregnancy to her mother. Not, thought Fleur, that things had been that good before then, in fact, she couldn't really remember when they had been close as a mother and daughter. Fleur's mind flashed back to the day at Garraiblagh when she'd overheard her mother telling her grandparents that they would be emigrating to New Zealand. Fleur had dealt with the move to New Zealand in her own way. She became 'difficult' as her parents described her and when old enough had taken the earliest opportunity to thwart their wishes by travelling into the vast landscapes of New Zealand with a group of other young people.

'So, you've come to your senses at last, have you. I'm glad. I'll contact Adamson the solicitor and we'll start the process of selling Garraiblagh.'

'No, we're not selling Garraiblagh! I will want to come back. It's just returning to New Zealand for a couple of years, to get Bryony up a little and hopefully for politics here to get themselves sorted out.'

For once, Rose did not argue. There was something in her daughter's voice that went deep. She knew that she had not been there for Fleur and somehow Garraiblagh had filled the gap.

'Well, at least you're coming home. I will speak to Adamsons in Belfast and see that they have the house properly secured. We can think about its future at a later date when you are both back over here. I'm glad you're being sensible.'

Fleur put down the receiver angrily. 'Sensible. When does she ever give a damn about anyone?'

Great-uncle Patrick agreed to keep an eye on the estate, but then Fleur had her doubts. 'He hardly ever leaves his animals even for a few hours and, much as he loves Garraiblagh, I think it will be too much for him. He's physically frail now as well as emotionally fragile.'

As they drove away in the taxi Fleur looked back up the drive towards the house.

Two female figures and a tall red headed man were standing, waving.

Without thinking, Fleur shouted to the taxi driver, 'Stop, please. I-I need to check on something.'

Getting out of the taxi she informed the driver that she would only be a few moments and ran back up the drive. There was no one there. No sign of anyone. Only a slight scent of roses and tobacco.

'Philip O'Brien was enjoying himself. He woke early each morning, had his usual breakfast and filled a flask, made sandwiches and walked with his back-pack along to his allotment'.

PART SEVEN

Rebirth

'To plant a garden is to believe in tomorrow.'
Audrey Hepburn

Chapter Forty-eight

Early summer 1998

HE'D NOTICED the gangly, long legged animal trying to reach into a bin near a cafe as he walked through the centre of Belfast. There had been a shout and a booted foot had been thrust out towards the dog. A yelp and then a further cry of pain as the animal cowered in a doorway. Michael had moved over towards him, sensing another of life's rejects.

Hey, boy, let's see ye.'

The dog had looked at him warily; ready to bare its teeth. Michael Wilson had then knelt down, talking softly, but not attempting to touch the dog.

As he sat there someone walked past and threw some coins at them. Another predictably cursed them as vagrants. Michael stayed quiet.

A wet nose pushed up at his hand and then a paw. He looked down and saw the fearful brown eyes searching his. He put out his hand and gently stroked the dog. No collar, but a gash on his head. The dog whimpered again. Another set of legs and feet stopped in front of them.

'You should get your dog some food. Here's some money. Don't drink it!'

He smiled to himself.

'So, that's what people think we are lad! Well, we'll use the money to get you some food and somewhere for us to stay for the night, then we'll see what we'll do. I'm calling you Fergus. Now remember you are named after a famous King of Ulster.'

He had been given the details for a hostel. So Michael and Fergus began to make their way there. Fergus stayed close, keeping his head focused on this new friendly human. Michael had never thought he would have to go to a hostel, but although he had been released under the Good Friday Agreement, he couldn't go home. It would be unsafe for him and for his parents.

The hostel was bleak, certainly from the outside, but it would have to do, thought Michael. As he entered there was a shout. 'Ye can't bring that dog in here mate!' Michael looked at the man behind the desk and then at the dog.

'That settles it.' Without another word, Michael and the dog left the building. Outside Michael leant down and stroked the dog.

'I don't have enough friends to give one up. We will manage, Fergus. I have a place in mind.' The dog wagged its tail.

With the money he had Michael stopped off at a corner shop and bought some cheap essential foods. Man and dog walked, ignoring looks. He ditched the heavy paper sack from the prison which held his belongings and stuffed them into the plastic bags the food was in.

As they walked Michael considered his options. It had been a war and what he'd done had been because of that though he knew that many people did not accept that. He needed to leave the city and its tightly knit streets and communities. Having been in prison for five years, he had not walked far in all that time and he realised it was taking him a while to get into a regular stride. Fergus paced himself to walk with this human whom he instinctively sensed was alright, however he also knew that humans could be fickle and deceptive. He would assess further before fully trusting him.

He was on the edge of the city where new housing estates now reached out into the countryside. Murals, flags and graffiti told Michael which areas to avoid. It soon became clear that the place he was looking for was no longer 'miles from the city and right out in the country' as his grandfather had described it to him as a child. It was in fact surrounded. If this was the place. On one side of old property union flags flew and in the estate on the other side tricolours flew. He stopped at old ornate gates. Seeing them he was sure this was the place from his grandfather's description. He moved closer and looked through them at an old gate lodge, windows boarded up, and weeds clustering around the door. The gates were well chained and padlocked. Michael stood back and looked at the floral pattern of the ironwork and what looked like flowers scrolled in metal. On the left hand pillar was a name, again in wrought iron but rusting, 'Garraiblagh'.

His grandfather had worked there as a gardener in the thirties and had many happy memories of the place which he had passed on to his grandson. Michael himself had never been inside the gates. His grandfather had always warned him never to go. 'I want ye to remember the way it was for me,' he said. Garraiblagh had become this magical land in his childhood imagination, like Tir na nOg.

Now in his mid–twenties he was about to break that spell. He had come to terms with so much disillusionment it wouldn't surprise him if this was yet another. The warm afternoon was now beginning to cool. He and Fergus followed the high boundary wall along to the right, down a minor road. The brick wall looked as though it had grown out of the grass verge beneath it. Parts of the wall were crumbling and needed re–pointing though it was still a strong deterrent to unwanted visitors.

Michael was beginning to think there was no end to the wall when he found the wooden door. If he hadn't been looking carefully he would have missed it. The ivy had created a shield, a curtain over the door, green paint peeling off it. He gave the door a shove. There was a little movement. Another push and the door opened.

He hesitated. He had a sense that there would be no going back if he stepped through. So many times in his life he had stood staring at doorways, endings and beginnings, more often endings. Michael made his decision and stepped over the threshold. In the distance he could see the remains of a terraced garden and beyond, a large sandstone house with part of it either demolished or fallen down.

'This must have been some place, boy. No wonder Granda liked working here.'

The field in front of him looked as though it had been cultivated at one time, almost as though it had been divided into smaller regular sections, he thought. There was an old barn and some smaller buildings, all of which looked unused. To the left were trees, the beginning of a wood, but one which had been under-planted with shrubs and smaller plants, now badly overgrown. He recognised rhododendron and azalea among them.

Michael and Fergus sniffed the air and listened. Both alert and ready to run. Dog and man were coming to rely on each other's instincts, each taking a lead from the other. A quick glance between the two confirmed it. They would go further in. The usual fear of places was overridden with a greater need, for somewhere to sleep. They had made their calculation.

Honeysuckle, bracken, old grass and lady's mantle. Plants entwined, wearing their Sunday best, determined to seduce, hoping for connection and friendship. Time seemed to have altered since he had entered the estate, Michael thought. He realised that he had no idea how long he had been standing there. There was something so attractive, mesmerising about the place. There was a beauty in spite of the dilapidation. He was glad he had finally defied his grandfather's rule. And after five years of experiencing the grey dullness of prison. He was happy just to stand there. It felt right; he couldn't quite work out why. It was purely an instinct, a feeling. He smiled wryly to himself. If he had described how he felt about this garden to any of his fellow combatants in the H Block they'd have thought he'd lost it and maybe, he had. Prison had been a shock. Crumlin Road had been bad enough when he was on remand. Then Court and the armoured police van into the Republican sector of the prison. Everything was run on military lines. He was like a prisoner in a prisoner of war camp which was how he and his comrades saw it. He was de-briefed by the Officer Commanding of the group.

His father attended all his court appearances and had seen him sentenced. His mother had stayed away, too upset by the whole situation.

Michael had felt overwhelming anger when his grandfather had been shot, in what had been yet another act of sectarian violence, people in the wrong place at the wrong time. His grandfather Paddy had been coming back from town after meeting up with his friends when someone had opened fire on group of people waiting at a bus stop. For Michael it had been the spark that had lit the fire. Until then he had been republican but not involved in the armed struggle. That changed. And what made it more complicated was the fact that his parents were in a mixed marriage, his father Catholic, from the Ormeau Road, his mother Protestant from the Cregagh Road.

Gardening was a love that his grandfather Paddy and Michael had in common. It had been Paddy who'd encouraged Michael to apply to Edinburgh Botanic gardens and the old man had been delighted when his grandson had been offered a place. His murder had come just after that celebration and Michael's plans to study horticulture evaporated along with his ideas for peaceful change.

Man and dog walked through the long grass towards the lower

terraced area. Michael had never considered his grandfather's history in detail. What had made him happy to work here? An estate run by rich and powerful Prods. Though, he thought to himself, looking around, not any longer. How strange it was that he was where his grandfather had worked as a young man. He tried to imagine the scene. Men with wheelbarrows and flat caps bantering with each other while the rich family sat on the terrace. He thought he saw his grandfather in his working clothes, hands on his hips and looking across the garden at his grandson.

Michael and had now reached an area that had obviously been a well–kept lawn at one time, flat, well drained. A pond, remarkably intact though the female statue no longer looked down on carefully pruned roses and peonies. Michael had never been in a garden so deserted, so forgotten. He had been used to his grandfather's allotment, his parents' small backyard and front garden, full of as many flowering plants as they could fit in. Looking at this garden was like peeling back history, a history so different from his own and in many ways representing all that he felt should no longer exist.

The upper lawn, with its shallow pond and the decorative parterres was, he had to admit, a work of art. He dropped to his knees to examine a plant that was struggling. He put his hands flat on the earth and thought he heard voices. With a start he looked around, but there was no one. He was alone. 'Did ye hear that Fergus?' The dog looked back at him quizzically. 'I thought dogs were good at that kind of thing. Come on, let's see if these people are still here.' They walked over to the old house.

'Somethin' happened here. It's not just an old building that's fallen down,' Micheal said to Fergus.

Warily they walked past the wrecked conservatory and past another large flower bed full of weeds to another high brick wall. Michael put his hand out to touch the rough brickwork, still in good condition though small wall ferns and sedums had found niches in the damper, mossy areas. Keeping his hand sliding along the wall's surface, relishing its texture he walked on until he reached a gate.

'A kitchen garden! Look at the size of it. I wonder how many people this fed?'

Fergus pushed his muzzle through one of the gaps in between the metal bars as though doing his own calculations. Michael could see that the area had not been cultivated for a long time. 'I think we'll leave exploring this for tomorrow Fergus. We need somewhere to stay overnight, preferably under cover.'

Fergus ran ahead of Michael following a scent, disappearing down a slope and through a tangle of overgrown climbing roses. Michael hurried after him, sliding down the slope. Dandelion clocks disturbed by the human sent seed heads floating up in front of him.

'What have you found, boy?' Fergus was sitting wagging his tail, his tongue lolling out. 'Somewhere for us to stay? Let's have a look.'

They had arrived at a small wooden house. 'A summer house,' Michael presumed. A broken window pane was the only obvious damage on the outside. The door opened easily. Inside surprised him. It wasn't what was in it, a few old pieces of furniture, the once heavy floral cotton covers mildewed and a number of dead insects littering the floor. It was the sense of tranquility, of happiness that the place exuded. Dust motes filled the air and Michael caught a mixture of scents — dry wood, roses and something else — a sort of oil.

'This will do grand for us. First things first though, we both need something to eat.'

Michael took out some dog food and a ready cooked pie.

'Do ye know this is the first time in a brave time that I've eaten something of my choice an' not had it dictated by others.' The dog wagged his tail in response. 'We can manage here.'

Looking through the cupboards he found old candles. As the evening darkened into night, long dark shadows were created on the walls, disconcerting, but still better than any prison cell. Michael knew there could be a darker element as yet unseen lurking in the garden and hearing a twig snap he listened, noting 's ears twitch to listen as well. Slowly he made his way to the edge of the widow and peered out just in time to see a fox disappear between two bushes.

In the morning Michael woke with a start. He was being held down, someone was holding his feet. He got ready to fight. Looking down he laughed with relief. 'Jees!, Fergus, thanks for keeping my feet warm, boy. Are ye as hungry as me?'

Michael took out more food from his bag and they took their meal outside, sitting on an old bench.

'I'd rather be sleeping here with ye than behind locked doors I can tell ye. We'll explore a bit further when we've somethin' in our bellies.'

The slow mist of rain created a luxurious dampness on the leaves. Still, with some warmth in the air, there was an undeniable scent of autumn.

The rain falling on the roof of the summer house woke Michael. Fergus wagged his tail, ready for any command. Looking out, the mist had obscured the normal view of the garden. The summer house hidden from the main garden gave them a feeling of security. Sometimes it seemed to Michael that the garden marked the boundary of the known world and the lough and hills beyond, a landscape awaiting discovery. Today they would have to rely on sounds and the occasional thinning of mist and clearing of sun that noted another living creature on the move. The nettle leaves, mottled red and green under the weight of water made Michael reflect on the everyday beauty of the place. Rosebay willow herb bent over in the long, corn coloured grasses. Vetches and bindweed securing their position as they strangled opposition.

The garden had begun to work on the man and his dog. A loose tendril of clematis demanded to be put back in its place. Small plants threw out shoots and a plant runner stopped Michael in his tracks as he stumbled, only to notice some potato plants that had found themselves a space to grow and were asking to be dug up. It occurred to him he was in an old and very overgrown vegetable garden and he began to pick vegetables that he knew by sight, vegetables that had become unruly and rowdy without the gardeners' attention.

Michael had never lived so close to nature, never had to rely on it and to be bound by its rules even though he'd been fascinated by plants. His grandfather had grown the usual veg in his allotment and relaxed in an old deck chair when taking a break. Michael could remember the battered singing kettle on the camping stove that he'd had in the allotment shed.

At the time Michael had taken it all for granted. His father had loved his garden, a small back yard in reality and he had made the most of it, plants in pots, scrambling up wall and fence and a few vegetables. Slowly but surely his father had created a place of beauty and productivity. Grandda Paddy would make suggestions and comments on his father's gardening which would be taken with good humour. He realised more clearly now that both his father and his grandfather had needed that space, working with the plants they grew. It was a world away from the anger and hatred that was threatening to snuff out anything good. Friends of his father had been killed in one of the bombs. His father had not said anything but had gone to the back yard and potted and planted until late into the evening when his mother had eventually gone out and brought him back in, his eyes red from crying.

There were times when Michael wished he'd taken up the place in Edinburgh but then he wished a lot of things had been different.

'Anyway,' he said to Fergus, 'I can't go home to them, I'll just cause more problems for them.'

His parents had stood by him. He'd been grateful for that but he didn't want to make their lives harder than they already were. 'I'll write when I'm settled.' That's what he had told them in the phone call on his release.

Michael and Fergus slowly walked their way around the different areas of the garden over the next few days. He was mystified that there were public housing developments surrounding the old Garraiblagh estate, but no one seemed to come into it. They left it alone. Ignored it. It was as if some unknown force was keeping people away.

Occasionally they left the garden to get food supplies which of necessity had to be very basic. The summer house gave enough shelter while the weather was good but the weeks grew into months and soon Michael realised in was late Autumn and at night he found it difficult to sleep because of the cold. By then the idea of leaving the garden became unthinkable. He felt cocooned within it, wary of making a choice to leave and go somewhere else and yet they needed to have some warmth and somewhere they could heat up food. Michael thought of the gardener's house. It should be far enough from public view that smoke from a chimney wouldn't be seen but he'd have to be careful. He could still use the small camping stove. Michael and made their inspection of the house and found an open window. Once in he found the key for the back door hanging up. They had a way in and out.

Something in Michael made him consider what he would do if the owner of the property returned. It was one thing camping out in the garden but he'd like to be able to say that he had given something to the garden, had worked and earned a place to live.

He decided he would work in the kitchen garden and slowly reinstate it. As time went on he realised that the rules of the gardens and seasons were rules he could work with. He began to notice more and more and watched as Fergus saw things his human senses could not.

The garden welcomed the two and kept all others at bay. Once again it was happy to have human company that did no harm, company that gave instead of taking. Someone who would clear the bindweed and cleavers and spend time tying back espalier branches that had long since forgotten their purpose. Unknown to Michael and Fergus the land had now adopted them as it had the Hendersons more than a century earlier.

In their different ways, Michael and Fergus felt an element of proprietorial pride in the careful and covert way they had managed and he was beginning to see the difference his work was having in the garden. He was beginning to remember his love of gardening and what he had hoped to do. For Michael it meant that he could breathe. He still had nightmares about the cell in the Maze. Other inmates shouting out. He wondered if there was anything that would ever really terrify him again. He thought not.

Sitting down with a cup of tea and a slice of bread he spoke to Fergus.

'I wonder what will change with this Agreement, eh boy?'

Fergus looked at Michael hopefully.

'Well, you're right there. It got me my freedom and without it we wouldn't have met. So I have to agree. We must look on the bright side.'

Chapter Forty—nine

1999

BRYONY HAD ARRIVED from New Zealand in Belfast the previous September to start her art college course. Garraiblagh was where she had wanted to go first, but her college course got in the way. She had spent the autumn and winter getting to know her way around the city, settling in with her flat-mates and concentrating on the new course and now in April she was finally ready to go to Garraiblagh.

It had been her idea to go to Art College in Belfast. There had been many reasons for choosing Belfast on the other side of the world, a city emerging from a thirty year long conflict, but like her mother Fleur, she felt a strong attraction to the ancestral home. There was also the possibility of finding her father. Her mother had told her very little about him though she only had to look at her mother to know there was still a yearning.

Bryony rode out to Garraiblagh on her bicycle. It had taken her a little longer than she had expected to get there. She had taken the less busy main road out of Belfast and found herself completely lost in the middle of a housing development. The flags and the painted kerbstones felt threatening. Her flat-mates laughed about the different colours that meant so much to local people of the different sides and some even used the symbols in their art work but Bryony didn't find it funny. She turned her bike towards what looked like the road out and pedalled fast. She felt uncomfortable.

Once she was on an ordinary road again she stopped and checked the map she had drawn out. From her mother's directions there should be more countryside before arriving at Garraiblagh but when she looked around her she noticed a high wall and gate posts not far away. Cycling over to the gate she saw the old metal sign Garraiblagh. Bryony was glad her mother had made sure she had keys with her for the different locks, including she hoped, the lock on the gates. She didn't think her chances of getting hold of the solicitor and asking him to bring the keys would result in anything positive.

Checking the lock on the gate she selected a key and tried it. It didn't work but the next one did and she unwound the chain to open the gate. She decided it might be a good idea to make it look as though it was still chained. Bryony didn't want anyone else getting in. She decided to wheel her bike up the drive. It allowed her to look around her and take in everything at a slower pace, but also, she had to admit, the potholes in the drive would have made cycling while looking around, pretty dangerous.

The rhododendrons crowded in on both sides, some beginning to come into flower. Pigeons cooing in the trees gave the place a restful feel.

Bryony gasped at the first sight of the house. She knew of the bomb damage, but seeing it was a very different experience. She hugged her jacket around her and made herself focus on the garden. It was overgrown without doubt, but she could still see its beauty.

Bryony turned her head towards the front entrance of the house and her eye was caught by a flash of blue in the woods beyond.

She remembered her mother telling her about the bluebells which carpeted the old beech trees. One of her favourite pictures that her mother had painted was of that bluebell wood. Her mother's pictures and stories had brought the place to life for her and now she would paint them herself.

Something would have to be done about Garraiblagh. It had lain empty, unloved for so many years. Eighteen years since she and her mother had left to live in New Zealand, sixteen since she had returned with her mother for the brief visit after the bomb. It still belonged to the family and her mother had left it to Bryony to make decisions. Now she was here. Fleur had been concerned about the bombs and was unsure of the new Agreement. However Bryony had been adamant and had reminded her mother that she had been brought to see a bombed out Garraiblagh at the age of three at the height of the Troubles.

As she approached the vivid blueness and exquisite scent of bluebells Bryony stood transfixed. She considered the drawings she would make in preparation for a series of canvases. The blues against the bright, vivid greens, the pools of shade and light. Bryony dropped down onto a fallen tree trunk and began sketching and making notes. She was so engrossed in her work that she didn't hear the sounds. It was the shock of a sudden presence that made her scream. Then she saw the face: two brown eyes, a lolling tongue and a wagging tail.

'Where have you come from, boy?' she whispered as she stroked the dog's thick black coat. Fergus had been investigating on his own and found this new human. His finely tuned instinct told this one was friendly. So he thought he'd make himself known.

Bryony looked for a collar and found none.

'Are you living here on your own? You seem in very good condition?'

Fergus nuzzled her and then lay down beside her.

'Well, you might as well join me while I work on these drawings. I appreciate the company.' Then a man's voice. 'Fergus where are you, boy?'

With a start Bryony looked up from her work and listened. She could hear leaves being trodden down.

'Are you being called?' she asked the dog who wagged his tail and stood up.

A man with wavy dark brown hair and a beard appeared. Bryony suddenly realised that she was very vulnerable. It had never occurred to her before. She was too thrilled to be in Garraiblagh. The garden had seemed so safe, but no one would hear her if she screamed and by then it might be too late. She thought about what she had that could be used in defence. A stick wouldn't be of much use. She would have to be ready to run, leave all her materials behind. Her eyes showed her concern. The sketchbook and pencils had fallen onto the ground.

'Sorry, I didn't mean to scare ye!' Fergus ran off and he doesn't normally do that.' Michael bent down and put the string around the dog's neck.

'Is he yours?' she asked. Bryony watched the stranger looking for signs of threat.

'Aye, well, we have a sort of partnership agreement.' He smiled.

Bryony relaxed a little but continued to watch the man's body language carefully. Who was he? This was after all, private property. Her family's property. No one seemed to come into the state. How come this man did?

'Do you live nearby? 'asked Bryony as she stroked the dog, not giving any eye contact, but watching carefully to see if the man's feet moved towards her.

Michael didn't answer directly.

'Aye, close by. How do ye know of this place?' Michael asked.

'My family own it,' said Bryony looking directly at Michael.

'Wow! Own? But sure it's derelict,' he said in surprise, looking around nervously. So it had finally happened, he thought. The owners were coming to take over.

'I know,' she hesitated,'It's a long story.'

'I like long stories,' Michael said with a nervous laugh 'Look, I'd better tell ye my story first. an' me have been sorta squatting. I didn't think anyone lived here or even owned it. We needed somewhere.'

Bryony looked at Michael. There was something guarded in the eyes, but not calculating or angry. Bryony rose to her feet, making jump backwards.

'I should be going. My flat mates are waiting for me.'

Bryony hoped that sounded realistic. Both her flat mates were away. In truth she had not told anyone where she was going. She cursed herself for being so stupid.

'You said squatting? So you live here?'

'Aye, I do.'

'But there's nowhere to live here. Where in the garden have you been staying?' She suddenly thought back to the bomb maker's use of the house. Those days were over weren't they?

'There's an old house in the walled garden and we've been bunking down in there. I've been working in the garden, clearing some of the weeds and fixing fences and things.

'How did you get in to the house?'

'There was an open window. I got in that way and then unlocked the door. I didn't break in. I haven't damaged anything. So what plans do ye have for the place?' Michael asked.

'Plans?' I don't have any plans. Sadly.'

Bryony looked at the pair and they looked at her.

'Look, if ye don't have plans could Fergus and me stay here for a while longer? I don't have much money but I could give ye some an' as I've said I've been beginning to clear a part of the garden. I could do more of that work.'

She hadn't planned on having to assert her ownership so quickly. This man was living in her gardener's house on the estate. Should she ask him to leave?

'I know nothing about you. I can't make a decision now. You can both stay here for the moment. I'm not in a position to stop you, but I want to think about all this. I hadn't planned on meeting any 'tenants'.'

They both smiled at the weak joke. 'I'm happy to meet with ye properly to discuss things,' said Michael hopefully.

'Meet?' asked Bryony. 'Meet where? I don't want to meet here in the garden. Somewhere public.'

They arranged to meet in Marshall's cafe in the city centre at the weekend. That gave Bryony time to contact her mother about this strange development.

Bryony picked up her sketchbook and pencils and walked her bicycle towards the drive watched by Michael and Fergus.

'Well, boy, we just have to wait an' see. We'd better be on our best behaviour for Saturday. A bath is in order I think.'

The dog gave Michael a look. 'Ok, I know. I'll have to tell her. She'll find out anyway.

Bryony began to relax as she did not hear any sounds or footsteps following behind her as she walked back down the drive. She had always prided herself on going by her intuition but there were times when she really needed to be sensible and this was one of them.

'I'll call mum and talk it over' she said to herself. 'It does make sense to have someone at Garraiblagh to watch over the place. But who is this guy?'

Bryony met Michael outside the cafe on Saturday as arranged. He looked nervous which suggested to Bryony that he wasn't a thug.

'Hi! Shall we go in?' Bryony asked and patted Fergus' head. Michael tied Fergus up to the nearby railing. 'Aye, sure,' nodded Michael and followed her in.

Although the place was busy they found a table a little apart from the nearest group, young people noisily talking about their night out. Michael stirred the sugar in his coffee thoughtfully and glanced across at Bryony . She was watching him but remained silent.

'Maybe I should start. I need to tell ye some things about my background. This is obviously a strange set up, ye finding me an' Fergus in the garden.'

Bryony nodded. Her mother had advised her to listen and not to say too much when she met Michael. Fleur had been wary of the meeting though at least glad it would be held in a public place. She wanted her daughter to ring her as soon as the meeting was over.

Michael hesitated, trying to gauge Bryony's likely response. 'This is Northern Ireland. It's a strange wee place as you probably know.' Taking a deep breath he said, 'Thing is I'm an ex-prisoner.'

Bryony sat back, an unconscious recoiling.

'Why? What for?' she said as her mind and heart rate raced through all the possibilities.

'How much of Irish politics do ye know?'

Bryony lent forward. 'I know some. Remember my family are from here.'

'Aye but you haven't lived here long, have you? Ye know the place has been at war for a long time.'

'I know there have been terrorists. I know there have been hundreds killed over the years and I know that in a small way, Garraiblagh was affected, part of the house blown up by men putting together a bomb and blowing up themselves instead.'

'Terrorists. Yeah. Some call them soldiers and others freedom fighters.' Michael gave her a long knowing look.

'Oh my God, is that what you were?'

'Aye,'

''What side?' she asked though in the back of her head she thought she probably knew the answer.

'I'm an Irish republican.'

Bryony looked at the man opposite her trying to grasp what he was saying, to understand that reality. She'd met some republican sympathisers at college and some from the loyalist side, some produced art work that reflected their experiences of living in Northern Ireland. She hadn't spoken to them at any great length.

'So what were you in prison for?'

'Armed robbery,' Michael said flatly. Bryony swallowed hard and considered making for the door. She'd never met anyone in her life that had broken the law, let alone robbed a bank with guns.

He went on, 'You need to understand that I was a combatant in a war.'

'A war against people living here, against the government?'

'No, there was no government, just a regime. An oppressive one. You got your news in New Zealand. Can ye accept that it may not have been truthful, not accurate about the place?'

Bryony considered.

'Tell me then,' she challenged. Michael thought he could see a genuine wish to understand in her eyes. A lot depended on his being able to come to an understanding with this young New Zealander. As he had been talking he'd realised just how much being at Garraiblagh had come to mean to him but on the other hand he didn't want to change his views to be acceptable to her.

Michael told his story, about his grandfather's murder and his plans to go to Edinburgh and the forces at work in Ireland that brought him to take up arms against the British. He could see the young woman was listening intently, her eyes fixed on him with amazement. She made noises like 'I see' 'Oh' and 'I'm sorry'

For Michael it was a kind of unburdening. He had never explained himself to anyone at length. He looked at Bryony again. She seemed genuinely interested.

Finally Bryony said, 'So that's the past. What about the present and the future? Do you plan any more violence?'

Michael wasn't sure whether she was joking or not. Bryony wasn't sure either.

'No, that's all finished with the Good Friday Agreement, for me anyway. At heart I'm not a violent person. I need to put my life back together again and that's where the estate came in for me. I hadn't figured it out. I had nowhere to go and I love gardens. That's all.'

'So your grandfather would have worked with my great grandparents Daisy and Tom Guthrie?' asked Bryony.

'Yes, he described the gardens in detail to me, almost as though he was walking through them in his mind. I think he would have gone on workin' there but my Granny wasn't a country girl. She liked the city. It was my childhood fantasy, a magical place. But he warned me not to go there.'

'Why not?' Bryony asked.

'I think he was worried that his memories of the place would be shattered if it had changed and I told him about it and that would shatter my dreams too.'

Bryony took a drink of her coffee and realised it was cold. She realised that she had forgotten all about the coffee while Michael had been talking. 'I'm going to get another coffee. Do you want one?'

Michael nodded and thanked her. As Bryony waited at the counter she thought 'What do I do! I'm really out of my depth. She also realised she'd had a very one sided view of the Troubles.

Bryony placed the cups on the table and Michael continued, 'I assumed that no one owned it any more when I saw the house. It just seemed right an' I'd just found Fergus in the middle of the town, on his own. The hostel I'd been told about wouldn't take Fergus so I decided it wasn't the place to stay We started walking. Understand this, I'm not a thief, a con man or a thug. I can do an honest day's work. I hope this Agreement means somethin'. I still want a united Ireland an' I hope with this agreement the system will be more equal. If people are right with me, I'll be right with them.'

'It's a lot to take in,' she said. 'I need to understand. I know I wasn't here and I know what happened to Garraiblagh and that was, as you might say, just collateral damage.'

Michael just smiled. A smile that Bryony realised was charming her.

'Look, I appreciate you telling me everything. I need to discuss this further with my mother.'

'I, we. Fergus and me would like to stay on at Garraiblagh. I'm happy to work, clearing, gardening. I did a lot of woodwork in prison and I'm quite expert. It could also be good to have a sort of caretaker there. I can't be the only one who has thought the place didn't belong to anyone.'

'Ok, Michael, I would like to meet up again here the middle of next week. You and Fergus can stay in Garraiblagh till then. I'm not making any promises. I'll let you know then.'

'Thank you, Bryony. I appreciate your time. I'll see you then.'

Bryony watched as Michael and Fergus made their way along Donegall Place.

After talking to Bryony, Fleur phoned the solicitor.

'Well, the place is a problem,' said the solicitor. 'There's no doubt about it. There may unwelcome interest in Garraiblagh now the troubles is over. Garraiblagh is a kind of border, a peace line between two sides. There's a Republican estate on one side and a Loyalist estate on the other. Garraiblagh was a no-go area. That may change now. Having someone like that Michael as a gardener/ caretaker could be positive. I've checked him out and his story stacks up, Ms Johnston. His grandfather, Paddy Wilson did work in the estate. So he has an attachment to the place perhaps which could be useful.'

'Well that's a happy coincidence,' said Fleur.

'Yes, you will be aware that Amelia and George Henderson left funds in a separate trust to help with the upkeep of Garraiblagh over the years.'

Fleur almost dropped the phone. 'No, I did not know! Are you telling me that there is money to help restore Garraiblagh?'

'Well, I wouldn't go as far as to say that but there is certainly a... substantial sum that can be drawn on. I'll send you details in writing.'

'Did my mother, Rose Johnson, know about this?'

'Yes, she was made aware of the trust. She never asked to draw anything from it though.'

'I'll bet she didn't!' said Fleur

Fleur rang Bryony, still angry about the information the solicitor had given her.

'Bryony, if you think this Wilson fellow can be trusted to work in Garraiblagh and act as caretaker then I think we should offer him a job. By the way we evidently have some money we can use to help reinstate or at least partially reinstate Garraiblagh then I think we see this as the first step. I'm going to be speaking to your grandmother and perhaps it's as well that you're on the other side of the world so that you don't hear the conversation!'

Bryony laughed. 'Remember I've heard you two argue since I was small!'

Fergus met Bryony on the drive as she cycled up. 'Hello, boy, have you started your guard dog work?' Fergus wagged his tail and ran alongside the bike to the house.

Michael waved and greeted her. Bryony smiled in return. 'I have a small map here of the estate. It will have to do for the moment, I'm afraid. I've got a copy for you. We should make a tour now and you can show me what you've been doing.'

'Let's start with where I've been working then, in the kitchen garden.'

Bryony could see the difference as soon as she stepped inside the walls of the garden. Half the area was overgrown, the other half was neatly weeded and fruit tree branches and bushes had been pruned and trained.

'Wow, I can begin to see what the garden must have looked like,' said Bryony, admiringly. Bryony and Michael made their way around to what was left of the house front. 'I know this was done,' Bryony pointed to the broken glass and rubble, 'near the beginning of the Troubles. It must have been beautiful inside.' Michael nodded without comment. For him this huge house was part of what had been wrong, part of the inequality.

' There used to be parterres here. My great-great-grandmother had them laid in blues and greens, using the shape of the linen flower, but now it would be difficult to see that.

Moving closer to the old patterns they saw lavender and thyme bushes had now thrown their stems out to the side. leaving an empty, bald spot in the middle. The circular pond, stagnant with weeds and topped by the moss covered statue and fountain looked forlorn. Bryony was aware that she and Michael were walking in comfortable unison.

'We'll go through the archway here.' Both needed to pull back pieces of yew and box to move into a different world. Taller, woodland plants had enjoyed the lack of attention. 'This was my great-grandmother's studio.'

'This is where Fergus an' I spent the first few weeks here. It's a grand place to be. It just got too cold for us, didn't it boy?'

Chapter Fifty

2000

IT BECAME A HABIT. Bryony would cycle out to Garraiblagh at the weekend and spend time drawing and painting. Often would find her and spend a few hours with her. She was glad that Michael kept to his work, acknowledging her when he saw her but keeping to the area he was clearing. She knew he was there and that was enough. She'd say goodbye before leaving and make some brief small talk then be on her way. She was glad to be able to find her own relationship with Garraiblagh and the garden without complications.

Until one day Michael sought to break the distance between them. 'How's it goin? I've put the kettle on if you would like a brew?' Bryony nodded, gathered together her satchel of painting materials and followed Michael. 'That would be great. You can share my sandwiches, although I think Fergus has his eye on one,' she laughed.

They sat on the old bench outside the gardener's cottage in companionable silence. Bryony found herself relaxing. It's a lovely garden and your work has made me realise how much work went into it over the years. 'Do you know any more about your grandfather's time here?' asked Bryony.'

'Aye I do now as it happens. I rang my parents the other day. I'd been meaning to do it for a while now. I told them what I was doing and where. My father remembered Grandda Paddy talking about Garraiblagh. He had started in the garden as an apprentice and worked until he left in 1935. He'd fallen in love with my grandmother and she lived out in Milltown, Belfast and didn't fancy living in the country so he left but he missed the place badly. My grandfather went to work in the Botanic Gardens in Belfast. He kept in contact with some of the lads who still worked here. The other thing my father told me was that the Guthries who owned the place, is that your great-grandparents?'

Bryony nodded.

'Well, the family always had a policy that politics and religion were no-go topics in the garden. They had both Catholic and Protestant gardeners and staff generally. I must admit that surprised me.'

Bryony smiled at Michael. 'And here you are in Garraiblagh, not the Garraiblagh that your grandfather worked in. He'd probably be horrified at what has happened to it. So perhaps my family wasn't too bad then?'

'Perhaps not,' he laughed.

'You know Michael, my background is perhaps not as clear cut as you imagine it is. My mother isn't married. She met my father here when she was looking after her grandmother. He was the grandson of her closest friend, Molly who worked here as the head gardener for many years. I've never met my father and I'm probably not likely to. The story goes that my father's grandfather was involved in the 1916 uprising, fought in the GPO and then the war of Independence. He was a republican of that era.'

Michael put down his cup and stared at Bryony. 'Jesus! That's a belter!'

'I thought you might like that!' laughed Bryony.

Michael shook his head and started laughing. 'So you're one of us! Nothing is ever as it seems, is it?'

'Partly, I suppose. My mum brought me to Garraiblagh when I was very small. I don't remember much but she told me stories and showed me pictures and drawings she'd made of Garraiblagh. Mum loved it here. She was heartbroken when my grandparents moved to New Zealand. I don't think she forgave them, particularly Granny. I always wanted to come back. I think my mother would too if she could find a way of working it. I also think she still wonders if she will ever meet my father again even after all these years.'

As time went on Bryony's studies at the art college claimed more and more of her time. Studies of the garden were being translated into pieces of screen printing and more complex ceramic pieces. It was becoming too difficult for her to travel out to the garden on a frequent basis. She realised that she was missing not only the garden but she had to admit she enjoyed Michael's company.

After a particularly gruelling week Bryony woke one Saturday with the strong sense that she needed to go to Garraiblagh. Packing some sandwiches and a flask, she set off. Bryony had grown used to being met by Fergus at the top of the drive but there was no sign of him. He's probably off somewhere with Michael. Perhaps they've gone to get some stuff from town she thought. But it didn't feel right. It was the wrong sort of silence. She gave a shout for Michael but there was no response, and no dog. She circled the side of the house and walked up to the gardener's cottage. There was no smoke, no sign of a fire. Bryony stood, undecided,'No sign of smoke from the chimney and it's cold enough for one, heaven knows,' she thought as she pulled her woolly hat lower over her head.

Knocking on the door there was no answering voice or barks

from Fergus the protector. Turning the handle she realised it wasn't locked. Hesitating, she called out again and listened. She had never come to the garden and not been met by them unless they had said they would be out somewhere. Bryony called out again, this time stepping over the doorstep. The house was cold. It didn't feel as though anyone was there. She thought she heard a scraping and then a low bark coming from upstairs.

Bryony made her decision. If Michael arrived and found her in the house she'd explain that she'd been concerned. She walked gingerly along the hallway and into the kitchen.

It was eerily quiet then she heard again a muffled growl. Slowly climbing the stairs Bryony listened for any sound. When she reached the landing there was another growl. At first she couldn't understand where it was coming from then a sound of frantic scratching led her to the hot press cupboard. 'Fergus?'

As she opened the door the dog raced out almost knocking her off her feet and ran to the bedroom. Michael was lying half on the bed with a huge gash on the side of his head and blood on his face.

'Oh my God! What's happened Michael?' Bryony touched his head.

'Michael?' She said again, shaking his shoulder while began to lick his hand.

'Bryony?'

'Yes, Michael, I need to get you to hospital. I'll phone. Thank God there's a signal.'

'What happened?' she asked.

'Fergus started growlin'. I didn't want him in the middle of anything so I shut him in the cupboard an' just as I was comin' downstairs to phone the police these two boys smashed the window. They were looking for valuables an' a bit annoyed they couldn't find any. Hence the beatin. I'm tough, Bryony. Don't worry, but I reckon I have broken ribs.'

The ambulance arrived, followed by the police car.

Bryony took to the flat and then hurried around to the Royal hospital to see Michael who was being kept in under observation. Sitting beside his bed she watched the monitors. She didn't like hospitals at the best of times and Michael's face, pale in some areas and bandaged in others seemed so unlike the man she knew.

'Bryony.'

'Yes, Michael,' she took hold of his hand. 'Thank goodness.'

'Where is Fergus?'

'Don't worry, he's with me in the flat and he's being spoilt by my flat mates. I'm just glad you're okay. You don't look too bad.'

'I don't look too bad, eh? There's hope for me then?'

Bryony caught his look. His eyes were asking something she wanted to answer.

'You'll have your good looks back in no time, then you'll be 'cooking on gas',' she said in her best Belfast accent.

'So you're starting to speak proper?' said Michael.

'It's the way I tell 'em!, said Bryony.

'Don't,' said Michael 'it hurts when I laugh.'

'Sorry.'

'Seriously Bryony, thanks for saving me.' He held out his hand and pulled her to him, kissing her on the mouth. There, I've wanted to do that for some time.'

'You're a cheeky blert, bai!' said Bryony in her best Belfast accent.

Chapter Fifty-one

2001

BRYONY'S DEGREE WAS FINISHED. The art show over and now the summer awaited. She had made a huge decision. She would not be returning to New Zealand to live. She'd made connections and friends and, more importantly, there was Michael.

She believed her world was here now in Northern Ireland and, more precisely, in the garden at Garraiblagh.

She prepared herself for the phone call.

'Mum, I want to stay here in Garraiblagh'.

It came out faster than she had wanted, less nuanced and considered, more confrontational. She listened for the response.

'I have been expecting it. Is it safe, Bryony?'

Bryony relaxed the grip on the phone.

'I think what I need to do is come over'.

'So, you don't think it's a bad idea?'

'No, I've been expecting it, as I said. I loved Garraiblagh. It was agony when your grandparents pulled me away from it. It was the place I felt at home in and inspired. My only worry is how

Garraiblagh and the area around it has changed and what can be done realistically with the estate. I would hardly be unhappy that it has affected you in a similar way.'

'Ok, Mum, thanks. I was worried what you'd say.'

'Let me sort out a flight over and then we can really talk and look at the future.'

Fleur put down the telephone receiver. She was right when she had told Bryony that she'd been expecting it. In truth she was pleased, but she also knew to listen between the words. That young man, Michael was in there somewhere. Fleur was worried that Bryony would be let down as she had been with Kevin.

Michael and Fergus were sitting on the step at the front of the summer house when Fergus began to wag his tail in greeting to Bryony as she came through the rose arbour.

'I didn't expect to see ye here today. Ye alright?'

Bryony sat down on the ground as Fergus threw himself down beside her.

'Yes in fact I think everything is very alright. Can we go for a walk?'

The threesome set off down the path and through the painting garden.

'Are we goin' somewhere in particular?' asked Michael.

'Aye, we are,' responded Bryony but kept walking. Fergus ran ahead across the lawn but then stopped, turning to check where they were and where he should go next. They crossed the stream and into the wilder part of the field, coming to a stop at the standing stone. The scent of the surrounding gorse blossom and the humming of the bees was intoxicating. Bryony picked daisies and sat down on the grass.

'I've rung my mother and told her that I'm staying here.'

'Here, where's here?' asked Michael.

'Yes, well I've told her I want to live here at Garraiblagh. I come from a long line of women who have wanted this garden to work. I don't want to let them down. I want to see what can be done with the place. It's been in decline for so long. I want to give it a chance to make a comeback of sorts. I'm hoping you would, what's the phrase? Give us a dig out.'

'Are ye suggesting a job?' he smiled, looking directly into her eyes.

'Mm, maybe more of a partnership? Garraiblagh was created by my great-great-great-grandmother and grandfather. They were young and knew what they wanted. I want us to keep Garraiblagh but I know it will be a very different Garraiblagh. With you and Fergus here it feels like life is returning.'

'What about your mother, your family?'

'My mother is flying over from New Zealand to talk about it.

Look Michael I need to know how you feel about me. And just so that I'm clear. I'm in love with you.'

Michael held back from taking her in his arms as he wanted to do.

'Jesus! Are all ye Kiwi women this direct? Look Bryony, your mother's not going to want a jailbird like me around. I'm not the hothead I used to be, but we're from different worlds, ye an' me. This is not New Zealand. This peace process may not work. What then, eh? My past may jump up to bite me an' ye with it!'

Bryony twirled a daisy between her fingers, listening.

'Truth is, it must be obvious how I feel about ye, Bryony girl. But how would it work between us?'

Bryony dropped her head. Fergus moved over to her, sensing her unhappiness.

'Bryony, ye must see what ye have meant to me this last while. Ye've given me life when I had none. A place to live. Ye saved me when I was attacked. Ye've turned my head. I love you but I need to feel I'm on an equal footing to ye or it won't work.'

'Yer a smooth talker, Michael Wilson.' Bryony walked over and putting her arms around him, looked into his eyes. 'If there can be a peace process for the country then there can be for us too.'

Fleur arrived at Belfast International at first unsure where she was. It was so different from her last memories. There, waiting at Arrivals was Bryony waving and hardly able to contain herself with excitement.

'Mum, I'm so glad you're here!' as she kissed her mother, wrapping her in a hug. Fleur saw a tall young man with curly hair and piercing eyes standing a few feet away, smiling at them.

'And you must be Michael!' said Fleur, holding out her hand.

'How are ye, Mrs Johnson. Good to meet ye.'

They drove back to Garraiblagh. Bryony and Michael had decided that Fleur should stay in the gardener's house while her mother was there and Michael and Bryony would camp out in the summer house.

Fleur sat down at the kitchen table with the two young people. She was still tired from the long plane journey and hoped that the coffee would keep her awake for little longer.

There's so much to discuss Mum. I've got some old plans of the place here and she unrolled the paper and smoothed it out over the table. She reached for the paperweights to hold it in place.

Fleur's eyes were caught by the glass objects. 'Those paperweights! Where did you find them, Bryony?'

'In a cupboard under the rubble. I suppose no one has taken them because it looked too dangerous or too uninteresting to go inside.'

'These belonged to Amelia and George. I always loved looking at them when I visited Garraiblagh. It's probably fitting that they are here when we discuss the future of Garraiblagh. Who knows, perhaps they used the paperweights for the same thing!'

'I found these plans in a box in the Gardeners cottage,' said Bryony.

'Of course they haven't been updated. That's something we need to do,' added Michael. After some discussion it became clear that Fleur was too tired to continue.

'Let's start again tomorrow,' suggested Fleur. 'We can have some food and coffee and begin properly.'

'It might be good,' Bryony suggested 'if we take a walk around the estate first and really look at all the different places before we try to remember from the maps and the plans.'

Fleur sat back in the chair with her arms outstretched on the table and looked at Michael. Then she sat forward, tapped her hands on the table and stood up.

'Right, now I need some sleep and to adjust my body clock!'

Fleur slept in late the following morning.

'I'll just go up to Mum.' said Bryony.

'Don't wake her yet. Mind she's had a long trip,' said Michael.

'Aye, You're right. It's just so exciting. I want to get going, look at plans, decide on things. I want you and Mum to get to know each other.'

Later they decided to start at the entrance and follow the drive before following on to the paths and lanes. It was the first time that Fleur had really walked the estate properly since childhood. The visit she had made when Bryony was a young child hadn't given the time and she had, in any case, felt too emotional at the sight of the house and the damage. Fleur stopped in the middle of the lawn and sighed.

'The house is obviously not habitable. It would cost a lot of money to restore it. We just don't have that kind of money.

'But perhaps that is not the best way forward anyway,' announced Bryony. 'It's a different world now, Mum. We can't put it back the way it was.'

Fleur looked at her daughter. She was right of course. She was the only one who had known the house as it had been, spent time in the rooms, remembered the warmth and the bustle.

'Something will have to be done about the house. It can't just sit there — its unsightly — and dangerous.'

'Perhaps the stones could be useful in building something else,' commented Michael, feeling his way into the conversation.

'Yes, true,' said Fleur,'there certainly is a lot to discuss. Can we go and sit down please!' urged Fleur. 'I'm still a bit tired and I realise I'm feeling hungry!'

In front of the fire in the Gardener's Cottage the three sat with their coffees and sandwiches. Bryony queried, 'What about the farm?'

'The farm is rented out,' replied Fleur, 'so that helps with some income and there is some money available to restore Garraiblagh through this Trust that the solicitor told me about. 'The estate is bigger than you think it is. From a purely practical point of view remember that at its height there were ten gardeners managing Garraiblagh.'

'Well Michael has been making great progress in the walled garden,' said Bryony proudly.

'We do need to think of ways we can get an income though,' said Fleur thoughtfully.

Bryony looked at Michael and then across at her mother who was scrutinising Michael.

'We want to keep most of the grounds and the garden, especially great-granny's painting garden and the studio summer house and you've told me so many stories about other parts of the garden. We don't want to give up any more than we have to!'

'We?' queried Fleur, wanting to get to grips with her daughter's relationship to this man. There was something attractive and reassuring about him, but Fleur had been fooled before with these romantic Irishmen.

'Michael and me. We're living together Mum. Actually we're planning to get married,' said Bryony waiting for her mother's reaction.

'Married!? Well, well, things are moving fast and no mistake,' said Fleur. She looked from her daughter to Michael who took Bryony's hand. They did look good together.

'Are you both sure? It's a big step.'

'We've known each other for good while now, Mum. This is not a sudden thing, you know,' said Bryony.

Fleur looked at Michael. He met her probing gaze.

'I really am happy for you, Bryony. This is turning into quite a trip. Michael I'm delighted to welcome you to the family. You're just what Bryony needs. Let me hug you!'

The hug between the two answered all her questions. Fleur realised he wasn't another Kevin and Michael could see she wasn't an arrogant member of the old gentry who saw him as just another peasant to order about.

'Bryony saved my life Mrs Johnson, in more ways than one. She means the world to me!'

'Well, I think a celebration is in order! Some wine. Not New Zealand, I'm afraid, but the best that I can find,' said Bryony breathing a sigh of relief.

Taking a first sip of wine, Fleur said, 'Well I also have some news for you, Bryony.'

'What is it?'

'Things are changing for me and my work can really be carried out anywhere. I've told you how Garraiblagh was for me, as a child.

It's never left me and now, hearing about it from you. Well... I want to come back'

'Come back? Leave New Zealand?' asked Bryony.

'I wouldn't want to cramp your style for you and Michael, I promise. After this morning's walk around I was wondering about one of the old cottages behind the house. I could make it quite cosy.'

'Yes, there are a lot of things that need to be fixed,' said Bryony, 'and I'd like a studio, a proper one, where I can work, but also exhibit. Michael would like to set up a plant nursery to sell plants alongside the rebuilding of the garden.'

Fleur opened her suitcase and removed an embroidered linen bag. She laid it on the bed and carefully folded back the cover to reveal a book. Pushing the pillows up against the wall she curled up on the bed and carefully opened the book, smoothing her hand gently over the page she had opened it at. Amelia's garden diaries had been handed down to Daisy but had not been left to Rose, instead they had been left to Fleur. Opening up the book Fleur looked again at the coloured images, the water colours of the various parts of the garden painted by Amelia. Slipped in between them were some early photographs of the house and gardens and a more recent diary obviously written and illustrated by Daisy.

Fleur had read the diaries before but tended to focus on the art work which had so reminded her of the far off gardens but the diary writing interested her too. She was particularly intrigued by the pencil drawings of who she knew to be George Henderson but also the delicate drawings of another man, a little older, bearded with red wavy hair. working with plants. Was this James Black?

'Come and help me look at the old cottages, Bryony,' said Fleur. 'Michael, are you coming too?' asked Bryony. 'No, sorry, I've got work to do,' said Michael, looking at Fleur. 'I'll see youse later.'

Fleur smiled at Michael. She was glad to see that he understood she needed this time with her daughter to talk over all the plans, including her marriage to Michael and was happy to see that he didn't feel the need to be there if his background or relationship with Bryony was discussed.

'I was wondering about this cottage in particular. It was Molly's.'

'I wish I'd known her.'

'You did know her, but you were too young to remember her.'

'She knew my father?'

'Yes, she did and you know it was through her that I met him.'

'I know I'm one to talk about marriage, Bryony. You never met your father and it's unlikely that you ever will. I just want to know, are you sure about everything?'

'About what in particular, Mum?' ' I mean Michael, in particular!'

'Mum, you know some of his history and that he was in prison. I'm not just walking into this without any thought. I am sure. His life was turned upside down by the Troubles. This isn't New Zealand. He means the world to me. He's not like my father.'

Fleur and Bryony walked on.

'Michael has asked me the same question, you know,' said Bryony. 'He's very aware of our differences. He's kind, he's intelligent and he's always been honest with me. I love him and he loves me. And no. I'm not pregnant. If that's what you would like to ask.'

'It had crossed my mind. But that's just me. Forgive me, love. You're not me and Michael is not Kevin. I can see that. You're old enough to make your decisions. I like him, it would be wrong of me not to check things.'

'Thanks, Mum.' said Bryony, squeezing her mother's hand. 'I

like the look of Molly's cottage. We'll have to get the key for it or get Michael to find a way in so that we can check inside.'

Fleur stopped at the gate. She moved her hand over the paint that was peeling off the old wood. It was reassuringly solid. She let out a long breath and forced herself to look towards the door. There was little to identify the cottage garden that had thrived there in Molly's day. Memories began to flood back in. She could feel her heart beating faster and to control it she made herself focus, to search out any plants that she could recognise.

'Plenty of thistles, that's for sure,' as she ruefully rubbed her leg where a strong nettle had stung her. 'Agapanthus, wonderful! It's obviously enjoyed being neglected — and hellebores! Well, that's at least two plants. I can work on the rest.'

Concentrating on the plants had helped. She had got to the door.

A flashback of Kevin opening the door to her, wild curly hair and blue eyes almost made her step back. Kevin with his winning smile who had broken her heart.

'This is the cottage I want, I'm not going to let memories stop me.'

A sound of scratching from behind her made her turn. A large black and white cat was waving its tail at her.

'Who are you? You're very like Molly's little cat Jo, but I know you can't be.' Fleur sat down on the doorstep to wait for the cat. The cat ran quickly to her, circling her legs and rubbing itself around her, purring.

'Well, if you haven't already got a home, you have one now. Come with me and let's look inside.'

The bunch of keys that they had found in the drawer of the desk in the gardener's cottage proved to have the right door key. Fleur opened the door and light flooded in. Dust motes danced, caught in the bright light. Fleur sneezed and noticed the dust covering everything but it felt dry, a good sign. The cat walked ahead of her into the sitting room.

'Strange,' she said to the cat, 'I can smell roses.' Fleur looked around, unable to work out where the scent was coming from.

'What do you think, cat? It seems a nice room and there is even some decent furniture here I can use. I can find the rest in auctions.'

On her way through the hall she noticed Molly's old desk.

'Oh how wonderful. I suppose this was all left. It was such a blur, Molly dying and me taking Bryony back to New Zealand. There might be stuff to check, perhaps plans of the garden to add to the ones we have found.' The cat looked at her as though it knew something.

Fleur looked at the complicated planting plans for the garden in its heyday and then the plans created by Molly for Daisy's rose garden and painting garden. She knew now having been back even for only a few weeks that Garraiblagh gave her the sense of place, of the family that she had craved for in other places. It would work and Molly's cottage would suit her well. She put away the crazy notion that if Kevin ever returned to find her that would be the place that he would remember. Sitting on the lawn with the maps and plans in front of them the three looked around them.

'So, it's agreed then, we keep the walled garden for our use,' said Fleur 'You two have the gardener' s cottage and we grow all our fruit and veg there.'

'It's still a lot of space to keep up,' commented Bryony.

'Yes, but I've been reading,' said Michael 'and I think we could lessen the upkeep a little by using more perennial vegetables. They wouldn't require that annual hard slog getting them going and then worrying when the season isn't warm enough.'

'Ok, but we should definitely consider how to use the greenhouses. They're not in too bad a condition.' said Fleur, 'and one of the things I remember most from childhood was helping grandpa Tom with the tomatoes. I think I'd like to start with them.'

'Aye, that sounds good, Mum. I'll work with Michael on getting a list together of all the fruit and veg we hope to grow then get started on the digging!'

'The garden needs some new life, new ideas as well,' commented Michael. 'Some of the old plants have had their day, some have completely disappeared. I think we should consider planting flowers in different ways, perhaps less formally. I'm going to go to the Blacks nursery and have a word with them, Perhaps see if I can get some advice and get them to Garraiblagh. Really want to do my horticulture course, the one I didn't get to when I left school.'

Bryony looked worried. 'You don't mean Edinburgh?'

'No, I can do the training over here an' it would be part time.'

'Great! I think it's great that you are going to do the training. It's what you wanted.'

'I've been thinking I would like to start a specialist nursery. Not yet, obviously. I need to learn more before then, but in the next few years. It's another reason for making contact with the Blacks.'

'That is a great idea, Michael!' both women agreed.

'Perhaps Grandfather Paddy would see that as a positive step.'

'I'm sure he would be delighted, love,' said Bryony as she took hold of his hand. 'Maybe all the ancestors are watching us.'

'I've no doubt of it. Ireland's full of ghosts. Who do you think brought us here?' said Michael.

Bryony laughed. 'Well then, we've nothing to worry about, big lad.'

'And the house?' sighed Bryony. 'What do we do about it?'

'We need to see what can be salvaged but I think we may have to have the building demolished,' said Michael.

'It would give us more space for a garden — or something else. I don't think we should try to work it all out now,' said Fleur.

'Yes, something will suggest itself,' responded Bryony. 'So we're agreed, we return Garraiblagh to the spirit of what it had been — a plantsman garden, a place for people and nature.'

'As well as a specialist plant nursery,' added Michael. 'And a garden for art — your art work, Mum and mine.' said Bryony.

Fleur picked up a piece old stained glass window. A blue piece she turned carefully in her hands. Then she bent and picked up other pieces; reds, yellows.

'There's enough here to create a new window or something smaller. I think I'll give it a go.'

Bryony found her mother later, crouched down beside the rubble wearing a pair of gloves, carefully selecting the best pieces of coloured glass. 'Wouldn't it be better just to get rid of all this?' asked Bryony. Fleur shook her head. 'No, the window it came from is part of my memories of this place. I want to see if I can create new ones. Something to put in Molly's cottage.'

Chapter Fifty-two

2002

THE CITY HAD SPREAD over the years since Garraiblagh had been built. It no longer stood in splendid isolation looking out across the lough on its own with only open fields and farm land bordering it on all sides. As the city had expanded so too had the trouble. Many people had been happy to leave the city, to have a distance between them and the brutality of the conflict that had ripped apart this part of the country but under the surface, came the problems, like a human bindweed, small sections creating problems, strangling the positive growth. The Agreement had brought the start of a peace process but the new estates housed people with old problems and no community to anchor them. The open green spaces around the houses soon became the place for bonfires, flags, murals, warnings. Trees were attacked and the planner's dreams lay in ruins. Like a parasitic plant, the organisations that had once been the communities' defenders had now turned inwards and become involved in a variety of rackets using threats and violence.

Sam Black was curious about his invitation to come to Garraiblagh to meet with Michael. He had heard that things were changing and that the family was set to restore all or at least part of the estate. Michael met Sam at the top of the drive. Sam looked at the tall, curly headed young man. He guessed he was in his late twenties and very fit from the look of it. Michael shook Sam's hand and began to explain what he wanted to do in restoring part of the garden but also looking at altering and introducing different designs and plants for other areas. Sam found he was soon caught up in Michael's enthusiasm. And while Michael kept pointing out that he didn't have a great deal of formal knowledge of plants and gardening, to Sam it was clear that Michael had a love for the garden.

Fleur was on her way back across the walled garden after collecting some rhubarb when she saw Michael talking animatedly to an older man. Both men were bent down investigating what looked like the leaves of some plant. Fleur's curiosity got the better of her and she walked towards them.

Michael and Sam heard her footsteps on the gravel and looked up. Michael stood up, followed more slowly by the red haired man.

'Hello again, Fleur,' said the man. At first Fleur was mystified then remembered. 'It's Sam, isn't it. Sam Black?

'Yes, I would have known ye anywhere,' he said. 'Have ye been back here long?'

Fleur began to chat in a way that she realised she hadn't for a long time. Something about this man made her feel as though she had known him forever.

Michael breezed into Bryony's studio in the summer house, grinning.

'You look pleased with yourself, Michael?'

'Aye, I am,' and reached down to give her a kiss. 'I like that,' he said looking at her drawing. 'Is it going to be a painting or something ceramic?'

'Ceramic I think. The wild geraniums have marvellous shapes and colours, just perfect for the pattern on a mug.'

'I think your mother has an admirer,' said Michael.

'An admirer, who? She's hardly been out of the garden,' said Bryony.

'Aye, but this admirer came here!'

'Don't keep me in suspense, who is it?'

'Sam Black. He was over helping me to check through the plants, advising me on which ones to leave and which could change when your mother joined us. I think they're still talking. Do you think I need to ask him his intentions?'

'Mum deserves some good luck in her life. I hope he's nice.'

'He must be about her age I think,' said Michael thoughtfully.

'You are just an old matchmaker, Michael!'

As Michael walked past the rows of large green leaves and trailing stems of the courgettes and squash he saw a movement. Stopping, he stood still, trying hard not to cause any disturbance and focused his gaze on the yellows and greens in front of him. Another glimpse of something, then an ear. He wanted to shout out in delight. A hare! Or rather, a leveret. Something must have made the animal notice him when it had not been concerned by presence before. It watched him, nose and whiskers twitching. Its fur a mixture of gold and browny grey. He thought it looked as though it didn't know where it could run to. 'It's alright. Ye stay where ye are. I'm going,' he whispered.

'Bryony, Fleur, I've been thinking and I have an idea,' Michael looked at Fleur, 'You've seen how changed the area is around Garraiblagh.'

Fleur nodded. 'I admit it was a shock. Garraiblagh was built when there was countryside for miles around. Now it seems homes are crowding up towards it.'

Michael nodded agreement. 'And while there is an Agreement

that doesn't mean that everything is settled. There are still strong emotions out there — hurt, anger, hatred and fear. Trust and the understanding needed to live together will be hard to build. I've learned a lot being here, working in the garden. I've been reading up on gardens and their history, how they've helped people in wars, post conflict situations and where there are even racial tensions. Garraiblagh is now sited between two housing estates, one Loyalist, the other Republican. We're right in the middle. But that could be a good thing. I think we have an opportunity to help the peace process in our own wee way.'

'How's that?' asked Bryony. Fleur looked on, listening carefully.

'What if we used the bottom fields and made them into a community garden, a garden that people from both estates could use.'

'That's pretty ambitious Michael. I don't know the politics like you, but wouldn't there be trouble?'said Fleur.

'I didn't say it would be easy. And with my background I understand that. I just think we have a chance. We're in the middle in more ways than one. We need this to be a safe and settled area for everyone especially us. I'm not saying it's goin' to fix everything. It's not. But, I think it could move things in the right direction.'

Fleur nodded.

'I've been thinking too. When the Blitz hit Belfast Granny Daisy and Grandpa Tom opened the bottom fields to what were in reality, refugees, people who'd lost their homes in Belfast. It helped some people, it made a difference. Thank you, Michael for reminding me of the things that were accomplished here.'

Later on in the afternoon, Bryony came into the kitchen of the Gardener's House with something in her hands. 'Look! I found this in the old gardeners' bothy. I think it would be perfect for the new community garden.' She unrolled the old piece of tapestry and gently smoothed it out. 'It was lying in an old wooden frame but the glass had broken and it would have damaged the stitches if I'd brought it like that.' said Bryony. Fleur turned it round to see it better and read the words out aloud.

'This is a garden. Leave your religion and politics outside its gates.' Murmuring her approval she studied the stitching and the embroidery more closely. 'It really is beautifully executed. The workmanship is very fine and whoever completed it loved flowers!'

Bryony lowered her head towards the canvas. 'There's a stitched signature here — Janet Black.'

'Oh my word! I think I know who that is — or rather, was! She was James Black's wife. I think she died rather tragically from what I can remember. That's probably 150 years old. It would definitely be a very appropriate piece to have hanging in the Community garden centre. It's proof of our legacy, our good intentions' said Fleur.

'I suppose I hadn't realised that religion and politics were as contentious then as now,' commented Bryony. 'Nothin' much changes here, Bryony.' said Michael in amusement.

'So do we go ahead and look into setting up a community garden in the bottom fields?' asked Bryony after they'd finished their evening meal.

Michael looked at the two women, wondering what their decision would be. As he'd read about the subject and thought more about it seemed for him that this was a way that he could move on, do something positive for others, possibly people like himself. At the same time he could understand if Bryony and her mother wanted to keep the place to themselves and not have any added problems. Bryony leant over the table and took Michael's hand.

'I say we should go ahead with the community garden.'

Fleur looked at them both. 'Yes I agree although it's going to take a lot of work and money. We need to make sure that we are still able to get the other things done in the garden that we agreed on and have a means of paying the bills.'

Fleur collected a bouquet of philadelphus, white and pink roses and freesia from the garden. Tying the flowers together with a white ribbon she thought back to the time since she had returned to Garraiblagh. A lot had happened. Bryony and Michael, the plans for the garden, and now Bryony and Michael's wedding. She smiled as she thought about it, not a moment too soon given that her daughter was now pregnant.

'Right, are we all ready?' asked Bryony. 'Down to the City hall for the ceremony and then back here for the celebration!'

'All ready,' said Fleur, ' and here are your flowers, my dear.'

Bryony took them in from her mother and hugged her hard. 'Thank you, mum.'

Fleur wiped away a tear. 'Sam's going to give me a lift down so you two can go on your own. Your parents are meeting us there, aren't they Michael?'

'Aye, an' ye make sure Sam is on time, remember he's my best man!'

Bryony, Michael and Fleur sat around the table in the gardener's house.

So, this is it. We seek funding just to get the structures and equipment in place for the community garden and we obtain charitable status for the community garden as a separate element of the estate. But we maintain control. We only lease the land to the charity. Are we agreed?' asked Fleur.

In the end the funding for the garden came at the wrong time of year, funding for something that those sitting in their offices did not understand. They would require a report at a time when plants would not have had a chance to grow or members recruited to join the garden. Bryony grimaced. It was yet another sign that in many ways for those in power what was being created was not the important thing. For them it was just the spending of money and a ticking of the boxes. As though money would end the problems. Creating a functioning garden was going to be difficult. They would be breaking the ice literally and figuratively. Bryony felt exhausted. She was glad that they had been able to get the funding to appoint a gardener to share the workload with the family.

Bryony and Michael conducted the interviews for the community gardener post.

'Steve Black's CV is impressive. He's well qualified and he has worked in some difficult places, bringing people together through gardenin'. We'd be lucky to get him.' said Michael.

'Aye, Steve is a good choice I think. It's lucky that he was back at the Blacks family home when we were looking for someone. It's interesting Sam and he are brothers, both involved in gardening and yet very different.' said Bryony. 'He has the practical gardening experience and he seems to be able to work easily with people. We should invite him to meet with us and make sure he understands what he's taking on. It's amazing to think that we will have a member of the Black family working with us again.'

Steve arrived early. He had been up early rehearsing what he was going to say and how he'd say it. Sam had told him just to tell Bryony and Michael outright. He wasn't so sure.

Steve waited for the couple to pour out the coffee and then began.

'There's something youse need to know.'

'You're not turning us down are you, Steve,' said Bryony with a worried look.

'No, but I need to tell you something about me that wasn't on the CV.'

Michael leant forward. 'Gawn ahead, Steve.'

'In my late teens I joined the UDA[33]. That was in the seventies. I thought I was defending my people. I spent a few months in jail. It made me think an' after that I left here an' went over to England to train. I've worked all over the place, in different countries an' I've enjoyed it but now, with the Agreement in place I want to come home an' work here. What youse're puttin' together here is exactly what I want to be involved with. I just didn't know when to tell ye.'

Michael looked at Steve and took a deep breath. Ye know my background. Can ye work with me?'

'Yes, I've learned a lot since those days, Michael. Can ye work with me?'

'It's no problem to me, Steve. I know as well as ye it's what we are now that counts. The past is dead and buried.'

'Bryony?' Michael turned to focus on his wife.

'If you can work with Michael, then it is the perfect solution isn't it? We need to show that people from both sides can work together.'

'That's settled then, Steve. We have a lot of work to do. There's one thing I am learnin' and that is that nothin' is ever simple and we're not one dimensional. There's more to us than a flag.'

The two men shook hands.

'We can get the structures for the garden in place fairly quickly. I need to talk to you Steve about the external plantin' and how we can make it look its best by the time the funders of the structural work come to check on progress,' said Michael.

'Fancy another coffee, love? I am suddenly very hungry! I suppose it's relief,' said Bryony.

'I can actually see how the community garden is goin' to work now,' Bryony said, putting her coffee cup down on the table with conviction.

'It had better. we've just convinced the council to fork out money

33 Ulster Defence Association is a British Loyalist paramilitary group formed in Belfast in 1971 to oppose the IRA.

for it,' said Michael. 'It's a good space. The land works and the site gives good access from both housing estates.'

'And that is one of the issues isn't it?' said Fleur.

'Yes,' agreed Michael, 'there needs to be good access and also a feeling of enclosure, of safety. We know people will be wary, or at least some will, for all sorts of reasons.'

Chapter Fifty-three

2003

STEVE HAD WANTED THIS JOB. He'd worked in many different gardens after his initial training at Kew. He nurtured the people in the community garden as he would the plants he'd learned to grow so long ago. A little praise here, a helping hand with a heavy wheelbarrow there, a new person requiring a more experienced person to help them grow, those who were only annuals, others were perennials, hardier, always willing to help. Then those who tended to spread themselves, greedy for space.

In their turn those in the garden welcomed Steve's leadership. They knew it was benign. They saw the way he worked the land and treated the plants. They felt that it was safe. Steve's quietness belied his determination and those who had seen him in action knew that he was fearless when the situation required it.

Garraiblagh was an interesting garden to be involved in. It wasn't decided by people who sat in offices and never knew what it was like on the ground. Steve was intrigued by Michael. he'd never met an ex-IRA man. If they could show how people from different communities could work together it would be a powerful motivator. Steve watched as the individual plot-holders decided where they wanted to site themselves — beside someone else or separate.

As he dug out the soil to plant an apple tree Steve waved over to Peter, one of the new gardeners who shyly responded. Peter looked to be in his mid-twenties though he had one of those faces that suggested he had experienced more than most. Steve knew that Peter didn't welcome long conversations or his name being shouted out; his concentration was always focused on what he was doing whether it was weeding or planting. Initially Steve had seen Peter look round warily whenever he heard a loud noise or a car stopping on the road outside. At times like that it was as though Peter lowered himself closer to the ground like an animal afraid of being hunted. Out there, once Peter closed the garden gate behind him, well, that was another matter. Steve hoped he was alright but he could only make the garden a place of sanctuary.

Peter looked across at Steve. He knew he was more relaxed when he was in the garden. He didn't look around waiting to hear his name being shouted, a car door screeching to a halt. In here he felt he was safe. He was proud of his garden and the vegetables he was managing to grow. He'd picked a few packets from the local shop — just veg he knew he might eat, nothing fancy. As the seeds had developed into seedlings, he'd become hooked. There were days when he'd just sit and look at them with a flask of tea in his hand, mesmerised by what he had achieved. When the carrots grew their ferny leaves and he could see the tops of the carrots he couldn't suppress a satisfied smile. As he stood, easing his back and taking a break, he noticed a robin watching closely. It bent its head to one side, its beady eyes intent on any insects or worms that had been uncovered. Peter was just about to welcome the robin over with a few breadcrumbs he had in his pocket when there was a flurry of wings. Another robin had moved onto the row of lettuces.

Flying at each other, beaks out, wings crashing against their opponent's small body it was an aerial fight in miniature. Peter looked in horror for a moment until he threw a clod of earth at them. They moved apart for a brief moment allowing the loser to fly away without further harm. 'No more fightin',' he shouted.

Michael sat looking around the newly planned Garraiblagh garden. His discussions with Sam Black had already taught him a lot and made him realise how important completing his own training would be. Sam had showed which of the original Garraiblagh plants and shrubs could be rescued and Michael had started, with help at first, taking cuttings and making divisions with infinite care. Now he was amassing rows of small flower pots, carefully labelled. He stretched his back and stood up. They had used some money to restore three of the greenhouses and Michael had one for his seedlings. He walked along the edge of the walled garden. Bryony was busily planting out some garlic for next year and further over near the wall; Fleur was collecting the last of the Cape Gooseberries. Waving to them both, he walked through the garden gate into the main gardens. He was always struck by the beauty of the place. A frost had caught the edges of leaves and small icicles hung from the ends of ivy climbing over the wall. An overgrown rambling rose still had a few flowers, palely caught in frost. The low light from the wintery sun illuminated the sadness of the garden neglected over time but Michael could see clearly in his mind's eye how it would change. Walking out through the gate and down the path he felt a warmth and scent of roses but there were no roses in sight. He stopped, trying to determine where the scent was from. A fox scurried away towards an old oak tree and the undergrowth surrounding it. The scent of rose followed him through his walk around the garden. The logical part of Michael's brain dismissed it. He was imagining it. He had seen no roses in flower apart from the old rose near the gate.

When word of the community garden and its allotments was announced Philip O'Brien had become excited. Now in his seventies, he'd moved into the sheltered accommodation at the top end of the housing estate. It was quiet enough. He kept away from the flags and the murals, as did most of the others in the housing association bungalows.

He put his name down for a place in the garden. He moved with difficulty, helped by the walking stick and while his hips gave him pain but he wasn't going to allow that to stop him working in the garden. Steve Black had seen Philip's physical difficulties and suggested he take one of the raised beds so that he wouldn't have to bend and dig. He was grateful for that and thrilled that he would be back in the old place, although where the community garden was sited was in an area he had not known well.

He had not told anyone about his history with Garraiblagh. The years that he had spent at Garraiblagh during the war had been some of his happiest, protected by the trees and the plants. Now here he was, back again. He smiled to himself. His life had come full circle. In his mind's eye he could see the way it had been, could clearly remember the gardeners and the others — Joe and Matt and Colin in particular, as though it was only a short time ago. Not almost sixty years ago.

He hadn't moved far after the war, he and his family had stayed in Belfast. He'd asked his father one time when he was home on leave from the RAF whether he had seen the message that Philip had made on Garraiblagh's lawn in stones. His father, nudged by his mother, responded that he had. Michael had led a fairly ordinary life he supposed. Things hadn't always quite gone the way he'd imagined they would but it hadn't been that bad either.

Steve walked down the path between the allotments, saying hello and exchanging a few pleasantries with different people. Bert's plot always made him smile He knew the elderly man enjoyed the garden, but that he liked his own space. Since taking ownership of his plot, Bert had ensured his area was surrounded with prickly shrubs he had planted around the edge. Within that space he was in charge and he grew his flowers.

'How's it going, Bert?' Steve called over. 'Not being bothered with greenfly yet?'

Bert shook his head. 'They know I'll be watching for them, boy!'

Steve laughed. Unbeknownst to Bert, Steve had watched him gradually become involved in the garden. While Michael and Steve had worked with contractors to lay out the garden sections Steve had noticed a lone figure that appeared every morning and sat beneath an old oak tree where, at twelve o'clock every day he took out a sandwich and unscrewed the lid of a thermos flask. It had not surprised Steve when he had recognised Bert signing up for an allotment.

Bert liked the fact that no one bothered him and the garden felt peaceful. His interest had been sparked when he had begun to see the garden being laid out, watching the progress as workers built raised beds and pergolas, erected a large wooden shed and created a paved area and, seeing how Steve and Michael worked, he felt it would be good place to be. He wanted to grow flowers; he had always wanted to grow flowers. Even as a child he had grown marigolds in a window box. Bert couldn't explain the pleasure he felt in tending the plants. His house, the one he'd been moved to after the destruction of the row he had lived in down in the town, had no garden and the back yard didn't have much sunlight. He'd tried putting flowers in a window box at the front, but they hadn't lasted long. A thump on the door late at night; a sound of something dropping and then a crash of bottles. Bert hadn't looked out. He'd waited until morning and then found his window box, broken and thrown onto the road. The marigolds had had their heads removed and been thrown carelessly down on the pavement. Bert tried again. He hated to be beaten by the yobs. A new window box, new plants. Then, a couple of weeks later; loud noises, shouts and arguments. Bert found the window box smashed. That was it. No more.

So, he had filled out the short application form to apply for his own allotment and celebrated with a beer when his application had been successful. Although he had planted the spiky coteanaster shrubs around the perimeter of his area he used the main part of the allotment to grow delicate flowers. Flowers he remembered from childhood, like marigolds, sweet pea and Sweet William and a few orange lillies. Bert's difficulty was what to do with the flowers he grew. He took some home and placed them carefully in the old vase he had inherited from his parents' house but he had more to spare. He did not know many people but he noticed the elderly woman who lived a little further up the street. She always said hello to him.

Bert picked a large bunch of flowers, arranging them as best he could then tied them with some twine. He walked up the street, reconsidering his decision. It might be foolish. Perhaps he should just go home. He'd never been at ease with women. Bert looked at the flowers. No, he would do as he'd decided. You're never too old. He knocked on the door. The elderly woman, her hair curled around her face stood there.

'I thought ye might like these?'

'They are beautiful, come in, the kettle's on and I've just made some cake.'

Steve was feeling unsettled. The garden was going well. They had a mixture of people renting allotments and some who just liked to potter about in the community garden planters, enjoying the chat as much as anything. What worried Steve was that there had been no confrontations, no vandalism. He didn't want it, but he also knew that often there needed to be a blow up of some sort in order for everything to settle more permanently.

Philip O'Brien was enjoying himself. He woke early each morning, had his usual breakfast and filled a flask, made sandwiches and walked with his back-pack along to his allotment. He had planted carrots and cabbage, in memory of his exploits as a child and was looking forward to harvesting them. He'd heard Steve talking about different vegetables he could try next year and was beginning to dream about what would be produced. There was an annual horticultural show in town and, 'just maybe,' he thought, he'd pluck up the courage to enter. The longer summer evenings had been wonderful and he felt much fitter and healthier than he had in years. Now, even at the beginning of autumn, he was busy. He didn't mind that others had gone home for the day and he was on his own, after all he knew the old estate inside out. Some people thought it was a little eerie but he had never found it so. He knew some people thought the place was haunted and maybe it was. He had never felt anything threatening. There were too many memories, good memories.

The youths came, late into the night. Drunk and high they intended to destroy anything they could. Fear vibrated through the plants. The leaves shook and petals fell. Hands grabbed the carrots by their necks and smashed them against the walls. Feet ground the delicate marigold seedlings into the soil. The apple tree lost branches and obscene words were brutally carved into its trunk. The garden shivered, urgent messages were sent through the root systems.

Philip was the first one to see the devastation. He had come in early to check on the plants and to bring some fleece to cover them with as the temperatures were dropping.

Steve and Michael surveyed the damage. Plants would be replaced. Ground cleared. The apple tree pruned. Both men were angry.

'I suppose we should've expected it,' said Michael.

'I was beginnin' to feel uneasy that we hadn't had any bother. Now it's happened at least we can work on it,' said Steve. 'At least they went more for the community area rather than the individual allotments this time.'

'Aye, this time,' said Michael.

Philip had seen enough of war in all its forms. This place had protected him and helped him when he needed it, he would do the same for it. Philip took up position in the garden, close to the tool shed. He knew they would come again, to gloat over what they had done and to cause further damage if they could. He also recognised that one of the trees that had not yet been attacked was the old cherry tree that he and Joe and the others had planted, where Willow the dog had been buried. He could not let anything happen to that. He owed the others and himself that.

Three of the boys arrived, kicking over anything that was in their way with shouts of bravado. They moved towards the cherry tree, threatening it and telling it what they would do to it.

Philip pulled himself up to lean on his stick.

'Do not touch that tree!' Philip was surprised at the strength of his voice.

'Oh aye, aul' man.'

A hard, long nosed face was just a few inches from him. Philip could smell the drink and saw the boy's pupils were enlarged. His eyes were dark holes.

'We'll do what we want. Why don't ye piss aff home?' There were giggles from them as they passed a bottle of Buckfast around. One of the boys, a shaggy headed, pimply youth kicked Philip's stick.

Another picked it up and started hitting the tree with it, thrashing the leaves which fell torn to the ground.

Philip looked at them, he realised that he was in a dangerous situation, but he couldn't back down now.

Philip's anger exploded. As a child he had known fear, German bombers obliterating the Belfast he had lived in, fears that his father or mother would not return home from work because of a bombing. But that had been external. It was the Germans, the Japs, someone somewhere else causing it. Then the Troubles, mates shot, imprisoned, more bombs and then a tentative peace. Everything closer. But now, now it was inside people. Philip thought. This is about good and evil. We've lost the knowledge of which is which. Something awoke in the frail, elderly man. From deep within him there was a growling, keening sound. The boys stopped, unable to work out what was happening.

'Get out ye evil bastards!'

Philip no longer cared what they did to him but this was a fight he could not leave. He looked directly at the shaggy headed creature in front of him.

'Here, I know ye! I knew your grandfather!' Philip pointed his finger at the first one.

'So what!' came the sarcastic response.

'Ye listen to me ye wee shit! Your grandad helped to plant that tree.'

'What de ye mean?' came the bored response from the youth.

'What I said. He an' I an' two others planted that tree back in 1944, during the war. Don't ye know anything about your family?'

'Fuck off, what does it matter?' The dark eyes looked at Philip threateningly.

'There's nothin' here, but plants and ye aul' boys.'

The sound of raised voices and the cries of despair made by Philip had carried in the cold night air. Fergus had been the first one to pick them up; a low growl from his throat had then disturbed Michael.

'I hear it, boy.'

Michael rose from his comfortable seat in front of the fire.

'I'm going to check out what's happening, Bryony. Stay here an' make sure the doors are locked after me.'

'No, I'm coming with you.'

Following Fergus as he ran through the shrubs and across the old lawn, Michael and Bryony made their way into the community garden. The sight of an old man being abused by a group of young men disgusted Michael. He flexed his knuckles and counted to ten before advancing.

His time in prison had left him less fearful of bullies. The sound of the dog and the accompanying footsteps made the straggly haired youth look round.

'What do youse want?' he spat. 'It's none of your business!'

The first youth looked at his mates for approval but was startled to find them backing off.

Fergus had two of them pinned against the wall and was growling ferociously.

'I think it has everything to do with me,' countered Michael who had moved to stand close to Philip.

The young man looked.

'Tryin' to be the hard man, eh?' said Michael in a relaxed tone of voice. 'So let's see how hard ye are!' he said, staring at the youth.

The youth turned to speak.

'Fuck. I know ye. Mickey Wilson.'

'Don't mess wi' him, Sean. He's RA[34],' warned one of the other boys.

For the first time fear seeped into the youth's mind. He had heard stories about this man; the rumours had gone around about what he had done back in the day.

---

34 A member of the IRA (Irish Republican Army)

Bryony, her heart thumping, had taken the opportunity to move to Philip's side as well. Holding his arm she helped him to a garden bench some distance away from the others.

Michael barked an order to one of the youths. 'Give the gentleman back his stick. There are two ways we can deal wi' this. Youse walk away and stay away or I make sure youse never walk again. Your decision.'

The youths shuffled their feet and meekly handed Philip his stick.

'So.... what will happen now is that youse.... will go home.'

The youths heard the disdain and disgust in Michael voice.

'An' in the morning I'll call on youse. Now get tae fuck! an' tell your dads that I'll be visitin' the morra... early.'

The boys walked away looking back to be sure Michael wasn't coming after them.

Michael and Bryony sat down beside the old man.

'Are you ok?' Philip nodded and looked down to find Fergus licking his hand. He stroked the dog and sat up straighter. 'I knew the grandfather o' one o' them. He'd be horrified to know what his grandson's doin'.' Looking into Michael's eyes Philip made a decision. He'd heard various rumours about the guy who was married to Miss Daisy's great-granddaughter, but he didn't like to judge and as far as he was concerned, actions spoke louder than words.

The three walked gently down the lane to the houses, finally turning off to Philip's home.

Waving goodnight to the old man, Michael and Bryony began the walk home; Fergus keeping close. They sat down in the arbour.

'Some of my best thinking happens here,' said Michael as he began to relax.

'You heard what that boy said. He knows of me from his father — and that will be a paramilitary connection. Steve and I will find a way of workin' wi' these boys from both sides, the ones who are at risk o' goin' the same way we went. Anyway, first things first I'll straighten things out in the housing estate. Then we need to have a meeting of all the people involved in the community garden. To defeat this vandalism we need everyone on board.'

Two days later, Bryony, Steve and Michael put out the chairs in the community garden hut and waited.

'I'm hoping we'll get a good representation of the individuals and families. The issue with those young guys is probably, well not quite a blessing in disguise, but... well, an opportunity to take the garden an' its runnin' on, to the next stage.' said Steve. 'It's always difficult to determine the timing of groups.'

Philip thought about it. He had listened carefully. 'I'd like to be on the committee if that's alright.'

'Very alright, Philip. I was hoping you would feel able to do that. Tell everyone a little about yourself, Philip,' said Michael.

'Not much to tell. I enjoy growing things. I spent years here, on the estate when I was a boy. I was evacuated from my home in Belfast after the Blitz.'

Someone piped up, 'I thought the Blitz was in London, places like that.'

'A lot of people do but it happened here in Belfast, Easter 1941. Anyway people were scared there would be more bombs an' ran out o' the city to places like this. They were well looked after by the Guthries. It seems to me that there are a lot of people who just want somewhere they can grow things and meet other people without any trouble. I live on my own. That's fair enough but I like to have company at times.'

'I know what ye mean,' said Bert. 'I'm new to the garden too. I'm a bit quiet I suppose. I don't want to chat all the time, but I like workin' next door to people an' see what they're growing.'

'Oh dear,' giggled a woman wearing old denims with a scarf tied round her wavy hair. 'I'm one of those chatty ones. I'll have to remember not to talk too much.'

'Don't worry, I like talking too,' said a small woman at the back of the room, nudging her friend. 'We're both a bit talkative!'

'That's fine,' said Bert. 'Youse go ahead, just realise that sometimes I'll be just working not talking.'

'Fair enough, we won't take it personally.'

Steve had been holding his breath until this, hoping that garden members would voice their opinions and be positive. Steve smiled over at them.

'Am I right in thinking everybody here believes the garden is something that we want to continue.'

There were nods and words of surprise. 'Of course we do.'

'That's good but we know from Philip's experience that not everyone the area feels like us.'

'It's our garden and we're not going to stop! said one of the women. Voices shouted out their agreement and the hall echoed with clapping.

The following morning Bryony walked down to the community garden.

'Steve, we have a new applicant for an allotment. Her name is Diba. She's from the Congo and finding it all a bit different here.'

Steve reached out his hand to Diba. 'It's good to meet you, Diba. Have you grown any vegetables or fruit before?'

Diba nodded shyly. 'In the Congo, not here.'

'Well, let's find ye a plot to start work on.' Steve took her to a plot. Diba put her hands in the loose soil and picked a fistful up in her hand and looked at it in delight. Letting the soil drop to the ground again through her fingers she reached inside the pocket of her dress and brought out some seeds.

'What are they, Diba? What are their names?' asked Steve.

'Matambele and bitter leaf,' she smiled, 'from home.'

Diba had had a long conversation with Bryony. She wondered how there could be so much rain and cold. She knew there were supposed to be four seasons here but she was finding it difficult to differentiate between them. This was an opportunity for her to grow her own food. She had been surprised that more people did not grow their own food in Ireland, but then, she thought, the earth was so different from where she came from. In the Congo plants could grow strongly and luxuriously almost before you had sowed the seed! She could not understand the reliance on packeted and prepared food that Irish people had. But she had to learn to be patient. The ground and the warmth from the sun were different. She wondered how everyone managed to grow things. She could see that everything, as far as she was concerned, grew slowly, and, she thought to herself, so would friendships. She wanted to show these people that she knew what she was doing.

As Diba settled into her allotment people became curious. She found people liked talking about the weather, what it was like, what it had been like, what it would be like so many times. She still found it difficult to understand why everyone was so interested in the weather. Diba's plants grew slowly, but they grew. She spoke to them in her native tongue as she moved the hoe slowly round them, urging them on. Food in Ireland seemed sweet to her. Tastes were different. She closed her eyes as she bit into the leaf and remembered the warmth of the land and the sounds of the people in the village where she had lived. Its bitterness made her mouth water as she thought of the stews she could make.

Sara had moved into the housing estate but the accommodation didn't stretch to a garden, only a back yard. She had kept her plants in pots for so long Sara had almost forgotten when she had first obtained them. She had promised her plants that they would be planted when she had come to the place where she would settle down, her own place, a permanent place. The plants however had other ideas. They were tired of travelling, tired of being in pots when what they wanted to do was feel their roots spread out and luxuriate in soil, not find their roots pinched and thwarted. They tried to make their feelings clear to Sara. Fuchsia kept throwing its pot over like a toddler throwing himself down in a tantrum. Sara watered the pot and placed it carefully in a position from which it could not fall. Fuchsia still managed to fall over and still Sara ignored its wishes. Blueberry wouldn't let its berries fruit, knocking them to the ground just after flowering. The rare blue geranium that Sara had obtained sat in its pot, sulking and worried. It knew that it couldn't last forever there. It wanted to cover the ground with its dusky purple blue flowers. In her heart, Sara knew the plants needed to be given their space. She so wanted it to be her own space though. She looked at the allotment she had in the Garraiblagh garden. It wasn't large. She decided she would have a word with Steve and see if she could rent more ground and check on the level of permanence.

Steve watched Sara as she walked towards him. Her shoulders looked hunched up. She looked worried. Her blond hair was tied up with a piece of green raffia and she had smudges of mud on her face. He had always noticed Sara. She wore bizarre combinations of colours and often accessorised them with earrings she had made herself but she could be aloof and difficult when it came to starting a conversation.

'What's wrong, Sara? Ye look bothered.'

She was surprised. She hadn't thought she was that obvious.

'Aye. I am. Look this probably seems silly, but I was wondering if I could have a larger allotment. It's just... this is where you will think I'm daft... but I have had plants that have been in pots for, literally years now. I promised myself and them that I would plant them in open ground when I found a permanent place to live, but that hasn't happened. I know they need to be planted out.'

Steve had watched Sara building up her allotment, preparing the ground, weeding and clearing. He'd heard her talking to the seedlings as she planted them and tended them.

He understood Sara's predicament and that of many allotment holders. They literally needed to put down roots. He was happy to grant longer term agreements to such dedicated gardeners and get them involved in their growing community.

Relieved Sara took a deep breath and upended the fuchsia. The plant was quivering with excitement as it saw the deep hole with the added manure to it. The shrub wriggled and placed itself in the soil. The cool of the earth welcomed the roots that had been held for so long. Watering it Sara could see that the shrub had already relaxed its branches and was looking fresher.

'Alright guys. If you are happy here then I am. Who knows what the future holds?' She smiled as she thought of the coffee Steve had said he'd have ready for her when she'd planted out the pots.

The festival celebrating Samhain had been planned as the culmination of the gardening year. It caught the imagination of the people involved in the garden. Guessing the size of the pumpkin had brought a lot of interest. Children and adults surprised that anything like that could be grown in the garden.

A small group of women had agreed to make apple tarts while two others battled with huge cabbages and carrots to make bowls of coleslaw. Everything, apart from some sausages and bread, was to come from the garden. Apart from the fun, everybody wanted to see how far they had come and what could still be achieved. Small turnip lanterns had been lit along the track, lighting the route from both estates. The ground was crisp with ice covered grass.

Through the old gate in the wall the scene was transformed. Fairy lights danced around the patio area attached to the new wooden community hut and a fire with a large pot hanging over it on a tripod gave off delicious, savoury smells. According to the ancient Celts this was the beginning of the year not the end. So this was a new beginning for the garden and its members. The squash and pumpkins had grown well, benefitting from the long spells of wet weather, grown in the community garden area rather than the allotments they were there to form part of the feast, roasted and carved.

The huge bonfire which had been carefully laid with the broken and rotten branches, clipped and sawn over the previous months blazed, sent sparks high into the night sky and the youths who had been confronted by Michael kept the fire going in between helping to serve the food and eat it. Fiddles and bodhran made wild dance music which vibrated around the garden. Michael was deep in conversation with Philip and Peter while Steve and Sara relaxed in the old chairs they had found. A group of youngsters lying on benches and upturned boxes chatted amongst themselves. The food or what was left of the delicious dishes lay on the tables. Apple tarts, potatoes in their jackets, blackberry muffins and a bitter leaf stew that Diba had put together. Diba felt pride and confidence being a part of this garden. The community garden had come a long way. It had the means to help people, change and grow mix and thrive. The bottom fields of Garraiblagh estate had found a permanent use.

In the undergrowth the foxes settled in to their lair and listened as they had always done. This time they weren't frightened. The sounds were not threatening and, when the humans had made their way back home and the fire had burnt down, foxes and other animals made their way into the garden and had their own supper.

A small turnip lantern placed on top of the standing stone which stood at the furthest corner of the community garden still flickered while at its base, among the long grasses a posy of elderberries and rowans with bright red fuchsia flowers rested. The ancients would continue to take care of the land.

2003

Garraiblagh estate was changing. Fleur, Bryony and Michael now had the money to maintain it. New designs had been drawn up by Michael and slowly the gardens were coming to life again, the old and the new combining. The topiary at the front of the old house had been reinstated but the old terraces were being planted with new colours and shapes, making them freer and less formal. The cutting garden was filling with plants, plants that would form the beginnings of Michael's plant nursery. The tulip tree planted back in 1870 now dominated the lower lawn and the pond and its statue while the path to the Japanese garden remained almost hidden by the magnolia planted so long ago.

In Molly's cottage Fleur sat working on a new children's story with Cleo the cat on her knee. The cottage and the garden were holding her, building new memories. She would find her way forward. She lifted up the old black and white photograph she had found among others when she had explored the remains of Garraiblagh House. It intrigued her. A formally posed Victorian studio portrait of a man and a woman. A Dublin photographer, dated 1900. The woman looked like other photographs she'd seen of Amelia Henderson and the man looked like James Black. She was struck by the likeness Sam had to his great-grandfather. Glancing at her watch she put down her pen and rose to go into the kitchen. Time to make the meal she had promised Sam Black. There was a knock at the door and opening it there he stood, a bottle of wine in one hand, flowers in the other and a smile on his face. This felt different. She would take her time getting to know this man with his love of plants and his sense of humour. She dared to hope he would be part of her future.

A thick mist covered the garden in the morning, softening shapes and sounds until slowly the sun began to burn through to a blue autumn sky. Bryony and Michael stood at the door to their home, mugs of coffee in their hands. Bryony breathed in deeply.

'There's a strange mixture of the scent of summers past and that unsettling smell of autumn in the air,' said Bryony.

A cool breeze brought a shiver to Bryony and Michael put his arms around her, his beard rubbing her cheek. Bryony holding her pregnant belly. 'I don't know about someone walking over my grave, but I've been thinking about this garden and everyone who has been a part of it through the years — and now here we are with twins on the way. I wonder what the world will be like when they grow up.'

'Well, they'll be fighters for sure!' said Michael. 'I can feel them kicking and thumping.'

'Aye, good fighters though,' said Bryony, 'fighting for a good cause in the right way, eh?'

'Not politicians I hope!'

'No, like us, guardians of the land.'

'I can smell roses!' said Bryony and as she said that a robin perched on the stone wall at the front, watching them, its bright black eyes looking deep into their souls.

The dew glistened on the grass and spiders' webs created tiny trip wires across the lawns and flower beds towards the trees and the lough beyond. It was as though the garden was celebrating in its own way. Chestnut trees were beginning to turn from green to gold, their conkers beneath them, glossy and brown. The box hedges now once again shaped and trimmed stood proudly in their place and there, beyond the newly restored topiary and steps, looking into the pond, stood a heron, a watcher, connector of the past, present and future.

Garraiblagh was weaving its magic again. It would work with these people as it had done before.

THE END

ABOUT THE AUTHOR

Jenny Methven lives in Fermanagh in Northern Ireland with her writer husband Willie, George the cat and Rosie, the collie.

She is inspired by the beautiful countryside she lives in for her writing and art.

Jenny grew up in Scotland, though her family are from Ireland. Following art college and teacher training in Wales, she moved to live in Ireland in her twenties.

She spent many years as a social worker and teacher, working with both adults and children and has an MA Education among her qualifications. Her MSc dissertation in Peace and Conflict studies is focused on the peace building powers of gardens and the natural world.

She has had poetry published in both online journals and print anthologies. Jenny's poetry collection '*Dancing in puddles with the Cailleach*' published in 2016 is a combination of her poetry and artwork.

Appendix

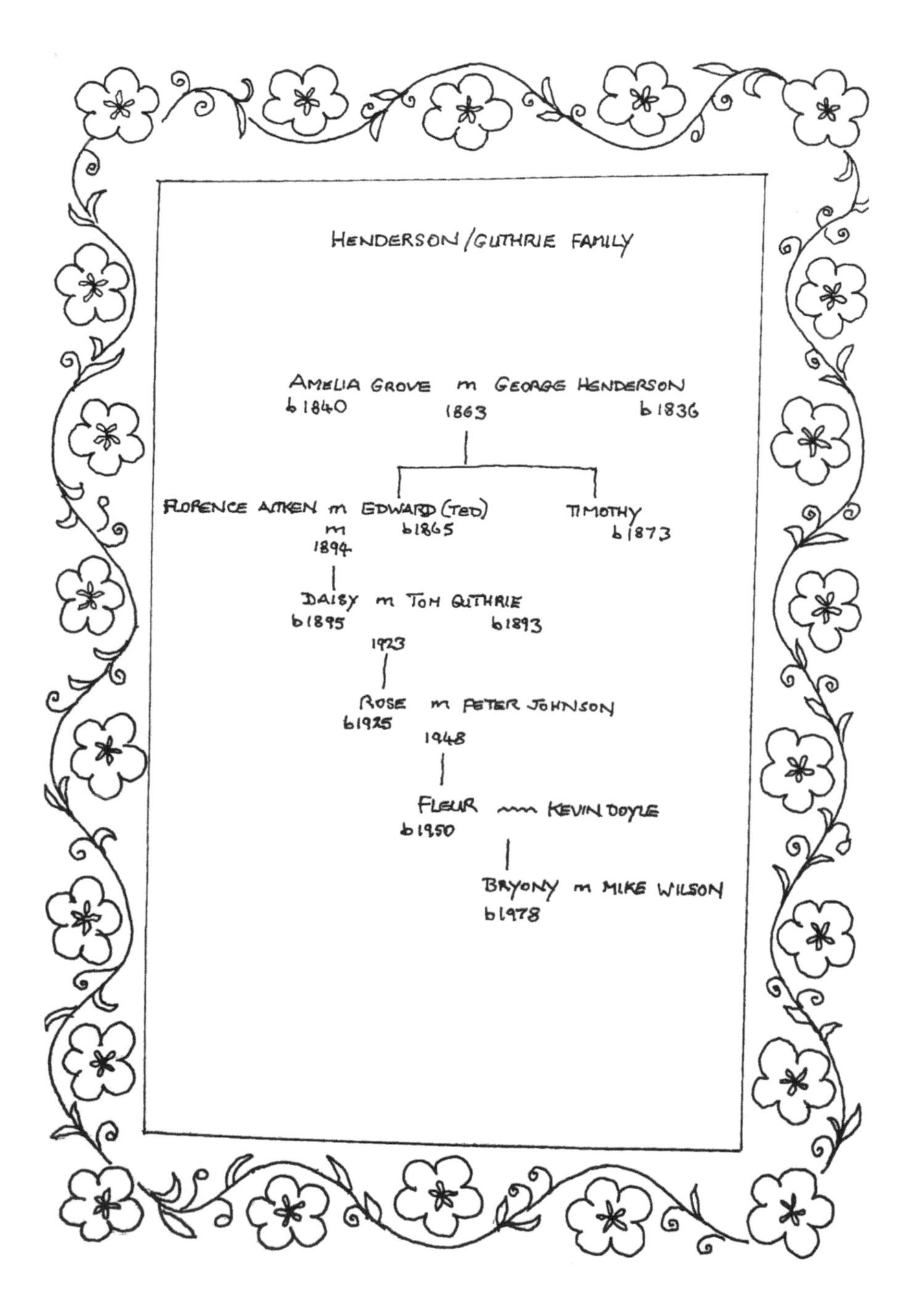
HENDERSON/GUTHRIE FAMILY
AMELIA GROVE m GEORGE HENDERSON
b1840
1863
b1836
FLORENCE AITKEN m EDWARD (TED)
m
1894
b1865
TIMOTHY
b1873
DAISY m TOM GUTHRIE
b1895
b1893
1923
ROSE m PETER JOHNSON
b1925
1948
FLEUR ~~~ KEVIN DOYLE
b1950
BRYONY m MIKE WILSON
b1978

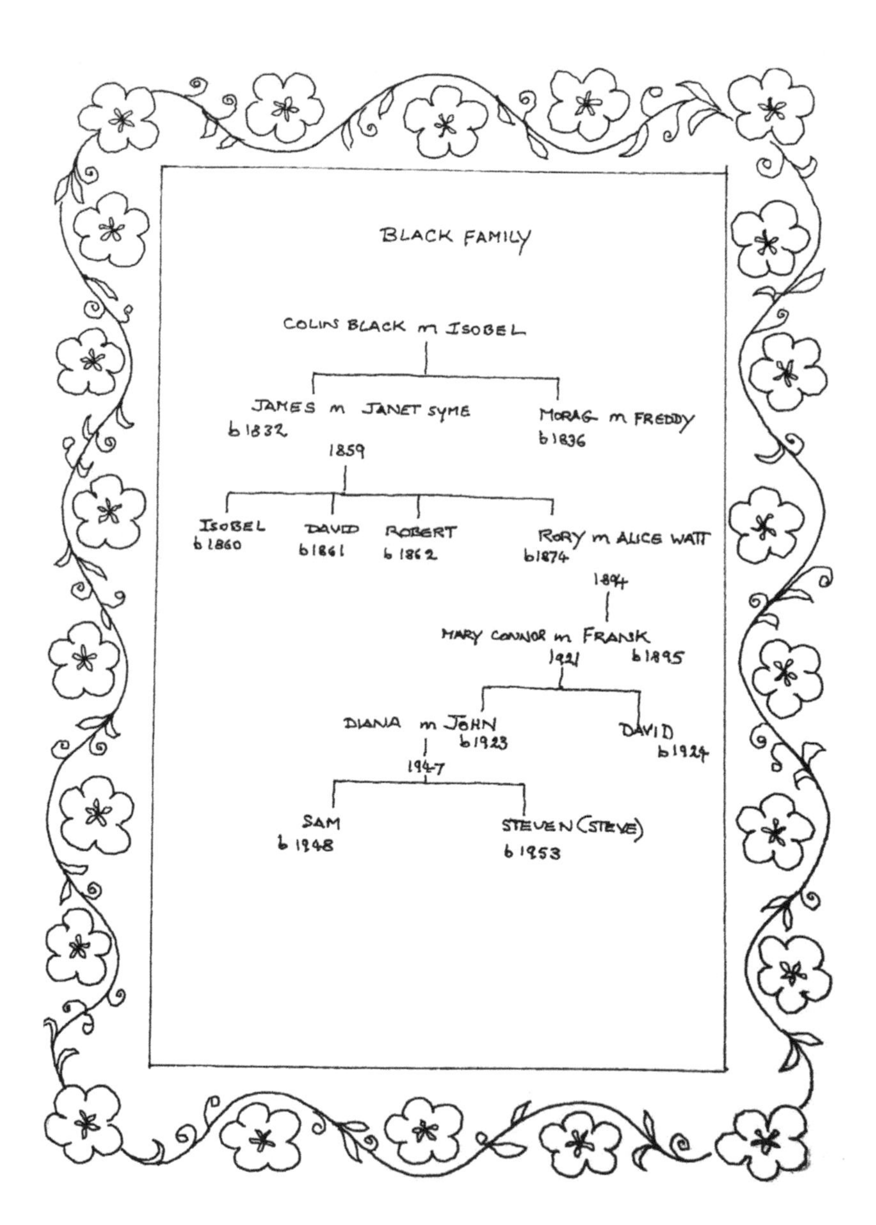
BLACK FAMILY
COLIN BLACK m ISOBEL
JAMES m JANET SYME
b 1832
1859
MORAG m FREDDY
b 1836
ISOBEL
b 1860
DAVID
b 1861
ROBERT
b 1862
RORY m ALICE WATT
b 1874
1894
MARY CONNOR m FRANK
1921
b 1895
DIANA m JOHN
b 1923
DAVID
b 1924
1947
SAM
b 1948
STEVEN (STEVE)
b 1953

Lightning Source UK Ltd.
Milton Keynes UK
UKHW022057101120
373159UK00006B/364